Canadian **Dani Collins** knew in high school that she wanted to write romance for a living. Twenty-five years later, after marrying her high school sweetheart, having two kids with him, working at several generic office jobs and submitting countless manuscripts, she got The Call. Her first Mills & Boon novel won the Reviewers' Choice Award for Best First in Series from *RT Book Reviews*. She now works in her own office, writing romance.

Born and raised in the Australian bush, **Miranda Lee** was boarding-school-educated, and briefly pursued a career in classical music before moving to Sydney and embracing the world of computers. Happily married, with three daughters, she began writing when family commitments kept her at home. She likes to create stories that are believable, modern, fast-paced and sexy. Her interests include meaty sagas, doing word puzzles, gambling and going to the movies.

D1146585

Also by Dani Collins

The Secret Beneath the Veil
Xenakis's Convenient Bride
Consequence of His Revenge

The Sauveterre Siblings miniseries

Pursued by the Desert Prince
His Mistress with Two Secrets
Bound by the Millionaire's Ring
Prince's Son of Scandal

Also by Miranda Lee

Rich, Ruthless and Renowned miniseries

The Italian's Ruthless Seduction
The Billionaire's Ruthless Affair
The Playboy's Ruthless Pursuit

Marrying a Tycoon miniseries

The Magnate's Tempestuous Marriage
The Tycoon's Outrageous Proposal
The Tycoon's Scandalous Proposition

Discover more at millsandboon.co.uk.

SHEIKH'S PRINCESS OF CONVENIENCE

DANI COLLINS

THE ITALIAN'S UNEXPECTED LOVE-CHILD

MIRANDA LEE

MILLS & BOON

First Published in Great Britain 2018
by Mills & Boon, an imprint of HarperCollins*Publishers*
1 London Bridge Street, London, SE1 9GF

Sheikh's Princess of Convenience © 2018 by Harlequin Books S.A.

Special thanks and acknowledgement are given to Dani Collins
for her contribution to the Bound to the Desert King series.

The Italian's Unexpected Love-Child © 2018 by Miranda Lee

ISBN: 978-0-263-93551-6

MIX
Paper from
responsible sources
FSC™ C007454

This book is produced from independently certified FSC™ paper
to ensure responsible forest management.
For more information visit www.harpercollins.co.uk/green.

Printed and bound in Spain
by CPI, Barcelona

SHEIKH'S PRINCESS OF CONVENIENCE

DANI COLLINS

To my fellow authors, without whom
the romance genre wouldn't exist. You have given me
hope and tears and guidance and passion, and best of
all a belief in happily-ever-after. Also a special shout
out to my fellow authors in this quartet—Tara Pammi,
Maya Blake and Caitlin Crews. I'm privileged
to have met each of you in person and
you are all wonderful in every way.

CHAPTER ONE

DO I LOOK PRETTY, Mama?

The reflexive question, one she had learned to suppress, still jammed in Galila's throat along with her heart when she turned and caught sight of an apparition.

She held herself motionless on the tiled platform in the center of the reflecting pool, staring at the woman who appeared against the window to her mother's lounge. With the subtle golden glow cast by the lights around the courtyard, it seemed as though her mother looked out at her, watchful and unsmiling.

As usual.

Galila wore a stunning tangerine gown, strapless and with a skirt of abundant shimmering silk. A long-sleeved tulle overlay was embroidered and bedecked with silver and glittering jewels—as suited a member of the royal family on the new king's wedding day. Her hair cascaded from beneath a tiara that only ever came out on special occasions, and until now, only on her mother's head.

The dress was too young for her mother, but those were definitely her mother's eyes, scrupulously emphasized with greens and gold, liquid eyeliner ending in a cat's tail. At one time, those doe-like eyes would have swept over Galila with indulgence. Affection.

So pretty, my pet. Her painted lips would have smiled with tender love as she stroked Galila's hair.

Tonight, Galila's mouth—as sensuously curved as her mother's had been and wearing her mother's signature glossy red—tightened. Her elegantly arched brows drew themselves together as she critically sought flaws, exactly as her mother would have done if she had still been alive.

Your skin looks sallow, Galila.

It was the yellow light and her imagination, but the reproach still had the power to sting. To make her yearn to correct the flaw and recapture the love that had dried up and blown away like sand across the desert.

She ought to be glad her mother wasn't here; ought to be grieving properly for a life lost. Instead, it was her secret shame that she was mostly grieving her chance to win back her mother's love. Or perhaps just to understand how she'd lost it.

What had she done that was so terrible—except to grow up looking exactly as beautiful as her mother had been? Was that her great crime?

Could she finally bloom freely now that she wouldn't overshadow her mother?

She lifted the glass she held, leaving another kiss print on the rim.

Not champagne, either, Mother. She directed that baleful thought to her image and received a dispassionate glance in return.

The brandy she had learned to drink at boarding school seared with blessed heat through her arteries, promising the numbing effect Galila sought.

In a perfect world, she would drink herself unconscious and possibly drown here in an inch of water, escaping the chaos raging around her.

Don't make a spectacle of yourself, Galila. That's Malak's purview.

"Your dress is getting wet."

The male voice, so deep and velvety it matched the caress of the warm night air, had her turning to peer into the shadows, expecting—well, she didn't know who she expected. A man, yes, but not *such* a man.

He leaned against the edge of an archway, features sharpened by the low light and framed by the drape of his *ghutra*. He was dangerous and handsome at once. Dangerously handsome with those dark, deeply set eyes and strong jaw beneath a short, black beard. Breath-stealing, in fact, in his gold-trimmed *bisht* that might have been the color of a good merlot. It hung open across wide shoulders to reveal his embroidered *thobe*, tailored to his muscled chest, collar closed at his throat and decorated by a yellow sapphire the size of her fist.

She told herself it was the alcohol that made her sway, but she suspected it was the impact of his virility.

He straightened and held out a hand. "Come. Before you ruin perfection."

He sounded indifferent, perhaps a little impatient, but her confused, bruised-up heart reached like a flower toward the sunshine of his compliment. She used her free hand to lift her skirt and carefully placed her feet on each round tile. She was a little too drunk for stepping stones and appreciated when he took the drink from her hand and clasped her forearm, balancing her until she was completely away from the water.

His touch undermined her equilibrium as much as

the brandy, though. More, perhaps. Brandy didn't make her chest feel tight and her eyes dampen with longing. Her ears picked up the distant sound of the wedding music, but all her senses were trained on him. Something in her flowed toward him. Sought...*something*.

He was tall, radiating magnetism while a force field seemed to surround him, one that made him seem untouchable. It cracked fissures through her that she couldn't begin to understand.

Maybe it was the brandy causing this overwhelming reaction.

He smelled the glass and his mouth curled with disdain. He set the glass aside.

"You don't approve of alcohol?"

"I don't approve of drunkenness."

It should have sounded too uptight for words, but she was ever so sensitive to censure. His condemnation cut surprisingly deep. Why? He was nothing to her.

But he was also like nothing she'd ever experienced—and she'd seen a lot these last few years, living in Europe. He wasn't like any of the urbane aristocrats or earnest artists she'd met. He didn't even match what she expected here, in her home country of Khalia. He was almost too iconic in his arrogant sheikh demeanor. She had long decided that if she ever did marry, it would be to a progressive, cultured man from abroad. Not one of these throwback barbarians from five centuries ago.

Yet he was utterly fascinating. A tendril of desire to impress him wormed through her. She wanted to stand here and hold his attention and earn his regard.

Quit being so needy, she heard Malak say in her head. He had learned to live without love or anyone's good opinion. Why did she think it was necessary?

She didn't, she told herself and reached for the glass. "It's my brother's special day. I'm celebrating."

"People do stupid things when they're drunk." Sheikh Karim of Zyria didn't raise his hand or his voice. He didn't even tell her not to drink.

Nevertheless, his deep tone carried the quiet command instilled by his station. It was evidently enough to make her falter and reassess him, perhaps understanding she would ignore him at her own peril.

He returned her scrutiny, taking advantage of the chance to do so up close. That's what he told himself he was doing, in any case.

He had watched the royal family all day and evening—the ones who were here, at least. Princess Galila, with her stark resemblance to her deceased mother, fascinated him the most. She flitted like a bird from perch to perch, joining this group and that, welcomed by all and animated as she spoke, flirtatious and not above rolling her eyes at anyone, including her brother, the groom and newly crowned King of Khalia.

Had her mother possessed that same sparkling energy? Was that how she had so ensnared his father? He had seen photos of all of them over the years, but in person, Princess Galila was not merely beautiful. She was potent and enthralling, pulling at him in a way he resisted out of principle.

Out of self-preservation, a voice whispered deep in the back of his mind.

Not that he was in danger of infatuation, he assured himself. She struck him as far too superficial, thriving on being the center of attention. The way she smiled and bantered told him she was fully aware of the power in her beauty and sex appeal. She used it without shame to steal the spotlight from every other woman in the room.

That's why it had surprised him when she'd slipped into the garden and walked away from the party into the family's private courtyard. He had followed because he wanted to understand how this woman's mother had destroyed and reshaped his entire life, not because he had been compelled to keep her in his sights.

Had her mother, Queen Namani, been this vain? He'd watched Galila preen in front of her own reflection like a lovebird, so deeply enamored with herself that she hadn't been aware of his presence.

He wasn't a stalker, lurking in shadows, spying on pretty maidens. He was a king, one with questions he had never been able to answer. Besides, he wanted to see her up close. Discover the secret of her allure.

He'd called her out of the pool—which was when he'd realized she was drunk.

Disappointing. He abstained, never wanting to be so far into his cups that he thought a leap off a balcony would solve his problems.

When he'd told her drinking was unwise, he'd thought for a moment that despair clouded her eyes, but she'd quickly switched to using her stunning looks to distract and mesmerize.

"What's stupid about enjoying myself?" she challenged lightly. She lifted her hair off her neck and let it flow carelessly off her forearm, watching to see if he followed the movement.

There was a man inside this royal casing. He felt desire the same as any other, but he knew when he was being invited to lose focus by ogling a breast. Much as he longed to eye the weight of her curves, he kept his gaze locked with hers.

"Exhibit A. You're on a tear of self-destruction." Locking horns with him was a grave mistake, he silently warned.

She was disconcerted by his unaffected response. She might even have been burned by it. Her brow flinched. She quickly lifted her chin in a rally of spirit, though.

"Perhaps I have reason. Did you think of that?" Her long lashes blinked in big, innocent sweeps.

"I'm sure your life is very fraught," he said drily.

"I lost my mother three months ago," she threw back at him with quiet anguish. "I'm entitled to grieve."

"You are." He dipped his head, but that was as much condolence as he was willing to offer. He hadn't been allowed any self-pity after his father's death. The circumstances had been far more disturbing and he'd been a child of six. "Drinking yourself blind will only make things worse."

"How is *that* possible?" she cried softly. "My father is so grief-stricken, he's like a shell. I can't reach him. No one can." She looked to the huge window where her own reflection had stood. "He misses my mother terribly."

Karim understood that affliction, too. No matter what he did, he had never been able to ease his mother's heartbreak over her loss, either. Protecting her from the fact that his father's death had been a suicide was the best he'd ever been able to do.

"She had an affair," Galila whispered. "He loved her anyway, but now we all know about it, which seems to have tripled his agony."

Karim's heart stopped. Even the breath in his lungs stilled.

As if she noted his jolt of alarm, she nodded to confirm her shocking statement, eyes wide and tortured.

"Your father knew but kept it from you?" Karim's mind raced. He had never confided in a single soul, no matter how long and heavily the truth had weighed on him—and it had. Endlessly. With the death of Queen Namani, he had thought that at least the secret of the affair would die when he did.

"He's known for years!" Her tone rang with outraged astonishment. "He helped her cover it up when she became pregnant. They sent away our half brother the day he was *born*."

Karim had to concentrate on keeping his face expressionless, his feet rooted to the marble tiles so he didn't fall over. His ears rang as though the soft words had been a cannon next to his head.

Galila gave a choking half laugh of near hysteria. "Explain to me how one processes *that* sort of news except to get roaring drunk?"

"You have a third brother? A half brother?" *He* had a half brother? His carefully balanced world wasn't just tilting on its axis. It was reaching such a sharp angle everything was sliding into a jumbled mess at his feet.

"Yes!" She didn't seem to notice his deep shock, too caught up in layers of emotional turmoil within herself. "My brothers and I should have been supporting each other, comforting our father, but *he* showed up at the funeral. Told us how our mother had been writing to him for *years*. How she regretted sending him away because she *loved him best*." Her eyes gleamed with a thick sheen of tears. "Because he was her only link to the man she truly loved."

Her fist went to the spot over her breast where she seemed to stem the cracks in a bleeding heart.

"Our father had a complete breakdown. Who wouldn't? We nearly all did! Zufar had to step in and take over… And now that's where Zufar's intended bride is, with *our half brother*." She spoke with livid bewilderment, arm flinging out to some unknown location. "Zufar wasn't supposed to marry Niesha. Amira's been promised to him since she was born, but Adir came back this morning and talked Amira into running away with him. I watched her go through the window. Adir said it was his revenge for being denied his birthright."

"Adir," Karim repeated faintly. That was the name of his brother? He barely heard the rest of what poured out of her.

"Zufar is so single-minded, he married our *maid* rather than admit there was anything wrong. Malak has quit the palace entirely, gone gambling or to work his way through a harem, I imagine. Where does that leave me? With *no one*. So excuse me if I take some comfort in a bottle of brandy."

When she started to drink, he stole it and tipped the alcohol onto the tiles. He had to. This news was utterly explosive.

"Who else have you told?" he demanded.

"No one," she muttered, giving a *tsk* of annoyance at the brandy puddle. "Now I have to walk all the way back for a fresh one."

"Who is Adir's father?" He kept his voice level but held the empty glass in such a tight grip he expected it to shatter in his hand, leaving him dripping blood onto the evaporating alcohol.

"No one knows." She gave her hair a flip. "Mother took *one* secret to her grave, it seems. Although, I have half a mind to ask around that crowd." She jerked her chin toward the balcony across the darkened expanse of the garden, where light poured out the open doors to the palace ballroom. "He must be there."

The elite from all the neighboring kingdoms mingled in a kaleidoscope of colored gowns and robes. Voices competed with the music in a din that suddenly grated on him more than he could bear.

"Why do you think that?" he asked, forcing a tone of mild curiosity while his blood prickled in his veins.

"My mother wouldn't take up with a servant. It had to have been someone of her stature, very likely one of those men congratulating my brother on his mismatched marriage."

She was right, of course. His father had been exactly at her mother's level, not that Karim would confirm it. Maybe the affair had started at an event like this, he imagined. His father and her mother would have been about his and Galila's age when they met, in their prime and bursting with biological readiness. Perhaps they had slipped away into the shadows to indulge their passion, as other couples were doing even now.

He was far too practical to wish, but he had an uncharacteristic longing to be one of those carefree couples with Galila. If only he could enjoy a simple dalliance, like other people, rather than listening to her sing his personal scandal to the night sky while racking his brain on how to most quickly prevent it going further than his own ears.

She was inordinately desirable, he noted with determined detachment. He almost understood his father's desolation at being rejected by such a woman. Of course, his father had been married and never should have started the affair in the first place, but Karim had no such restrictions.

In fact, remaining close to this pretty bird was exactly what he ought to do. He had devoted his life to ensuring his mother never learned the truth about his father's death. He wasn't about to watch it all come apart through one woman's brandy-lubricated tongue. In fact, he had to ensure the entire family's silence on the matter.

Hmm.

"We should get back to the party," the mysterious stranger said.

Through her haze of growing infatuation, Galila distantly realized she shouldn't be loitering alone with a man, let alone spilling family secrets in his ear, but there was something exhilarating about holding his attention. For weeks, in many ways *years*, she'd been an afterthought. Female, and therefore less than her male brothers. Princess, not queen.

"Mmm, yes, I'd love to fetch a fresh brandy," she said with a cheeky slant of her lashes at him.

No smile of answering flirtation, only a circumspect look that made her heart sink under the feeling she had disappointed him.

"I don't need your permission," she pointed out, but her confidence was a stuttering thing in her chest.

"We'll see," he said cryptically and took her arm to steer her around the pool.

His touch sent a shock of electricity through her. She

jolted and nearly turned her ankle. It was disconcerting, made even worse by his disapproving frown.

I'm not that drunk, she wanted to claim, but all coherent thoughts seemed to have left her brain.

Her entire being was realigning its magnetic poles with something in him. She wasn't just aware of him. His presence beside her seemed to surround her in a glow that tingled her skin and warmed her blood. It compressed her breaths while making her feel each one come into her like scent, except it was his aura she was taking into herself.

In a daze, she let him guide her toward the path that would lead them into the garden and back to the wedding reception.

"You don't drink at all?" she asked, trying desperately to ground herself in reality.

"Never."

"Oh, please," she teased, leaning into his firm grip on her elbow. "Let me be the one to initiate you."

Some dim instinct for self-preservation warned her that provoking him was a terrible idea. Something deeper, even. A sense that her gentle mockery not only failed to impact him but was misplaced. He wasn't weak at any level. Nor innocent. He was worldly to the point of cynical, and inimitably strong because he allowed no one to influence him.

Looking up at him as they entered the garden, she noted that his mouth was a work of art. Despite how very serious it was, his lips were full and sensual. How would they feel, crushed against hers?

The flush that went through her at that thought was pure lust, hitting in all her erogenous zones and making her feet tangle into themselves again.

He stopped and steadied her, frowning. "Do I have to carry you?"

She laughed at the thought of it. She was worldly enough to have fooled around with men, but she knew who she was. She had kept her reputation intact along with her virginity for the sake of her family. Maybe even to avoid one more harsh criticism from her mother. The deep-down truth, however, was that she'd never been overcome with enough desire to give her body to anyone.

The compulsion to throw herself into the arms of this man, tonight, was intense enough to unnerve her. A drunk and stupid idea, indeed, but exciting. She didn't even know his name!

"What were you doing over here? Following me?"

"Same as you." A muscle in his cheek ticked. "Reflecting."

"On?"

"Responsibility."

"How boring. I'm surprised I didn't find *you* drunk and facedown in that pool."

The severity in his expression didn't ease. His hold on her arm sent glittering sensations through her bloodstream. She ought to shake him off. What would people think if they returned together? Nothing good, that was certain.

Such a remarkable man, though. One she really didn't want to share with a party full of beautiful women. She wanted him to be hers. To look on her with adoration and desire.

His expression in the moonlight was cool and decidedly intent. Ruthless, even. But there was hunger buried deep beneath his layers of control. Avid male need that she had seen often enough to recognize it. His narrowed eyes focused on her mouth, telling her his speculation was along the same lines as her own.

"Don't you want to throw caution to the wind sometimes? I do." She flipped her hair behind her shoulder again. *Look at me. Want me.* "Malak gets away with it all the time. I'm tired of being the good girl."

"Are you?" Something in his silky tone and the way he flicked his gaze down her front wound around her like ribbons, exciting and wicked. Tightening and binding, compressing her breaths, yet making her feel free.

"Am I tired? Or a good girl? I'm both." She thought of her charity work, her carefully cultivated image of kindness and purity, her endless striving to earn her mother's approval and her stalwart presence beside the men in her life as they took their own self-destructive paths.

All her life, she had tried to be like her mother. They had all thought Queen Namani so perfect, but she hadn't been. Why should Galila live up to something that was an illusion? Live up to the expectations of a woman who not only hadn't held herself to such high standards after all but was also *dead*.

"I'm ready to do what I want." She pressed herself to his front and lifted her mouth.

"I don't take advantage of inebriated women," he said, but with a glance toward the light of the party. His cheeks hollowed, giving his profile a chillingly ruthless appearance. His hands on her arms tightened in some internal struggle.

"I'm not that drunk," she dismissed in a sultry voice. She was low on inhibition, certainly, but more intoxicated by the excitement he made her feel.

They were in a faraway, unlit corner of the garden, where the scent of roses and herbs, orange blossom and frangipani coated the air, making it feel thick as a blanket around her.

"Kiss me," she demanded when he hesitated.

His hands almost began to push her away, but he only held her like that, staring into her uplifted face. For three heartbeats that shook the entire world, they stood like that, as he debated and came to a decision.

With a muttered imprecation, he circled his arms around her. His fingers dove into her hair, tilting back her head as his mouth came down to cover hers.

For another pulse of time, that was all it was. One mouth against another while the universe seemed to open itself, leaving her utterly vulnerable yet transfixed by the vast beauty of it.

With a harsh noise in his throat, he dragged his lips across hers. Instantly they were engulfed in a kiss that was beyond anything she had ever experienced. Intimate and passionate. Hot and damp and demanding. A statement of possession but with a quality that swept her into abandoning herself willingly. Joyfully.

The texture of his tongue met her own, boldly erotic. She reacted with a moan and mashed herself into him so hard her breasts hurt, but it felt good, too. The contact assuaged the tips that stung like bites. When he started to ease back, she whimpered and pressed her hand to the cloth covering his head, urging him to continue kissing her with this mad passion. She wanted to feel his hair, taste his skin, strip naked and know the weight of him over her.

She wanted to know how that hard flesh that was pressing against her belly would feel stroking inside her.

With an abrupt move and a ragged hiss of indrawn air, he pulled back. "Not here."

Had he read her mind? Her body?

"My room," she whispered, already plotting their discreet path through the halls of the palace.

"Mine," he stated. She couldn't tell if it was a preference of location or if he was staking a claim on her. Either way, she let him take her hand and drag her from the garden toward the stairs that led up to the balcony outside the ballroom.

She balked in the shadows at the bottom of the steps. "My lipstick. People will know."

"I thought you were ready to take control of your own life?"

In the slant of light, she saw a mercilessness curl at the corner of his mouth. He pivoted them a few steps into the shadows beside the wall of the steps.

She was more than ready to give herself to him, but this was her home. Her brother's wedding. She was the Princess of Khalia. She was sober enough to know that she had to be discreet about having an affair, not parade it through the middle of a state ceremony.

But as her would-be lover pressed her to the stones that had barely cooled in the hours since sundown, she forgot her misgivings. Her hands found the heat of his neck and she parted her lips, moaning as he kissed her again.

He transported her to that place of magic they seemed to create between them.

As she lost herself to his kiss again, he stroked her hip and thigh, urging her to pick up her knee and make space for him between her legs. Cool air grazed her skin as he shifted her skirt up, up and out of the way, touching—

She gasped at the first contact of fingertips against the back of her thigh. Arrows of pleasure shot into her core, making her yearn so badly her eyes grew damp along with her underthings. She arched her neck as he trailed his mouth down her throat.

It was exquisite and joyful and…

Wait.

He was hard where he pressed between her legs, but something was off.

She touched the side of his face, urging him to lift his head. There was heat in his glittering eyes, but it was banked behind a cooler emotion. Something deliberate. His skin might have been flushed with arousal, but his expression was dispassionate.

He wasn't as involved as she was.

Hurt and unease began to worm through her, but before she could fully react, she heard a gasp and a giggle above them. Someone said a pithy, "Get a room."

"That's the princess!" a female voice hissed.

"With who?" She knew that demanding masculine voice. She looked up to see several faces peering down at them over the wall of the balcony, one of them her brother's. He did *not* look pleased.

Did her lover release her leg to find a modicum of decorum? Not right away. Not before she caught a dark look of satisfaction in his hard features.

Gaze solely on her, he very slowly eased his hold on her leg so his touch branded into her skin as she lowered her thigh. Humiliation pulsed in her throat, made all the more painful by the way he had gone from passionately excited to…this. Remote. Unaffected. Perhaps even satisfied by her public set down.

Angry and embarrassed as she was, her abdomen

still tightened in sensual loss as he drew away from their full-frontal contact, which only added to her mortification.

"You were right," he said. "We should have gone to your room."

She had no choice but to take refuge there. Alone and *fast*.

CHAPTER TWO

GALILA WOKE TO a dull headache, some low-level nausea that was more chagrin than hangover and a demand that she present herself to her brother *immediately*.

Despite what she would have hoped was a fulfilling wedding night, Zufar was in a foul mood and fifteen minutes in, didn't seem to be tiring of tearing strips off her.

"You can't bring that sort of shame down on the palace and think it doesn't matter."

"What shame?" she cried, finally allowed a word in edgewise. "A few people saw us kissing. Malak behaves far worse *all the time*."

"And you hate it when he gets the attention! You couldn't put your own silly need to be in the spotlight on hold for one night? The night of my wedding? Is anyone talking about our ceremony or my bride? No. The buzz is all about the fact you were seen behaving like a tart."

"You're welcome," she said with a glance at her manicure. "Because the things they were saying about your marriage to the maid weren't all that flattering."

"Mind how you talk to your king, little sister," he said in a tone that should have terrified, but she refused to take him seriously. It was just the two of them in here and he was behaving like a Neanderthal.

"I don't know what you want me to do," she said, throwing up her arms. "I can't undo it."

"You could start by promising you'll show more decorum in future. This shouldn't even be happening. Why Mother let you go this long without marrying you off to someone who can control you, I will never understand."

"Can't you?" she bit out sharply.

"What is that supposed to mean?"

"She saw me as competition, Zufar." It was plain as day.

"Get over yourself, Galila. *You* are the one who sees everyone as competition. Take heed now. I won't have you upstaging my queen. You will learn to take a back seat."

"I wouldn't—"

They were interrupted by a servant. He entered after a brief but urgent knock and hurried to lean into Zufar's ear. All Galila caught was "…very insistent…"

Zufar's expression hardened. "Show him in." As she turned, Zufar added, "Where do you think you're going?" He glared at Galila's attempt to exit.

"I assumed we were done."

"You wish. No, I have no idea why he insists on speaking to me, but I imagine it concerns you, so you'll stand here while he does."

"Who?" She looked to the door the servant had left through.

"Sheikh Karim of Zyria."

"Is that his name?" She had imagined he was one of their more illustrious guests but hadn't realized—

Zufar slammed his hand onto his desktop, making her jump. "Do not tell me you didn't even know the name of the man who had his hand up your skirt."

She looked to the corner of the ceiling, biting the insides of her cheeks.

"Do you honestly think my life has room for your childish antics?" Zufar demanded.

She started to scowl at him, but *he* came in. Sheikh Karim of Zyria. He had exchanged his ceremonial garb of last night for a Western-style bespoke suit in slate gray sans headdress.

If possible, he was even more knee-weakeningly handsome. The crisp white of his shirt and blood-red tie suggested a man who commanded any world he occupied. He stole the breath from her body in a psychic punch, utterly overwhelming her.

His gaze spiked into hers as though he'd been waiting to see her again, but before her heart fully absorbed that sensation, he offered a terse nod and turned his attention to her brother, leaving her feeling promptly dismissed and inexplicably bereft.

After ensuring Princess Galila had indeed retired for the night, Karim had gone to his own guest apartment, somewhat disgusted with himself. He had been telling the truth when he'd claimed not to take advantage of women in a weakened state. He considered himself an honorable man.

But he hadn't been able to take the chances that she would leak his secret to someone else after her next sip of brandy.

He had been wrestling with his conscience over whether he should seduce this tipsy woman to his room, where he could at least contain her, when she had thrown herself against him in the darkest corner of the garden.

Their kiss had been the most potent drug imaginable, jamming into his veins and bringing him throbbingly alive at the first taste of her. As if he'd been dead for three decades. Existing, yet not seeing or tasting or smelling. Not *feeling*.

Then, for heart-stopping minutes, he had been resurrected. Sunlight had dawned upon him, shaking him awake from a long freeze. Everything in him had wanted to plunge into that world and never leave it.

Somehow, he had pulled back, much the way any sane man would catch himself before teetering like a crazed addict into a hallucinogenic abyss.

That shockingly intense reaction had been a lesson. One he would heed. Now he knew *exactly* how dangerous she was. It meant he was now prepared to withstand the power of her effect on him.

He kept telling himself his abominable actions were for honorable ends. He was protecting her family as much as his own. His deliberately public display had worked beautifully to put an end to any inquiries she might have made about the man who had impregnated her mother.

Temporarily.

The rest of his strategy would play out now.

With one brief glance, he took in her suitably demure dove-gray skirt and jacket with a flash of passion-pink blouse beneath. Her hair was rolled into a knot behind her head, but she was every bit as beautiful as she'd been last night, if looking a little haunted around the eyes and pouty around the mouth.

He didn't allow his gaze to linger, even though the flush on her skin was a sensual reminder of her reaction to him last night. She had worn a similar color when their kisses had sent the pulse in her neck racing against the stroke of his tongue. That response of hers had been as beguiling as the rest, and not something he could allow himself to recollect or he'd embarrass himself.

For the most part, Karim kept his emotions behind a containment wall of indifference. It wasn't usually so difficult. He'd been doing it his whole life.

Last night, however, this woman had put more than one fracture in his composure. Those tiny cracks had to be sealed before they spread. His reaction to her would be controlled. His command of this situation would be logical and deliberate. Effectual—as all his actions and decisions were throughout his life.

He started by refusing to react with any degree of emotion when her brother offered a blistering, opening attack.

"I expected better of a man in your position, Karim." Zufar didn't even rise, lifting only one sneering corner of his mouth. "You should have had the grace to be gone by now."

"Allow me to make reparation for any harm to your family's reputation," Karim said smoothly. "I'll marry her."

Galila gasped. "What? I'm not going to marry *you*."

Karim flicked a glance to her outraged expression. "Do not tell me you are promised elsewhere." He had to fight to control his reaction, never having experienced such a punch of possessiveness in his life. He would shed blood.

"No." She scowled. "But I'm not ready to marry anyone. Certainly not a stranger. Not just because I kissed you. It's ridiculous!"

"It's highly practical and a good match." He had spent much of the night reasoning that out, determined emotions wouldn't enter into this arrangement. "You'll see," he assured her. Her flair of passion could wait for the bedroom.

"I will not see!"

"Quiet." Zufar held up a hand, rising to his feet.

Galila rushed forward and brushed it down.

"Don't tell me to be quiet," she hissed. "I will decide whom I marry. And while it's a kind offer—" she said in a scathing tone that suggested she found Karim's proposal anything but, she stared Karim right in the eye as she said emphatically, *"No."*

Her crackling heat reached toward him, licking at the walls he forced himself to keep firmly in place.

"Clearly your sister has a mind of her own." She was the kind of handful he would normally avoid, but greater things were at risk than his preference for a drama-free existence. "Was that the problem with your first bride?" Karim asked Zufar with a blithe kick below the belt. "Is that why she ran off with your brother?"

"What?" Zufar's voice cracked like a whip, but Karim kept his gaze on his intended bride, watching her flush of temper pale to horror.

"Half brother, I mean," he corrected himself very casually, despite feeling nothing of the sort. This was high-stakes gambling with a pair of twos he was bluffing into a straight flush.

"Galila." Zufar's tone was deadly enough that Karim shifted his attention—and the position of his body— to easily insert himself between the two if necessary.

Incensed as her brother looked, he didn't look violent. And culpable as Galila grew, she didn't look scared. She was glaring blame at Karim.

"Why are you doing this?" Her voice was tight and quiet.

"I am in need of a wife. Or so my government takes every opportunity to inform me." It wasn't a lie. "You are of suitable... What was the word you used when describing your mother's lover? Station? Stature. That was it."

"This goes beyond even your usual nonsense," Zufar said in a tone graveled with fury. "A moment ago, you didn't even know his name, yet you talked to him about our family's most intimate business?"

"I was drunk." She looked away, cheeks glowing with guilt and shame. "That's not an excuse, but it's been a very trying time, Zufar. You know it has. For all of us."

Zufar's eyes narrowed on her and his cheeks hollowed, almost as if he might accept that as reason enough for her imprudent behavior.

"Allow me to assure you," Karim said with scalpel like precision, "that if you agree to our marriage, your family's secrets will stay between us."

The siblings stood in thunderous astonishment for a few moments.

"And if I don't agree to the marriage?" Zufar asked, but Karim could see they both already knew the answer.

"Blackmail?" Galila asked with quiet outrage. "Why would you stoop so low? Why do you *have* to?" she challenged sharply.

He didn't. He hadn't made marriage a priority for a

number of reasons, most of them superficial and convenience-related. He was a workaholic who barely had time for his mother, who still very much needed him. Women expected things. Displays of emotion. Intimacy that went beyond the physical.

"I'm not going to hurt you, if that's what you're suggesting," Karim scoffed. "I'll treat you as gently and carefully as the pretty little bird you are."

"In a gilded cage? You know, you could ask me to marry you, not trap me into it."

"Will you marry me?"

"*No.* I would never have anything to do with someone as calculating and ruthless as you are."

"You already know me so well, Princess, you're practically made for me. It certainly seemed that way last night."

Zufar made a noise of outrage while Galila stomped her foot, blushing deep into her open collar.

"Stop talking about that! There are other women," Galila insisted. "Pick one."

"I want you."

"I won't do it."

Karim only swung his attention back toward her brother. "I've made it clear what I'm prepared to do to get her."

"Why? What else do you want?" Zufar flared his nostrils in fury.

Above all, Karim wanted to forestall any speculation about who might be the mysterious man their mother had fallen for. If it became known that Queen Namani's lover had been his father, King Jamil, the news would not only destroy his mother, but it would rock both kingdoms right down to their foundations. Not to mention what this newly discovered half brother might do with the knowledge.

So Karim only asked, "Is it so remarkable I might want her?"

"You didn't even introduce yourself. Last night was a setup," Zufar said.

"Oh, thank you very much," Galila interjected hotly, but hurt and accusation lingered behind her glossy eyes as she glared at Karim. "I don't care what you threaten. I'm not some camel you're trading."

Karim had given his explanation some thought as he had lain awake last night, having anticipated that Zufar would be a man of intelligence, capable of seeing his sister was being used for reasons that went beyond her obvious charms.

"I'm not the only man who noticed last night that the princess is very beautiful," he said to Zufar. "She's unmarried and much is changing in Khalia with you taking your father's place. An alliance with the sister of the new king could only be an advantage to me."

"And you think I want to form an alliance with a man of your methods?" Zufar scoffed.

"If I'm married to your sister, yes. I think we will both work toward aligning our countries' goals. And I believe, in the long run, you'll appreciate my methods. I'm saving you months of fielding offers from lesser men and having to play politics in refusing them."

"Such magnanimity," Zufar said with venom-like sarcasm, adding darkly, "But I can't refute the logic."

"Try harder, Zufar," Galila said scathingly. "Because I won't marry him and you can't make me."

"I'm your king, Galila." He said it flatly, but not unkindly.

As she tried to stare down her brother, her cross expression slowly faded into something disconcerted. She clearly began to realize what she was up against and grew pale.

"Zufar, you can't."

"I am not Mommy and Daddy whom you can manipulate with your crocodile tears. You have stepped way over the line this time. I can't put this back in the box for you."

It was tough love in action, something Karim would normally subscribe to, but he sensed genuine distress in the way she reached for a tone of reason, though her voice trembled.

"This isn't like our parents' time when everything was arranged and Mommy was promised to Daddy from when she was a girl. We are allowed to marry for love—"

"Did *I* get the bride I wanted?" Zufar interjected. "The time we are in, Galila, is one where we all have to make sacrifices for the crown of Khalia. You made this bed you're already half in." He sent a dark look at Karim. "Whether you were seduced into it or tricked or went there of your own volition."

Karim didn't bother explaining that as far as that side of it went, she had been a willing partner. He might not be a man who indulged his passions, but he and Galila certainly hadn't lacked any. That was the one thing that made him cautious about this arrangement, but that was a worry for a later time, after he got what he wanted.

Which was *her*.

Even though she looked shattered by his demand for her hand. She visibly shook but found the courage to turn and confront him. "I refuse. Do you understand me?"

"Come," Karim responded, holding out his hand, almost moved to pity by her anxiety but not enough to change his mind. "It is done."

"It is not," she insisted. "I'm going to talk to my father."

"You should inform him," Karim agreed. "Do that while I negotiate our marriage contract with your king."

Her father offered no help whatsoever. He gave her a halfhearted pat on her cheek, eyes red and weary.

"It's past time you married. Listen to your brother. He knows what is best for you."

No, he doesn't!

Malak didn't even answer her text. Her friend Amira was gone—seduced into running away with Adir. Galila was jealous of her friend. Amira's escape might have been dramatic, but at least she wasn't forced into a marriage she didn't want.

Galila felt as though she was being kidnapped in slow motion. Even her one trusted ally within the palace, Niesha, had gone from being someone who might cover for her long enough for a getaway to being her *queen*. Galila wasn't allowed to see her without an appointment and didn't have time to make one. A travel case had already been packed for her and Karim was knocking on the door to her apartment while she flittered back and forth in a panic.

"Ready?" The detached question made her long to dismiss him as a robot, but there was something deeply alive about him. He was a lion—all-powerful and predatory, completely unfeeling in what he pursued or how much pain he caused, so long as he could feast on whatever it was he desired.

"I will never forgive you for this," she said in reply.

"Let's save our vows for our wedding day."

"There won't be one." She used a glare that unfailingly set a man in his place, but he was impervious, meeting her icy gaze without flinching.

Much to her chagrin, as she maintained the eye contact, she felt the tug of desire all over again. His eyes were such a dark brown they were almost black, velvety and holding far more depth than she initially gave credit for.

The whole time he had been blackmailing her brother and admitting that he had manipulated her last night to capture her hand before anyone else could, she had been thinking about how delicious he had made her feel.

She had thought about him *all* night, mostly feeling disappointed that they'd been caught and interrupted, not nearly as mortified as her brother had wanted her to feel when he had criticized her behavior.

But the enigmatic stranger who had kissed her was gone. He had turned into this disinterested man who had used her. His complete lack of reaction toward her, his utter indifference, reminded her that all the feelings and attraction had been on her side. That thought carved a hole right next to the ones already leaving a hollow feeling inside her.

Even if it was about time she married, even if she absolutely had to succumb to marriage, it should be to a man who wanted *her*. Not Zufar's sister. Not the Princess of Khalia. Not the politically expedient ally. *Her*.

He ought to at least offer her the adoration her mother

had had from their father. No one should expect her to accept *this*.

And yet, as they walked outside to the cars, a polite round of applause went up.

For appearance's sake, her brother had announced that their engagement had been kept secret for weeks, so as not to overshadow the coming wedding. If Zufar thought the departing wedding guests believed that, there were several bridges in America he could purchase at an excellent price.

Repulsed as she was by the lie, she didn't make a scene. Far too late for that. She accepted congratulations with a warm, delighted smile. Let them all think this was as grand a romance as her brother tried to package it.

The better to humiliate Karim when she left him in the dust.

"Are you really a sheikh?"

Oh, had his fiancée finally chosen to speak to him? He glanced up from his productive hour on his laptop.

She hadn't cried or begged as they left the palace, which he had half expected. She had thrown waves of cold, silent resentment at him, making it clear that if he hadn't personally escorted her into the car and then his helicopter, she wouldn't be here.

As a man highly in demand and averse to theatrics, Karim told himself that receiving the silent treatment was a gift. At the same time, he had to acknowledge her strength of will was more than he had bargained for. He wasn't someone who thrived on challenge and overcoming conflict. He didn't shy away from it, either. He met obstacles head on and expected them to get out of his way.

This woman, however, with her royal blood seething with passion, wasn't cowed by the mere timbre of his voice. On the surface, she appeared soft and delicate, but he was beginning to see the length of steel in her spine.

He hoped like hell that didn't portend clashes. He had no time for tantrums.

"I am," he answered mildly.

Her skeptical gaze left the window to scan the interior of the helicopter cabin, then dropped to the clothes he'd changed into for travel. He'd worn a suit for his high-stakes meeting with her brother but wore typical Arab attire as often as possible. Not for religious or political reasons, but because he found it the most comfortable.

"I was not expecting company when I left Zyria," he explained of his helicopter and its lack of attendant. It only seated four in the cabin, but very comfortably. "This aircraft is the fastest and most flexible." He could fly it if he had to and regularly did, to keep up his skills. He would be doing so now, if she wasn't here, not that she seemed to want his company.

Her brows lifted in brief disdain as her attention went back out the window. Her frown increased and he almost smiled, realizing why she was skeptical.

The metropolis of his country's capital, Nabata, was not appearing beneath the descending helicopter. Instead, all she would see out there was a speck of a palace in the rugged desert.

"My mother is looking forward to meeting you. She spends much of her time at the palace my father built

for her away from the city." She liked to escape grim
memories.

It almost felt an insult to bring the daughter of his
father's lover to meet his mother, the Queen Mother
Tahirah. She had no idea of her husband's infidelity,
of course. Keeping the knowledge from her was why
Karim had orchestrated to marry Galila, but *he* knew.
It grated against his conscience along with the rest of
the secrets he kept.

Galila noted his expression and asked, "What?" with
a small frown. She looked hurt as she touched the scarf
she had tucked beneath her popped collar, then glanced
down to ensure her skirt and jacket were straight. "Is
my hair mussed?"

He cleared whatever shadows had invaded his expression. "No. You're beautiful. Perfect."

Her thick lashes swept down and she showed him
her profile, but he knew she was eyeing him, suspicious
of his compliment.

"You are and you know it," he chided. "Don't expect
me to pander to your vanity."

Her painted mouth tightened. "Because I'm not a
person whose feelings you care about or even an object
you desire. I'm a rung on a ladder."

He pursed his lips, weighing her words and the scorn
beneath them.

"Our marriage is expedient, yes. That doesn't mean
it can't be successful. Many arranged marriages are."

"When both parties agree to said marriage, I'm sure
they are."

They landed and disembarked, forestalling further
debate—which was unproductive at this point. She was
going to marry him and that was that.

"This is very beautiful," Galila said, gazing on the pink marble and intricately carved teak doors.

While Karim agreed, he found the extravagance of the palace disturbing. Clearly his father had been eager to please his wife with it. This wasn't a guilty conscience. He had built it before Queen Namani had come into the picture. Sadly, whatever he had felt for Karim's mother had been overshadowed by what he had felt for the other woman. And Karim and his mother hadn't been enough to live for, once Queen Namani ended their affair.

What, then, must his father have felt for Queen Namani if his first—and supposedly lesser—infatuation had produced this sort of monument? It was a depth of passion—of possession—Karim couldn't wrap his head around. He instinctively shied away from examining it too closely, maintaining a safe distance the way he would a conflagration or other life-threatening force.

As Galila started up the steps, he touched her arm, halting her.

She stilled and seemed to catch her breath. A soft blush rose under her skin.

Her reaction caused an echoing thrill inside him, one that warned him that he was tying himself to a ticking bomb and had to be very careful. On the surface, this physical compatibility might be exciting and promise a successful union, but he knew what indulged passion could do to a man.

He yanked the reins on his own response, hard, especially as he realized he was taking advantage of every opportunity to touch her and still had his palm on her arm. He dropped his hand to his side with self-disgust.

She was looking right at him and whatever she read

in his expression made a tiny flinch cross her features. It was gone so fast, he could have been mistaken, but it slid an invisible wall between them, one that niggled at him.

She lifted her chin to a haughty angle. "Yes?"

"You'll be kind to my mother."

Her spine grew tall with offense. "I'm always kind." She flipped her hair. "I was being kind last night when I let you kiss me."

It took him a full second to understand that the unfamiliar sensation in his throat was an urge to laugh. He couldn't recall the last time he'd loosened up enough for *that*, and fought it out of instinct.

At the same time, a deeper reaction—not ego, but definitely something that had roots in his masculinity—was affronted at her dismissal of their kisses last night. He knew exactly how potent they had been and didn't care for her trying to dismiss that inferno as "kindness."

The impulse to *show* her… But no. He refused to allow her to disarm him in any way. He waved her forward. "I'll look forward to your next act of kindness, then."

She narrowed her eyes.

"Come." He broke the eye contact. He could not, under any circumstances, become enamored with her. He had seen with his own eyes what falling for her mother had done to his father. He would not be another casualty to a Khalia temptress.

Despite its compact size and remote location, expense had not been spared on the desert palace. Galila was no stranger to wealth, but even she had to appreciate the effort of transporting marble and teak doors.

Inside, a fountain provided a musical ripple of noise and cooled the air. Columns rose three stories to a stained-glass dome. Mosaics in green and blue covered the walls to eye height before switching to delicate patterns in golds and blues and tangerines. Wrought iron marked the second-and third-floor walkways that encircled this grand foyer.

"I don't know what this is. A genie's lamp?" She was in love. "It's too beautiful for words."

Karim drew her up some stairs so thickly carpeted their shoes made no sound. They entered his mother's parlor where he introduced her to the Queen Mother Tahirah.

The older woman rose to greet them, her face holding deeply etched marks of grief that reminded Galila of the ones her father wore.

"It's like Queen Namani has come to visit me. Her beauty survives, if not my dear friend herself," she said, taking Galila's hands as she studied her features. "I'm so sorry for your loss."

"Thank you," Galila murmured, returning Tahirah's kisses against her cheeks, genuinely touched by her condolence. "I didn't realize you knew my mother, but of course you must have met her at some point through the years."

Was it her imagination that Karim stiffened? She glanced at him, but only saw the aloof expression she couldn't read. The one that stung because it felt like a condemnation for reasons she didn't understand.

"When we were young, yes," his mother said, drawing her attention back to her. "We often met up after we were both married, but lost touch after my husband passed. My fault. I ceased most of my royal duties and rarely went on social visits. I couldn't face the responsibilities without my soul, Jamil. Thankfully Karim's uncle was able to manage things until Karim was old enough to take his rightful position. And now my son has found happiness." Her faint smile was a weak ray of light in her otherwise anguished expression.

Oh, yes, they were both quite giddy and could hardly contain themselves, Galila thought, but she *was* kind to the less fortunate. Tahirah might be surrounded by extravagance, but she was the living embodiment of money not buying happiness. Her heart was clearly broken and had been for a long time.

"I expect we will both be very content as we go into the future," Galila prevaricated, adding a silent, *separately*. Read the news, gentlemen. Times had changed.

"And the wedding?" Tahirah asked.

"Within the month," Karim said firmly. "As soon as it can be arranged."

Galila stiffened, wondering if he had been planning to ask her about the timeline, but kept her pique to herself as Tahirah drew her across to the satin-covered loveseat.

"There's time for you to wear my engagement ring, then. I had it brought out of the safe."

"I...don't know what to say." Galila looked from the velvet box that Tahirah presented to her, then looked up to Karim, completely taken aback.

He nodded slightly, urging her to accept it.

She opened it and caught her breath.

An enormous pink diamond was surrounded by white baguettes. The wide band was scrolled with tendrils of smaller diamonds, making it as ostentatious as anything could be, but it was also such a work of art, it had to be admired. Coveted and adored, as every woman would want to be by her fiancé as she anticipated joining with him for a lifetime.

Her heart panged at the love that shone from such a piece, something she would never have if she married this man. She swallowed, searching for a steady voice.

"This is stunning. Obviously very special. I'm beyond honored." And filled with anguish that this was such a farce of a marriage when this ring was clearly from a marriage of total devotion. "Are you quite sure?" She looked again to Karim, helplessly in love with it but not wanting to accept something so precious when she was quite determined to abandon him at the first opportunity. She couldn't be kind *and* lie to this poor woman.

"I am," Tahirah said with a husk in her voice. "I haven't worn it in years, but it is beautiful, isn't it? Karim's father loved me so much. Spoiled me outrageously. Built me this palace…" She blinked nostalgia-laden eyes. "Losing him still feels as raw today." She squeezed Galila's hand. "And I'm quite sure Karim is as enamored with you. He has always told me he was waiting for the right woman. I'm delighted he finally found you."

Galila conjured a feeble smile that she hoped his mother interpreted as overwhelming gratitude. She felt very little conscience in defying her brother or even Karim, but misrepresenting herself to Tahirah was disrespectful and hurtful. She was genuinely sorry that she was going to disappoint her.

Karim took the ring from the box and held out his hand for Galila to offer hers.

His warm touch on her cool fingers made her draw

in her navel and hold her breath, but it didn't stop the trickle of heat that wound through her, touching like fairy dust to secretive places, leaving glittering heat and a yearning she didn't completely understand.

Yet again, she experienced a moment of wishing there could be something more between them, something real, but he was being entirely too heavy-handed. She was a modern woman, not someone who would succumb to a man because she'd been ordered to by another.

At the same time, she reacted to Karim as he bent to kiss her cheek. The corners of her mouth stopped cooperating and went every direction. She thought he drew a deliberate inhale, drinking in the scent of her skin when his face was that close, but he straightened away and she was lost at sea again.

She looked to her hands in her lap, pulse throbbing in her throat and tried to focus on the ring. When she finally saw it clearly, she was utterly taken with it—as she was by all sparkly, pretty things. But it was legitimately loose on her, not even staying on her middle finger without dropping right off.

"I would feel horrible if anything happened to it," she said truthfully to Karim. "Would you please take custody of it until it can be resized?"

"If you prefer."

"Do you mind?" she asked Tahirah before she removed it. "I would be devastated if I lost it. It's so beautiful and means so much to you."

Tahirah looked saddened but nodded. "Of course. It's even loose on me these days. It fit me perfectly through my pregnancy and Karim's childhood, but I haven't had a proper appetite since losing his father. Once I took it off, I couldn't bear to wear it again. It reminded me too starkly of what I'd lost. Everything does."

This was why Karim was marrying Galila, this anguish that his mother still carried three decades after her loss. How could he take the grief she attributed to a tragic accident and reveal that her husband had deliberately left her? That he had thrown himself off a balcony, rather than face life without the *real* object of his love?

Fortunately, Galila asked about the palace and other things, not letting his mother dwell too far in the darkness of the past. Karim had been worried when the topic of her mother had come up as they arrived, but now they were moving on to a recap of her brother's wedding and other harmless gossip.

At a light knock, his mother said, "I've had a luncheon prepared. Shall we go through to my private dining room?"

Galila excused herself to freshen up.

"She seems lovely," his mother said as Galila disappeared.

"She is," Karim said, relieved to discover Galila was so skillful at small talk. Their marriage was expedient, and he had spent a restless night thinking that having her as a wife would be a sexually gratifying, if dangerous, game, but he was seeing potential in her to be the sort of partner who fit into his world as if made for it.

She was royal herself. Of course she understood the niceties and other social finesses that were required, especially with women and the older generation. He wasn't sure he wanted to like her for it, though. He needed his guard up at all times.

A servant started to come in, saw they were still in the parlor and quickly made apologies for interrupting them, turning to exit just as quickly.

He noticed what the girl held and waved her to come in and attend to her task.

"Haboob?" he asked his mother as the maid crouched to set the seals in place around the door onto the balcony. He'd been too distracted this morning to check the weather, but the dust storms came up very suddenly, which was probably why his pilot hadn't said anything.

"I'll have rooms prepared for you," his mother said, taking his arm as he led her into her private dining room. It overlooked the oasis next to which the palace was built. The wind was already tugging at the fronds of the palms and whirling sand into small devils.

"I need to return to Nabata this afternoon. Perhaps we'll skip the meal—" He glanced up as a different servant appeared, wide-eyed and anxiously wringing her hands. Thankfully, she stood behind his mother so his mother didn't see her.

Karim knew instantly what the trouble was. Galila should have rejoined them by now. He scratched his cheek, not revealing his instantaneous fury.

"You'll have to excuse us, Mother. We'll stay ahead of the storm. I hope you'll join us in Nabata very soon and have a proper chance to get to know Galila before the wedding."

"Of course," she said with disappointment. "Be careful. I should say goodbye."

"No need." He kissed her cheek and strode from the

room, taking the maid into the hall with him. He asked which car Galila had taken, then hurried outside the palace to snap his fingers at his pilot.

They had to catch his runaway princess before she was caught in the coming storm.

CHAPTER THREE

GALILA'S GETAWAY WAS an exhilarating race down a straight stretch of paved road through the desert. If the sun seemed to dim, she blamed the tinted windows, not her mood. She didn't have any gloomy feelings about leaving Karim. Zero. She couldn't do it fast enough.

Then the light pouring through the sunroof really did change. It became a strobing flash as a helicopter hovered over the car, casting its shadow on the hood. The *rat-a-tat* chop of the blades cut into the otherwise luxuriously silent interior.

"So what?" she shouted. "I have a full tank and an open road."

She would get herself to the border into Khalia and once there, she would be her own person again. She would fly to Europe and stay there. Pull a Malak and quit the family. Do whatever the hell she wanted.

She jammed her foot even harder onto the accelerator. The road was straight and clear, not another car in sight.

He raced ahead, staying low, then stopped and landed in the middle of the road.

"Bastard!"

She had half a mind to ram the car straight into him.

With a muted scream of frustration through gritted teeth, she lifted her foot from the accelerator.

As her speed dropped off, she searched for a way around the helicopter, but it blocked both lanes. This car wouldn't get very far off-road, unfortunately. The soil might look hard-packed, but pockets of loose sand could swallow a tire in a heartbeat. This was the sort of sedan built for a paved highway, not scrubby desert. It would spin in the dirt until it ran out of fuel.

Turn around? The only place to go was back to his mother's palace.

Oh, she was frustrated as she braked! She came to a reluctant stop as she reached the helicopter while its blades were still rotating.

She flung herself from the car. The wash off the rotors caught at her hair. She used a finger to drag it out of her eyes.

"I *will not* marry you," she shouted in single-syllable blurts when Karim came out of the helicopter, expression thunderous.

"Look," he said with a stabbing point to her left.

That was when she realized why the sky had been growing darker. A red-brown cloud rose like a tsunami against the sky. *Haboob.*

She didn't normally swear out loud, so she swallowed the words threatening to fall from her lips.

"We'll outrun it. I want to be in Nabata when it hits." Karim threw his arm around her, using his body to shield her as best he could while he more or less dragged her toward the helicopter.

Much as she wanted to fight him, windstorms could be deadly.

"What about the car?" she shouted.

His pilot was already leaping out of his seat. Galila presumed he would take the vehicle back to the palace and allowed Karim to push her into the copilot's seat.

"This isn't an agreement to marry you," she told him as she buckled in and accepted the headphones he handed her.

He ignored her statement as he quickly buckled in himself and put on his own headset. Maybe he didn't hear her. He lifted off in seconds, perfectly adept as a pilot, which was kind of sexy, not that she wanted to notice.

Within moments, they were racing toward the rocky hills in the distance.

She eyed him, trying to gauge how angry he was. It was difficult to tell when his body seemed to move with natural precision and that stern mouth of his had probably never smiled. She hadn't expected to get caught so she hadn't worried too much about his reaction to her escape, but he wasn't her father and her brothers.

Until this morning, she had been confident she could cajole nearly anything out of anyone—schooling in Europe, Thoroughbred horses, designer clothing. When it came to her charity work, she was a money-raising machine, squeezing record donations out of men and women alike. With very few exceptions, she always got what she wanted.

Things had changed, however. Her stupid brother had put her at the mercy of this wretched man and Karim didn't strike her as the indulgent sort, his mother's remarks notwithstanding. In fact, the longer she watched him, the more her uneasiness grew.

He swore, sudden and sharp as a gunshot, loud enough to make her jump because it came into her head through the earmuffs, crystal clear. For one second, she thought the curse had been aimed at her, then he made a sudden veering motion that tilted them as he avoided something.

She looked forward where visibility had become severely reduced. Despite his efforts, the storm was wrapping around them, buffeting the helicopter. They were running out of time. And options.

He went lower, searching for a safe place to land, but the rotor wash kicked up more dust, making it nearly impossible to see what was on the ground.

"There!" she said as she saw a flash of blue and green, black and yellow—colors and symmetries that didn't belong in the rust-red of the desert. It was a Bedouin camp, men running around securing tents and corralling the camels.

Karim set down on the nearest flat piece of land and turned off the engine, but the rotors continued to turn and whine.

"I have to tie down. Wait here." He leaped from the helicopter.

One of the Bedouins clutched his head-covering and ran to greet him. She saw the shock and flash of a wide smile of recognition before the man hurried to help, shouting at one of his fellow tribesmen that their sheikh was among them.

"Tell the women," she heard him shout. To prepare food and suitable lodging, Galila surmised.

She pulled off her headphones and drew the scarf from around her neck to drape it over her head and prepare to wrap it across her face. Zyria wasn't a country where face covering was demanded, but she would have to protect herself from the blast of dust.

That was when she realized her purse was in the car and she didn't have her sunglasses. Her toothbrush was with her luggage, though.

She went through to the passenger cabin, having to catch her balance twice because the wind was trying so hard to knock the helicopter off its footings. The luggage compartment was easily accessed and she quickly retrieved her necessities along with stealing the shaving kit out of Karim's case. Such things were always the last into the luggage so it was right on top.

Then she shamelessly dumped his laptop bag onto an empty seat. She began filling it with the contents of the onboard pantry—coffee and tea, fresh oranges and bananas, nuts and dried figs, cheese and crackers, chocolates and Turkish delight. Caviar? Sure. Why not?

"What the hell are you doing?" he bit out as he came through from the cockpit.

"Food." She showed him the bag, swollen with his travel larder. "Our toothbrushes are in here, too. Time to run?" She buttoned her jacket and drew her scarf across her face.

He clearly hadn't expected this. He glanced at her heeled shoes. Yes, well, she hadn't made a priority of digging out her pool sandals. She'd been too busy making herself useful.

The helicopter jerked again. They couldn't stay here. The very thing that kept this bird aloft was liable to topple it in the wind. The Bedouins had spent centuries learning how to wait out these types of storms, however. She and Karim would be safer in one of their tents.

Karim leaped out the side door, not bothering with the steps. He reached back to take her by the hips and lift her to the ground while one of the Bedouins stood by and slammed the door behind her.

She dragged her scarf up to peer through the layer of silk, relying more on Karim's hard arms around her to guide her than the ability to actually see. She had only ever watched a storm through a window. It was terrifying to be in it, making her anxious when Karim pressed her into a tent and left her there.

A handful of women were moving around inside it, efficiently smoothing bright blue sheets and plumping cushions on a low bed, setting out a battery-operated lantern on a small dining rug and urging her to sit at a washing basin.

The walls and roof of the tent fluttered while the wind howled and sand peppered the exterior. She removed her scarf and jacket, grateful to wipe away the worst of the dust with a damp cloth. She wound up changing into the silk nightgown she had thrown into the bag since all of her clothes felt so gritty. It wasn't cold in here, not with the sunbaked earth still radiating heat and so many warm bodies in here, but she accepted the delicate shawl one woman handed her.

The entire camp had been informed that the sheikh's intended bride, the Princess of Khalia, was among them. They were pulling out all the stops, eager to praise her choice of husband.

Choice? Ha!

But they wanted to make her comfortable so Galila bit her tongue. She had done enough work with the underprivileged to understand that her problems were not the sort that most people identified with. These women had chapped hands and tired smiles. Everything they owned, they carried.

She let them fuss over her, rather appreciating the motherly kindness of the old woman who wanted to brush her hair. After she had washed her face and hands, she gave her moisturizer to the old woman. The woman laughed and said nothing could erase her wrinkles, but she was pleased all the same.

The other women were excited by the fresh fruit and other treats, insisting on adding a selection from the bag to Galila's meal of stew and lentils.

That was when Galila realized the dining mat was set for two.

What had Karim told them? They couldn't share this tent! They weren't married.

Karim was their sheikh, however. When he entered the tent, the women scattered with gasps and giggles, not a single protest for Galila's honor.

It was fully dark outside by then, despite the still early hour. The tent was lit only by the small lantern over the meal they would share. The wind howled so loudly, she couldn't hear any voices in the neighboring tents.

Now she realized why the women had been so admiring of this silly nightgown, intent on ensuring her hair was shiny and tangle-free as it flowed around her bare shoulders and fell just so across the lace on her back. That was why they had praised him and called him lucky and said she would make him a good and dutiful wife.

They thought she was consummating her wedding night!

She hugged the delicate shawl more closely around her. Her pulse throbbed in the pit of her belly. She curled her toes into the silk nap of the rug beneath her feet, clammy and hot at the same time. Her mind trailed to the way he'd made her feel last night, kissing her so passionately, while the rest of her fluttered with nerves.

He took a long, leisurely perusal from her loose hair to the hem of her ivory nightgown.

Without a word, he removed his robe and scraped his headwear off, tossing the dust-covered garments aside without regard. He wore a white tunic beneath that he also peeled off, leaving him bare-chested in loose white pants that hung low across his hips. He stepped out of his sandals.

She swallowed.

His mouth might have twitched, but he only turned and knelt with splayed thighs on the bathing mat, using the same cloth she had run down her throat and under her breasts to wash his face and behind his neck.

She shouldn't be watching him. Her pulse raced with a taboo excitement as she gazed on the burnished skin that flexed across his shoulders. Her ears picked up the sound of water being wrung from the cloth, and his quiet sigh of relief. Those sounds did things to her. Her skin tightened and her intimate regions throbbed.

She imagined replacing that cloth with her hands, smoothing soap along the strong arm he raised, running slippery palms up his biceps, over his broad shoulders, down to his chest and rib cage. If she snaked her touch beneath his arm to his navel, would she be able to trace the narrow line of hair she had glimpsed, the one that disappeared into the waistband of his trousers?

What would he look like completely naked? What would he *feel* like?

As wildness threatened to take her over completely,

she tried to forestall it by blurting, "You shouldn't be in here."

"Worried about your reputation? We're married." He stayed on the mat with his back to her, continuing to stroke the cloth along his upraised arms and across his chest.

"I don't know how to say this more clearly, but—"

"They have already given up one much-needed tent for me," he interjected, pausing in his bath to speak over her. "I won't ask them to prepare one for you as well. We share this one. Therefore, we must be married. We are."

"Just like that?" she choked. "The sheikh has spoken and thus it is so?"

"Exactly."

She didn't even have words for the weakness that went through her. She told herself it was the deflation of watching her childhood dreams of a royal wedding disappear in a poof, but it was the way her life had changed in the time it took for him to make a declaration.

"You can't." She spoke so faintly she was surprised he heard her.

"It is done, Galila. Accept it." He rinsed the cloth and gave it a hard wring.

"I can't."

She had avoided marriage for many reasons, one of the biggest ones being that she wanted a choice in how she lived her life. At no time had she been satisfied with the idea of putting her fate into the hands of any man—particularly one who didn't love her and didn't seem to even *like* her. She barely knew him!

What she did know was that he was strong and powerful in every way. No one would come to her aid here even if they heard her scream over the wailing wind.

In a matter of a few words, he had stripped away all the shields she possessed—her family name, her station as Khalia's only princess, even the composure she had taken years to construct. There was no affection or admiration or infatuation to leverage here. This was all about expediency. About what *he* wanted.

She tightened her fists at her sides, throat aching while the backs of her eyes grew hot, but she refused to let him see she was terrified.

"You are an educated man with intelligence and—I would hope—a shred of honor." Perhaps that wasn't true, considering he'd used her at the wedding and seemed to have no conscience about behaving like a barbarian from centuries ago. Realizing that made her tremble even harder. "You can't just declare us married and force yourself on me."

"I'm not going to attack you," he said sardonically. "Quit sounding like a terrified virgin."

"I *am* a virgin." She spat it out with as much angst as anger.

He froze, then dropped the cloth and rose, pivoting so neatly on the ball of his foot, the rug gathered beneath him into a knot.

"How?" he asked, sounding very casual with his inquiry, but the intensity that seemed to grip him caused the hot coil in her belly to tighten and glow while her heart teetered and shifted. It thumped in wavering beats, unsure whether to feel threatened or excited under his laser-sharp regard.

"What do you mean, 'how'?" She grew prickly with self-consciousness, face scorched even though virginity was nothing to be ashamed of. "The usual way. By not having sex."

"You're twenty-*five*."

"Six."

He gave his head a small shake, as if he didn't understand the words passing between them.

"How have you not been with a man?"

"I've dated. Had boyfriends. I'm not…completely inexperienced." None of her relationships had lasted, though, because she didn't put out. Not much, anyway. She confined things to kissing and a bit of petting. She knew what happened between the sheets. Girlfriends had described the process in profound detail over the years, which truth be told, hadn't always been a selling feature. The process sounded both incredibly intimate and kind of ridiculous.

"Weren't you curious?"

"Sure." She shrugged, trying to appear offhand when this conversation was equally intimate and awkward. "But not enough to sleep with a man just to know what happens. It's not a book where you can skip to the end and make sure it will satisfy before you wade through all the exposition."

He made a noise that might have been a choke of amusement, but his face remained a mask of astonishment.

"What?" she demanded. She had wanted more. So much more than the tepid feelings that most men inspired in her. Even when her suitors had been adoring and dazzled by her, it hadn't been enough. She hadn't trusted their infatuation to last. She needed *more*.

Karim hung his hands off his hips. "You were going to take me to your room last night," he reminded.

"I was drunk," she claimed, even though with him, it had been different. She had felt the "more" that she'd been craving. At least, she'd thought she had. Now she was so confused, she didn't know what she felt.

He barked out a single harsh, "Ha!" and came toward her.

She stumbled backward in alarm only to have him catch at her arms and steady her.

"You're about to step into our dinner."

She shrugged off his touch, disturbed by the way her whole body was now tingling, and lowered to the rug with him, the food between them.

He stretched out on his side, propped on an elbow. His stern face relaxed a smidge. Maybe. She watched him closely, but wasn't sure.

"Are you laughing at me?"

"No." He reached for an olive in a dish. "Us, maybe. I don't care for lies," he stated. "Tell me now if it's not true. You're really a virgin?"

In the low light, his eyes were more black pupil than brown iris as his gaze came up to take hold of her own, refusing to let it go.

"I am," she said, wondering why her voice had retreated behind a veil and came out shy and wispy. She cleared her throat, searching for the confident woman who usually occupied her skin. "Are you?"

"No." Flat and unapologetic.

She managed to break their stare by rolling her eyes. She had fully expected that answer, but a pang struck in her chest all the same. Jealous? That would be a ridiculous response when she kind of hated him.

Didn't she?

He ate another olive, still watching her. "Be thankful I'm familiar with writing compelling exposition."

"Don't be smug." The pang went through her again.

She wanted to splay her hand over his face and give him a firm shove.

His mouth twitched. "You've been living in Europe for years. I would have thought you would have been drunk before last night."

She had, but she ignored the dig inside his comment and asked, "How do you know where I've been living?"

He shrugged. His gaze lowered to scan the food, but it seemed like a subterfuge.

"Big fan of gossip sites, are you?" she prompted.

"My advisors have kept you on my list of prospects for years. Ours has always been seen as an advantageous match. I would have thought it had been viewed that way in Khalia as well. Your father never suggested me when discussing your own marriage plans? Frankly, I'm surprised you're still single, never mind a virgin."

"Names came up, yours among them," she admitted. "I wasn't interested in marrying so I never bothered to look at photos or read any of the advisements I was sent. Being in Europe, I didn't attend many events to meet any bachelors, either. My mother always sided with me that I didn't have to hurry into marriage."

"That seems odd. Why not?"

Galila shrugged, curling her knees under her, trying to get comfortable but feeling as though she sat on sharp stones. It wasn't the ground beneath the floor of the tent, however. It was the rocky relationship with her mother that was poking at her.

Karim reached a long arm to the bed and handed her a cushion.

"Thank you," she murmured and shoved it under her hip.

"Your mother didn't encourage any match? Or just

not ours?" He seemed to watch her with hawk-like attention.

"It wasn't personal." She told herself she was reading more intense interest from him than the topic warranted because she was feeling so sensitive. She took her time arranging her nightgown so it covered her feet, not wanting him to read the layers of mixed feelings she carried when it came to her mother. They were far too close to the bone to share with a stranger. She wasn't drunk tonight, and she had learned the hard way that he used every weakness for his own gain. "She was sensitive to the signs of age. Preferred to put off being called Grandmother as long as possible."

It hadn't been about her daughter's well-being, but it had suited Galila to avoid the shackles so she had been grateful.

He made a noncommittal noise and accepted the bowl of stew she served him.

"Karim," she said, boldly using his name and finding it a caress in her throat. "I am a modern woman with a liberal education. You cannot expect me to give you my virginity simply because you declare us married."

"Galila." Somehow, he sounded as if he mocked her solemnity, yet turned her own name into an endearment. "You caught fire in my arms when your senses were dulled by alcohol. Your sober brain is now regretting your impulsiveness, but I expect we'll be even more combustible when we lie together. You will give me your virginity because you want to."

She couldn't move, felt caught in amber, her whole being suffused with thick honey that suffocated with the aim of creating something eternal.

"I had hoped that would be tonight," he added in a

voice that seemed to roll into her ears from far away, barely discernible over the noise outside the swaying walls of this tent. "But your inexperience changes things. We'll wait for your trust in me to grow. I've given my staff two weeks to arrange a wedding ceremony and reception at the palace. We can wait until then."

She choked. A whole two weeks? Wow.

"How am I *ever* supposed to trust you when you tricked me into this?" she asked, voice cracking with emotion. "How am I supposed to feel confident— proud—to be your queen when I'm only a strategic political move?"

That was his cue to profess a deeper interest in her as a woman. It wouldn't be a lie to say he was intrigued by the facets she kept revealing. He had thought her impulsive and spoiled, not given to thinking of others. That was certainly the impression she had left last night. Her brother's disparagement of her actions this morning had more or less confirmed it.

But she had put his mother at ease and it didn't escape him that she had ensured the family ring stayed in his possession while she plotted her foiled escape.

He had been prepared to let loose with his riled temper when he confronted her on the highway, but she hadn't kicked up a fuss at their emergency takeoff. She had evacuated with as much awareness of their danger as required. She wasn't balking at camping with the Bedouins, either. Instead of acting like she was above these rough conditions, she had ensured they contributed to the community food supply, guaranteeing she reflected well on him and the union he had made and knowing full well it would affect his country in subtle, unalterable ways.

The worst complaint he had so far was that she had cost him a favored laptop bag, since he wouldn't dream of asking for its return. Even her escape had worked to his advantage, providing him a reason to shift their marriage from intended to a *fait accompli*. He had been on fire since he had spoken the words.

Now he had discovered she was a virgin? He had neither expected nor particularly wanted an untouched bride, but having one was an inordinate thrill. A primal possessiveness gripped him, chest and belly and groin. He would be the only man to stroke and taste and mate with her. She was *his*.

His inner barbarian howled with triumph, recalling the way she had ignited in his arms, demanding to stoke that blaze into an all-consuming inferno *now*.

The very fact he hovered so close to losing his rational brain to the primal one, however, told him he had to slow things down. For her sake and his own.

So he was careful to keep his tone even, not betraying how craven desire licked like flames inside him. "You're very beautiful, Galila. Of course I desire you."

Every man she had ever come into contact with must have desired her. It defied comprehension that she had never physically shared herself with one of them. He wasn't in the habit of disbelieving people, but he genuinely couldn't understand how a woman of her naturally sensual nature hadn't indulged her passion to its fullest extent. *He* had.

Or rather, he had always believed he had. She might have already reset the bar—which was yet another disturbing layer to this thing between them.

All of these thoughts he held to himself behind an impervious mask.

She studied him, picking apart his words and seeming to grow more and more skeptical of them as the seconds passed.

"My beauty has nothing to do with this. You don't care if I'm beautiful. You're beautiful. Do you want me to believe you chose me so we can make beautiful babies?"

He felt his eyebrows jump. The topic of an heir hadn't entered his mind beyond the abstract, but now she had brought it up...

"We should talk about that."

"How beautiful you are?"

"Children."

She scowled and shifted to hug her knees. "Politically expedient broodmare. Is that what I am? How romantic. A thousand times yes, I wish to be your wife, Karim."

He ought to curtail that sarcasm. No one else in their right mind would speak with such casual disrespect toward him, but he found her temper revealing. She probably didn't realize how much of her genuine thoughts and emotions she betrayed with that barbed tongue of hers.

"You had other plans for your life? Tell me how I've derailed them. Perhaps there's a compromise."

"Yes, you strike me as a man who compromises all the time."

Ah. That was what she was afraid of.

"I rarely have to," he admitted. "From the time I was old enough to grasp an adult conversation, I sat with my father in his meetings. He died when I was six and my uncle continued to include me in every decision he made on my behalf, explaining his reasoning. By the time I was fourteen, I was effectively running the country with his guidance and support. *He* carried out *my* wishes until I was officially crowned."

She blinked wide eyes at him. "Zufar is barely ready for that level of responsibility at thirty-three."

"He has the luxury of a father who still lives."

She cocked her head with curiosity. "What happened to your father? It was an accident, wasn't it? I don't recall exactly."

"He fell from a balcony at the palace." He repeated the lie by rote, even though it grated on him to this day that he was forced to carry such a dark secret. He hated lies, probably because his father had burdened him with such earth-shattering ones. "He'd been drinking."

"Ah," she said with soft compassion. "That's why you were so disparaging. I see now why you resent anyone who fails to appreciate the destructive power of alcohol."

He resented a lot of things—his father's affair with her mother, her mother for leaving his father and causing his father to pursue a desperate act. Now Karim learned there had been a child? It wasn't as though he hadn't considered that possibility over the years—and again in the last twenty-four hours specifically where Galila was concerned. She had been born long after his father had died, however. There was no chance they were related, which was quite possibly the only bright spot in this otherwise three-act tragedy.

"Do you want to tell me about him?" she invited gently.

"No." He didn't regret his abrupt response. He rarely spoke about his father, but the way she closed up like a flower, showing him her stony profile, caused him to sigh internally.

Women. They were as delicate as thin-skinned fruit, bruising at the least thing.

"Your father left you without a choice," she summed up, still not looking at him. "So you're comfortable imposing a lack of choice on others."

He wasn't so soft he felt stung by that remark, but he did feel it, maybe because the fact she was striking out that hard told him how deeply her own resentment ran at what he was demanding of her.

"You weren't planning to avoid marriage forever, were you?" People in their position couldn't.

"I was waiting to fall in love."

Ah. Something like regret moved in him, but he wanted there to be no false hopes between them.

"It's true that I will never expect or offer you love," he agreed. "That particular emotion is as treacherous and devastating as alcohol."

"You've been in love?" Her pupils exploded as though she'd taken a punch.

"No. Like alcohol, I don't need to imbibe to see the inherent risks and have the sense to avoid it."

A small flinch and her lashes swept down, mouth pouted.

"It doesn't mean we can't have a successful marriage. In fact, going into this union with realistic expectations ensures we won't be disappointed in the long run."

"Is that what you think?" She took a cube of cheese. "Because the problem isn't whether you can grow to love me. It's that I expected to choose my own husband, not have one forced upon me. I *expected* to make a family when it felt right, because I wanted to see something of my husband in the children I made. If you give me sons and daughters, I'm sure I'll love them, but I don't desire your children."

That one did land in a previously unknown vulnerability. Why?

"Meanwhile, you expect me to give up my freedom so you won't have to go through the inconvenience of renegotiating a few trade agreements with the new Sheikh of Khalia. The two most important decisions any woman will make are whom she will marry and whether she will have children. You expect to make both of those decisions for me. That's not fair."

"As I said, we can talk about children." He wasn't a monster. He had already said they could curtail the sex, hadn't he?

"You still expect me to breed with you eventually," she said with a sharp angst. "You gain on every level with this marriage and I gain nothing. In fact, I lose everything. And I'm not even allowed to feel disappointed? *Your* expectations are the ones that are too high, Karim."

CHAPTER FOUR

"I CAN GIVE you pleasure."

The wind had died down, the light was off, and the sound of a gently plucked string on a *rababeh* carried from one of the other tents. They weren't expected to appear before morning so they had turned in early. Galila had formed a dam down the center of the mattress with a rolled mat and a few cushions before asking Karim which side he wanted.

"Everything that happens in bed between us will be your choice," was his response.

She had sat there stunned by what sounded like a vow, trying to understand why she felt both moved and overwhelmed. It felt like too much responsibility for a woman who knew so little about the things she might want from her marriage bed.

And now, in the darkest dark, he was telling her he could teach her.

She wanted to say something cynical but couldn't find any words, let alone form them with her dry mouth and even drier throat.

"Are you awake?" he asked in a quieter voice.

"Yes." She probably should have stayed silent and let him think she had missed hearing what he said, but she revealed her wakefulness and died a little inside. She threw her wrist across her eyes, wanting to go back thirty hours or so and never take a single sip of brandy at her brother's wedding.

The silence between them grew with expectation.

"I can give myself pleasure," she pointed out, glad for the dark so he wouldn't see her blush at the admission she was making.

Silence was his answer, but she swore she could hear him smiling.

"Don't even pretend you don't…" She couldn't finish the sentence.

"Read the footnotes?" he suggested.

"Oh, yes, you're a delight in bed. So glad I can share this one with you." She turned her back on him and clenched her eyes shut. Her fist knotted in the edge of the blanket and nestled it tight under her chin.

After a pensive few minutes, he said, "I had to take advantage of the opportunity you presented me, Galila."

"Yes, well, I'm not presenting one now. Perhaps give me some quiet so I can get my beauty sleep."

"For various reasons, I never thought you and I would be a good fit, despite the fact my advisors consistently brought you to my attention. You seemed young, wayward and superficial."

"Are you sure you're not a virgin? Because you're offering very little pleasure with remarks like that."

"No one else appealed to me, though." He sounded almost as if this was a surprise revelation only occurring to him now, one that dismayed him. He sounded disturbed, even.

She sighed. "Please don't make this about my looks,

Karim. That's no better than using me for political gain."

"I didn't come to the wedding intending to make an offer for you. I wouldn't have kissed you if you hadn't kissed me first. But when we did…"

"Karim." She was glad for the dark because she was wincing with mortified agony. "I know you weren't as involved as I was. I felt your…" She swallowed. "Distance. Before we were seen."

"That only proves how attuned we are to one another. Physically."

"No! It proves you can manipulate me with my body while I have no such power over you."

He shifted abruptly, voice now coming from the space above and behind her shoulder, telling her he was propped on an elbow. "Did you want me to lose myself and make love to you against the wall where everyone could see us?"

"I wanted you not to use me!"

"I'm offering you a chance to use me."

"You're not that simplistic. Or generous. You're going to get me all worked up, then say, 'Why don't we go all the way?' Not my first rodeo, cowboy."

"Am I?"

"What?"

"Going to get you all worked up? Because I know how to settle myself down. You have no fear I'll prevail on you to provide *my* happy ending."

"Oh!" She buried her cry of frustration into her pillow. "Fine," she declared with the impulsiveness that had earned her a reputation for being exactly as spoiled and wayward as everyone thought her. "Go ahead and prove there's something in this marriage for me. Give me all this pleasure you're so convinced you can provide."

Nothing. No compliments or commands. He didn't move.

She suspected he still hovered over her, but it was too dark to tell. She turned to face him, one hand inching just enough to feel the silk tassel on the cushion still between them.

He drew the rolled mat out of the way and his hand bumped hers when he sought the cushion. He kept hold of her hand.

She didn't know what to do. Pull away? Let her hand rest in his? She was nervous. Curious. Furious. Frustrated in more ways than one.

He lifted her hand and rubbed his lips against her knuckle. The short whiskers of his closely trimmed beard were silky soft where the backs of her fingers brushed against them.

"This isn't about how you look, Galila," he breathed across her skin. "I can't see you. It's about how we make each other feel."

"How do you feel?"

His humid breath bathed her palm before he spoke into it. "I'll let you know when you get there."

The light play of his mouth exploring her skin, the dampness when he opened his lips, sent heady tingles through her entire body. When he pressed a kiss into her palm and set his blazingly hot mouth against the inside of her wrist, tongue swirling against her pulse, she gasped at the wave of arousal that throbbed through her. It sent heaviness into her loins, stinging tightness to the tips of her breasts, and a helpless sob to catch in her throat.

"How are you doing this to me?" He was touching her *hand*.

"What am I doing? Tell me. I can't see you."

"You're—" She didn't want to admit he was seducing her. "I can't breathe. My heart feels like I've run miles."

He moved her hand to his neck, setting the heel of her palm against his smooth throat, next to where his Adam's apple moved as he swallowed. The artery there held a powerful pulse, one that was quick and hard.

"You're excited?" she asked.

"Of course."

No. He was tricking her again. But she found herself doing what she had last night, acting out of instinct, but this time her fingers were in his thick, silky hair. She urged him down and somehow their mouths found each other despite the blinding darkness.

The lack of light amplified the acuteness of her senses. Such a rush of heat went into her lips, her mouth stung under his, assuaged by the lazy way he settled into the kiss, easing her lips to part. She was the one to seek a deeper kiss by searching for his tongue with her own and moaned as their kiss grew fully involved.

His arm snaked around her and he tucked her half beneath him, weight settling more heavily on her. Then he lifted his head just enough to say, "Say yes," against her lips.

He wanted this to be her choice and it was. His bare chest pressed where the straps of her nightgown left her upper chest bare and she had never felt anything like that specific heat and texture. It was intoxicating.

"Yes," she whispered, arching to pull her hair out from beneath her.

It brushed against his skin, and he made a noise that suggested he had to reach for restraint.

"This might become my obsession," he said, gathering the long waves and burying his face in it. When he turned his head, his mouth was against her nape. He licked into the hollow beneath her ear and sucked on her earlobe, making her whimper in delight.

His touch moved to play his barely there fingertips against the silk of her nightgown, following the band of lace beneath her breasts where it hid her navel, coming back to climb the slippery silk alongside the swell of her breast. By the time his touch met where his lips had strayed, and he began to ease the narrow strap down her shoulder, her breasts were swollen and aching. She was so needy, she was feeling wild. Her own hands were moving restlessly across his shoulders, excited but apprehensive.

"I'm going to make love to you with my mouth," he said in a voice that barely penetrated the rush of blood in her ears. "That's not a pleasure you can give yourself."

Was that what she wanted? She didn't know, but she was too caught up in the sensation of his beard across the top of her breast. He bared it and she stopped being able to think straight. The heat of his breath warned her just before his mouth engulfed her nipple, but nothing could have prepared her for the way electricity seemed to shoot through her, stabbing into her heart so she thought it would burst. Sexual need raced in sharp lines to her loins, making her tingle and tremble as he pulled and laved and cupped the swell in his big hand and flicked his tongue against the turgid tip.

She could feel herself growing damp and slick. Heard wanton noises escaping her throat. She wanted him to keep sucking her nipples, but wanted to kiss him, too. It was the sweetest torture and she actually lifted and offered herself when he eased the other strap down, desperate for the delicious torture on her other breast.

Oh, he was making her crazy. She swirled her hands through his hair, over his damp neck, across his shoulders. The dip of his spine was an intriguing place and she even wickedly slipped her hand down to touch his chest, finding his own nipples sharp as shards of glass.

He rose to kiss her mouth again, hard and thorough. She moaned her approval, body rolling into his of its own volition, knee crooking.

When he ran his hand down her hip, he pushed the blankets away at the same time. Then he gathered the skirt of her nightgown, drawing it up so her legs felt the cool night air. It was erotic and almost a relief, she was so hot, but it was a moment of truth. Was this really what she wanted?

The darkness was a wonderful place, allowing her to hide and somehow protect her modesty as his touch strayed inward and brushed the damp hair between her thighs. He caressed her swollen lips, more of tease, so entrancing she allowed her thighs to relax open.

He didn't get the message and continued being so gentle, she wanted to sob with frustration. She was nothing but an agony of anticipation, waiting, longing, yearning for a firmer touch.

He shifted and slid down, pressed her legs wider, beard brushing the sensitive skin of her inner thigh, sweeping in brush strokes that made her gasp and quiver with need. When he turned his face against one thigh and the other, refusing to make contact where she pulsed with molten heat, she sobbed, "Karim."

"You want my mouth here?" His wide palm settled on her mound, the pressure not nearly firm enough.

He wanted her full surrender. She instinctively knew this wasn't compromise. It was his way of forcing her to accept his will, but it was such a wickedly delicious way. Seductive. Impossible to resist.

"I do," she admitted, feeling as though she gave herself up to him with the words, binding herself irrevocably to him. "I do, I do."

Openmouthed kisses edged closer. He parted her with delicate care, then wet heat slid along her most intimate flesh. Glittering pleasure suffused her, waves of growing arousal that rose as his attentions deepened. In fact, her level of involvement skyrocketed so fast and high, she didn't know how to handle it.

He paused, causing her to open her mouth in a silent scream of agony. Only his hot breath caressed her as he spoke in a graveled tone.

"Use your words, my pretty bird. I can't tell if you're struggling because you don't like it or you like it too much."

"Too much," she gasped. "So much. Please. Keep going."

He held her thighs open with firm hands, muting the buck of her hips as he took his time, seeming to recognize when she was on the brink of climax, then slowing to hold her on that plateau, forcing her to languish in that place of mindlessly unbearable perfection.

She stroked her fingers into his hair again, thinking this was ridiculous and far too personal, but she didn't care. She only wanted him to keep doing this forever, yet she could barely withstand the intensity of this pleasure. Not much longer. Couldn't. Absolutely couldn't bear it.

He pressed his mouth over her with firm possession, causing her to hit the crest of her wave with a cry of loss and triumph. Her entire body shuddered as the climax rolled through her in powerful waves.

He remained attentive, ensuring every last pulse was teased to its fullest degree, until she was spent and splayed, panting in the dark. She felt the dampness on her lashes against the arm she threw over her eyes. Yes, that had been so good, she had wept from the power of it.

He lifted away from her but remained between her legs so she couldn't close them. She was aware of his rapid movements, heard his shaken breath, then his long, jagged, relieved sigh.

She dropped her arm and blinked, trying to see him in the absolute dark.

"Did you—?"

"Yes." He stretched out beside her.

She felt a little cheated. Her hands itched to explore him.

He only turned her so she was spooned into his front. Her nightgown was still up around her hips, but he stopped her from trying to pull it down between them.

"Let me feel you against me." His hand smoothed up her hip, then down to settle on her abdomen. His lips touched her shoulder. "Think about how good it will be when I'm inside you and we come together."

When? Did he really want to wait until after their formal ceremony?

The naked contact with him was delicious. In fact, latent desire made the flesh of her mound tingle at the

proximity of his hand. He might have given himself release, but he was still firm against her bare buttocks and
she was already wondering how it would feel to have
him moving inside her while she shattered. She didn't
know if she wanted to wait until tomorrow morning,
let alone two weeks from now.

Which had no doubt been his plan all along. Ruthless, vexing man.

His arm around her grew heavy as he relaxed into
sleep, but she continued to blink into the darkness. She
was starting to realize the power she had handed him
by letting him take her to such heights. He was in her
head now, making her eager to feel exactly what he had
suggested. Him, moving inside her while they shattered
in unison. He was making her want what he willed.

How would she take herself back from that?

Karim left his wife sleeping soundly beneath the light
blanket. He was hard as titanium, more than primed to
fully consummate his marriage, but *he* was master of
himself. Not her. Not this need he had stoked by plea-
suring her last night.

It was a toss-up as to which of them had enjoyed
that more, much to his consternation. Had it been self-
indulgent to offer himself like that? Absolutely. When
he had settled beside her, he had had no intention of
touching her.

But he did want this marriage to work. He did expect
progeny from her. And yes, maybe his ego had been
stinging from that remark she'd made about not desiring his children. He had definitely wanted to remind
her that she desired *him*. That there was something he
offered her that no one else could.

Maybe he had needed to prove it to himself, a dark voice whispered. Maybe he had wanted to prove he could pleasure her without losing command of himself—which he very nearly had. If she had invited him to deflower her, he would have been lost completely.

No, all he had proved last night was that the sexual connection between them was so potent, he couldn't entirely trust himself to be alone with her. It was exactly the depth of irrational passion he refused to succumb to the way his father had.

He *would* wait until they were formally married, if only to prove he could.

To that end, he steeled himself and stepped out to the cool morning air, found clean clothes for both of them in the helicopter, then did his preflight check while tribesmen brushed the sand off the blades and footings. He was drinking coffee with the men on the far side of the camp when Galila emerged from their tent in the linen pants and T-shirt the women had taken in to her.

Her gaze scanned the encampment until she found him. Pink stained her cheeks and sensual memory softened her expression. Her tentative smile invited him to smile back.

It took everything in him to stay rooted where he was and not cross to touch her. A nearly overwhelming pull urged him to move forward and press her back into their tent for the kind of lovemaking that drummed like a beat in his groin. A kiss, at least.

He confined himself to a cool nod of acknowledgment.

He was already glancing away when he saw her expression stiffen. He glanced back and her lashes had swept down. She quickly gave her attention to some children who approached, but her cheer seemed forced. She didn't look his way again as she was drawn into the circle of women and children.

His blood stayed hot with memory as he watched her. Her response to him had been exquisite. Explosive. Everything he could want in a wife—if he wasn't a man who knew there was a high cost to high passion. Seducing her had been a pleasure and a strategic move, but it had also been something that could all too easily take him over if he wasn't careful.

He watched her charm that side of the encampment as he continued his discussion with the elders in this tribe.

Karim might not have known Adir al-Zabah was his half brother, but he had heard the name through the years. Adir was renowned in the desert for his toughness and strong leadership, very much revered among the nomads. They couldn't tell Karim what family Adir had come from, however. His parents were unknown.

They asked why he was inquiring, but he brushed aside his questions as idle curiosity. The burden of secrets was his alone to carry.

The way the women and children adulated her was a much-needed balm to Galila's ego after Karim had barely acknowledged her this morning. She knew it was pathetic that she drank up this sort of starstruck wonder like water, but it filled a hollow spot her mother had carved with the hot-cold sway of her affections.

Sometimes Galila wondered if her desire for validation and appreciation ran deeper than that, and was a shared character flaw she had inherited from her mother. Perhaps it wasn't just an enjoyment of being recognized, but an expectation of glorification. Her mother had always acted as if the way her husband doted on her was natural and something to which she was entitled.

That certainly wasn't something Galila could anticipate from *her* husband, she acknowledged with a clench of hurt when he sent a young boy over to relay the message that it was time to leave.

She made promises to the women of supplies and aid as she said goodbye, enjoying the way they blessed her and touched her arms, asked her to kiss a baby and pray for a good marriage for the unmarried girls among them.

Karim waited until they were airborne and waving down at the Bedouins before speaking to her. They were connected via the microphone on the headsets again, making the communication feel almost more like a phone call. "You don't have to send anything. I asked the men. They don't need anything."

She heard something like her brothers' disparaging cynicism in his tone. *They* didn't buy regard with magnanimous acts the way she seemed to try to.

"It is a mark of pride among them, I'm sure, to insist that they meet the needs of their women without help," she responded. "It's little things. Teething gel for the boy who was crying. Feminine supplies for the young girl who is too embarrassed to ask for it. Things that aren't easy to come by out here. If you don't want to pay for it, I will." She had ample funds that had been set aside for her as part of her marriage contract.

"Of course, I'll pay for it," Karim said impatiently.

She curled the corner of her mouth. All men were

created equal when it came to impugning their pride, apparently.

He didn't realize how happy she was to spend other people's money on the needs of the less fortunate, however.

She quickly accepted his offer, adding, "I would appreciate very much if I could say you underwrote the things I send, since I also want to include some books for the girls. There seems to be controversy as to whether education is for all the children. It would go a long way if you made it clear you expect everyone to learn to read, not just the boys."

"I do." He wore a scowl as they approached the outskirts of Nabata, as if the remark struck a nerve.

Someone hailed him and he relayed an expected time of arrival, then returned to speaking to her.

"I realize we've fallen behind our neighbors in some ways. When my father was alive, my mother spearheaded women and children initiatives, but she has largely been not much more than a figurehead since his death. Without strong leadership, things have stagnated, rather than continuing to progress. Would you take up that mantle?"

Her first instinct was to leap on the opportunity. In Khalia, she had been her mother's envoy, often earning the credit but not receiving it. There were many times when she hadn't agreed with her mother's decisions, but had had to go along with her because she was a loyal subject of the queen and a dutiful daughter.

"Would I have to run everything by you?" she asked.

"Is that so unreasonable? I'm all for advancements, Galila, but at a pace people can adapt to."

She supposed that was fair, but: "Are you just offering me this role because you know I like it? As a way to persuade me into accepting our marriage?"

"What I offered last night wasn't enough?" he asked in a silky tone that caused a shiver to trickle down her spine.

She refused to look at him.

A moment later, he clicked a button and spoke again to the voice she presumed was at the landing pad. The palace appeared and captured all her attention.

It was clearly the product of centuries of additions. The highest dome dominated the center structure while annexes stretched in four directions, each with a variety of smaller domes, flat roofs, solar panels and even an arch of solarium windows over a great hall of some kind. From each of these four legs grew smaller additions, apartments perhaps—there were a number of small pools and courtyards with palms and fountains.

He landed in a circle on one of the highest rooftops where three other helicopters of various sizes were already tethered. They were hanging their headphones on the hooks above the windscreen when he spoke again.

"How you come to terms with our marriage is up to you, but it is a fact. You may weigh in on the details of our celebration as you see fit, but my staff is perfectly capable of making it happen without your input. As for representing the women of my country—*our* country— I would like you to be their voice, if you're willing. Is that something you would enjoy or not?"

She hesitated, drew a breath and admitted, "Each time I say yes to you, I feel a piece of me fall away. It's not the same for you, though, is it?"

People were approaching to tether the helicopter, but he didn't look away from her, only said a quiet, "No."

It hurt a lot more than she had braced herself for, pushing a thickness into her throat and a pressure behind her eyes.

"Is this still about love, Galila? Look at my mother. You don't want that. Be practical and accept this marriage for the beneficial partnership it can be."

To whom? Everyone *but* her.

She was being offered the chance to elevate the living conditions of a country full of women for the low price of her own freedom and the loving marriage she had always promised herself.

"I've never understood how people live without love." Her brothers did, maybe because they hadn't been loved in the first place. She had, though, and maybe that was proof that Karim was right. She had grown addicted to being seen as special and valuable and wanted. Losing her mother's love was still a deep and agonizing wound.

She knew better than to fall into another situation where she was yearning for feelings that weren't there, yet here she was, distantly hoping he would come around and feel something toward her.

"It's not that difficult," Karim replied drily, essentially driving a coffin nail into her heart. "Come. Let me show you our home."

"Well, I guess I don't have a choice, do I? Not unless I want to throw myself off the edge of this roof and end things right now."

"Why would you say that?" His voice lashed at her, quick and snapping sharp as a whip. "Don't ever say anything like that. *Ever.*"

His vehemence had her recoiling in her seat, heart hammering. She recalled with chagrin that his father had fallen from a balcony here. "I didn't mean—"

He cut her off with a chop of his hand through the air between them and disembarked, then impatiently demanded she come out behind him, picking her up and releasing her with abrupt motions.

He exchanged a few words with someone, then hurried her out of the heat and into the relief of air conditioning where a handful of personnel awaited them, all wearing attentive expressions.

"Cantara." He introduced a middle-aged woman in traditional dress with heavily made-up eyes, a wide smile and a tablet and stylus at the ready. "My mother's assistant, when she's here at the palace. Cantara will show you around and help you hire the staff you need. I'm required elsewhere."

He strode away. The rest of the staff flowed into position behind him like birds in a flock, making him seem to disappear.

She waited, but he didn't look back. Last night's intimacy was forgotten. It certainly hadn't changed anything in *his* agenda.

"I've had tea prepared in your chamber. May I show you there?"

Galila found a polite smile and dutifully followed where she was led.

Karim forced himself not to look back, but he still saw Galila. Heard her.

How did each word she spoke have such power over him? She loaded a single glance with a thousand emotions, saying, *I've never understood how people live without love,* while a kaleidoscope of despair and confusion, yearning and wistfulness took their turn across her angelic face. Somehow, she caused those feelings to be reflected in him, twisting his conscience at the same time, which was distinctly uncomfortable.

And when he tried to move her past her melancholy, she thrust a knife from a completely unexpected direction, flippantly suggesting she throw herself to her death the way his father had done.

Whatever pangs of guilt had reverberated through him had been slapped out by that statement, sparking his temper with the power of a lightning strike.

That slam of energy had had its roots in a white-hot fear. He would never wish his experience on anyone, certainly could never face witnessing something so traumatic again, but somehow knew it would be especially devastating if she did it.

He'd smacked a hard lid on that sort of talk, seeing how wary his outburst made her, but he didn't even want her to dare think of doing something so horrific, let alone threaten it.

The entire five-minute conversation had left her limpid eyed and looking abandoned as a child when he left her with an assistant and turned away.

Perhaps she was entitled to some bewilderment. Their lovemaking had been so powerful, he had stooped to reminding her of it himself, unable to dismiss it from his mind. He wanted her to recall every twitch and sigh and caress. It was all he could think about.

But it was completely reckless to let himself be so distracted and preoccupied by carnal desires. He had married her to keep a secret that could rattle swords in both their countries—upend the entire region, even. Not to mention the personal cost to all of them. Her mother's affair was already a sore topic with her and her siblings.

He didn't want to force painful discussions on them any more than he wanted them himself.

No. She might open herself to him and offer a type of pleasure he had never experienced, lure him like a bee to a nectar-laden flower, but he had to remain stoic and indifferent. And after the way she had behaved at the wedding? Getting drunk and spilling what she had to *him*? There was no way he could entrust her with the rest. Too much depended on him keeping their parents' affair a secret.

To do that, he had to keep her contained, yet at a distance. In his palace, in his apartment, but not in his bed. It was best for all their sakes.

CHAPTER FIVE

TEN DAYS LATER, Galila was fed up with being ignored.

Not that she was ever left alone. Rather, maids and clerks and advisors hovered constantly, asking for her preference on *everything*, right down to which side of the gold-plated bathroom tap her cut-crystal toothbrush cup should sit.

She was changed at least four times a day, from silk pajamas to comfortable breakfast wear, then to casually elegant midday wear, then sophisticated evening wear and finally back to pajamas. If she and Karim were entertaining, there might be poolside wraps while amusing the wife of a visiting diplomat, cocktail attire before dressing for dinner or something ceremonial for an official photograph.

They were always entertaining. Or meeting with some dignitary over a luncheon. Even breakfasts were business meetings, where she and Karim ate across from each other, but staff hovered with tablets and questions, asking for replies on emails and finalizing their schedules for the rest of the day.

The strange part was, she didn't mind the demands. She found it invigorating. There was something both thrilling and satisfying in making seating arrangements or setting a menu or suggesting a blue rug would look better in this room, and seeing her wishes carried out promptly and without question.

As a princess in Khalia, she had had influence, but even Malak's disinterested male opinions had held more sway than her own. She had nearly always been contradicted by her mother, which Galila had sometimes thought was purely a desire on her mother's part to reinforce her own position, not a genuine partiality to whatever suggestion of Galila's she had decided to overrule.

Now, as Queen of Zyria—and that title made her choke on hysterical laughter because she had yet to properly sleep with her husband, the king—Galila discovered the power of her position. At first, she'd been tentative, expecting to hear that the Queen Mother Tahirah ought to be consulted or had always preferred this or that.

To her amazement, Galila was assured that such courtesies as consulting the Queen Mother were at her discretion. The only voice that might veto her own was her husband's. What a heady thought!

So she tested the extent of her privilege. She sought out her husband unannounced and said she would wait for the king in his anteroom.

She was not turned away. She was offered refreshments. His highest-ranking assistant offered to interrupt the king's conference call if it was an urgent matter.

"It's not. Merely a private discussion I'd like to have before our guests arrive. I'll ring if I require anything."

She was left alone to explore the private library. It was a retreat, a place for Zyria's ruler to freshen up between meetings, since there was a very luxurious bathroom and a small walk-in closet with a spare of everything.

It ought to smell like Karim in here, she thought, as she lifted the sleeve of a robe to her nose.

She was actually craving the scent of him, some lingering evidence of their intimacy. Her nights were agony as she relived the way he had pleasured her in the tent, then fantasized all the other things they might do to one another if he came to her. Why hadn't she at least pleasured him the same way when she had had the chance?

In the darkest hours, when she was sweaty and aching with desire, she rose and walked to the closed door between their apartments but couldn't bring herself to knock.

Was he being honorable? Giving her time to adjust to their marriage as he had promised he would? Or had he completely lost interest in her?

She always went back to bed bereft, wondering what she had done to turn him off.

As brutal as the nights were, the days were far worse. Each time she was in his presence, she fought lust. His lips on the rim of a coffee cup made her shake with desire. His voice stroked across her skin, causing her pulse to race. If she caught his scent, she had to close her eyes and take control of herself.

Even now, anticipating being alone with him, her intimate regions were tingling with anticipation. Her one-track mind turned to fantasies of making love on the floor of his very closet, his naked weight upon her. His thick shaft piercing—

Flushed and impatient with herself, she went back into the main area.

The only thing worse than suffering this constant yearning would be his discovering how deeply she felt it and feeling nothing in return.

She shook herself out of her mental whirl by taking a more thorough look around the main room. Did he even come in here? There wasn't a speck of dust in sight, but she had the sense he spent very little time in here.

A sofa and chairs were arranged to face a television, should there be breaking news he needed to watch, but the cushions were undented. The liquor cabinet held nothing, not even nonalcoholic choices.

When she looked at the books, they were also dust free and arranged with precision, but who read actual books anymore? Especially dry nonfiction. Give her a romance and she would sneeze her way through the most yellowed pages, but biographies and history? No, thanks.

She couldn't help touching the mane of the gold lion that lounged on an ebony bookend. His one front paw was relaxed and dangling off the edge. His tail appeared about to swish. It was an eye-catching piece, one that looked vaguely familiar, making her think she'd seen something like it, perhaps by the same artist. She would have remembered if she'd seen this one. It was not only startlingly lifelike, with the animal's musculature lovingly recreated, it emanated power along with the innate playfulness of cats. The lion peered around the edge of the upright slab of ebony that he lounged against, as if waiting on his mate. Inviting her to come to his side of the books.

Galila looked for the match, but there was only the one. Strange. Bookends came in pairs, didn't they? That was why there was an expression about things being "bookended."

She looked on the desk for it, then realized the heavy curtains behind the desk hid a pair of tall doors that led onto a balcony. She pulled them open.

Was this where his father had fallen?

She wasn't a morbid person, but something drew her to open the doors and step onto the shaded balcony. The heat crushed like a wall, but the view of the sea was stunning. There was a broader balcony on the other side of the palace that was used for ceremonies. It overlooked a public square and had been a means of addressing the masses before television.

This one, like the room behind her, was a place for reflection.

With an unforgiving courtyard a fatal distance below.

"No," Karim said, startling her into gasping and spinning. She clutched her chest where her heart leaped.

Mouth tight, Karim pointed her back into the center of the room.

"I didn't—I was just—"

He closed and locked the doors, then drew the drapes across with a yank on the cord. The room became cooler and darker, but she was still hot and flustered.

"Karim." She had come in here on a wave of temper, determined to confront him, but found herself in the middle of the carpet with her hands linked before her, apologies on her tongue.

"It's not up for discussion," he stated.

She didn't have to ask him if that was where the accident had happened. She could see the truth in his severe expression. He'd been six. How was it such a painful, visceral memory for him?

As she searched his expression, her infernal attraction to him began to take root and flourish through her. She noted how handsome he was in his business attire of pants and a button shirt. Nothing special, but it was tailored to his strong shoulders and framed his hips just so. He was as sexy and casually powerful as the lion she had admired.

He also had a thorn in his paw. She yearned to be the one who pulled it, she realized. The one he cherished for healing him.

"The ambassador and his wife will arrive soon. You should change."

It was a dismissal.

They were alone for the first time since the tent and he didn't have any use for her. Just like that, her temper flared. She remembered why she had been so infuriated, why she had hiked the distance across the massive palace to confront him.

"I need to talk to you." She folded her arms, chin set.

"It can't wait?"

"Until when? Do you propose I discuss my doctor's appointment over the dessert course so our guests can weigh in?"

His whole body tightened, as if bracing himself. His brows slammed together and his gaze swept her up and down. "What's wrong?"

"Nothing," she admitted, realizing she had alarmed him, which was a tiny bit gratifying since he hadn't given her any indication of even a mild passing concern for her health and well-being since he'd poured out her brandy the night they met. "I mean, it's not a health problem, if that's what you're thinking."

He made an impatient noise and flicked his hand

at her. "That's exactly what I thought. But if you're healthy, then what?"

"I want to know why you told the doctor I could go on whatever birth control I would prefer."

His head went back with surprise. "You said you didn't want children right away."

How was it possible for him to become *more* inscrutable? He pushed his fists into his pockets. The motion drew the fabric of his trousers tight across his fly, which revealed the hint of his masculine flesh.

She had been spending way too much time wondering about that part of him and her guilty conscience pushed heat into her cheeks. She forced herself not to stare and looked instead to the hardness in his jaw. Something in his stance made her think he'd been offended when she had told him she didn't have a particular desire to have his children, which had been true-ish at the time.

Now, she folded her arms, defensive because she was so—oh, she was going to have to own it. She was frustrated. Sexually.

"Aside from the fact it is not *your* decision what I put in *my* body," she declared hotly and for all womankind, "I don't understand why you think birth control is necessary when you seem to have decided on abstinence."

He blinked. His face relaxed with a hint of satisfaction that made her think of the lion swishing his tail, pleased he wouldn't have to run her to ground because she was edging close enough he wouldn't have to make any effort to chase her at all.

Oh, he read her agitation like it was a neon sign, she could tell. She blushed even harder.

"Hot and bothered, are you? We agreed to wait until after the wedding ceremony next week."

"Is that what we agreed? I thought you stated it and I have been given no opportunity to discuss it. What happened to it being my choice what happened between us in bed?"

His eye ticked, then his jaw hardened.

"If you can't wait for our wedding night…" His hands came out of his pockets and he waved them slowly at himself in offering. "Help yourself."

As bluffs went, it almost worked. She was still a virgin and already feeling very scorned by him. This was daylight, not the safety of a pitch-black tent. Years of reading sexy romance novels, a rich fantasy life and curiosity were all a far cry from the reality of staring down a fully dressed man whose mouth was curling with smug knowledge that he was getting the better of her.

Because he thought she was some trembling wallflower who wouldn't make advances.

Well, he thought wrong. She was sick of feeling like his dalliance. A flame of fury glowed hot within her, refusing to be at the mercy of his whims. She would not be the only one obsessing about how they would feel together. *She* could give *him* pleasure.

She was determined to prove it.

When she walked up to him, however, and he loomed over her despite the heels she wore, her heart began to beat fast with apprehension. This was a dangerous game.

He didn't lower his head to cover her offered mouth. He made her set a hand behind his head and draw him down into *her* kiss. Then he had the gall not to respond to her first uncertain advances. *All* men wanted to kiss her. Didn't he realize that?

She forced her tongue between his lips and pressed

harder, rocking her mouth under his as she pulled his tongue into her own mouth.

He made a growling, primal noise and encircled her with hard arms as he took over the kiss with passionate roughness. It lasted for a few uncontrolled, thrilling heartbeats before he caught her arms in a firm grip and set them apart from each other.

His gaze clashed into hers with accusation, as if she'd forced him to react in a way he didn't care for.

But that brief crack in his control only fueled her resolve. She brushed his hands off her arms and pressed his wrists behind his back, meeting his fierce glare with a scolding one.

"You just gave yourself to me, didn't you? Are you going back on that? What are you afraid of?"

Her breasts grazed his chest and their thighs brushed through the fabric of her skirt and his pants. She could feel he was aroused and that bolstered her confidence even more.

"I'm not afraid of anything." His voice was gritty, his words pushed through clenched teeth. "But what are you planning to do? Lose your virginity here on my desk?"

"I'm going to make love to you with my mouth," she dared to say, and felt the jolt that went through him. The muscled wrists in her hands became rock-hard, strained tendons as he bunched his hands into tight fists.

She smiled under a rush of feminine power.

"Do you like that idea?" She drew back a little and brought one hand to his fly. She caressed his hard flesh through the fabric. "I think you do." *She* did. Her hand was trembling.

His nostrils flared, but he held himself very still. She couldn't tell if he was trying to act unaffected or if they were playing a game of chicken and he was waiting for her to lose her nerve first.

She might. She'd never done anything so boldly wicked.

With two shaking hands, she unbuttoned his shirt and spread it wide, indulging herself by splaying her hands across his hot skin and the light sprinkle of hair. She turned her face back and forth against the contours of his pecs, played her touch over his rib cage before she licked at his nipples to see if he reacted.

He did. He made a harsh noise and his fist went into her hair, but he didn't force her to stop. When she offered her mouth this time, he took it like a starving man, without hesitation, greedy and rapacious.

She almost lost herself to that kiss. Her blood was running like wildfire, her oxygen all but eaten up. She longed to let him take control, but she also needed to prove to both of them that she wasn't alone in this sea of lust.

She ran her hands over his buttocks, then traced her fingers beneath the waistband of his pants until she came to the front.

She unbuckled and unzipped, stepped back enough to open his pants and push them down his hips. Then she eased the black line of his shorts down, exposing the thick flesh that had been keeping her up nights. Her breaths were coming in deep pants, like she'd been running for an hour, breasts rising and falling.

"You've taken this far enough," he said grimly, catching her hand before she touched him.

"You don't want me to?" She looked up at him with craving nearly blinding her.

Whatever he saw in her expression caused his own

pupils to expand. The heat between them was like flames, licking back and forth, scorching. Shadows of struggle fought with a glaze of desperate hunger in his eyes.

"I want to," she assured him in a husky whisper, sinking to her knees before him.

She didn't know exactly what to do, but there didn't seem to be a wrong move as she lightly caressed and explored, getting to know his shape. Her first touch had him sucking in a breath. His flesh seemed to welcome her grasp with pulses of enjoyment. He muttered imprecations between ragged breaths, but didn't stop her.

He watched her with a fierce, avid gaze that only encouraged her to steady him for the first dab of her tongue.

Then he tipped back his head and groaned loudly at the ceiling, like it was pain and pleasure combined. She lost herself then, did everything she could to pleasure him with exactly as much devotion as he had shown her in the Bedouin tent. And when he was reaching the peak of his endurance, when his hand was in her hair and he was warning her he couldn't last, she was so aroused, she couldn't resist touching herself and finding release at the same time he did.

Karim left his stained, sweat-damp clothing on the floor of the closet and dressed in fresh pants and a shirt, shaken and stunned—utterly stunned—by what his wife had just done to him.

He came back into the main room and she was already gone from the bathroom where she had retreated moments after taking him to such heights of ecstasy that he had thought he was dying.

What a way to go.

He looked around the room he passionately hated and knew his regard for it had been completely rewritten. He would always think of her now, when he was in here. Galila on her knees before him, hair a silk rope that bound both his fists to the back of her head. Her mouth working over his tip, her slender fingers a vice of pleasure around his shaft. And then, when his fantasy-turned-reality could not possibly have become more erotic, she had burrowed her hand beneath her skirt and pleasure had hummed in her throat as they found satisfaction together.

How could any man withstand such a thing?

He ran his hand down his face, trying to put his melted features into some semblance of control before he had to rejoin his staff, let alone ambassadors from around the world.

He had been avoiding her, it was true. The more he wanted her, the more he fought against going to her. Making himself wait until their "wedding night" had seemed a suitable, if arbitrary way of proving he could control his lust and resist her.

Like hell. He had lost the battle the second he'd been told she was waiting for him, never mind when she had sidled up to him and kissed him.

This had been a defeat, one he already regretted, even as his blood purred in his veins and every bit of tension in his body had left him.

With regret, he squatted and swept his hand across the nap of the carpet, erasing where his own footprints faced the impression of her knees.

As he squatted there, from this vantage, he was the height he had been when his father had sat at that desk, rambling about things Karim hadn't even comprehended.

I love her. Do you understand? Your mother can never know. She doesn't know. Doesn't understand what this kind of love is like. Pray you never experience it, my son. It destroys your soul. And now she says it's over. How do I go on? I can't. Do you understand, Karim? I cannot live without her. I'm sorry, but I can't.

Karim hadn't understood. But the memory was a timely reminder as to why he had been trying to avoid giving in to his desire for Galila. Such intense passion could very easily become addictive. Obsessive and soul-destroying.

As he straightened, he pulled on the cloak of control he'd been wearing since bringing her here, determined to set her at a distance and keep her there. Permanently this time.

It wasn't easy. An hour later, she arrived at his side wearing a hijab, since the ambassador and his wife were Muslim. Somehow her conservative gown and face framed in closely draped indigo were more provocative than one of her knee-length skirts with a fitted jacket.

Galila was beautiful no matter what she wore, but he could barely keep his gaze off the lips that had left a stain of pink on his flesh, or the lashes that had framed the wide eyes that had looked up at him.

He quickly made a remark about a political situation and drew the ambassador aside so he wouldn't embarrass himself by becoming freshly aroused.

This constant flow of dinners and entertaining had been partly a series of prescheduled meetings, but also a necessary means of introducing his wife to key dignitaries before the celebration that would cement her as his wife and queen. Their marriage had been surprise enough. With all the rumblings of concern at lower levels, he had to ensure she was accepted.

Galila, he had to acknowledge, had a particular gift for charming people onto her side. She flowed effortlessly from small talk over the best shoe designer in Milan to a policy discussion. If she had a question, she asked it in a way that never seemed impertinent. If she had an opinion, she always managed to voice it in a way that was nonconfrontational but made her point.

As for the reports he received daily on the various decisions she was making as queen, well, he was grateful to have fewer things to worry about so he could concentrate on the ones that had broader impact.

"Oh, you know my father?" she asked with surprise now, voice drawing Karim back to the dinner and the conversation.

"That's an overstatement," the ambassador said with an embarrassed wave of his hand. "I met him, well, it must have been thirty years ago? I was quite young, just starting my first career as a translator. He came to our country as part of a diplomatic tour. He has such a sharp mind. I very much admired him and only wanted to express my concern for his health, given he stepped aside recently. I hope he's well?"

"Grieving my mother." Galila stiffened slightly, just enough for Karim to notice, but this was another area where she seemed to finesse her way without a misstep.

"I expect he was quite heartbroken. I'm sure you all are, but, well, it was obvious to me, even back then, how much he loved her. He cut short his tour to be with her. I remember it so clearly because I couldn't imagine having a woman in my life whom I couldn't bear to be apart from. Then I met one." He smiled at his wife.

She blushed and told him not to embarrass them.

Galila offered a smile, but it didn't reach her eyes. She stared off into the middle distance a moment, murmuring, "I didn't realize he had ever been apart from her for any length of time. It certainly never happened in my memory, but that would have been before I was born."

If she did the math and realized Karim's father had killed himself roughly thirty years ago...

"We need to add a discussion on your country's foreign banking regulations to tomorrow's agenda," Karim cut in, changing the subject.

Moments later, the women had moved on to an innocuous topic and the rest of the evening passed without incident. He realized, however, that this was another angle of vulnerability he had to protect himself against. His marriage of expedience was a minefield of potential disaster.

Galila excused herself the moment their guests were gone. She had a lot to think about. Deep down, she was still reeling from her experience with Karim, feeling self-conscious about the way she had behaved.

When she saw him at dinner with the ambassador, he had once again been the remote man who revealed only the barest hint of regard toward her. His indifference crushed her soul into the dust, but she hadn't allowed herself to look him in the eye or her gaze to linger on his expression. She had fought all evening to hide her aching soul, asking mindless questions and pretending an interest in the wife's dog-breeding techniques.

Then the ambassador had made that remark about her father's trip thirty years ago.

She had enough going on with her new marriage that she shouldn't have room for obsessing over her mother's lover, but she couldn't help but wonder. She couldn't ask her father about his trip, but she sent an email to both her brothers, keeping her inquiry very vague, asking if they knew anything about that particular trip their father had taken. She doubted they would. Malak hadn't been born and Zufar had been a toddler.

Still, she sighed with disappointment when she received their blunt "No" replies the next morning.

"What's wrong?" Karim asked as he nodded to accept more coffee.

"Nothing. I asked my brothers if they knew anything about that diplomatic tour my father went on, the one the ambassador mentioned. They don't."

"Why?"

She looked at him, conveying with a flick of her lashes that it probably wasn't a topic that should be raised in front of the servants. "I'm curious about it."

He knew exactly what she was telegraphing and said dismissively, "I don't see that it matters."

"With all due respect," she said in a carefully level tone, "it wouldn't seem important to you because it doesn't concern your parent. I have questions, however."

The listening ears would think she was still talking about her father, but she meant her mother and Adir. Perhaps Karim took offense at her remark despite her attempt to maintain a suitable amount of deference. His fingers tightened on the handle of his coffee mug.

"Surely you have more important things to do with your time. How are the reception plans coming?"

She knew when she was being patronized and flipped her hair. "Perfectly. Your excellent staff would provide nothing less." She smiled at the hovering assistants.

The party was only days away, and much as she enjoyed being the center of attention, she was quite nervous. Everything would be exquisite, she had no doubt at all, but Karim intended for them to consummate their marriage that night and she was having mixed feelings about that.

She had wanted to prove something to him yesterday, but she wasn't sure what. That she was brave? That she would be a lover who would satisfy him? That he couldn't resist her?

What she had discovered was that even when she took the initiative, she had no control over her reaction. No modesty or inhibition.

In fact, the more she thought about their encounter, the more anxious she became. She kept seeing herself as besotted as her father was with her mother. Loyal as a hound, he'd loved his spouse into her death despite the fact she had committed adultery and never gave more than passing consideration to the children she had made with him.

Even more of a fearful thought was that she might become as dependent on Karim's regard as she had been on her mother's. For a time, she might be his sexual pet. There was a certain novelty within a new marriage, she was sure. They might both indulge themselves, but he had already demonstrated that his desire was fickle. He could turn his emotions on and off on a whim.

She couldn't bear to invest herself in him, grow to care for him, only to have that rug pulled. How would she withstand years of his casual indifference?

At least as a daughter, she'd been able to escape to Europe and distract herself with schooling. But charity work and its accompanying accolades only went so far in filling up the void inside her. She needed more.

Karim, however, would never offer the "more" she sought.

Why? What was wrong with her? What was her great flaw? She had convinced herself that her mother's fading beauty had caused her to grow jealous as Galila's allure ripened, but Karim was behaving with the same ambivalence toward her.

Perhaps that meant there was a deeper shortcoming inside her that kept people from truly loving her?

She was a kind person, an obedient daughter. She was trying to be a loyal wife, but Karim didn't even seem to value that much in her. It was agonizing.

She had no choice as far as attending the reception went, but she didn't know if she could become his wife in every sense of the word afterward. He would surely break her heart.

CHAPTER SIX

CORONATIONS WERE NOT a lavish affair in this part of the world. Galila knew that from her own country and had been told that Karim had a cousin appointed as his successor should he fail to produce one. That designation and the allegiance of all his cousins and other dignitaries had been handled with public, verbal pledges witnessed by the rest.

Recognizing Galila as his queen had been a matter of Karim stating that he had chosen her that night in the Bedouin encampment. It was all the people of Zyria had needed to accept and recognize her as their monarch, but they would feel cheated of a party if he didn't host one.

That was all that this day was—a formal celebration here in the palace, but one followed by all. Festivities were extended across the country, providing the entire population a reason to take a day to enjoy themselves.

Galila was nothing if not scrupulously adept at planning this sort of event. Along with charity work abroad and at home, she had always led the charge on family events—to a point. Her mother had liked Galila to do all the work of choosing menus and decor, then always swooped in at the last minute to change the color scheme or the order of the speeches, putting her own stamp on it.

This time, every single detail was Galila's own.

As part of that, she had carefully considered the message the event would send. Obviously, she had to convey that she was pleased to be Karim's wife and that she embraced her new country. She needed to highlight the advantage of a union with Khalia, too. It was a celebration and needed to be lavish enough to reflect their position, but she didn't want to pin *spendthrift* to her lapel and require years to remove it. She wanted it known that she was eager to begin charity work, but didn't want to appear critical and suggest Zyria was failing to meet the needs of its people.

The guest list had been its own Gordian knot to unravel and there had also been kosher meals and other diverse religious observances that had to be considered.

In the end, Galila pulled a small cheat by adding some well-respected professionals to the mix. She seated doctors and teachers next to ministers and other dignitaries with appropriate portfolios. Everything in the swag bags from silk scarves to gold bangles to a jar of spices had been sourced in Zyria, showcasing their best merchants.

Within the speeches, she had the treasury minister praise her for being under budget with this party. He announced that she had asked for the savings to be donated to a traveling medical unit that would service some of the most difficult to access places in Zyria. It was met with an appropriate round of appreciative applause.

Her husband promptly upstaged her by announcing that a hospital wing to service women's health issues would be built in her name. Her reaction must have been priceless because everyone laughed and applauded even harder while she covered her hot cheeks with her hands.

It was a political gesture, she reminded herself. A means of ensuring she was accepted and welcomed and cemented into Zyria's history books.

She was still touched by the gesture, perhaps because he looked at her with sincere regard as he said, "I'm hoping you'll take an active role in this project. Your instincts and attention to detail are excellent."

"Did you mean that?" she asked as he seated himself next to her again.

"Of course." He seemed surprised by her question. "I've been kept apprised of every decision you've made here so far."

That was news. She had been quite convinced he hadn't thought of her more than twice since they'd met.

"You've done an excellent job," he said, sounding sincere. His gaze skimmed across the four hundred people dressed to the nines, jewelry sparkling and gold cutlery flashing as they dined on their first course beneath faux starlight. Landmarks were projected onto the walls beneath swathes of fabric to resemble looking out from a Bedouin tent on Zyria's landscape. The centerpieces were keepsake lanterns amid Zyrian flora and the scent of Zyrian incense hung on the air.

"I don't know that anyone will dare eat these chocolates, but they will certainly enjoy showing them off. Very ingenious." He tilted the treat that decorated each place setting. It was made of camel milk by a Zyrian chocolatier and shaped like Zyria and Khalia stuck together as one piece, the border only a subtle shift in color, not a dividing line. She had prevailed on her brother to send coffee and cinnamon from Khalia to flavor their side of it while the Zyrian was spiced with nutmeg and cardamom.

"It's a subtle yet brilliant touch."

Brilliant?

Don't be needy.

But she was. In her core, she was starved for validation. Which was exactly the problem with this marriage. She wanted—needed—to believe Karim valued her. That whatever he felt toward her was real and permanent.

He was in demand at all times, however. It was somewhat understandable that after his brief compliment, his attention went elsewhere. They didn't speak again until the plates had been cleared and they moved to the adjoining ballroom to begin the dancing.

Here she'd been a little freer with the Western influences, bringing in colored lights and a DJ who played current pop tunes from around the globe, but included many of the hits by Arab bands.

Their first dance was an older ballad, however, one Karim's mother had told her had been played at her wedding to Karim's father. It was meant as a reassurance to the older generation that things were changing but only a little.

Karim wore his ceremonial robes and she was in several layers of embroidered silk over a brocade gown with jewels in her hair, at her wrists, around her neck and even a bejeweled broach worn on a wide band around her middle.

Karim had to be very careful as he took her into his arms. He muttered something under his breath about hugging a cactus.

"I understood it to be an heirloom that all Zyrian

queens wear on special occasions," she said, affected by his closeness despite the fact he had to maintain enough distance not to catch his robes on the piece.

"My staff was too shy to explain it was designed as a chastity belt, worn when the king was not around to protect his interests."

"Talk about putting a ring on it," she said under her breath.

He snorted, the sound of amusement so surprising, she flashed a look upward in time to see the corner of his mouth twitch.

"Yes, well, the king is in the house so we'll dispense with it as soon as possible."

Her heart swerved in the crazy jitter of alarm and anticipation she'd been suffering as this day drew nearer. It was so silly! They were familiar with each other. She knew she would find pleasure with him.

But what happened after that? Would he go back to ignoring her? She wouldn't be able to stand it. How could she give herself to a man who would only rebuff her afterward?

Karim stole her away to her apartment as soon as he could, dismissing the staff that hovered to help undress her. He could handle that himself, thank you very much.

On his instruction, the rooms had been prepared with a fresh bath, rose petals, candles, cordial and exotic fruits. The music of gently plucked strings played quietly in the background. Silk pajamas had been left on the bed for both of them—and would be swept to the floor unused if he had his way.

Alone with his wife for the first time since she'd

blown his mind in his library the other day, he was fairly coming out of his skin with anticipation—not that he would admit to it. Oh, he knew damned well that part of him had been counting the minutes until he could release himself from his self-imposed restraint, but he barely acknowledged that. It was pure weakness to feel this way, damn it, but he couldn't put off consummation forever.

In fact, he had begun to rationalize that the reason he was growing obsessive about the moment of possession was merely because he hadn't yet done so. Once they made love, he wouldn't be so preoccupied by how delicious it might be.

That was the only reason urgency gripped him and put a gruff edge on his voice when he commanded her to turn around. "Let me relieve you of that thing."

She jolted a bit and didn't meet his eyes as she turned so he could remove the elaborate belt.

Her spine grew taller as he released the dozen tiny hook-and-eye fasteners. She drew a deep breath as he set it aside, then, when he touched her shoulders to remove her outer robe, she stiffened again and glanced warily over her shoulder.

He hesitated, but she shrugged to help him peel it away. It was surprisingly heavy with its detailed embroidery locking in pearls and other jewels. If anything, her tension grew as he eased it away, however.

She turned and folded her arms, now in a strapless gown bedecked with a band of silver and diamonds beneath the extravagant necklace that had been his wedding gift to her. She pressed her lips together, conveying wary uncertainty.

"What's wrong?"

"Nothing," she said a little too quickly, shoulders coming up in a shrug and staying in a defensive hunch.

He moved closer and had to tilt her chin up, then wait for her gaze to come to his. A tiny flinch plucked at her brows and her gaze swept away, anxious to avoid his.

"Galila," he murmured. "Are you being shy?" It seemed impossible, considering the intimacies they'd shared, but her mouth twitched.

She hitched a shoulder, nodding a little, lashes dropping to hide her gaze again.

"There's no rush," he assured her, even though it felt like a lie. Standing this close to her, feeling the softness of her cheek under the caress of his thumb, he didn't know how he had managed to wait this long. The starving beast inside him was waking and stretching, prowling in readiness to go on the hunt.

When he started to lower his mouth to hers, she stiffened with subtle resistance.

He drew back, experiencing something like alarm. Was she teasing him on purpose?

"I'm nervous, it's fine," she insisted, but she was still avoiding his gaze.

Her crown had been fitted with a silver and blue veil that draped over the rich, loose waves of her hair. She reached to remove it.

"I'll do it." He searched out the pins that secured it, distantly thinking he should have delegated this task to the one who'd put them in. It was an intricate process and she winced a couple of times, even though he was as gentle as he could be.

He persevered and finally was able to leave the crown and veil on a table. She ran her fingers through her hair—an erotic gesture at the best of times. Tonight, she was especially entrancing. The smooth swells of her breasts lifted against the blue velvet. Her heavily decorated ivory skirt shimmered, merely hinting at the lissome limbs it hid.

"You're so beautiful, it almost hurts the eyes." The words came from a place he barely acknowledged within himself, one where his desire for her was a craven thing that he could barely contain.

She dropped her hands in front of her. "I can't help the way I look."

"It's not a drawback," he said drily, moving to take up her hands and set them on his shoulders. His own then went to her rib cage, finding her supple as a dancer. Her heels put her at exactly the most comfortable height to dip his head and capture her mouth with his own.

A jolt of electricity seemed to jump between them, reassuring him even as his mouth stung and she made a sound of near pain. He quickly assuaged the sensation with a full, openmouthed kiss. The kind he'd been starving for. The kind that should have slaked something in him, but only stoked his hunger.

She began to melt into him and he felt mindlessness begin to overtake him, the same loss of control that had pinned him in place while she stole every last shred of his discipline that day in his library.

He tightened his hands on her and started to set her back a step, needing to keep a clear head.

She made a noise of hurt and the heels of her hands exerted pressure, urging him to release her altogether.

His reflexes very nearly yanked her back in close. Some primitive refusal to be denied was that close to overwhelming him.

The push-pull was startling enough to freeze him

with his hands still keeping her before him, so he could read her face.

"Do you not want—?" He had to look away, not ready to hear that she was rejecting him.

"I do, but—"

She did break from his hold then, brushing his hands off her and pacing away a few steps. The action raked something cold across him.

She turned back to hold out a beseeching hand. "I can't bear the games, Karim."

She looked stricken enough to cause a sharp sensation to pierce his heart.

"Make love to me if you want to. But don't… Don't tell me I'm beautiful, then act like you can't stand how I look. Don't kiss me like you can't get enough, then push me away as though I'm someone you dislike. Don't tell a roomful of people that you think I'm wonderful when you clearly think I'm not. I can't go through those ups and downs again. I can't."

He narrowed his eyes. "What are you talking about? I don't dislike you."

She closed her eyes. "It doesn't matter how you feel, just be honest about it. And consistent. Please. It's fine that you only want me a little, the way any man might respond to any available woman. Don't pander to me and act like…"

"What?" he prompted, bracing because he was afraid that he might have betrayed too much somewhere along the line. Definitely when she'd taken him in her mouth.

"I don't know," she said with a break in her voice. "I don't know how you feel. That's the issue. Sometimes you act as though you like me, but then…you don't."

"Of course, I like you, Galila." He swallowed, thinking he understood the issue here. In a gentler tone, he added, "But I told you in the beginning not to expect love from me."

"I'm not talking about love, Karim! I'm talking about basic regard. You've barely spoken to me since the day in your office. You act like it didn't even happen! Then you think saying a few nice things tonight—that I'm so beautiful you can't stand to look at me—and think that makes me want to…" She waved at the bed, then her arm dropped in defeat.

His heart skewed in his chest. "That's not the way I meant it, Galila."

"The worst part is, I still want to have sex with you. But be honest about how it will be afterward. If you're only going to ignore me until the next time an urge strikes, then don't arrange rose petals and candles and act like you want me to *feel* something tonight. Don't act like this is a special moment for either one of us. Not when you're only going to pretend I don't exist afterward."

He pinched the bridge of his nose. This was special. It was her first time. Did she think he didn't have some nerves about that? The responsibility to *make* it special?

"I wanted you to relax."

"Well, I can't." She shook off whatever melancholy was in her expression and reached to remove her earrings. "Let's just get it done so you can lock yourself back in your room."

"Get it done?" he repeated as a sick knot tightened in his gut. "I want our lovemaking to be a pleasure for you, Galila. Not a chore."

"I'm not like you! When we…do things, I feel it. Emotionally." She pressed her curled hand between her breasts. "And you're manipulating me with that. Maybe not on purpose. Maybe you don't even realize how badly you're knocking my feelings around, but you are. I can't do that for a night, Karim, let alone a lifetime. I accept that this is an arranged marriage, not one based on love. But don't act like you care and then prove that you don't. I can't bear that. Not again."

If she had plunged a knife into his lung, he wouldn't have winded him this badly. Her accusations were bad enough, but suddenly he was wondering if she had given her heart to another and been rejected. And if she had, why was he taking that far worse than he would have if she'd had other lovers physically?

"Who else did that to you?" He needed to know.

"It doesn't matter," she muttered, turning away to work bangles off her wrists.

"It's affecting our marriage. Our relationship." What the hell did he care about such things? She was handing him a free pass to make love to her and withhold any investment of deeper feelings. He ought to rejoice. Instead, he was aggrieved by the idea of her coming to their marriage bed withholding anything from him, especially the genuine excitement and delight she had seemed to take in their congress before.

Running a hand over his head, he demanded, "Who?"

She sighed and stayed silent a long time, while her jewelry went into a dish with soft clinks.

"In light of what we've learned about my mother recently," she began in a subdued voice, "I understand better why she was so ambivalent with my brothers. Why she pushed them away. She had given away a child she wanted to keep. That has to break something in you.

Maybe that's even why she eventually pushed me away, but it wasn't always like that. For years…"

Her shoulders slumped under an invisible weight.

"None of this really matters, Karim," she said faintly.

His ardor was well and truly doused. Short of an invasion that required him to protect his country, he could not imagine anything more important to him than what she was telling him right now.

"Continue," he commanded.

"It makes me sound very pathetic. As superficial as you think I am." She kept her back to him and spoke to her feet. "When I was a child, I felt very special. It was obvious to me that I was the one Mother loved. Father worshipped her and she gave him nothing. The boys learned to live without affection from her, but she adored me. She brushed my hair and dressed me so we looked alike. She took me everywhere with her and was always so proud and happy when people said I was pretty and looked like her."

"That makes you sound more like a pet than her child."

"I was. A living doll, maybe. If only I had stayed that way."

"What way? Young?"

"Preadolescent, yes. Once I started to become a woman, it stopped."

"What did?"

"Her love."

She clutched her elbows in clawlike fingers, manicured nails threatening to cut into the skin of her bare arms. He moved across to touch her, drawing her attention to it so she would stop hurting herself.

She gave a little shiver and flashed a distressed glance up to him, then stepped away, averting her face.

"How do you know she stopped loving you? What happened?"

"Instead of saying, *You're so beautiful*, she would say, 'Your perfume has soured.' Instead of saying, *I love how your smile is exactly like mine*, she would say, 'Your laugh is too high-pitched. That lipstick is not your color.'"

"Did you do something to anger her?"

"If I did, she never said outright what it was." Her tone grew bitter.

"Then why do you think—? Ah. You told me before that she didn't want to be called Grandmother," he recalled.

"She said those exact words one time when my father was telling me over a family dinner that I ought to marry."

"So she was jealous of your youth."

"Maybe even that my life was ahead of me. I've been thinking about her all day today, thinking she would have died rather than attend *my* wedding. She hated it when I was the center of attention and would always say, 'You're acting like Malak.' She really did hate him and wasn't afraid to show it."

Galila had never acknowledged that out loud, but it felt weirdly good to do so. Like lancing a wound so it could begin to heal.

"And now you have no opportunity to ask her about it. I do understand that frustration, you know."

She sent him a helpless look, one palm coming up.

"You see? You're doing it again. Making it seem like we have something in common, that you care what I might have been through. What happens in ten minutes, though? In an hour? In the morning? Will my feelings become inconsequential again?"

He looked away from her, uncomfortable as he viewed his behavior in a fresh light. He had been protecting himself—his whole country, he could argue— since Zyria had been impacted when his father threw his life away over a broken heart. But he hadn't seen that in protecting himself, he had been injuring her.

"Is it me, Karim?" she asked in a voice thick with dread. "I had nearly convinced myself that my mother's hurtful behavior was her own issue, but if you're doing the same thing, then there must be a flaw in *me*." Her voice cracked as she pointed at her breastbone. "Something that makes me impossible to love. What is it?"

Galila stood in a vice of agony while her husband stood unmoving, as a man made from marble. She didn't even think he breathed. Was he trying to spare her? Because he was alleviating none of her fears with that stoic expression.

Finally, he blinked and muttered, "There's nothing wrong with you. That's absurd."

"There you go. I'm absurd!" She felt exactly as she had in those first dark years when her mother had begun to pull away. "I know I'm a ridiculous person. My brothers told me all the time that I shouldn't be so needy and want to feel loved. I know that with some people, like you, there's no getting into their good graces, even when you once were loved by them. But I don't understand how I *lose* it. Is it things that I say? Am I supposed to stand in silence and allow myself to be admired? But why would anyone want to look at me? I'm not beautiful *enough*. My neck is too long and I have my mother's thighs. Is it because my nose is too pointy? Help me understand, Karim! I can't fix it if I don't know what the problem is."

"There is no problem," he said so firmly she could only take it as a knife in the heart because he clearly wasn't going to tell her.

She threw up her hands in defeat. "Fine. Let's just—" She waved at the bed, but tears came into her eyes. She didn't know if she could go through with it. All she could do was stand there, crushed by anguish, fighting not to break down.

"Galila. There is nothing wrong with you," he insisted, coming across to take her hands. "Look at me." He dipped his head and waited until she was looking into his eyes. "You're very engaging. Very easy to…"

His mouth tightened and she could see him pulling himself back behind some invisible wall.

She tried to pull away, but he tightened his grip on her hands.

"Listen. I find myself letting down my guard with you. That's not something I ever do. Not with anyone except perhaps my mother. Even then…it's not comfortable for me."

"Well, it's not comfortable for me to let down my guard only to be shut out afterward. That's why I'm still a virgin. That sort of intimacy isn't easy for me, either. Not unless I'm convinced my heart will be safe." She pulled her hands free and quarter-turned away. "Maybe that's what all relationships are, though? Maybe I am a fool, thinking there's some way to feel safe in one." She spun back. "But your mother and father were in love. It's possible, Karim."

He was the one to walk away this time, hand drawing down his face as he let out a harsh breath.

"I know what you're thinking," she said with despair frosting her insides. "That I'm ruining our honeymoon night. I don't mean to set ridiculous standards. I just…"

Find it all very disappointing. Heartbreakingly empty.

"I don't know how I'll live in this state of hurt for the rest of my life. How do you not care, then? Teach me *that*, Karim."

His shoulders flexed as though her words had struck like a whip across them. He shook his head, voice disembodied when he spoke.

"I have trained myself not to care, Galila. To keep my thoughts to myself and control my desires. A man in my position can't give in to urges and open up doorways to vulnerability. I can't, Galila. The kingdom depends on my strength." He turned to deliver that bad news in a voice that was calm and factual but kind, at least.

Her mouth trembled and she nodded. "I know. Look at my father, abdicating because he was so devastated by losing my mother, even after what she had done. I just don't know how to be like you, Karim, instead of like him."

"I don't want you to be like me," he said in a voice that was low and quiet, but carried an impact that seemed to go through her as a shock wave, shivering all her pieces into new alignments. "I like who you are, Galila."

"You don't even know me, Karim." Her eyes were hot, and she wanted so badly to believe him.

"Untrue. Look at this party tonight. It was a ridiculous expense, one where you could have made it all about yourself. Instead, you gave it meaning. You *are* beautiful, so beautiful you trick the mind into thinking that's all you are. Then you display intelligence and kindness and you navigate all aspects of my life—a life I fight to control every minute of every day—you walk through that obstacle course with a graceful lack of effort. It's astonishing to me how well you fit in."

"My mother should get the credit for preparing me for this life, not me," she pointed out, throat abraded by emotion.

"And humble on top of the rest."

"Karim, it's very nice of you to say these things, but—"

"I don't do platitudes, Galila," he cut in flatly. "I'm telling you what I have learned of you during our short union. You have qualities I didn't expect, but I never expected to have a partner at all. A wife, yes, but not someone who is a genuine support. It's the strangest thing to me. Do you understand that? I don't want to grow accustomed to your presence at my side. I never needed you before. Why should I need you now? But there it is. You make it easier to carry out my duties, even as I feel weak for allowing you to lift any of the load. It's a paradox I haven't worked out how to solve."

She was soaking up the mud with the rainwater, feeling the contradiction inside her while watching the dismay battle with resignation in his brutally handsome features.

"Do you understand that it's your reluctance to allow me to share in your life that is killing me? Every time you push me away and act like I'm more annoyance than necessity, I hurt. How do I relax and give myself to you tonight, then face your withdrawal tomorrow? When you've decided I've seen too much of you?"

His cheek ticked.

"I'm sorry," she whispered, shaking her head in defeat. "I don't think I can—"

"I won't," he cut in, tone thin and sharp as a dagger, one corner of his mouth pulling down into the deadly curve of a *jambiya* blade. He was tensile steel, pupils expanding and contracting with inner conflict—a warrior on the defensive, but ready and willing to attack.

"Won't…?"

"Shut you out. I won't," he vowed.

She searched his expression, anguished by the struggle she could see in him, disheartened by how clearly it went against the grain for him. "That's not a promise you want to make. I can see that much, Karim."

Why didn't he want to share himself with her?

His lips pulled back against his teeth.

"But I will." He came across to cup her cheek. His gaze dropped to her throat, where her pulse throbbed fast. His palm slid down to cover it, so her heartbeat was hitting the heel of his hand. "Because I would do almost anything to touch you." His voice was both graveled and velvety. "That is the crux of it. And I can't believe I am handing you that weapon."

He looked tortured, but if his statement was a weapon, it was one that disarmed her as thoroughly as him. Her eyes burned and the rest of her grew weak. With her own tentative trust building, she set her hand on his chest, where his heart hammered in fierce pounds that made her own echo in her ears.

"It's the same for me. You know it is," she whispered.

"Our souls may be destined for hell then, because I have tried to resist—"

He dipped his head and this time, when he dragged

his mouth across hers, she melted. The harsh truth was, she wanted him far more than she feared the detriment he might become to her well-being.

And how could she deny the hunger in his kiss? He was so unabashed it was as if he'd let himself off leash. His lips demanded while his tongue took and gave, making her whole body feel gripped in a force that was both energizing and weakening. The pulse that had raced in her throat grew to something she felt in the pit of her belly and at the juncture of her thighs. It was nervous anticipation. Knowledge that *this was it*.

Neither of them could be torn from the other now.

She clung to him, growing so hot, she whimpered in frustration because she didn't want to let him go to remove the rest of her clothing. Her one hand went to her back and tried to work the zipper.

He lifted his head, eyes glowing and avid, cheeks flushed, mouth wet and pulling in a nearly cruel grimace.

"We have time," he said roughly.

"I don't feel like we do," she said breathlessly, feeling overcome and anxious and—

With a feral noise, he scooped her up and strode to the bed. His angular features were warrior sharp, hawkish and fierce.

"This," he said as he set her on the mattress and leaned on the hands he braced beside her shoulders. "This is what scares the hell out of me. It's your first time and I feel like an animal. If I don't control it, who will, Galila?"

"Come here," she demanded. Begged. And set her hand behind his head, moaning in tortured joy when his weight came down on her along with the heat of his lips against hers.

They attacked each other with erotic passion, legs tangling in her gown as she tried to make space for him. Her fingers caught at the collar of his robe, pulling at it so she could taste his shoulder when he dragged his tongue down the side of her neck. Somehow her teeth set against his skin and she had to restrain herself from biting down, but she wanted so ferociously to mark him, it was a fight to keep herself to a scrape and a threat of pain.

"Go ahead," he said, lifting his head and revealing a dark smile that was so transfixing, she felt it like the sun hitting her bare skin. It lit her up inside and out, nearly blinding her. "Claw at me. Bite me. I want all of it. Whatever is inside you."

She dragged her nails down his back through his robe, then dug them into his buttocks, hard as steel but flexing at her touch to drive his firm flesh against her sensitive mound.

He cupped her head and held her still for another rapacious kiss. Again and again, he feasted on her, satisfying yet stoking. Driving them both wild until she was ready to cry, she was in a state of such heightened arousal.

"I need to feel you," she panted when his hot mouth went down her throat again. "Please, Karim."

His answer was to yank at her bodice, baring her breast to his greedy mouth. She arched, crying out at the sharp pull on her nipple.

"Too hard?" His breath bathed her skin in a tease.

"Never," she gasped, and dragged at his robe, trying to get beneath it.

He shifted, went after her other nipple with equal fervor while he began gathering her gown up her thighs. The second he found skin, his hand climbed unerringly to the lace that shielded her most intimate flesh.

He groaned as he traced over it. She whimpered at the caress that was desperately needed and not nearly enough.

"Karim," she begged.

"So ready for me." He rose to kiss her, but his hand stayed beneath her gown. "Do you think about that night my mouth was here? I do. All the time."

His finger slid beneath the silk, parting and caressing, making speech impossible.

"I think about you in my office, touching yourself as you pleasured me. I'm jealous." He probed gently, licking at her panting mouth as he carefully penetrated. "I think about being here like this with you, having you in every way possible because I want you to be *mine*."

"I am," she swore, opening her legs to invite his touch deeper.

"I take care of what's mine." He pushed the silk firmly aside, his thick finger making love to her while his thumb teased the knot of nerves that made her writhe in pleasure.

She was going to die, held by his caress on a molten ledge, teased and stroked, heat building until that was all she was. Heat. Blistering heat. She bit her lip, wanting the release but fighting it.

"Karim," she managed to breathe, stilling his hand. "I want to feel you. Do this together."

His cheekbones were sharp above cheeks drawn taut. All of him was tense and flexed. Even his lips were pulled back from his teeth in effort.

"Yes," he hissed and very, very carefully withdrew, then he began to tug at her gown.

It took forever. They kept stopping to kiss. To groan. To caress bared skin and whisper, "Oh, yes. You smell so good. You're so smooth here. So lovely. So strong."

Somehow, they managed to strip and she made a keening noise in her throat as they rolled together. The aching swells of her breasts flattened by his hard chest, the roughness of his thighs abrading the insides of hers was sheer magic. She hadn't known that being naked, skin to skin, sex to sex, would make her so weak. She hadn't known that his muscles and overwhelming size could be its own aphrodisiac, making her writhe in ecstasy simply because he was against her.

"Galila." His voice was an abrasive husk, savaged by the same limits of arousal that gripped her.

"I'm ready." She was going to weep. She was so achingly ready.

He slid against her, parting her folds, lined up for entry. And kissed her as he held himself there. He kissed her as though she was the most precious thing he had ever seen.

"No one else will ever give you this," he vowed against her mouth, brutally possessive, but truer words had never been spoken.

"No one could."

There was pressure, invasion. She stiffened a little in surprise, anticipating pain, bracing for it, but he kissed her so tenderly as he exerted that steady pressure.

For one second, as his implacable demand threatened pain, she thought, *I can't.* Then it was done and he seemed to become a part of her, mouth open over her trembling lips, thumb caressing her cheek. His hard shape inside her was strange, yet deeply wonderful.

"No one else will ever give me that," he said with awe and pride. He nibbled her jaw, brushed his lips at her temple, then kissed her once, very sweetly. Then again, this time with more purpose. When he came back a third time, she clung to his mouth with her own.

Their bodies shifted. There was tenderness where they were joined, but nothing more than she could handle, not when arousal was returning with inescapable tingles and clenches of desire.

He was right. This was a type of pleasure she couldn't give herself, couldn't have even imagined. She rubbed her face against his neck, wallowing in the weight of his hips, the way smoothing her inner thighs against his hips made him groan.

When he began to withdraw, she clung on with everything in her and he returned with a rush of sensation so acute she gasped.

"Oh," she breathed, beginning to understand.

"Yes," he said tightly, eyes deep pools, atavistic and regressive, yet he never lost control. He kept his pace slow, letting her get used to the feel of him forging his way, holding her well inside the concentric circles of pleasure that rang through her with each thrust.

She couldn't bear it, it was so good, and she turned her mouth against his iron-hard biceps, biting him. Only then did he make a primal noise and pick up the pace. The intensity redoubled. Her body undulated to receive him. The struggle to reach the pinnacle became a fight they fought together with ragged breaths and fisted hands and every ounce of strength they both possessed.

Then she was there, right there, the cataclysm a

breath away. She locked her heels at the small of his back, determined to keep him inside her forever. At least while the waves of pleasure rolled over her.

He pressed deep, holding himself flush against her as culmination arrived.

They clung then, holding on to each other as the acute tension released in a near painful rush of heat and such encompassing waves of pleasure she could hardly breathe. If her eyes were open, she was blind. If he said things, she only heard the rush of blood in her ears. What happened to him happened to her, stopping time and holding her transfixed. They were one in a way she hadn't known was possible.

It was utter perfection that couldn't be maintained forever, which was a tragedy, she decided, as the rush subsided and the pulses began to fade and she discovered tears on her cheeks.

That supreme ecstasy could be replicated, however. They pleasured each other into delirium twice more before she fell asleep, bound to him in a way that could never be undone.

Which made waking to an empty bed that much more excruciating.

He had promised not to rebuff her, but here she was, forsaken, abandoned and alone. Again.

CHAPTER SEVEN

KARIM HAD MADE a terrible mistake. He had known it as he was offering a vow to Galila that put fissures in his defenses against her. He had known it as he chose to make that vow rather than put off consummation of their marriage—which would have proven his mastery over his corporeal desires.

He hadn't had the strength. Waiting until his wedding night, hanging on to control while he tried to understand her hesitation, had taken all his willpower. When he had been pushed right up to the edge and given the choice to protect himself or have her, he had chosen to have her.

Which told him everything he needed to know about how dangerous she was to him. Devastatingly dangerous.

Once hadn't been enough, either. Maybe if she had expressed some reluctance or said she was tender, he might have restrained himself, but she had been as eager as him to bind their flesh irrevocably.

It wasn't until he woke in the dawn hours, aching to take her a fourth time, that sanity had intruded on the euphoria of honeymoon madness. She was slender, delectable, infinitely erotic but new to lovemaking. He *had* to find a shred of control, if only to continue calling himself human.

He left for his own apartment where he did everything he could to put himself back inside the armor he had worn until Galila had smashed him apart. He watched the sun come up, letting the brightness burn from his retina the image of her nubile curves. He listened to the morning numbers from overseas, drowning out the memory of her pleasured moans and cries. He showered the scent of her from his skin, then hated himself for all of it and wished himself back in her bed, feeling her warm, smooth skin stretching awake beside him.

He ordered their usual breakfast and had it served in the common dining room between their apartments, as it always was. He should have been sated and mellow. Instead, he was short on sleep and impatient with the staff as they hovered, each with their schedules and correspondence, their headlines and coffee urns.

Was the queen expected? Should they allow her to sleep? The questions were unending and struck him as unbearably intrusive. He gritted his teeth against ordering all of them out.

Despite his conflict, he lingered over his breakfast, full of self-loathing at the weakness he was displaying. His schedule had been emptied for the day after their reception as a courtesy. There was endless work in his office to be attended to and he shouldn't dally here like some besotted suitor, hoping to catch a glimpse of the object of his affection.

He was a man. One who ought to be in complete command of himself and the world around him. As he became aware of stirring behind the door to her room, he rose to leave.

* * *

Galila had barely been able to look at her own wan face in the mirror, feeling quite a chump for falling for Karim's promise. At least she had slept well past the time when he normally left for the far side of the palace. She would have the breakfast room to herself.

When she entered the small dining parlor, however, he was standing by the table, reviewing something on the tablet his aid was showing him. He flicked her a glance, one that lasted barely a second, but she saw the consternation in it. Read the lack of welcome in his stiff posture.

Waking alone had been a slap. Walking in here to see he had resumed his cloak of indifference was a kick in the stomach. Having all that play out before the usual assortment of hovering staff added insult to injury. Was it really necessary that she parade her deflowered self before a dozen people?

A case of acute vulnerability struck. Physically, she was fine. She'd had a bath and was only feeling as though she'd pushed herself with stretching poses, not particularly tender from their lovemaking. But memory of their intimacy thinned her skin. She couldn't bear to look at him, she was so dreading the coolness in his eyes.

"Good morning." She gathered her shredded composure and found a distant smile. "I thought you would be across the palace by now."

Silence.

She had the sense he was waiting for her to look at him, but she pretended to take enormous care with selecting cut fruit to add to her yogurt. She brushed away the serving hand that would have poured date syrup over her flatbread.

When she reached for the coffee urn, one of the staff hurried to fill her cup, but Karim said sharply, "I'll do it. Leave us."

His tone was so hard, Galila started, then remained on her guard, gaze on her untasted breakfast.

The room cleared in a quick shuffle of feet and a closed door.

She sat with her hands in her lap, discovering she was afraid to move. Not because she feared him, but because she had silently wished they were alone and now discovered the downside of that. No one to hide behind. She didn't want to move and draw his attention.

"You're angry with me," he said.

She was angry with herself.

"Why would you think that?" she murmured, picking up her spoon.

"You're not looking at me."

She should have looked at him then, to prove she wasn't avoiding it, but her eyes were hot. She feared he would read the anguish in them. She had poured out her heart to him last night. She had shared her body in a way she had never done with any other man and now...

"Even if I were..." *It wouldn't matter*, she wanted to say, but couldn't face that harsh reality so head-on. It would hurt too much. "Just go, Karim."

"I would have made love to you all night, Galila," he said through his teeth. "Until we were both too weak to move. As it was, I was far too rough with you. How do you feel?"

He hadn't sat down again and she only had the nerve

to bring her gaze as far as the embroidery that edged his robe.

"Fine."

He sighed in a way that made her flinch, he sounded so impatient. Then he threw himself into the chair and his eyes were right there, leveled into hers like a strike of sunlight off water, penetrating so deep it hurt. Her eyes began to water and she blinked fast.

Through her wet lashes, she still saw the accusation behind his eyes. The way he searched her face as though trying to find a reason to hate her.

"I know a prevarication when I hear one," she said, her voice a scrape against the back of her throat. "You left because you'd had enough of me. Just go, Karim. It will be easier to stand being ignored if you're not doing it in person."

His hand closed into a fist. With a muttered curse, he unfurled it, then reached to take her wrist, the one that held her spoon. He tugged her to her feet and around the table where he pulled her into his lap.

She landed there stiffly, one elbow digging with resistance into his ribs, face forward as she gritted her teeth.

"What is this?" she demanded. "Some new form of torture where you assume that if I succumbed to you once, I'm yours whenever you want me?"

She very much feared she was. Her bones were already threatening to soften, her whole body wanting to relax into supple welcome, longing to melt into him, skin tingling for the sensation of his hands stroking over her.

"Definitely torture," he said, rubbing his beard into her neck so she shivered and squirmed in reaction.

His arms stayed locked around her, keeping her on his lap.

She put a little more pressure behind the sharpness of her elbow. "I'm actually hungry," she said pointedly.

"Eat, then," he invited, opening his arms and relaxing beneath her, but the way his hands settled on her hip and thigh told her he would restrain her if she tried to rise. "I will hold my wife and consider my inner failings."

"Sounds like I'll have time for dessert and a second cup of coffee." She didn't relax, still defensive even though his hands were settling, smoothing and massaging in a way that was kind of comforting, as though he wanted to offer and take pleasure in equal measures.

"Karim—"

"This is new territory for me, Galila. Don't expect my ease with this to happen overnight."

She let out a choke of humorless laughter. "Even though it was the deal you agreed to for that particular type of night? Are you just angling for more sex right now?"

His hands stalled. "Sex can wait until tonight."

Disappointment panged inside her even as he sighed toward the ceiling.

"I can stand depriving myself. Hurting you so badly you won't even look at me? That I cannot bear." His hands moved again, reassuring now then clenching possessively on her curves. "This level of passion isn't normal, you know. If you had had other lovers, you would know that and be as wary of it as I am." He dipped his head forward so his mouth was against her shoulder, whiskers tickling her skin.

She considered that as she spooned yogurt into her mouth. He wasn't offering her the open heart she wanted, but he was talking, at least. He had dismissed their audience. It was a small step, she supposed. One that allowed her to relax a little on his lap and enjoy the way he cradled her.

"You resent desiring me? That only makes me begrudge feeling attracted to you. That's not healthy, is it? Are we supposed to apologize for the pleasure we give each other?" She set petulant elbows on the table while she scraped at her yogurt bowl, deliberately jamming her buttocks deeper into his lap at the same time.

His hands gripped her hips and he drew a harsh breath.

She sent a knowing smirk into her bowl.

"Do you understand what you're inviting?" he asked mildly, opening his thighs a little so the shape of his aroused flesh dug firmly against her cheek.

"I believe you demonstrated that in great detail last night. Why do you think I'm so hungry? You'll have to let me finish my breakfast, though, before we satisfy other appetites. Otherwise, I'm liable to faint on you. Tell me something about yourself while you wait. What was your childhood like?"

"I didn't have one."

She started to rise, wanting to shift back to her own chair so she could look at him and gauge his expression as he spoke, but his hands hardened, keeping her on his lap. Keeping her with her back to him, she suspected.

"I didn't mean that to be an insensitive question," she said gently. "I thought, well, I supposed you might have played with cousins when you were young? Perhaps traveled when you were finishing your education?"

"My university was the throne of Zyria. When I wasn't with my tutors, I sat with my uncle, learning how to run my country. What did you do as a child?"

"Compared to that, it seems beyond childish. One of my favorite pastimes was learning pop songs. I have a decent voice and performed them for my mother's friends. I'm good with languages, too, which was another parlor trick she liked me to show off. I rode horses with my brothers and we camped in the desert with family sometimes. My childhood was fairly ideal. My teen years were more challenging."

"Why is that?"

She bit into the flatbread. It tasted like cardboard. For a moment, she thought about changing the subject, but maybe if he understood why she found his distance so hurtful…

"That's when she began to criticize me. I became obsessive about earning back her approval. I spent a ridiculous amount of time learning about fashion and makeup, trying to look more like her, thinking it would please her. I asked her to make every decision from my shade of lipstick to the shoes I wore. I kept thinking she couldn't disapprove of the way I looked if she made all my choices, but then she would say I was badgering her. Too needy. Everyone said it, my brothers especially. I felt like everyone hated me. It was awful."

Her scalp tickled as he idly played with her hair. "Did she send you away to Europe?"

"I begged my father to let me finish my schooling there. I couldn't take her moods. Even then, I was so careful to only be in the tabloids for good reasons.

Helping a children's hospital or whatever. Anytime I received good press, though, she would say I was upstaging her. Begging for attention. There was no pleasing her."

She tried to twist and look at him, but he didn't let her. He continued playing with her hair, lightly tugging, dipping his nose to inhale, breathing out against the side of her neck.

"How are we talking about me?" she asked. "Tell me what you like about ruling Zyria."

"I like providing stability. No ruler can make an entire populace happy all the time. The best I can do is avoid war and ensure my people are not suffering in poverty. If they can eat and send their children to school, get the care they need and a new refrigerator when the old one breaks, then I am winning the game."

"That's true. You can't *make* someone happy. Do you ever wish you had brothers or sisters?"

He didn't answer. When she tried to turn her head to look at him, his hand tightened in her hair, preventing her. She gave a little shrug of warning, but he wasn't hurting her. He didn't let go, though. After a long minute, he answered.

"There are times I have thought my life would have been easier if I'd had an older brother and the responsibility I carry had gone to him," he spoke with a hint of dry humor, but his tone was also very grave. "Perhaps a lot of things would have been different. I don't know. But I can't make a sibling happen, so there's no point wishing for it."

She waited, but he didn't say anything else.

She pushed aside her emptied plate and sipped her coffee. When she set it down, he shifted her sideways so her legs were across his and they were finally looking at each other.

His face was impassive, difficult to read, but she understood him a little better. He carried a country on his shoulders and had for a long time. If he was lonely, he had made it his friend. That was why he was having such trouble turning to her.

Smoothing her hand over the silky hairs on his jaw, she said very sincerely, "Thank you for telling me that." She pecked his lips with hers.

The light kiss turned his dark eyes molten. "Are you sufficiently rejuvenated?"

"I could be talked into returning to the bedroom."

"Here will do."

Karim had to be extremely careful with his inquiries, but he had learned more about Adir. In the three weeks since Zufar's wedding, Adir had married Amira, the bride who had been promised to Galila's brother. Rumor had it they were expecting.

An odd pang had hit him with the news. For years, Karim had been ambivalent about procreating. More than one of his cousins had the temperament to rule. Was it latent sibling rivalry that prompted a sudden desire to make an heir?

"What's wrong?" Galila's soft voice nudged him back to awareness of the view off her balcony as her scent arrived to cloud around him.

He glanced back into her apartment and discovered her maids had finally left them alone.

In another lifetime, which was mere days ago, he would have brushed off her inquiry with a brisk and conscienceless "Nothing." He wasn't required to explain his introspective moods to anyone.

But Galila's slender arms came around his waist as she inserted herself under his arm. Her pointy chin rested on his chest and she gazed up at him. The pretty bat of her lashes was an invitation to cast off his pensiveness and confide in her.

"There are things I would discuss with you if I could, but I can't," he said, surprised to discover it was true. He wanted to confide in her. It was yet another disturbing shift in his priorities. "It's confidential." He stroked the side of his thumb against her soft cheek to cushion his refusal.

"Hmm," she said glumly. "Bad?"

"Not violent, if that's what you mean."

"Trade embargoes or something," she guessed.

Did not acknowledging his potential successor to Zyria's throne count as an embargo? "Something like that."

"You can trust me, you know. I know I behaved indiscreetly the night we met, but I'm not usually so reckless. That was a special case. With a special man," she added, lips tilting into the smile that he fell for like a house of cards.

She hadn't had a drop of alcohol since the night they met, he had noted.

She shifted so they were front to front and rested her ear on his chest, sighing with contentment. His hands went to her back of their own accord, exploring her warm shape through the silk robe she wore over her nightgown.

This was becoming the norm for him—holding her. He wasn't a dependent man, but she was so tactile and affectionate, seeming to thrive on his touch, he couldn't resist petting and cuddling her.

"I don't regret telling you about him that night. Adir, I mean," she murmured.

He stalled in stroking across her narrow shoulders.

"I'm glad you're willing to listen. That *I* can trust *you*," she went on. "I'm still so shocked by Mother's affair and Adir. I keep wondering about Amira. How she even knew Adir well enough she would run away with him."

He almost told her the woman was married and expecting, but she would wonder how he came to know it.

"Did you know her well?" he asked instead, resuming his massage across her back.

"Her father is one of my father's oldest friends. She was promised to Zufar since she was born. I was looking forward to having her as a sister-in-law. And Zufar—you saw him on a really bad day. He can be gruff, but he would have done his best to be a good husband. I've asked him what he has learned of Adir, but he's so angry, he wants nothing to do with it. I don't know what to do. I want to be sure Amira is well and happy with her decision, but I can't very well make inquiries without spilling our family secrets, can I?" She leaned back to regard him. "See? I am capable of discretion."

"I'll see what I can learn," he promised, pleased when she grew visibly moved.

"You will? Thank you!"

He was growing so soft. He very much feared he was becoming infatuated with his wife, constantly wanting to put that light in her expression and feel her throw her arms around him like he was her savior.

He picked her up and took her to the bed, distantly wondering what she would say when he told her he had learned her friend was pregnant.

I don't desire your children.

He didn't know why that continued to sting when they made love so passionately every night. It was early days in their marriage and he ought to be pleased they were making love frequently without morning sickness or other health concerns curtailing their enjoyment of each other.

Still, as they stripped and began losing themselves in each other, he was aware of a deeper hunger that went beyond the drive for sexual satisfaction. Beyond his need to feel her surrender to him and take such joy at his touch. He wanted all of her. Every ringing cry, every dark thought, every tear and smile and whispered secret.

He suspected he wanted her heart.

Do I look pretty, Mama?

Galila was in the gown she intended to wear to stand next to her mother at the children's hospital gala. This used to be one of their favorite events, but for months now, her mother had been growing more and more critical. Galila didn't understand why.

She had tried very, very hard this time to be utterly flawless. Her gown was fitted perfectly to her growing bust and scrupulously trim waistline. Her hair fell in big barrel curls around her shoulders. Her makeup was light, since her mother still thought she was too young—at sixteen!—to wear it. Nail polish had been allowed for years, though. She had matched hers to the vibrant pink of her gown and wore heels, something the queen had also been arguing were too old for her.

She thought she looked as beautiful as she possibly could and smiled with hope, trying to prompt an answering one from her mother's stiff expression.

Her mother winced and gave her a pitying look. *I expect you to have better instincts, Galila. The green would be better and a nude shade on your lips.*

Rejection put a searing ache in the back of Galila's throat. She turned away to hide how crushed she was, waiting until her mother went back into her own closet before she reached for a tissue on the shelf and dabbed it beneath her eyes, trying to keep her makeup from running.

Why was her mother being so cruel lately? She stared blindly at the bookshelf, trying to make sense of her mother's change in attitude. She used to be all purrs and strokes, now she was claws and hisses. Just like…

The object before her blurred eyes came into focus. It was a bookend. Two slabs of ebony with a bright gold figure upon it. A lioness. She stood on her hind legs, one paw braced against the upright wall as she peered over the top, as if looking for her mate—

Galila sat up with a terrified gasp beside him, jolting Karim awake.

"What is it?" He reached out a hand in the dark, finding her naked back coated in sweat. The bumps of her spine stood up as she curled her back, hugging her knees protectively. Her heartbeat slammed into his palm from behind her ribs, drawing him fully out of slumber.

"Nightmare?" he guessed. "Come here. You're safe."

She only hugged herself into a tighter ball, tucking

her face into her knees, back rising and falling as she dragged long breaths into her lungs, as though she was being pursued.

He came up on an elbow, and rubbed her back, trying to ensure she was as awake as he was. "Are you in pain?"

"Just a bad dream." She didn't let him draw her under the covers, though. She pressed a clammy hand to his chest and pushed her feet toward the edge of the mattress. All of her shook violently, her reaction so visceral, his own body responded with a small release of adrenaline. He caught at her arm, ready to protect her against frightening shadows and monsters under the bed.

"What was it about?"

"I need a minute. Let me—" She left the bed and found her silk robe, pulling it on before she disappeared into the bathroom.

He was sleeping inordinately well these days, thanks to their regular and passionate lovemaking. The sated, sluggish beast in him wanted to lie back and drift into unconsciousness again, but he heard water running.

Concerned, he rose and followed her into the bathroom where the light blinded him. She had turned on the tap and buried her face in a towel to muffle her sobs. The cries were so violent, they racked her shoulders.

His scalp tightened. This reaction was off the scale. "Galila."

She hadn't heard him come in and gasped, lifting a face that was so white, his heart swerved in his chest.

"You look like a ghost," he said. Or she'd seen one. He tried to take her in his arms, but she wouldn't allow it.

"I'm sorry. I can't—" Her words ended in a choke. She set aside the towel and splashed the water on her face, then dried it only to hide behind the dark blue cloth again.

Her desire for distance surprised him. Stung, even. He was used to her turning to him for the least thing. He liked it.

"What was it about?" he insisted. "Tell me."

She couldn't. She was barely making sense of it herself. She wasn't even sure if it was a genuine memory. Dreams were pure imagination, weren't they?

Clenching her eyes shut, she tried to recall her mother's boudoir. Her bookshelves. Was it possible the lioness she had pictured so clearly had been conjured by the curiosity that was plaguing her? She wanted to know who her mother's lover had been, so she was inventing scenarios in her sleep.

Or was it real? The palace of her childhood was full of objets d'art. Masterpieces in oil, ivory, ceramic and yes, some were sculptures cast in gold. Could she mentally picture all of them? Of course not, especially the ones that had been in her parents' private rooms. She hadn't entered those much at all.

But she *had* gone to her mother that one afternoon, ahead of the children's hospital ball. That was a real memory. She distinctly remembered it because the ball had fallen right after her birthday. The pink gown had been a present to herself, one she had been certain her mother would approve of.

None of that was the reason she could hardly catch her breath, however.

What if it is true? What if her mother had owned the

other side of Karim's father's lion bookend? Did that prove Karim's father had been her lover? Or was it a bizarre coincidence?

"Galila."

Karim's tone demanded she obey him.

She opened her eyes and searched his gaze, but couldn't bring herself to ask if it was possible. How would he know? He'd been a child. And the suspicion was so awful, such a betrayal to his mother, she didn't want to speculate about it herself, let alone put it on him to wonder.

What would such an accusation do to this tentative connection they had formed? She couldn't bear to lose what was growing between them. He had married her to be a link between their two countries, not the catalyst for a rift that couldn't be mended.

With lashes wet with helplessness, she said very truthfully, "I don't want to think of it." She held out her hand. "Make love to me," she whispered. "Make me forget."

He was too sharp not to recognize she was putting him off, but he let her plaster herself across his front and draw his head down to kiss him.

Within seconds, he took command of their lovemaking, taking her back to bed where they were both urgent in a way that was new and agonizing, as if he felt the pull of conflict within her. Impending doom. He dragged his mouth down her body, pleasured her to screaming pitch and kept her on the edge of ecstasy, then rolled her onto her knees. She gripped the headboard in desperate hands as he thrust into her from behind, but even after she shuddered in release, he wasn't done. He aroused her all over again, his own body taut and hotter than a branding iron when he finally settled over her and drew her thighs to his waist.

Now he was everything, her entire world, filling her, possessing her, driving her to new heights that they reached together, so intense she sobbed in glory.

Spent, she fell asleep in his arms, clinging to his damp body as if he could save her from her own subconscious.

But the lioness stalked her into the morning light.

When she woke, she knew what she had to do.

"Are you sure you're all right?" Karim asked twice over breakfast. It was usually a private meal now. He let their aids in when they were nursing their second cup of coffee, rarely before. "You'll feel better if you talk it out."

"It's silly," she prevaricated, but couldn't find the dismissive smile she needed. "Just a silly dream."

He knew she was lying to him. She could tell by the grim frown overshadowing his stern gaze. It chilled her heart to disappoint him and even worse, deserve his consternation.

"I don't want to relive it," she said, miserable at not being able to share.

His mouth twitched with dismay, but he let the subject drop. A few minutes later, he rose to start his day.

When she was certain he was on the far side of the palace, she texted Niesha, Zufar's wife and the new Queen of Khalia. With so much going on, she had barely absorbed her brother's email yesterday concerning his new wife and the startling possibility she could be the lost Princess of Rumadah.

It wouldn't have surprised her in the least if Niesha hadn't returned her message, preferring to take time to absorb her own life changes, but she video-called Galila a short time later. Galila dismissed the maid in her room and answered, forcing herself to strike a casual pose on the end of a sofa, as if she wasn't wound so tightly with nerves she was ready to snap. It took everything in her to get through a few gentle inquiries after Niesha's situation and well-being.

"Thank you so much for calling me back," Galila said when she felt she could steer the conversation to her own interests. "I don't know what made me think of a particular keepsake of my mother's, but I wondered if it was on the shelf in your room? Would you be able to show me? It's an ebony bookend with a lioness cast in gold."

"I'm so sorry," Niesha said. "All her rooms have been completely redecorated, but your mother's things were boxed up and put into storage. Nothing was discarded. It's all safe."

"No apology is necessary. Of course, you made it your own." Galila spared a brief thought for how odd it must be for Niesha to be living as a queen, rather than a maid. They were equals now and Galila had to remember that, but she was fixated on learning the truth. "Do you recall seeing a bookend with a lioness, though?"

"I don't recall it, no. Let me check with Zufar. I'm sure he'll agree you should be the one to have her things. I'll have them shipped to you."

It wasn't exactly the answer she wanted. Galila had hoped to solve the mystery in seconds. Instead, she had to act like it was a trifling thing, not an obsessive worry.

"Whenever you have time," she said with a flick of her hand. "I don't want to disturb you when you have so much going on."

The more Galila thought about it, however, the more she was convinced that Karim's father, King Jamil, had been her mother's lover. The timing fit with Adir's age and her own father's diplomatic tour. A brief glance at Zyria's history online confirmed that Karim's father had died very shortly after her father had returned to Zyria.

Had his death been a catalyst for her mother telling her father about her pregnancy? Had Jamil's accident even been an accident?

She couldn't help dwelling on every possibility as she waited for the boxes to arrive.

What if Karim's father had been her mother's lover? That would mean Adir was Karim's half brother, too. How would he react to *that* news?

Not that she could burden him with any of this. Definitely not until she had more evidence than a spooky dream.

But if it did turn out to be true, was it wise to tell him? He would have to keep it from his mother, who still held Jamil so close to her heart. What of the political ramifications? Zufar was already dealing with an embittered man who blamed him for the loss of his birthright. She couldn't subject Karim to the same.

A sensible woman would leave the mystery unsolved, but she couldn't let it go. At the same time, keeping all of this inside her was like trying to ignore an abscess. It throbbed and ached in the back of her throat, flaring up and subsiding as she pretended to Karim that she was fine, all the while waiting on tenterhooks for news that the shipment of boxes had arrived.

A week later, rather than bother Niesha again, she

had her assistant speak to the palace in Khalia. The boxes had finally left and should arrive in a day or two.

Somehow, knowing they were on their way was far worse than if they hadn't left.

"Should I cancel our dinner engagement tonight?" Karim asked over breakfast.

"Pardon?" Galila's gaze came back from staring at nothing and focused on him. She seemed to become aware that her coffee was halfway to her mouth and set it down without tasting it. "Why would you do that?" she asked.

Because she had been positively vacant the last few days. He wanted to know why. This was usually her favorite time of day, when she had him all to herself. She usually flirted and chattered, reminded him to call his mother and asked if he had any preferences for upcoming menu choices. She might sidle up to his chair and kiss him if she was feeling particularly sensual.

She'd become downright remote of late, though.

He hated it.

"You're not yourself. Is there something we should discuss?"

"What? No! I'm completely fine." A blatant lie. "Just…distracted. Should I let the staff in?" She rose to do it.

"Does it have to do with Adir? Because I have news."

"You do?" She swung back, interest sharp.

"He married Amira. She's expecting. Sooner than one would anticipate, given she was supposed to marry your brother a month ago," he added drily. "My reports are that they're quite happy."

"Oh. I thought she must have had some sort of relationship with him, to be willing to go with him like that. It's good to know she's well." She stood with her hands linked before her, still taking it in, chewing her lip and pleating her brow. "That's all you learned?"

For some reason, the way her gaze searched his caused the hair on the back of his neck to stand up.

"Yes." The word *why?* stayed locked in his throat.

With a thoughtful nod, she let in their staff, curtailing further discussion.

Galila wanted the lion on hand to compare to the lioness when—*if*—it arrived. Would Karim miss it if she removed it from his study? At the very least, she needed a fresh look at it. She wanted to search for a signature or an identifying engraving or seal—anything that might prove it was one of a pair.

She would take a few photos on her phone, she decided, as she crossed to the far side of the palace.

Karim had left their breakfast room about an hour ago for his day of royal duties. Would he cancel their dinner? She wasn't sure how she felt about that. Her mind was a whirlwind these days, one where she could barely take in what Karim had said about Adir and Amira when she was so focused on discovering who Adir's father was. Obviously her distraction was beginning to show, but she couldn't tell Karim what was bothering her until she could provide a definitive answer.

Much like the first time when she had arrived without warning, she was invited to wait in his study. She again insisted he should not be interrupted. She wanted to be alone for this.

The bookend was exactly where she had seen it the

first time. It was surprisingly heavy. She turned it this way and that on the shelf, taking photos, then tilted it to look at the bottom.

There was a date that fell a few weeks into Galila's father's trip away. The artist was someone she didn't know, but she would look up the name later. Where was he located? Zyria? Khalia? Somewhere in between where lovers might meet?

Most tellingly, the piece was called *Where Is She?*

Her heart began to thump as she instinctively guessed the other would be called *Where Is He?*

"They just told me you were waiting."

Karim's voice startled her so badly she dropped the bookend, narrowly missing her foot and crying out with alarm as she leaped back from it.

"Did it hit you?" Karim grasped at her arm to steady her, then crouched, trying to examine her foot.

Galila stumbled back, certain her guilty conscience gleamed bright as full moon on a clear night. "I'm fine," she stammered. "Did I break it? I'm so sorry. I didn't hear you come in."

"Worry about your foot." He picked up the bookend and rose, turning it over and weighing it in his hand. "I don't think a nuclear bomb could hurt this thing, but you would be in a cast if it had landed on your toes. What was so engrossing about it?"

"I don't know," she babbled, finding it increasingly impossible to lie to him, especially when she had been working so hard to coax him to open up to her. "It's just a very well-crafted piece, don't you think?"

He narrowed his eyes and studied it more closely, reading the bottom before slowly setting it on the shelf and nudging it up against the books.

"It belonged to your father, I imagine? I would feel horrible if I had dented it."

"It's fine." He folded his arms and frowned at her. "What did you need?"

"I—" She couldn't say *Nothing*. Not when she had said she needed to speak to him and would wait here for a private audience. Last night, when she had decided to come here to examine the bookend, she had conjured a question about Adir and Amira, but he had answered that this morning. They had private conversations every day over breakfast. She had no good excuse for being here.

Fighting to keep her gaze from drifting back to the lion, she racked her brain.

"Is it whatever you've been hiding from me?"

Her heart took a hard bounce, causing her voice to stutter. "W-what?"

She knew damned well her gaze was rife with culpability as it rose to his. She watched his own narrow like a predatory bird swooping into a nose dive.

"You think I can't tell? We're so attuned, I sense the slightest shift in the cadence of your breath and the change of scent on your skin. You're worried about something. You avoid my eyes—" He muttered an imprecation. "You're doing it now. *Look at me.*"

She couldn't. Guilt weighed her lashes along with her shoulders and even her head on her neck. She couldn't tell him, though. Not until she knew for sure.

This morning, when he had mentioned Adir, she had wondered if he had learned Adir was his half brother. Now, through her panic, she recalled something else that had penetrated the edges of her mind during that conversation. A suspicion that had been overshadowed by her turmoil over a pair of bookends.

It was something she wasn't quite ready to acknowledge because she could be just as wrong about that as she might be about his father. But she would rather speculate on that than the other.

"I think I'm pregnant."

CHAPTER EIGHT

KARIM HEARD THE words but they didn't make sense. They weren't bad, just astonishing. "How?"

She rolled her eyes. "Do not tell me to have 'the talk' with you. Not the way we've been carrying on."

He couldn't help smirking at that, but then frowned in confusion. "I said you could use birth control. You said you wanted to."

"Yes, well." She wrinkled her nose and gave her hair a self-conscious flip. "I was annoyed with you the day I came in here to discuss that. The doctor was very patronizing, making it sound like I *had* to take something. As if it was your decision that I shouldn't conceive. You'll recall that we weren't even having sex at the time…" She looked at her manicure, embarrassed by her pique that day, but also blushing at how uninhibited she'd been with him.

"I remember." His voice held a warm, delicious undertone, one that made her toes curl. "So you didn't go on anything?"

"I had a small tantrum about it at the doctor's, then came here. I kept thinking I should go back and get it sorted, but I don't care for him, so I never did."

"He's been my doctor all my life. He's very thorough."

"And I'm sure you would enjoy discussing your personal life with my female doctor back in Khalia, who is also very thorough," she said pertly.

"Point taken. See if she wants to relocate."

"I've had preliminary discussions about the women's health center and met some excellent female doctors here in Nabata. I only have to ask my assistant to book me an appointment, but—you're going to think me the biggest idiot alive, Karim. You're going to say I'm the one who needed 'the talk.'"

"Why?" He frowned.

"I honestly didn't think it would happen so fast," she admitted with a groan. "I've been ignoring the signs because I feel quite stupid for thinking I could have sex and get around to starting birth control when I felt like making a visit to a new doctor a priority. I'm a grown woman. *I know better.*"

He laughed. It was a brief chuckle that was more of a pair of staccato exhales, but it made her insides blossom in sweetly smug triumph for squeezing that carefree noise out of him.

His amusement lingered in his expression as he shook his head in wry disbelief at her. In fact, he was so handsome in that moment, she tipped a little further into love with him.

A little further? Oh, dear. Yes. She was quite in love with him, she realized with a stutter of her heart. She looked to the floor, letting her hair fall forward to curtain her face and hide that she was coming to terms with a *lot* lately. How had she been so foolish as to do that though? The very thing she feared most—yearning for someone she loved to love her back—was now the definition of her marriage.

With that burning ache for a return of her affections pressing outward in the base of her throat, she asked, "Are you angry?"

"Of course not! I'm astounded, but thrilled. You told me you didn't desire my children."

"I was angry." She wrinkled her nose in apology. "It turns out, I do want your baby, Karim. Very much." So much, the magnitude of it pushed bright tears into her eyes.

His expression of utter bemusement turned tender as he cupped her face. His gaze was quite solemn.

"I've been thinking lately that we ought to be trying to conceive, waiting for the right time to bring it up. I'm very happy with this news, Galila. I only wish you had felt you could trust me with it sooner. Is this why you've been so distracted? You thought I wouldn't approve?"

She shrugged, feeling evasive as she buried her face in his shoulder, but enormous feelings were overtaking her. Love, a kind she had never before experienced, had a breadth and depth that terrified even as it exhilarated her. Anticipation of their growing family swelled excitedly in her while profound despair countered her buoyancy. He had said he would never love her. Overshadowing all of that was the secret of his father's possible affair with her mother, the weight of it heavy enough to crush her flat.

He closed his arms around her, though, and kissed her with such incredible sweetness, her world righted itself for a few precious seconds.

"I'm glad you're pleased," she said against his mouth.

"That's two good memories you've given me in this room to replace my bad one."

She was so startled by that statement she drew back and studied him.

He clearly regretted his remark at once. She watched his expression close up. His jaw hardened and his lips sealed themselves into a tight line.

Ah, this man of hers. He was capable of opening up, but only in very brief and narrow peeks. She traced the hollow of his rigid spine through his shirt, saying quietly, "I wondered."

He grimaced and his gaze struck the curtains that hid the balcony beyond.

"Do you have many memories of him? Six is so young."

"Too young for a memory like that," he said flatly, almost as if he'd seen his father's body, but surely not. Who would allow such a thing?

She started to ask, but he kissed each of her eyes closed. "Shall we make another pleasant memory in here?" His mouth sought hers.

She let him erase the troubling thoughts lingering in her psyche, but it was temporary. She hadn't been completely honest with him and couldn't be.

Not until she had found the lion's mate.

Galila belatedly realized how tasteless it was to have her mother's things shipped to her in Zyria. She wound up requesting they be left in a storage room in the lower palace, rather than in the royal chambers.

Then she had to wait until she had a free afternoon, which didn't happen until she had had her doctor's appointment and her pregnancy confirmed.

That had prompted a flurry of additional appointments with key staff who would keep the news confidential but begin preparations for the upcoming heir. She and Karim even squeezed in a day trip to inform his mother, who was beside herself at the news.

Finally, five days later, Galila was able to go with her assistant down to the roomful of boxes and begin sifting through them. They were labeled but very generally—Books, Art and Heirlooms—all words that could indicate the box held the bookend she sought.

Her assistant was beginning to nag her about being on her feet too long when she squeezed something hard and vaguely animal-shaped through a careful wrapping of linen. She asked her helpers to leave her alone for a few moments.

Stomach tight and curdling, she lifted out the heavy piece. Her hands shook as she unwound the linen.

It was the lioness, exactly as she had dreamed it.

Not risking her foot this time, she kept it on the table and tilted it enough to see the same artist's signature, the same date and the inscription *Where Is He?*

She drew a shaken breath. What should she do now?

Galila was still not herself. Was it the baby? Karim wondered.

She had had the pregnancy confirmed and the obvious signs were there, now that he made a point to notice them. She hadn't had a cycle and her breasts were tender. A brief glance online told him moodiness and forgetfulness weren't uncommon.

If he didn't know better, however, he would think she was drunk, she was so absentminded, leaving the making of conversation with their guests to him. He could tell the older couple was surprised by her wan smiles and quiet introspection. They had met her before and knew she was typically animated and engaging.

Finally, the wife of the minister said something about Galila suffering the pressure of producing an heir. Galila snapped out of her daze to blush and Karim was certain they immediately put her distraction down to pregnancy. They left with smug smiles, convinced they held a state secret.

"Our news will be rumored on every station tomorrow," he said as he followed her into her rooms.

She gave him a startled look. "What news?"

He stared at her. "What is going on with you?"

Her entire being seemed to deflate. "I have to talk to you about something and I don't know how."

The anguish in her expression made his heart lurch. "Is it the baby?"

How could he be instantly devastated when he'd barely begun to absorb this new reality?

"No. I'm perfectly fine. Not even iron deficient or suffering much morning sickness. The baby and I are completely healthy. No, this is something else entirely." She touched her forehead. "Come. I have to show you something."

They dismissed the staff and she took him into her bedroom where she knelt to open a lower drawer. She lifted out a wrapped object that was obviously heavy.

He bent to take it from her and saw the anxiety that leaped into her expression as he picked it up, as if she wanted to snatch it back.

"What is it?" Its density and bulk felt vaguely familiar.

She waved at the bed and he set it there to let her unwrap it. She did, slowly. With dread, even. He heard her swallow as she revealed glimpses of ebony and gold.

It was a bookend, one he recognized as similar to the one that had so engrossed her in his office. The two polished black slabs set at an angle were identical to his, but the lioness cast in gold on this one was in a different position, peering over the top of the wall, rather than around the side.

She had distracted him with pregnancy news, but that had been subterfuge. *This* had been her reason for coming to his office last week. He didn't care to be lied to, but that wasn't what made his scalp prickle so hard it felt as though it was coming off.

"An early birthday present?" He wasn't a flippant man. The remark came out abraded by the gravel in his throat. The pit of his gut was turning sour. "Where did it come from?"

He already knew, even before she looked up at him with misery and regret pulling at her features. Her knuckles were white and sharp as teeth where she clutched the linen in her fist.

"It belonged to my mother."

He closed his eyes. Now came the fury.

"Who else have you told?"

Galila frowned in confusion. "What do you mean, who have I told? Karim, do you understand what I'm telling *you*?"

"Yes," he clipped out.

She had expected more disbelief and shock, not an immediate leap to damage control. She had agonized all day, since pulling this from the box, about whether to tell him. She had then braced herself for having to convince him, once he realized what she suspected. This was, after all, circumstantial evidence. Strong but not definitive. Of course, he would have doubts. She still wasn't ready to believe it.

How could he get there so fast without working through all the reasons that this proved nothing?

"Maybe you should sit down," she said. "Because I don't think you realize what this might mean."

"It matches the one that belonged to my father. *I know what it means*, Galila. I didn't think there was proof of their affair. That there was a way for it to be pieced together. What did you tell them in Khalia about this?" His voice was scythe-sharp, cutting off her reach for other explanations and leaving her weak excuses on the ground. He was so tall and intimidating in that moment, she stumbled back a step.

She kept going, backing away until her knees found the chair where she threw her robe when she climbed into bed. She plopped into it.

"Am I to understand you *knew*?" She was like a fish gasping for air, jaw working, eyes goggling.

"Of course I knew! Why do you think I married you?"

She was glad she was sitting down. His words bowled her over. She felt each of the buttons in the upholstery digging into her back.

"That's why you came on to me at Zufar's wedding? Why you coerced him into agreeing to our marriage? To hide this secret?" She thought being a political pawn had been bad. She wasn't even *that* expedient! Their marriage was a gag order, nothing more.

"Do you understand the ramifications if this gets out?" he went on. "It could start a war!"

She had never seen him this aggressive, shoulders bunched, face so hard there was nothing of the tender lover she had slept beside. He was not a man at all. He was a warrior defending his kingdom.

"My parents' marriage was a peace treaty with tribesmen who backed her father," he added in a clipped tone. "They support me, but grudgingly. If they found out my father cheated on her? That he had a child with another woman? Who knows what sort of retaliation they would take against me. Or Adir."

He paced away and his hand cut through the air.

"Who even knows what kind of man Adir is? He's already shown himself willing to take revenge against your brother for your mother's actions. What would he do to me and Zyria? Then there is your brother Zufar."

He spun to confront her.

"Zyria and Khalia have been in a cold war for years. Your mother's doing, I am sure, since my uncle's overtures after my father's death were always shut down. *I* knew why the relationship between our countries went stale." He tapped the center of his chest. "I never tried to reach out when I took the throne, knowing there was no point. But after your mother passed, I was suddenly invited to your brother's wedding. We are finally in a position to mend fences between our countries and you want to tell him *this*?"

"No!" she cried. "I haven't told Zufar or anyone. I've been agonizing about telling *you*." She had been trying to protect him, didn't he see that?

"How you even—" He ran his hand down his face and glared at the bookend.

"How did *you* know?" she asked.

"My father told me," he spat with great bitterness. "The night he died. Your mother cut off their affair and he got himself blind drunk. If only he had blacked out, but no. He sat there and told me in great detail how deeply he was suffering a broken heart. Said he loved my mother, but not the way he loved Namani. His feelings for her were beyond what he thought possible."

His tortured memory of that night threw harsh shadows into his face.

"He'd thought she felt the same, but she broke it off. He couldn't go on without her. Refused to."

Galila tried to speak and realized her hand was over her mouth. She lowered it. "You were six years old. What was he thinking, putting all of that on you?"

"He wasn't thinking. He was out of his mind with agony."

Karim's own agony was written in deep lines of anguished grief, painful memory and a lifetime of confusion and regret.

"It was years before I understood it properly, but he wanted me to know why he was leaving it all in my hands. He couldn't leave a note. My mother would have seen it."

"Are you saying—Karim," she breathed, gripping the arms of her chair and leaning forward. "His death was deliberate." *Please, no.*

He flashed one tortured flare of his gaze her direction, then showed her his grim profile. "My mother can never know. I've always let her believe he stumbled."

"You *saw* that?" The words tore a strip from the back of her heart to the back of her throat, leaving a streak of burning anguish on his behalf. "That's horrible! He never should have—"

Her entire composure was crumpling in empathy for him. She rose anyway, but he stiffened as she approached, telling her he didn't want her comfort. It was an excruciating rejection.

"Karim…" She held out a hand. "I had to tell you, but I would never, ever tell anyone any of this. Certainly not your mother."

He jerked his chin in a nod of acknowledgment, but when she came closer, he again stiffened and held up a hand this time, warding her off.

His harshly voiced declaration came back to her. *Why do you think I married you?* Surely, they had built something beyond that, though? She was carrying his child.

"I'm going to put that in my personal safe," he said. "I don't want anyone else to see it and come to the same conclusions you have."

"Of course." She moved to take up the linen, but he took it from her and wrapped it himself, disappearing to his own side.

She stood there waiting for his return. And waited and waited.

He didn't come back.

Galila entered the breakfast room to find a handful of aides doing exactly what her husband wanted them to do—they were creating a buffer between him and his wife.

She had spent a restless night missing his heat beside her in the bed, trying to take in the fact Karim had known all along that his father had had an affair with her mother. That he had lied to her about his reasons for marrying her and hadn't trusted her enough to tell her the truth. Not until she figured it out for herself.

Now she had, he was turning his back on her again. Why? Shouldn't this shared secret draw them closer?

As she sank into her chair, he rose, almost as if they were on different ends of a child's seesaw.

"I have a busy morning," he said, looking to the door rather than at her. "If you have questions about our schedule with the duke and duchess, we should cover that now, before we greet them at the airport."

Why do you think I married you?

They had grown close despite his initial motives, though. Hadn't they? He had seemed happy about her pregnancy. Until last night, they had made love unreservedly. That meant she was a source of pleasure for him, didn't it? Surely, he felt *something* toward her? He wasn't going to reject her out of hand, now that she had uncovered the truth about his father's infidelity. Was he?

He didn't give her time to ask any of her questions, rushing out to start his day. They were both tied up for the next few days as they hosted several dignitaries around an international competition for child athletes recovering from land mines and other war-related injuries.

Galila did what she had done for years. She ensured her appearance was scrupulously balanced between flawless elegance and warm benevolence. The cameras adored her. All of Zyria praised Karim for his choice in bride. They dubbed her the Queen of Compassion.

She was miserable, taking no pleasure in the adulation. Thankfully, the car windows were tinted and the madly waving crowd couldn't see that she wore such a long face.

Karim finished his call beside her, one he hadn't needed to make. It was yet another brick in the wall he was building against her.

Before he could cement another into place, she asked,

"Are you so angry with me for figuring it out that you can't even speak to me about it?"

He paused in placing another call. "There's nothing left to say."

"Is there nothing left of our marriage, either? Because you're avoiding me. You're—" He was avoiding their bed.

He sighed. It was the sigh that cut through her like a blade. *Don't be needy,* it said.

"Why aren't you sleeping with me?" She swung her face toward him, refusing to guess at his reasons. "Is it because I'm pregnant? Because you don't trust me? Because you're angry? What did I do to make you turn your back on me, Karim?"

"Nothing," he said from behind clenched teeth. "I was simply reminded by our…discussion the other night that…" He polished the screen of his phone on his thigh. "This passion between us is dangerous," he stated more firmly.

She studied his craggy profile. He was staring straight ahead at the closed privacy window. There might as well be one between them, holding her apart from his thoughts and feelings. From his heart.

"Is that all it is?" She felt as though she inched onto thin ice. "Because I had begun to hope it was more than merely passion."

His jaw pulsed. "I told you not to expect that."

Don't be needy.

Swallowing, she looked to the palm trees that lined the boulevard as they approached the palace. The archway and fountain, the flower garden and flags, the columns and carpeted steps that formed the impressive entrance of the Zyrian palace.

He offered her a home as beautiful as the one she'd grown up in, and as equally empty of love.

"Why?" Her voice broke. "I don't understand why I should never expect to feel loved, Karim. What is wrong with me that I must lower my expectations and stop believing I deserve that?"

"It's not you." The car stopped and he said, "I don't want to talk about this right now."

"You don't want to talk about it ever. Be honest about that much, please." She slid out of the car as the door was opened for her.

Karim threw himself from the far side and flashed her a look across the roof of the car, one that accused her of pushing him to the very limits of his control.

"You want me to be honest? Come, then." He snapped his fingers at her as he started down the walkway alongside the palace.

She knew eyes followed them, but they were left to walk alone through the garden and around the corner of the public wing to the side of the palace that faced the sea. Here the grounds were a narrow band of beach, a triangle of garden and a courtyard—

Oh. She realized where they were when he stopped in the middle of a ruthlessly straight path and looked upward.

"Karim," she breathed. The sun beat down on them so hot it dried the air in her lungs. Her shoulders stung through the silk of her dress and her scalp tingled as though burning along the part in her hair.

"He was so *in love*—" his inflection made the emotion sound like a case of leprosy "—he could not live without her. He preferred to plunge to his death, *in front of his son*, than face another day without her. Is that what you want me to feel for you, Galila? Unable to live without you?"

The reflection off the building was so hot it burned her face, even though the sun was behind her.

"They weren't able to be together." And she knew her mother. There was every chance she didn't love Jamil in the same way, not that she would dare say so. "Our situation is different. I—I'm falling in love with you."

His body jolted as though struck. "Do not," he said grittily. "We have the foundation for something that can work. If we hold ourselves at arm's length."

"No, we don't!" She grabbed his sleeve and shook his arm, as if she could shake some sense into him. "We almost did and now you're pushing me away again. Karim, are you really saying you will never love me? That you would rather break *my* heart by refusing to? By your logic, that means I should go drown myself right now." She thumbed toward the nearby waves washing the shore.

His gaze flashed from her to the water. He flinched, then his expression hardened. "I'm putting a stop to your feelings before they get any worse."

Worse? He really didn't understand love at all. Which was, perhaps, the real problem.

"You aren't just refusing to love me, you *can't*. Can you?" He didn't know how.

"Cannot and will not. I'm protecting both of us. All of Zyria."

He had told her this before, but some tiny thing inside her—smaller even than the child she carried—had hoped. Now she knew how foolish that hope had been. Now she believed him when he said he would never love her.

Her next breath was deep. It was the kind one took to absorb the sting of a deep cut or the reverberation from a cracked head. The kind that felt like a knife going into her throat and staying there.

"Very well, then."

CHAPTER NINE

KARIM ROSE AND prowled through the dark to the door to Galila's bedroom, paused, turned back and sat in the chair, elbows braced on his splayed thighs.

He was hard, so hungry for her he was sweating and panting with need, but he made himself resist the lure of her. The weakness that going to her would represent.

She might not welcome him anyway. He had ground her heart beneath his heel a few days ago and she'd been walking around like a ghost ever since. He loathed himself for doing it, but clung to the truth he had spoken. They had a child on the way. He had to keep a level head on his shoulders for the next two decades, at least.

Two decades of meting out their lovemaking in small measures to prove to himself he didn't need her like air and water. Twenty years of averting his gaze from her laughing expression so he wouldn't be tempted. Of listening to the falsely cheerful tone she used when she was hurting and trying not to let it show.

Of knowing he was breaking her heart.

She had said she was falling in love with him.

He closed his eyes, savoring those words before

pushing them to the furthest reaches of his consciousness. Whatever she felt was so new, she would be able to recover from his rejection. He was sure of it.

He had to believe it.

Unable to sleep and quite sure he would go to her if he stayed, he dressed and went to his office across the palace. It wasn't even sunrise. He ate an early breakfast in his library, a room where she permeated the walls, layering over old memories like a clean coat of paint, then started his work day.

He was little better than a ghost himself, unable to say later what he had accomplished. The entire day was an exercise in deprivation. He counted the minutes until he would see her. It was exactly the sort of weakness he dreaded in himself, but he finally began to breathe again when he entered his apartment to dress for their dinner with a general and his wife.

That was when he was informed Galila wouldn't be joining them.

"The queen was feeling under the weather and canceled all her engagements for the rest of the week," her assistant informed him.

Shock and concern washed through him in a sickly wave.

"Why wasn't I informed?" He started to brush past her into Galila's rooms.

"She's not here, Your Highness," the woman quickly said. "I thought—it must be my mistake. I understood she intended to speak to you before she left."

Something inside him snapped. Broke. Exploded. "Where the hell did she go?"

The girl fell back a step, eyes wide. "I believe she went to stay with your mother."

* * *

Galila was beating herself up for being the neediest wimp alive, scurrying off for TLC in the desert palace.

She discovered, however, that being needy could be a good thing. Sometimes a person needed someone to coddle and fuss over. Galila's low spirits pulled a maternal instinct from Karim's mother that put a smile of warmth on the older woman's face. A brightness of purpose.

"I'm so glad you came to me. Of course, you should come anytime you feel a need to get away," Tahirah said in response to Galila's apology for imposing. "You'll be a new mother soon. Learn to let people take care of you."

Her spoiling and attention was so sincere, Galila wanted to cry with gratitude. Here was the mother she desperately needed. They talked pregnancy and babies and the challenge of running a palace and the endless social obligations of royal duties.

She was still scorched by Karim's refusal to love her, but at least she had someone who seemed genuinely happy to bond with her. Her heart would still be in two pieces, but at least those pieces could be offered to his mother and the child he gave her. Her life would not be completely devoid of love.

Those broken pieces of her heart jangled when Karim rang through on a video call as she was dressing for dinner. She dismissed her maid and answered.

He looked surprisingly incensed. "What are you doing there?" he snapped.

"I was going to discuss this with you over breakfast this morning, but you weren't there." Completely true, but rather than seek him out or text him or try to inform him via the many other avenues of communication available at the palace, she had slipped away like a criminal. "I'm not here to tell her anything, if that's what you're worried about. I just needed some time."

"For what?"

"To think about how I'm going to accept the kind of marriage you've offered."

"We went over this in the early days, Galila. It will be fine."

"For you. But I fell in love with you. I didn't expect that to happen, but it did. And you don't feel the same. Can't. So I need to think about all of that."

"And do what?" His tone sharpened. "If you think you're going back to Khalia, or taking my child to Europe—"

"If I wanted to do that, I would already be there, wouldn't I? I came to your mother's, Karim. That's as far as I plan on taking your child without your permission. We're having a lovely visit so let me be."

His mouth tightened. "When are you coming back?"

"I haven't decided."

"I'll send the helicopter tomorrow."

"I just got here! Why would you even want me to come back? We're not sleeping together. You barely speak to me. I'm surprised you noticed I was gone."

His nostrils flared as he drew a deep, patience-seeking breath.

"What?" she goaded. "You don't even like when I help with your royal duties. You said so. I make you feel weak. You never needed me before we married and still don't want to, judging by the way you've been treating me. Go back to your old life, then. Pretend I don't exist."

"Galila, if you're trying to provoke some kind of reaction—"

"I know that's impossible! You feel nothing, Karim! We both know you're not going to kill yourself if I stay a few days with your mother so that's exactly what I'm doing."

She jammed the button to end the call.

Then she threw the phone across the room. It hit a marble column, shattering the screen.

"Her Highness has broken her phone," Galila's assistant informed Karim the next morning. "A new one is on its way. She'll be back online this afternoon, I'm sure. In the meanwhile, you'll have to message her through your mother. May I also ask...? There are a number of agenda items I needed to discuss with her, but in her absence, will you approve these?"

Karim went through them quickly, resenting every second of it. Why? Not because he didn't want to review the preliminary budget for the women's health center. He would have to do that eventually anyway, but because he was staring at an empty chair, speaking instead of listening.

We both know you won't kill yourself...

He forced himself to proceed through his day, thinking of her constantly. He kept making mental notes to share things with her only to realize he wouldn't see her later. He wouldn't watch her painted mouth as she entertained their guests, wouldn't stand with pride beside her, wouldn't set his hand in the middle of her back just so the silken fall of her hair would caress his skin.

By the time he was alone in his library, he was thinking for the first time in his life how good a shot of whiskey might taste.

Furious, he yanked open the curtain and glared at the balcony. Instead of seeing his father there, he saw Galila, tall and strong, chin up, eyes on the horizon.

By your logic, I should drown myself.

Was she hurting? Was that why she had run away? Breaking her heart had never been his intention. Collateral damage was inevitable in life, but he tried not to purposefully hurt anyone. Galila, with her spirit and compassion and sharp intelligence, deserved every speck of the adoration she earned.

She had definitely earned his respect, not only solving the mystery of her mother's lover, but protecting that secret as diligently as he always had. She had been reluctant to tell *him*, and he knew how heavy the load was on that.

It was considerably lighter these days, he realized. Because he had shared it with her? Or because he was carrying a different load on his conscience? Her bruised heart crushed like a piano atop his own.

He turned to stare at the lion on the bookshelf, the one engraved with the words *Where Is She?*

The same question clawed inside him. His mate was in a palace in the desert. She might as well be locked in a vault the way the lioness was. Locked in the dark for safekeeping. Endlessly searching for her mate while this one eternally waited here.

Apart.

Why? Why did it have to be this way?

With a snarl, he grabbed the bookend, tempted to throw it through the glass doors and over the balcony, into the sea.

Instead, he carried it with him to his empty bedroom.

* * *

Galila was treading water in the infinity pool that overlooked the oasis when she heard her maid make a startled noise. She dragged her gaze from the sand dunes and palms, swirling in the water to face the paved courtyard that surrounded the pool.

Her husband picked up her robe off the chair while her maid scampered away.

Her chin was in the water and Galila very nearly sucked a mouthful into her lungs, managing at the last second to merely swallow a taste of chlorine.

"Come," Karim said, shaking out her robe. "I want to talk."

She hesitated, then kicked herself into a glide toward the steps, self-conscious as she climbed them. Her body hadn't changed. She was barely pregnant, but she didn't know which would be worse—his avid gaze or a disinterested one.

He gave her a rapacious one. His features hardened as his attention followed the flow of water off her shoulders, between her breasts and across her quivering belly, over the triangle of green-blue bikini bottoms and down her thighs and calves.

Shaken, she couldn't find a voice to ask what he was doing there. She turned to thread her arms into the sleeves of the robe, then caught the edges and folded them across her front. The silk clung to her wet skin, warm despite being in the shade.

He didn't let her step away. His arms closed around her and held her before him, damp hair under his chin. He trapped her arms in a crisscross before she could get the belt tied.

"Karim—"

"Shh," he commanded softly. "Let me feel you. I need to know that you are here."

"You knew exactly where I was." She didn't know why, but her heart began to pepper even harder in her chest. Her body twitched with uncertainty. Relax? Remain on guard? "Why are *you* here, Karim?"

"To tell you that we don't have to repeat history. We shouldn't."

"In what way? Because you've already made it clear you won't allow yourself to feel anything toward me," she said with a jagged edge on her voice. Most especially not the depth of love his father had felt for her mother.

His arms tightened and his beard brushed her wet cheek as he spoke against her skin. "I don't know that I had a choice in how I feel about you. From the moment I saw you, I was transfixed."

Her insides juddered in reaction while she recalled that luminescent moment of turning to see him watching her.

"So was I," she whispered in stark honesty.

"The difference is, you were willing to accept how I made you feel. I was never going to allow myself to be this vulnerable, Galila. I knew I couldn't afford it. I had to fight it."

"Because you don't trust me." She pushed out of his arms and turned to confront him.

"Be careful," he said through gritted teeth, glancing toward an upper balcony to indicate they could be overheard by his mother at any moment.

"I know," she hissed. "But that secret is the reason you married me, yet you withheld it from me. Even when things changed. At least, I thought things were changing." She touched where her heart was a cracked and brittle thing in her chest. "You made me think we were growing close, that we could trust one another, but no. You were keeping secrets, refusing to care…" Her voice trailed into a whisper. The despair that had been stalking her crept close enough to swallow her whole.

"Galila." He tried to reach for her.

She held him off with an upraised hand, too raw to accept his touch without crying under the agony of a caress that wasn't genuine tenderness or affection.

He flinched at her rejection.

"I trust you," he said gravely. "If I didn't, I wouldn't have let you stay here like this. I know you'll guard what you know as carefully as I do. I wouldn't be having a child with you if I didn't trust you."

"But you don't trust me with your heart! What do you think I'm going to do with it? Treat it as badly as you treat mine?"

He snapped his head back, breath hissing in with shock, as though she had struck far deeper than he had imagined anyone could.

There was no satisfaction in it. It made her feel small. She looked to the arid sands of the desert, a perfect reflection of their future.

"I'm not trying to hurt you," she murmured. "I'm just not ready to be with you and act like I'm happy when I'm not."

"You won't be until you come back to me, Galila. We have to be together."

She started to shake her head, but he spoke with more insistence.

"The denial is what does the damage. Pushing you

away is killing me." His tone was an odd mix of vehemence and tenderness.

She glanced at him, not wanting the unfurling of hope again, only to open herself for a stomping.

"You were right," he continued. "I won't kill myself over your absence."

And there it was. Her heart went into free fall toward a shattering impact.

"I will come after you and fight to keep you. I *am* fighting for you." His possessive words, the light of anguished need in his expression, was a hand that thrust out and caught her heart before it hit the ground, dragging it into his possession so it would be his forever. *"Come home."*

Her mouth trembled. "I want to, but—"

"I love you, Galila."

Her knees weakened.

He caught her with real hands this time, grasping her upper arms and holding her in front of him so all she saw was him. His features were hard, but cast in angles of concern and repentance. His eyes gleamed dark and solemn, but they were open windows to his soul, holding back none of the brilliant light within him. A light that shone with ardent, aching love as he scanned her features.

It was such a startling, intimate look into his own heart, hot tears of emotion brimmed in her eyes and a lump formed in her throat.

The rest of her crumbled. Not in a bad way. In the best possible way, even though she was quite sure it was her least elegant look ever. Her chin crinkled and she had to bite her lips while tears of joy and love overflowed her eyes. Her face was clean of makeup, her hair skimmed flat, her robe damp and ruffled as she hugged herself into him. Hard.

"I love you, too," she choked. "So much."

She lifted her mouth and he brought his head down. Their lips met in a kiss that made her cry out at the power of it. The sweet perfection. He kissed her the way he had that first night in the garden outside the palace of Khalia. Like he was released from years of restraint.

She returned his passion with her own overwhelming need for him, ignoring the aching tenderness in her breasts in favor of pressing closer and closer—

"Karim!" his mother called sharply from an upper terrace. "*The servants*. Take that to your room."

He pulled away from their kiss as they both broke into laughter.

CHAPTER TEN

KARIM WOKE DISORIENTED in the darkness of a tent. He was quickly distracted by his wife's exploring touch over his body. She was staking a claim here in the dark, taking her time, teasing him with the swish of her hair across his skin, kissing and arousing him.

His hands sought her breasts and he remembered at the last moment to be extra gentle, letting her press into his touch as much as she could bear.

"I thought you were too tired for this," he whispered in the dark, longing to suck on her nipples, but he could only tongue them or she cried, they were so sensitive.

"I was." She sighed. "Then I woke up and I didn't want to sleep. *I want you*."

She straddled him so he felt her nest against his shaft. It had been a long day of travel finding this particular tribe. They'd been welcomed warmly and given the royal treatment, but Galila was in a delicate condition and had turned in early.

She was proving very resilient now, though. He held himself in position as he felt her seeking to take him inside her heat.

They both sighed as she seated herself on him, her heat snug around his pulsing shaft. She began an undulation that made him bite back a groan of supreme pleasure. They didn't have wind and the pepper of whipped sand to disguise their carnal noises this time.

Catching back her own moans of pleasure, she gave herself to him without reserve. He did the same, lifting his hips to meet the return of hers. Her fingernails dug into his chest where she braced herself and hit her peak quickly, the power of it so acute, she pulled him over with her.

He was sorry for it to be over so quickly, but they were practically in public. It was close to dawn and the arrival of other royal guests could happen any time. Today, tomorrow. It might be in a few days, they had been told, but eventually Adir would show up with his wife.

As their personal storm receded, Galila lay sleepily upon him, still joined with him. Her lips grazed his damp skin as she spoke.

"What do you think he will say?"

"I don't know," he said truthfully. That was what he was here to find out.

Galila was watching a new mother demonstrate the proper way to swaddle an infant when excited voices drew her attention to the arriving party.

"Amira!" She leaped to her feet with excitement. Her friend was considerably further along than she was, showing well into her second trimester.

Amira hugged her warmly, but it was the beaming smile on her face that put Galila most at ease. She hadn't seen Adir since the shocking morning of Zufar's wedding. He still had the dangerous air about him and watched her closely as she reunited with Amira, but when he gazed on his wife, he revealed a glimpse of tenderness that warmed Galila's heart.

That softness disappeared between one blink and the next as he flicked his gaze from her to Karim. His stance shifted imperceptibly, almost as if he felt Karim was an enemy he had to watch for sudden moves.

Karim wore the same air of armed caution, unabashed in the way he took Adir's measure.

"Meet my husband," Galila invited Amira, stepping back to Karim's side as she made the introductions.

The resemblance between Karim and Adir wasn't obvious, but she was looking for it and saw the way Karim noted their similar height and scanned a brow and a jaw that matched his own. Seeing their profiles reflected like that, the similarity was undeniable to her. Strange and endearing, especially because she saw a hint of her brothers in Adir as well.

"What business do you have with me?" Adir asked Karim.

"My wife wanted to see her friend, to assure herself she was well." He nodded at Amira.

"Very," Adir said flatly. "As you can see."

Amira patted her baby bump. "All three of us are very happy."

"I'm glad," Galila said. "But we also wanted to speak with you, Adir. About…" She looked to Karim. This was such a delicate matter. "It's a private matter. We have something for you. But I think…" She looked between Adir and Amira, able to see the obvious connection between husband and wife. "Amira, you should come, too."

They entered the tent that Galila and Karim occupied. Amira accompanied them, a confused look on her face. Galila gave her hand a small squeeze and offered a smile of reassurance as she lowered to the cushions with her.

Adir waited while Karim brought the parcel they'd carried into the desert with them, then sat as Karim did.

The bookends were both wrapped carefully in linen. Galila helped Karim unravel them until the lion and lioness were both revealed.

Karim set the lion on the mat before Adir. Then he took the heavy lioness from Galila and braced the two upright walls back to back.

Now it looked as though the male lion gazed on his mate with a casual check-in. *Stay close, sweetheart.* She peered over at him. *I'm right here, darling.*

"A wedding gift?" Adir said, voice somewhere between dry sarcasm and suspicion. But it was clear he saw the value in the pieces and found it odd they were offering such a treasure to him.

Galila licked her lips. "This one belonged to my mother."

Karim's cheeks went hollow before he nodded at the lion. "The other was my father's. We think you should have them."

Adir's brows slammed together.

Amira gasped. "Are you saying…?"

Karim nodded once, curt. He was wary, she could tell, because she knew her husband well these days. She wanted to take his hand, but there were still times where he needed his walls. This was one of them.

Adir looked between them, astonished. He picked up both pieces and turned them over.

"There's nothing to prove it," Karim said. "Except that I know it to be true."

"That your father is—"

"Was. He passed away when I was six. A few months before you were born."

Adir drew a harsh breath. "You're saying we're brothers?" He was clearly astounded, but studied Karim with more interest.

Karim was doing the same to him. "I didn't know there was a child. Not until the night of Zufar's wedding, when Galila told me."

"These are so beautiful," Amira murmured, taking up the lioness.

"Are you sure you want to give them up?" Adir looked between them.

"It's best if questions aren't asked in my palace about how we found the mate," Karim said. "And it seems right that you should have something of them."

Adir nodded and set aside the lion, thoughtful. "Volatile information, indeed. Thank you for entrusting me with it." He shot a look at Galila and the corner of his mouth quirked. "Good thing I never intend to talk about this, since I would have to tell people that my brother and sister are married."

She gave his knee a nudge. "Exactly the sort of misplaced remark I expect from a brother."

His mouth quirked and he looked to Karim again. "I've always wondered who my father might be. What was he like?"

"That was a wonderful trip, but it's good to be home," Galila said as they entered their apartment. The doors between their rooms were rarely closed these days.

"What are you most excited for? A proper bath? Or Wi-Fi?"

"Privacy with my husband," she said, pinching at his stomach as she walked past him toward the bathroom. "Join me in the bath?"

"Love to. I'll be in as soon as I check—" He cut himself off with a sharp curse.

Galila swung back, instantly concerned. "What's wrong?"

"I don't know if it's *wrong*, but your brother has abdicated."

"Zufar? *Why?*"

"To rule Rumadah, Niesha's home country."

"What?" Her ears rang under the news. "Then who is king of Khalia?"

His head came up. "Your brother Malak."

She blinked in shock. "God help us all."

* * * * *

THE ITALIAN'S UNEXPECTED LOVE-CHILD

MIRANDA LEE

To my daughter Veronica, who has read all my books
and said nice things about every single one.

PROLOGUE

LAURENCE SHOOK HIS head as he read the investigator's report for the second time. Frustration consumed him, along with dismay. He'd assumed his daughter would be married by now. Married with children. She was twenty-eight, after all. Twenty-eight and beautiful. Very beautiful.

His eyes moved over to the photo attached to the report, his heart filling with pride when he saw that his genes had produced a truly gorgeous creature. Gorgeous, but childless.

Such a waste!

Sighing, he returned to re-read the report.

Veronica had been engaged three years earlier to a doctor she'd met at the children's hospital she worked in. She was a physiotherapist and her fiancé an orthopaedic surgeon. Tragically, he'd been killed in a motorcycle accident two weeks before their wedding. After that, there was no evidence of her ever dating anyone again. She didn't even seem to have many friends. She'd become a loner, still living with her mother and not doing much of anything besides work, which she did from home now, rather than in hospitals.

Laurence understood grief. He'd been devastated when his wife of forty years had died several years ago, not of the cancer—which they'd both expected would take her, given she'd carried a dangerous cancer gene—but of a stroke. He'd retreated into himself after that, retiring permanently to the holiday home they'd bought together on the Isle of Capri, never looking at another woman, never wanting to move on, as the saying went. But he'd been seventy-two at the time of her death, not in his twenties. His daughter was still young, for pity's sake.

But she wouldn't stay young for ever. Men could father children for a long time, but women had a biological clock ticking away in their bodies.

As a geneticist, Laurence knew all about human bodies and human genes. His in-depth knowledge on the subject was the reason behind his having donated his sperm to Veronica's mother in the first place. His gesture had been inspired more by hubris than caring, however. Male ego. He hadn't wanted to go to his grave without passing on his oh-so-brilliant genes.

Laurence shook his head from side to side, remorse filling his soul, as well as guilt. He should have contacted his daughter after Ruth died. Then he would have been there for her when her fiancé had been killed.

But it was too late now, he accepted wretchedly.

He was dying himself—ironically, of cancer. Liver cancer. Too late to do anything, really. His prognosis was not good. Advanced liver cancer was not very forgiving, though he only had himself to blame. After Ruth had died, he'd drunk far too much for far too long.

'I did knock,' a male voice intruded. 'But you didn't answer.'

Laurence looked up and smiled.

'Leonardo! How lovely to see you. What brings you home so soon after your last visit?'

'It's *Papa's* seventy-fifth birthday tomorrow,' Leonardo said as he walked along the terrace and sat down in the afternoon sunshine, sighing appreciatively as he gazed out at the sparkling blue Mediterranean. '*Dio*, Laurence. What a lucky man you are to have a view like this.'

Laurence glanced over at his visitor with admiring eyes. How well Leonardo looked. How handsome. And how full of life. Of course, Leonardo was only thirty-two, and a man of many talents—not least of which was everything women would find both fascinating and irresistible.

This last thought evoked a deep thoughtfulness.

'*Mamma* said she invited you to the party but you declined. It seems you have to go back to England tomorrow to see your doctor.'

'Yes, that's right,' Laurence agreed as he folded the report carefully so that Leonardo couldn't see it. 'My liver's playing up.'

'You do look a little jaundiced. Is it serious?'

Laurence shrugged. 'At my age, everything is serious. So, have you to come to play chess and listen to some decent music, or to try to buy my home again?'

Leonardo laughed. 'Can I do all three?'

'You can try. But my answer to selling this place will be no, as usual. When I'm dead and gone you can buy it.'

Leonardo looked startled, then uncharacteristically sombre. 'I hope that won't be for some years yet, my friend.'

'That's kind of you to say so. Now, do you want me to open a bottle of wine or not?' he asked as he rose from his chair, carrying the report with him.

'Are you sure that's wise, under the circumstances?'

Laurence's smile was wry. 'I don't think a glass or two is going to make much difference at this stage.'

CHAPTER ONE

VERONICA SMILED AS she accompanied her last client of the day to the front door. Duncan was eighty-four, and a darling, despite suffering terribly from sciatica. But he wasn't a complainer, which Veronica admired.

'Same time next week, Duncan?'

'Can't, love. Wish I could. You keep me going, you really do. But it's my granddaughter's twenty-first next week and I'm flying up to Brisbane for her party. Thought I might stay a week or two at my son's place while I'm there. Be warmer, for starters. This last winter in Sydney has got right into my bones. I'll give you a call when I get back.'

'Okay. Now, you have a good time, Duncan.'

She watched Duncan shuffle his way down Glebe Point Road in the direction of the small terraced house where he lived. Most of her clients were locals, elderly people with lots of aches and pains, though she did treat a smattering of students from nearby Sydney University. Young men, mostly, who played rugby and soccer and came to her for help with their various injuries.

Frankly, she preferred dealing with her older male clients. They didn't try to hit on her.

Not that she couldn't handle the occasional pass. Veronica had been handling male passes since she'd reached puberty, the natural consequence of having been born good-looking. No point in pretending she wasn't. She'd been very blessed in the looks department, with a pretty face, dark, wavy hair, good skin and large violet eyes.

Jerome had called her a natural beauty.

Jerome...

Veronica closed her eyes for a few seconds as she tried

to wipe all thought of that man from her mind. But it was impossible. Jerome's sudden death had been hard enough to handle, but it was what she'd learned after his death that had truly shattered her.

She still could not believe that he'd been so...so wicked.

Naive of her, she supposed, given what her mother had suffered at the hands of the man *she'd* married. Still, as she'd grown up, Veronica had never bought into her mother's cynicism towards the opposite sex. She'd always liked men. Liked and admired them. Yes, she'd grown up understanding that some men were players. But she'd always steered well clear of those. When a couple of her boyfriends had proved to be a bit loose on the moral side, neither of them had lasted long.

Veronica wasn't a prude. But she couldn't abide men who flouted society's rules just for the hell of it—who were disrespectful, insensitive or downright reckless. Her perfect man—the one she'd always envisaged marrying—would be none of those things. He'd be successful, and preferably handsome. But most importantly he would be decent and dependable. After all, he wasn't going to be just her husband. He was going to be the father of her children. At least four children, she'd always pictured. No single-child family for her.

When Jerome had come along, she'd thought he was perfect husband-and-father material.

But Jerome had not been perfect at all. Far from it.

Veronica gritted her teeth as she walked down the hallway towards the kitchen. She supposed she still had her work. Her personal life might be a non-event, with her dreams of a happy family shattered and her trust in relationships totally destroyed, but her professional life was still there. There was a lot of satisfaction in easing other people's pain.

Veronica was just filling the kettle with water when her mobile rang.

Probably someone wanting to make an appointment, she thought as she pulled her phone out of her pocket. She didn't get many personal calls these days.

'Yes?' she answered a little more abruptly than usual. Thinking about Jerome had left a residue of simmering anger.

'Is that Miss Veronica Hanson?' a male voice asked; a rich male voice with a slight accent. Possibly Italian.

'Yes, speaking,' she confirmed.

'My name is Leonardo Fabrizzi,' he said, at which point Veronica almost dropped her phone. Her fingers clutched it more tightly as she tried to get her head around who was on the other end of the line.

Because surely there couldn't be too many Italians called Leonardo Fabrizzi in this world?

It had to be him. Though perhaps not. The world was full of coincidences.

'Leonardo Fabrizzi, the famous skier?' she blurted out before she could think better of it.

There was dead silence for a few tense seconds.

'You *know* me?' he said at last.

'No, no,' she denied quickly, because of course she didn't *know* him. Though, she'd met him. Once. Several years ago, at an *après ski* party in Switzerland. They hadn't been properly introduced, so of course he would not recognise her name. But *he'd* been very famous at the time, a world-champion downhill racer with a reputation for recklessness, both on the slopes and off. His playboy status was well deserved, she'd learned that night, shuddering at how close she'd come to becoming just another of his passing conquests.

'I… I've heard of you,' she hedged, her voice still a little shaky. 'You're famous in the ski world and I like skiing.'

More than liked. She'd been obsessed with the sport for a long time, having been introduced to it as a teenager by a classmate's family. They'd been very wealthy and had taken her along on their skiing holidays as company for their very spoilt but not very popular daughter.

'I am no longer a famous skier,' he told her brusquely. 'I retired from that world some time ago. I am just a businessman now.'

'I see,' she said, not having skied herself since Jerome had died. Her interest in the sport—and most other things—had died along with the man she'd been going to marry.

'So how may I help you, Mr Fabrizzi?' It suddenly occurred to her that maybe he'd come here to Australia on business and was in urgent need of treatment after a long flight. He might have looked up Sydney physiotherapists online and come up with her website.

'I am sorry,' he said in sombre tones, 'But I have some sad news to tell you.'

'Sad news?' she echoed, startled and puzzled. 'What kind of sad news?'

'Laurence has died,' he told her.

'Laurence? Laurence who?' She knew no one called Laurence.

'Laurence Hargraves.'

Veronica was none the wiser. 'I'm sorry, but that name means nothing to me.'

'Are you *sure*?'

'Positive.'

'That is strange, because your name meant something to him. You're one of the beneficiaries in his will.'

'What?'

'Laurence left you something in his will. A villa, actually, on the Isle of Capri.'

'*What?* Oh, that's ridiculous! Is this some kind of cruel joke?'

'I assure you, Miss Hanson, this is no joke. I am the executor of Laurence's will, and have a copy of it right in front of me. If you are the Miss Veronica Hanson who lives in

Glebe Point Road, Sydney, Australia, then you are now the proud owner of a very beautiful villa on Capri.'

'Goodness! This is incredible.'

'I agree,' he said, with a somewhat rueful note in his voice. 'I was a close friend of Laurence and he never mentioned you. Could he have been a long-lost relative of some kind? A great-uncle or a cousin, perhaps?'

'I suppose so. But I doubt it,' she added. Her mother was an only child and her father—even if he knew of her existence—certainly wouldn't have an English name like Hargraves in his family. He'd been an impoverished university student from Latvia who had sold his sperm for money and wasn't even on her birth certificate, which said *'father unknown'*. 'I'll have to ask my mother. She might know.'

'It is very puzzling, I admit,' the Italian said. 'Maybe Laurence was a patient of yours in the past, or a relative of a patient. Have you ever worked in England? Laurence used to live in England before he retired to Capri.'

'No, I haven't. Never.' She had, however, been to the Isle of Capri. For a day. As a tourist. Many years ago. She recalled looking up at the hundreds of huge villas dotted over the hillsides and thinking you would have to be very rich to live in one of them.

Veronica wondered if Leonardo Fabrizzi was still rich. And still a playboy.

Not that I care, shot back the tart thought.

'It is a mystery, all right,' the man himself said. 'But it doesn't change the fact that you can take possession of this property once the appropriate papers are signed and the taxes paid.'

'Taxes?'

'Inheritance taxes. I have to tell you that, on a property of this considerable value, the taxes will not come cheap. Since you are not a relative, they stand at eight percent of the current market value.'

'Which is what, exactly?'

'Laurence's villa should sell for somewhere between three-and-a-half and four million euros.'

'Heavens!' Veronica had a substantial amount of money in her savings account—she spent next to nothing these days—but she didn't have eight percent of four million euros.

'If that is a problem, then I could lend you the money. You could repay me when you sell.'

His gesture surprised her. 'You would do that? I mean... it could take some time to sell such a property, couldn't it?'

'Not in this circumstance. I would like to buy Laurence's villa myself. I often visited him there and I love the place.'

Veronica should have been grateful for such an easy solution. But for some reason she was reluctant just to say *yes, that would be great, yes, let's do that*.

He must have picked up on her hesitation, despite her not saying a word.

'If you're worried that I might try to cheat you,' he said, sounding somewhat peeved, 'you could get an independent valuation. Which amount I would be happy to pay in full. And in cash,' he added, highlighting just how rich he was.

Veronica rolled her eyes, never at her best when confronted by people who trumpeted their wealth. Jerome's parents had been very rich. And had never let her forget it, always saying she was a very lucky girl to be marrying their one and only child.

Hardly lucky, as it turned out.

'Perhaps you would like some time to think about all this,' the Italian went on. 'I imagine this has all come as a shock.'

'More of a surprise than a shock,' she said.

'But a pleasant one, surely?' he suggested smoothly. 'Since you didn't know Laurence personally, his death won't have upset you. And the sale of his villa will leave you very comfortably off.'

'Yes, I suppose so,' she mused aloud.

'I do hope you don't think me rude, Miss Hanson, but I noticed your birth date on the will. I know women don't like to talk about their ages but could you please confirm for me that the details are correct?' And he rattled off the date.

'Yes, that's correct,' she said, frowning. 'Though how this Laurence person knew it, I have no idea.'

'So you were twenty-eight as of last June.'

'Yes.'

'You're a Gemini.'

'Yes. Though I don't think I'm all that typical.' According to a book on star signs she'd once read, she could be light-hearted and fun-loving one day, and serious and thoughtful the next. That might have been true once but she seemed to be stuck these days on the serious and thoughtful. 'You believe in star signs, Mr Fabrizzi?'

'Of course not. It was just an idle remark. A man is master of his own destiny,' he stated firmly.

Spoken like a typically arrogant male, Veronica thought, but didn't say so.

'You're sure you know of no one called Laurence Hargraves?' he persisted.

'Absolutely sure. I have a very good memory.'

'It is all very curious,' the Italian admitted.

'True. I'm finding it pretty curious myself. So, do you mind if I ask *you* a few questions?'

'Not at all.'

'Firstly, how old was my benefactor?'

'Hmm. I'm not quite sure. Let me think. Late seventies, is my best guess. I know he was seventyish when his wife died, and that was some years back.'

'Quite elderly, then. And a widower. Did he have any children?'

'No.'

'Brothers and sisters?'

'No.'

'What did he die of?'

'Heart attack. Though I found out after the autopsy that he also had liver cancer. He told me the weekend before he died that he was going to London to see a doctor about his liver. Instead, all he did was make a will, then dropped dead shortly after leaving his solicitor's office.'

'Goodness.'

'Perhaps a mercy. The cancer was end stage.'

'Was he a heavy drinker?'

'I wouldn't have said excessively so. But who knows what a lonely man does in private?'

Veronica was taken aback at how sad he suddenly sounded. This evidence of empathy made her like Leonardo Fabrizzi a little bit, which was a minor miracle. Playboys were not her favourite species.

Though maybe she was doing him an injustice. Maybe he *had* changed. It was, after all, several years since the night he'd cast his charismatic eye on her and casually suggested she join him and the blonde dripping all over him for a threesome.

No, she thought with a derisive curl of her top lip, men like that didn't change. Once a player, always a player.

'If you give me your email address,' he continued, 'I'll send you a copy of the will and you can get back to me with your decision in a day or two. Alternatively, I could ring you at this time tomorrow and we can talk some more. Would that be suitable?'

'Not really.' She and her mother always went down to the local Vietnamese restaurant for dinner early on a Saturday evening. 'What time is it in Italy at the moment?' she asked, not liking the idea of waiting to make a decision. 'You are in Italy, aren't you?'

'*Si.* I'm in Milan. In my office. It is nine-twenty.'

He really did speak beautiful English, very polished with correct grammar, all in a mild but disturbingly attractive accent. Veronica had always found Italian men attractive, having met quite a few during her obsessive skiing years.

One, however, stood out amongst all the rest…

'Right,' she said crisply. 'The thing is, I would like to talk to my mother first. Ask her if she ever knew a Laurence Hargraves. Maybe she can clear up this mystery for us. But, no matter what I find out, I can't see there will be any problem with your buying the villa, Mr Fabrizzi. Much as it would be lovely to have a holiday home on Capri, I really can't afford it. I will ring you back in about an hour or so. Okay?'

'*Certo*. I will look forward to your call, Miss Hanson.'

They exchanged relevant details, after which he hung up, leaving Veronica feeling slightly flustered. Which irritated the hell out of her. She thought she was over being affected by any member of the opposite sex, especially one with Leonardo Fabrizzi's dubious reputation.

Giving herself a mental shake, she retreated down the hallway and made her way up the stairs to the extension her mother had had built a few years back, a necessity once Nora had started up her home-help business on the Internet. The upstairs section included a small sitting room, a well-appointed office and a spacious bedroom and *en suite*. As it turned out, the extension had become a real blessing after Jerome's death, with Veronica able to convert her mother's old front bedroom into a treatment room for her own home-based physiotherapy business.

It wasn't until Veronica reached the upstairs landing that her thoughts returned to the annoyingly fascinating Italian and the astonishing reason behind his call. All of a sudden, an idea of who Laurence Hargraves might be zoomed into her head. An astonishing idea, really. Not very logical, either, knowing her mother. But the idea persisted, bringing with it a strange wave of alarm. Her heartbeat quickened and her stomach tightened, sending a burst of bile up into her throat. She swallowed convulsively, telling herself to get a grip.

What you are thinking is insane! Insane and illogical!

The man was English, not Australian. Besides, Mum would not lie to me—not over something like this.

Finally, after scooping in several deep breaths, she lifted her hand to tap on her mother's office door, annoyed to see her hand was shaking. Her mouth went dry. And her heart started pounding again. Not quite a panic attack, but something close.

'Yes?' came her mother's impatient query.

It took an effort of will to turn the knob and go into the room.

'Mum,' she said on entering, pleased that her voice wasn't shaking as well.

Her mother didn't look up from where she was frowning at the computer screen.

'Yes?' she repeated distractedly.

Veronica walked over to perch on the corner of her mother's desk, gripping the edges with white knuckles. 'Mum, does the name Laurence Hargraves mean anything to you?'

Veronica had seen people go grey with pain in the course of her work; seen all the blood drain from their faces. But she'd never seen her mother go that particular colour.

Strangely enough, as she watched her mother's reaction, Veronica no longer felt panic. Just dismay. And the fiercest disappointment. Because now she knew the answer to the mystery, didn't she?

'He was my father, wasn't he?' she said bleakly, before her mother admitted to anything.

Nora groaned, then nodded. Sadly. Apologetically.

Veronica groaned as well, her face screwing up with distress, her hands balling into fists in defence of the flood of emotion which threatened to overwhelm her. Not since she'd discovered the awful truth about Jerome had she experienced such shock and anger. Funny how you could suspect something, but when you were actually faced with some awful truth your first reaction was still pained disbelief, quickly followed by outrage and anger.

'Why didn't you tell me the truth?' she threw at her mother in anguished tones. 'Why give me that cock-and-bull story about my father being some impoverished sperm donor from Latvia? Why not just tell me you had an affair with a married man?'

'But I didn't have an affair with Laurence!' her mother denied, her face flushing wildly. 'It wasn't like that. You don't understand,' she wailed, gripping her cheeks with both hands as tears filled her eyes.

For the first time in her life, Veronica felt no pity for her mother's tears.

'Then how was it, Mum?' she asked coldly. 'Make me understand, especially why you didn't tell me the truth about my father's identity.'

'I… I couldn't tell you. I gave Laurence my word.'

Veronica could not believe she was hearing this. She'd given her word to some adulterer? The mind boggled.

'Well, your precious Laurence is dead and gone now,' Veronica snapped. 'So I don't think your giving him your word matters any more. I dare say you'll also be surprised to hear that my errant father has left me something in his will,' she finished up caustically. 'I've just received a call from the executor. I'm now the owner of a villa on the Isle of Capri. Lucky me!'

Nora just stared at her daughter, grey eyes blinking madly.

'But…but what about his wife?'

'She's dead too,' Veronica said bluntly. 'Quite a few years ago, apparently.'

'Oh…'

'Yes. Oh.'

Her mother just sat there, stunned and speechless.

'I think, Mum,' Veronica bit out, her arms crossing angrily as she tried to contain her emotions, 'That it's time you told me the truth.'

CHAPTER TWO

LEONARDO EMAILED OFF a copy of the will then settled back down at his desk, trying to put his mind to studying the designs for next year's winter range. But his mind wouldn't cooperate. It remained firmly on the call he'd just made to Sydney, Australia.

Who in hell *was* Veronica Hanson? And why had Laurence never mentioned her?

A great-niece, perhaps? Leonardo speculated. Most people did like to leave their estates to relatives.

Though, if that were the case, why not leave her some money as well? Why just leave her the villa, then leave the rest of his considerable portfolio of cash, bonds and shares to cancer research?

It was a mystery all right.

Hopefully, Miss Hanson's mother would provide some pertinent information.

Glancing at his watch, Leonardo saw that less than ten minutes had passed since he'd hung up. He could hardly expect a call back this soon.

Unfortunately.

Leonardo's sigh was one of exasperation. He had no hope of concentrating on anything until he heard back from Miss Hanson. Patience had never been one of his virtues. But he had no alternative on this occasion but to wait.

Still, he didn't have to wait in here, at his desk, pretending to work. Jumping up, he decided to get himself some coffee, bypassing his PA's offer to get it for him with the excuse that he needed some air.

Leonardo needed some air a lot. He'd described himself as a businessman to Miss Hanson. But whilst Leonardo had quite enjoyed setting up his top-of-the-range sportswear company—and making a huge success of it—being *just* a businessman was not the way Leonardo ever saw himself. He was a sportsman, a man of action. A doer, not a pencil pusher. He actually hated offices and desks. Loathed meetings of any kind. And despised sitting for too long.

His spirits lifted once he was outside the building and into the fresh air. The sun was shining and a mild breeze was blowing. Milan in late August was glorious, though too busy, of course, the streets filled with tourists.

Leonardo breathed in deeply and headed for his favourite cafe, which was tucked away down a cobbled side street and never too crowded. There, his espresso was already waiting for him by the time he reached the counter, the female *barista* having spotted him as he strode into their establishment. He drank the strong black liquid down in one gulp, as was his habit. She smiled at him as he smacked his lips in appreciation, her big brown eyes flashing flirtatiously. She was a very attractive girl, with the kind of dark eyes and hair which Leonardo especially liked.

'Grazie,' he said, then placed the empty cup back on the counter, keeping his own smile very brief and not in any way flirtatious. Best not to encourage the girl. She might think he wanted more from her than good service.

There was a time in his younger years when he would have jumped into bed with her weeks ago. But he had more control over his hormones these days. And he was miles more careful, having narrowly escaped being trapped into marriage by a fortune-hunting female a few years back, shuddering whenever he thought of how close he'd come to being shackled for life to a girl he didn't love.

Leonardo shuddered anew as he strode from the cafe and headed back to his office.

Of course, he could have refused to marry the girl, even if she *had* been pregnant. Which it had turned out she wasn't. But Leonardo hadn't been brought up that way, having it drummed into him as a young man that, if he ever fathered a child, he'd better marry the mother *pronto*. Because if he didn't do the honourable thing then he wasn't ever to bother coming home again.

Such an outcome would have been untenable to Leonardo. His parents meant the world to him. So, yes, he would have married the girl. And loved his child. But his life would not have been the life he'd planned for himself, which was no marriage and children until he was ready to settle down. Which he certainly hadn't been back then.

Thank God his uncle had stepped in and demanded another pregnancy test by an independent doctor. Leonardo's relief at the news there was no baby had been a lesson well learned. After that he never believed a girl when she said she was on the pill. And he always used a condom. *Always!*

As an added precaution, he only dated women these days who were less likely to be looking at him as a meal ticket for life. Women with careers of their own. Money of their own. And minds of their own.

On Leonardo's part, he had no intention of marrying until he met the love of his life. Which he hadn't so far. Strange, given all the clever and attractive girlfriends he'd had. But none had captured his heart. None had inspired the kind of wild passion he'd always imagined being truly in love would engender. Yes, sex with them was satisfying. But not mind-blowing. It never compared to the thrill of hurtling down a snowy mountain, knowing that he was going faster than any of his competitors.

Leonardo sighed. Ah, those were the days. Days which would never be repeated, his many falls and injuries having caught up with him by the time he'd turned twenty-five, forcing his retirement from the sport. Yes, he'd been a famous skier, as Miss Hanson had pointed out. But fame was fleeting and life moved on. Seven years had passed since then; seven successful but, perversely, frustrating years. He should have been satisfied with his life. Fabrizzi Sport,

Snow & Ski was doing very well, with stores in all the major cities in Europe. He'd become a wealthy man in his own right, not just the spoiled only grandson of a billionaire.

But Leonardo wasn't satisfied. Sometimes he was consumed with the most awful emptiness, the result perhaps of not having been able to fulfil his ambitions on the ski slopes, injury always having got in the way of success in major championships. There was a restlessness living inside him, a manic energy at times which refused to be quelled, no matter what he did.

And he did plenty. He still skied in the winter, though not competitively. He went yachting and waterskiing in the summer, along with mountain climbing and abseiling. Recently, he'd gained his pilot's licence for both small planes and helicopters. His frequent holidays were hectic with activity, but he inevitably returned to work still burning with a fire undimmed.

The only time Leonardo had really relaxed was when he'd been on Capri, sitting on Laurence's terrace, looking out at the sparkling blue sea and sipping one of his friend's excellent wines.

Thinking of Capri sent his mind back to Laurence's mystery heiress. Hopefully she would ring him soon and tell him that he could buy the villa. Because he not only wanted it, he *needed* it. Life without Laurence's company would be bad enough. Life without the calming influence of his friend's beautiful home would be a bitter disappointment.

Leonardo glanced at his Rolex once more, then headed back to his office, not wanting to take Miss Hanson's call in the street.

CHAPTER THREE

VERONICA LAY ON her bed, her head whirling with what she'd discovered. She found it almost impossible to process her feelings. Was she still angry or just terribly sad? What her mother had told her had sort of made sense, and was much better than her mother having slept with a married man. And, yes, she understood why her mother had promised to keep her father's identity a secret, even if it still upset her.

What puzzled her the most, however, was the will. Now, that *didn't* make sense. Why leave her anything at all? Her father must have known it would stir up trouble and leave so many questions unanswered.

Her father...

Tears filled Veronica's eyes. She'd had a father. A real father, not some unnamed sperm donor. He hadn't been a nobody, either. He'd been a famous scientist, a groundbreaking geneticist with a brilliant brain. Oh, how she wished her mother had told her years ago.

But of course she hadn't been able to. She'd given her word. Down deep, Veronica understood that. Good people honoured their promises. And her mother was a good woman. But, dear God, her father was dead now. Dead and gone. She could never see him or talk to him. Never know what he was like.

'Are you all right, love?' her mother asked tentatively from the doorway.

Veronica blinked away her tears then turned her head to smile softly at her very stressed-looking mother. She was well aware that her mother had suffered a big shock too. She had to be worried that her much-loved daughter might never forgive her.

Whilst Veronica still harboured some natural resentment at the situation, she could not blame her mother for what she'd done. If anyone was to blame, it was Laurence Hargraves. The stupid man should have gone to his grave with his secret intact and not left her anything at all! Then she could have gone on being blissfully unaware of having a father whom she would now never have the opportunity to know.

'I'll be fine,' she said with feigned composure. 'It's just a shock, that's all.'

'I know. And I'm so sorry. I don't know what possessed Laurence to put you in his will. I truly don't. It was sweet of him, in a way, but he must have known that the truth would come out, and that then you'd be upset.'

'People do strange things when they're dying,' Veronica said with a degree of understanding. She'd seen it time and time again in her work. Once, when she'd been treating an old lady, the woman had confessed she was dying and on impulse had wanted to give Veronica a beautiful ring she was wearing. Veronica had declined, knowing that the woman had a daughter who would have been most hurt by such a gesture. But the old lady hadn't thought of that. Maybe this Laurence hadn't thought through the consequences of his will.

Or maybe he'd known *exactly* what he doing.

The trouble was she would never really know either way. Because she didn't *know* the man.

'Would you like me to make you some coffee, love?' her mother asked.

'Yes, that would be nice,' she replied politely, thinking what she really wanted was to be left alone. She needed to think.

Her mother disappeared, leaving Veronica to ponder the reason why her father had chosen to make his identity known at this late stage, when he could no longer be a living presence in her life. What she wouldn't have given to have a real father when she'd been growing up, when she'd been at school, when her bitchy so-called *friends* would tease her about having come out of a test tube. She'd laughed at the time. But she hadn't found their jibes funny at all. The hurt had struck deep. Teenage girls, she'd found, had a very mean streak. It was no wonder she'd always gravitated to boys when making close friends.

Thinking of boys reminded Veronica that there was one very grown-up boy she would have to ring back shortly.

Leonardo Fabrizzi.

She wasn't looking forward to telling him that Laurence Hargraves was her biological father. He was sure to ask her lots of questions.

Still, she had lots of questions she wanted to ask him. After all, if he was close enough to her father to have been made executor of his will, then he had to have known him very well. Maybe he had a photo or two that he could send her. She would dearly love to know what this Laurence looked like.

Veronica was nothing like her mother in looks. Nora Hanson was quite short with brown hair, grey eyes and a rather forgettable face and figure. In truth, she was on the plain side. Veronica had always assumed she'd inherited her striking looks from her biological father. Maybe now she'd have the opportunity to see the evidence for herself.

This last thought propelled an idea into Veronica's brain which had her sitting up abruptly then scrambling off the bed. She raced out into the hallway and bolted down to the kitchen, where she snatched up her phone which she'd left lying on the counter.

'Goodness!' her mother said, startled perhaps by her sudden exuberance. 'Who are you ringing?'

'The Italian I told you about. Leonardo Fabrizzi. I promised to ring him back once I'd talked to you.'

'Oh,' Nora said, looking pained. 'You're not going to tell him everything, are you? I mean, does he have to know about your being Laurence's daughter? Can't you just sell him the villa and leave it at that?'

'No, Mum,' Veronica said firmly. 'I can't just leave it at that. And I *am* going to tell him I'm Laurence's daughter. For one thing, it makes a difference to the inheritances taxes if I'm a relative. On top of that, I won't be selling Mr Fabrizzi the villa straight away. There's something else I have to do first.'

'What?'

Veronica told her.

CHAPTER FOUR

LEONARDO'S HEART JUMPED when his phone finally rang, then began to race when he saw it was her at last. Why was he suddenly nervous? He wasn't a nervous person. On the ski slopes, he'd been known for his *nerve*, not his nervousness. The press had called him Leo the Lion because of his lack of fear. When he'd retired, he'd chosen the image of a lion as the logo for his sportswear company.

'Thank you for calling me back, Miss Hanson,' he answered, putting the phone on speaker as he leant back in his leather chair and did his best to act cool and businesslike. 'Was your mother able to tell you anything enlightening?'

'She certainly did.' Her answer was crisp, her voice possibly even more businesslike than his own. 'It seems that Laurence Hargraves was my biological father.'

Leonardo snapped forward on his chair. '*Mio Dio!* How did that happen?'

'It seems Mr Hargraves came to Australia about thirty years ago to do genetic research at the Sydney University. He was given a house as part of the deal and my mother was hired as his housekeeper.'

'And what? They had an *affair*?' Leonardo found the concept of Laurence being unfaithful hard to believe. Laurence had been devoted to his wife. They'd been an inseparable couple, their love for each other very obvious to everyone who knew them.

'No, no, nothing like that. Though my mother said that she and Laurence became quite good friends during the two years she worked for him. With Ruth too. She said she was a lovely lady. No, they didn't have an affair, or even a one-night stand.'

'I don't understand, then.'

'Mum had me through IVF. I thought my biological father was an impoverished law student from Latvia who sold his sperm for money. That's what I'd always been told. But it was a lie. Laurence was the sperm donor.'

'I see… Well, that explains everything, I suppose. Though not the secrecy.'

'Did you know that Laurence's wife couldn't have children?'

'Not exactly. Though I did know they'd never had children. I didn't know which of them was the cause of their childlessness. Or whether they'd just decided not to have children. It's not something you can ask without being rude. Obviously, the problem was Ruth's.'

'Yes. Mum told me Ruth had very bad cancer genes which ran through her family and had killed off all her relatives. She decided as a young woman not to pass any of those genes on and had a total hysterectomy. She met Laurence through his work on genes and they fell in love. He told my mother he didn't overly mind about not having children as his love for Ruth was all-consuming. And so was his work. In fact, his work was the reason behind his becoming my biological father.'

'His *work* was the reason?' Leonardo was not quite getting the picture.

'Yes. When my mother confided to Laurence that she planned to have a baby through IVF at this particular clinic, he was appalled.'

'Appalled? Why?'

'Because he thought they didn't know enough about the prospective sperm donor's genes. Yes, the clinic records showed the one she'd chosen was tall, dark and handsome. *And* intelligent. But Laurence questioned his medical and mental backgrounds, the details of which he said were superficial at best. He said she was taking a risk because she didn't know enough about the sperm donor's DNA, whereas his own had been thoroughly checked out. By *him*.'

Leonardo nodded. Now he understood what had happened.

'So he offered his own sperm instead,' he said.

'Yes. When Mum initially refused, he argued with her about it. Made her feel that if she didn't agree she was being silly.'

Leonardo nodded. 'Laurence could be very persuasive when he wanted to be. He introduced me to classical music. And opera. I told him I hated opera but he proved me wrong in the end. Now I love it. I can well understand how he talked your mother into using his sperm. He would have convinced her that she owed it to her child to make sure she wasn't carrying any unfortunate genes. But what about Ruth? I gather she didn't know anything about this arrangement?'

'No. He insisted they keep it a secret from his wife. He said it would upset Ruth terribly if she found out. Mum had to promise to put "father unknown" on the birth certificate and go along with the charade of my father being a Latvian university student.'

'That makes Laurence sound a bit heartless.'

'That's what I thought. Mum said he wasn't but I don't agree. Okay, so he bought her the house we live in. Big deal! She still had to live on the single mother's pension until I went to school and she could go back to work. I mean... Okay, so he didn't want to upset his childless wife... I get that, I guess. But why didn't he contact Mum and me after his wife died? Why leave me to find out he was my father after he was dead? What good was that?'

'I'm sorry, I cannot answer those questions, Miss Hanson. I am as baffled as you are. But at least he left you his villa.'

'Yes. I've been thinking about that too. Why leave me anything at all? And why this villa? On the island of Capri, of all places. He must have had a reason. He was a highly intelligent man, from the sounds of things.'

Something teased at the back of Leonardo's mind. Something about the last day he'd talked to Laurence. But the thought didn't stick. He would think about it some more later, when he was calmer.

'Maybe he just wanted to give you something of value,' he suggested.

'Then why not just give me money? From reading his will, I gather he had plenty.'

'I must admit that thought had occurred to me too, Miss Hanson.'

'Oh, please stop calling me that. My name is Veronica.'

'Very well. Veronica,' he said, and found himself smiling for some reason. 'And you must call me Leonardo. Or Leo, if you prefer. I know Australians like to shorten names.'

'I prefer Leonardo,' she said. 'It sounds more… Italian.'

Leonardo laughed. 'I am Italian.'

'You speak beautiful English.'

'*Grazie.*'

'And *grazie* to you too. Now… I have made a decision about the villa. I appreciate your offer to buy it, Leonardo. And I will sell you the villa. *Eventually.* But, first, I want to come and stay there for a while. Not too long. Just long enough to find out all I can about my father…'

CHAPTER FIVE

EXCITEMENT FIZZED IN Veronica's stomach as the ferry left Sorrento on its twenty-minute ride to Capri. The day was glorious, not a cloud in the sky, the water a sparkling and very inviting blue.

It had taken two weeks for her to organise this trip. She hadn't wanted to leave her patients in the lurch by departing abruptly so she'd seen them all one more time—or contacted them by phone—telling them that she was taking a much-needed holiday.

Naturally, she hadn't been about to blurt out the truth behind her trip to Italy. That would have set a cat among the pigeons, sparking far too many questions. They'd all been sweetly understanding, bringing her to tears on a couple of occasions, because they mistakenly thought she was still grieving Jerome's death.

Which she had been, in a way. For far too long.

But not any more.

Finding out about her real father had been a big shock. But it had also given her the impetus to stop living her life like some mourning widow. Hence her new and rather colourful wardrobe, which had put a serious dent in her savings. But how could she come to this gorgeous and glamorous island looking drab and dreary?

Veronica refused to concede that the effort she'd made with her appearance had anything to do with Leonardo Fabrizzi. As nice as he'd been to her on the phone, he still was what he'd always been. A player.

Curiosity had sent Veronica looking him up on various social media sites and there'd been plenty to look at. Since his retirement from competitive downhill racing, Leonardo had made a name for himself in the world of fashion, Fabrizzi being considered *the* name in active wear. His company had boutiques in all the main cities in Europe, as well as one in New York. Veronica noted that the press articles didn't call them shops or stores. No. *Boutiques* they were called, the kind where only the rich and famous could afford to shop.

Aside from news about his business acumen, it showed Leonardo had also led a very active social life, his name connected with many beautiful women of the type wealthy playboys invariably attracted. Models. Actresses. Heiresses. He'd had countless gorgeous creatures on his arm over the years—and undoubtedly in his bed. Leopards didn't change their spots. And neither had Leo the Lion.

It was feminine pride, Veronica told herself, which had made her put her best foot forward today. And her best face. All women liked to feel attractive, especially when in the company of a man as handsome and as charismatic as Leonardo Fabrizzi.

And she would be in his company within the next half an hour. Leonardo had made all the arrangements with Veronica over the phone. He was going to meet her at the dock then take her straight to the villa which, she'd learned, was perched above the Hotel Fabrizzi, a small establishment which Leonardo's parents had been running for over a decade.

This news had surprised Veronica as she'd learned via the Internet that the Fabrizzis were from Milan, Leonardo's grandfather having set up a textile manufacturing company after the war, becoming extremely wealthy over the years. He'd had two sons and heirs, Stephano and Alberto. What she hadn't learned—though admittedly she hadn't looked very hard—was what had happened after the grandfather had died. After all, she was coming to Capri to find out about her own father's history, not Leonardo's.

Thinking once more of the reason behind this trip made

her heart beat faster. Soon, hopefully, she'd have answers to all the questions this unexpected inheritance had raised. Soon, she'd find out everything she wanted to know about her biological father. What he'd looked like. What he'd liked. What he'd been *like*!

Veronica no longer harboured any lingering anger over her mother's lies. What was done was done. No point in going on and on about it. The blame—if there was any blame—lay at her father's feet. Okay, so she was still upset at his not having contacted her earlier. After all, if he had wanted to keep his identity a secret, why leave her his home in his will?

This was the question which bothered her the most. His leaving her this villa.

Why, Dad? Why?

Her heart caught at finding herself calling him Dad like that. Caught, then turned over. She'd never called the student from Latvia *Dad*, not even in her thoughts. He'd just been the sperm donor. Not a real person. Just some tadpoles in a test tube. She'd never tried to picture what he looked like. She'd blanked her mind to him. Not so Laurence Hargraves. He was real in her head. Very real. She couldn't stop thinking about him.

Tears pricked at her eyes, filling them quickly then threatening to spill over. When the girl seated across from her on the ferry started staring at her, Veronica found a smile from somewhere, blinking the tears away before pulling her phone from her straw bag. She'd promised her mum she would take photos of everything and send them to her.

So she did, starting with the ferry, the sea and the approaching island.

Leonardo wasn't on the pier waiting for her. Instead there was a middle-aged man holding a sign with her name on it. He looked very Italian, with curly black hair and dark eyes. Clearly, he didn't know what Veronica looked like, as he was scouring the crowd of tourists with a worried look on his face.

When she walked right up to him and introduced herself, his face broke into a radiant smile.

'Signora Hanson,' he said with a thick Italian accent, dark eyes dancing. 'Why, you are *molto bella*! Leonardo should have told me.'

Veronica smiled. She didn't speak Italian but she could recognise a compliment when she heard one.

'Where is Leonardo?' she asked, disappointed at his no-show.

'He said to tell you he is sorry. He was held up. Business. He is flying in soon.'

'*Flying* in? But there is no airport on Capri.'

'There is a helipad. At Anacapri. I am to give you a sight-seeing tour then take you there to meet him. Here. Let me take your luggage.' He tossed the sign with her name on it in a nearby bin.

Veronica didn't have the heart to tell him she didn't really want a sightseeing tour, so she just smiled and said, 'How lovely,' then climbed into the back of a long yellow convertible that looked like a relic from an early Elvis Presley film.

She was glad after less than a minute that she'd put her hair back into a secure ponytail. The breeze coming off the sea—plus the wind caused by Franco's rather cavalier driving—would not have made for a pretty result. Veronica tried to appreciate the sights but she really wasn't in the mood. She'd been so looking forward to meeting Leonardo her disappointment was acute. She politely declined a visit to the Blue Grotto, admitting at that stage that she had been to Capri once before, many years ago, her one-day tour having included a visit to the grotto.

'It's a lot busier these days,' she said, noting the long line of boats waiting to go into the famous cave.

Franco frowned. '*Too* busy. But, come the end of September, things will be better. The cruise ships. They will stop coming. Will you be here then?'

'Unfortunately not.' September had only just arrived and her return flight was for just over three weeks' time.

'It is too warm for the top to be down,' Franco decided at this point, and pressed a button which sent a canvas top up and over, shading her from the sun. Which was perhaps just as well, Veronica's pink-and-white striped top having a deep boat neckline which might catch the sun on her neck. She always lathered herself in sunscreen. She didn't want to burn.

Once Veronica put aside her disappointment over Leonardo's no-show, she enjoyed the tour. Franco was a very agreeable guide, his knowledge of the island that of a man born and bred there. It turned out he was also married to Leonardo's older sister, Elena. They had three children, a boy and two girls.

She wondered if Leonardo had told him she was Laurence's daughter. Possibly not yet, she decided, swallowing back the questions she was dying to ask about her father. Maybe another day…

Finally, after getting a text on his phone, Franco headed for Anacapri and the helipad.

Despite telling herself there was nothing to be nervous about, Veronica's stomach tightened and her heartbeat quickened. By the time Franco reached the top of the hill and parked, she found she could not sit in the back of the taxi any longer. Leaving her straw carryall on the back seat, she climbed out and walked around, lecturing herself all the while about her upcoming meeting with Leonardo.

Yes, he's very attractive, but he's a playboy, Veronica. Quite a notorious one. Don't ever forget that. Play it cool when you come face to face with him. Don't, for pity's sake, let his good looks—and his undoubted charm—distract you from your quest. You've come here to find out about your father, not flutter your eyelashes at Leonardo Fabrizzi.

A helicopter approached from the direction of the mainland. Veronica shaded her eyes to watch it, despite already wearing sunglasses. The helicopter was black with red writing on the side and tinted glass, so she couldn't see who was sitting in it. As it came in to land, the wind from the huge rotor blades hit her like a mini tornado. Thank God she'd chosen to wear her new white jeans, and not the sundress with its gathered skirt. As it was, a few strands of hair came loose from her ponytail, whipping across her face. Finally, the helicopter's noisy engine shut down and the blades slowed. A side door on it slid open and out jumped a man, a tall dark-haired man in a pale grey suit and a blinding white shirt open at the neck with no tie.

Veronica recognised Leonardo instantly, despite his hair—which he'd worn disgracefully long back in his skiing days—now being cropped short. It suited him, however, showing off his face to better advantage, highlighting his sculptured features and strong jawline. Still, she'd already known about his new haircut, having studied many images on social media during the last two weeks.

He was, however, even better looking in the flesh than in recent photos, two-dimensional images not able to capture the total essence of this man. He was, Veronica accepted as she watched him stride towards her, not just the stereotype of tall, dark and handsome. Leonardo was more than that. Much more, as evidenced by the way her heart began racing within her chest. Aside from his looks, there was the way he moved. The way he walked. The set of his broad shoulders. The angle of his head. He was the total male package. Arrogant. Confident. And super sexy.

As he drew nearer, her heartbeat accelerated further.

Did he do this to all women? she wondered with exasperation. Did he make them forget everything that life had taught them about males of the 'player' species? Did he make them want to act like fatuous female fools?

Possibly.

Probably!

Veronica sarcastically renamed him 'tall, dark and dangerous' in her head.

It was a good thought to have. A sensible, soothing thought, giving her the willpower to draw in several deep, gathering breaths, consciously slowing her heartbeat and untangling the knots in her stomach. No way was she going to have her head turned by Leonardo Fabrizzi. She'd avoided that trap all those years ago. Surely she was better equipped not to fall for it this time.

All you have to do is think of Jerome...

He was staring at her, she knew, despite his sunglasses hiding the expression in his eyes. She could sense his penetrating gaze behind the opaque lenses, perhaps because his dark brows were drawn slightly together, forming two little frowning lines. It made her glad she was wearing sunglasses herself. That way he wouldn't see into her eyes which she knew were, indeed, the windows to her soul.

Not that her *soul* was bothered by Leonardo Fabrizzi. It was her body which was bothered currently. Her silly, possibly frustrated female body which had been too long without the comfort of a man's arms around her, without the wonderful feeling of being held, kissed and caressed.

'Veronica?' he said in that sexy voice which by now she was familiar with.

Her smile felt forced. 'Yes,' she confirmed.

His smile was light. And wry. 'I should have known you'd be beautiful,' he said. 'Laurence was a very handsome man. Welcome to Capri,' he added, stepping forward to draw her into a very Italian hug.

Her arms were trapped by her side as he pulled her close, the strength and warmth of his body bypassing her resolve to be sensible around him. *Oh, God.* She could feel herself melting in his arms. Feel her blood charge hot and heady around her veins. Her neck flushed. So did her face.

'Goodness!' she exclaimed, pulling back out of his embrace before she combusted. 'I'd forgotten how very demonstrative Italians were.'

Leonardo's eyebrows arched. 'You don't hug hello in Australia?'

'We do. Though usually just relatives and close friends.'

'How very odd. If I overstepped the mark, then I apologise. Come. It is too hot to be standing out here in the sun.' He took her elbow and turned her back towards where the taxi waited for them, Franco still behind the wheel.

She resisted pulling her arm away, thinking that would be too rude. And too telling. He was just being a gentleman, after all. But, oh, it worried her, that wildly pleasurable sensation which had charged up her arm at his touch.

'You don't have any luggage?' she asked when he dropped her arm to open the back door of the taxi.

'No need. I keep spare clothes here at my parents' hotel. My Capri clothes, I call them. No business suits for me when I stay here, isn't that so, Franco?' he said as he handed her into the car and climbed in after her.

'*Si*, Leo. You are a different man once you come here.'

'Have you been looking after our visitor? Shown her the more famous sights?'

'*Si*. But Veronica, she not want to go to Blue Grotto.'

'I've seen it before.' Veronica jumped in before Franco could say anything further. 'I came here as a day tripper when I was in my early twenties. It's a very beautiful cave but I didn't want to queue up to see it again.'

Leonardo nodded. 'Understandable. Actually, the only way to see Capri is by air. I will take you up in the helicopter tomorrow.'

'Oh,' she said, thrilled and terrified by his offer. 'You don't have to do that.'

'But I want to. And you will love it. Let's go, Franco. I'm sure Veronica is anxious to see her father's villa.'

Oh, Lord, Veronica thought as the taxi moved off. Her

father's villa. The reason she'd come here. And the last thing she'd been thinking about since the very handsome Leonardo Fabrizzi had stepped off that helicopter less than five minutes ago.

CHAPTER SIX

LEONARDO SETTLED INTO the back seat of the taxi and tried to act normally, not like a man who was finding the girl next to him disturbingly attractive. Disturbing, because he wasn't in the mood to be attracted to *any* girl at the moment, having decided after today's fiasco in Rome that the female sex was nothing but trouble.

At the same time, he owed it to his friend's memory to be hospitable to his daughter. And to satisfy Veronica's very natural curiosity about the father she'd never known. It was a pity, however, that she had to possess the type of allure which he'd always found difficult to resist. He adored tall, elegantly slender brunettes, especially one whose hair was long and which, once released from a ponytail prison, would cascade down her back in loose curls like the tresses of some mediaeval princess. Combine that with a delicate oval face, clear porcelain skin and a lush mouth and you had a package which would tempt a saint.

And he was no saint.

Hopefully, when she took her sunglasses off, she would have small squinty eyes and a bumpy nose, but he doubted it. Laurence's eyes had been one of his best features and his nose had been nicely shaped. If his daughter took after him—and he suspected that she did—she would be a classical beauty, with a superb brain and an enquiring mind.

The many hours Leonardo had spent with Laurence stood out as some of the most enjoyable times of his adult life. It hadn't been just his house he'd enjoyed but the man himself. His company. His knowledge. His probing questions.

Leonardo sighed as he was reminded how much he missed his friend.

'I'm sorry I wasn't there to meet you off the ferry, Veronica,' he said. 'I had some unexpected trouble at my boutique in Rome which I had to attend to.'

She turned to glance his way, her jeaned thigh briefly brushing against his. 'Something serious?'

'Yes and no. The manager was…what is the expression?…dipping her fingers in the till.'

'That's dreadful. Did you have her arrested?'

Leonardo's laugh was very dry. 'I would have liked to, but she threatened to ruin me if I did that.'

'How could she ruin you?'

Leonardo shrugged. 'Perhaps "ruin" is an exaggeration. She threatened to accuse me of sexual harassment if I had her arrested. In the end, I paid her off and she left quietly. But I'm not sure I trust her to keep her silence. She might still put something nasty on social media about me.'

'Like what?'

'She could say that to get her job in the first place she had to sleep with me.'

'But that's slander!'

'Not exactly. I did sleep with her. Once. It was a mistake, but I could not take it back after it happened, could I?'

'Well, no. I guess not.'

Leonardo noted the dry note in Veronica's voice. She probably thought he was a playboy. Which he was, in some people's eyes. But not of the worst kind. He tried not to hurt women's feelings, but unfortunately the opposite sex often equated lust with love. He glanced over at Veronica and wondered if she was that type.

This thought brought another one.

'I didn't think to ask over the phone if you had a boyfriend,' he said. They'd talked about their professional lives but hadn't touched on the personal. He'd told her about his sportswear company and she'd explained that she worked from home as a physiotherapist, treating mostly elderly patients. She'd sounded oddly spinsterish over the phone. He could see now how wrong that impression had been. A beautiful woman like her would surely have a love life.

Her face betrayed nothing. But she stiffened a little.

'No,' she replied after a small hesitation. 'No one at the moment. No one serious, at least,' she added with a wry little smile.

'Ah. You like to play the field.'

Her laugh was both light and amused. 'If you like…'

He did like. Oh, yes, he liked that idea a lot, forgetting all about the antagonism towards the opposite sex that this morning's confrontation had evoked in him. Suddenly, the prospect of keeping this lovely lady company this coming weekend was not a duty but a pleasure.

'We have arrived,' he announced when Franco turned his taxi through the high stone walls into the courtyard of the Hotel Fabrizzi. 'What do you think, Veronica? Is not my parents' hotel a delightful little establishment?'

CHAPTER SEVEN

HARDLY *LITTLE*, VERONICA THOUGHT, glad to turn her eyes away from this extremely handsome and annoyingly charismatic man. Lord, but he could charm the pants off any woman!

Except me, she reassured herself, blithely ignoring her thudding heartbeat.

'It's lovely,' she said as the taxi came to a halt in front of a columned portico.

The hotel itself was two-storeyed and dazzlingly white, with terracotta tiles on the roof and dark wooden frames around the windows and doors. To their right as they alighted was a large pergola covered in grape vines, under which sat a long wooden table with equally long benches on either side and two large cushioned chairs at each head of the table. The closest was occupied by a huge ginger cat, basking in the dappled sunshine. When Leonardo walked over to stroke it, it purred loudly but did not get up.

'This is Gepetto. He's my mother's cat and very old. He was here when my parents bought this place thirteen years ago. The previous owners abandoned him.' Leonardo smiled a rueful smile. 'He's not de-sexed. Mostly because we can never get him into a cage. He doesn't mind being stroked but don't ever try to pick him up. He can be quite savage. I'm told there are many ginger kittens on Capri.'

Veronica looked at Leonardo and wondered how many offspring *he'd* sired over the years. Though perhaps he was too careful for that. Wealthy playboys would learn to practise safe sex from an early age, she imagined. There certainly hadn't been anything about paternity suits levelled against him on the Internet.

'Must go, Leo,' Franco called out as he dropped Veronica's case onto the portico then climbed back into the taxi. 'I will see you tonight,' he directed straight at her.

'Tonight?' Veronica echoed but Franco was already gone.

'My parents will invite you to dinner,' Leonardo explained. 'The whole family will be there to meet you. They are very curious over the long-lost daughter of their friend and neighbour.'

'Oh.' It sounded like there would be a daunting lot of people gawking at her.

'Don't say no,' he advised. 'They would be most offended if you did.'

'I wouldn't dream of saying no,' she said, just as two people emerged from the hotel out into the sunny courtyard.

Veronica saw immediately where Leonardo got his looks, because this had to be his parents. Both of them were surprisingly tall for Italians. Despite being obviously in their seventies, they both stood with straight backs, their faces beaming with happiness at the sight of their son.

'Leonardo!' his mother exclaimed, and hurried over to throw her arms around him.

'*Mamma*,' he said warmly, holding his mother's face and covering it with kisses.

His mother laughed and smiled, hugging him even tighter.

Veronica watched with a tightness in her own chest. Was it jealousy she was feeling? Or just envy? She and her mother loved each other dearly but they weren't much into physical demonstrations of their love. The occasional hug, maybe. Her mother had kissed her goodbye at the airport. Just one kiss. On the cheek.

Of course, Italians were like this. They were a passionate people, given to touching and kissing at the drop of a hat. Australians not so much, though they were improving when it came to showing affection—especially in Sydney, where immigration was the highest, with people from other cultures bringing with them new and possibly better ways.

Finally, Signora Fabrizzi disentangled herself from her son's arms and turned to face Veronica whilst Leonardo's father had his turn at hugging and kissing his son.

'And you must be Veronica,' she said, her Italian accent not as heavy as Franco's. 'Laurence's secret daughter. I am Sophia, Leonardo's *mamma*. And this is Alberto, his *papa*. My, but you are lovely, aren't you? Let me see your eyes,' she added, and without a by-your-leave stepped forward and swept off Veronica's sunglasses.

'Mamma!' Leonardo chided, but laughing. 'Don't be rude.'

'I just wanted to see if she had Laurence's eyes,' his mother explained sheepishly. 'See, Leonardo? They are the same violet colour. The same shape. Now I believe she is really his daughter.'

Leonardo muttered something in Italian, having removed his own sunglasses, perhaps so that he could see the colour of Veronica's eyes more clearly. Their eyes met, with nothing now to mask their feelings. Veronica stiffened at the naked desire which zoomed across the space between them. It was the same way he'd looked at her that night all those years ago. She'd resisted him then. But could she resist him now? Did she even *want* to?

Hopefully, he wouldn't put that question to the test. Because, for whatever reason, she didn't feel as strong today as she had back then. Which was odd, really, since she had her experience with Jerome to help immunise her against the attractions of men such as Leonardo Fabrizzi. She wished now that she hadn't suggested she was the free and easy type when it came to men. The urge to seem sophisticated in his presence had been acute. Female vanity, she supposed. But it had been a mistake.

Leonardo finally extracted them from his parents' overwhelming welcome with the excuse he should take Veronica up to see her villa.

'I will see you soon, *Mamma*,' he said, shepherding them both back inside whilst he retrieved Veronica's luggage, and her sunglasses, at the same time. 'After I've got Veronica settled in I'll come back down and you can tell me all the gossip.'

His mother called out something from the hotel foyer in Italian. His reply was in Italian also. Despite only knowing limited Italian, Veronica gleaned it was about dinner tonight.

'Haven't you been home for a while?' she asked as he handed over her sunglasses, which she popped into her shoulder bag. Their eyes met again and something lurched inside her. He just stared at her for a long moment, and she stared right back, thinking how beautiful he was. Not just handsome. Beautiful.

Oh, dear…

'It's been a month since my last visit,' he said at last.

Not so very long ago, Veronica thought. She'd been imagining it must have been much longer, judging by the prodigious joy of his parents' welcome. Clearly, Leonardo was the apple of his *mamma's* and *papa's* eyes.

'This way,' he said, then took off through the paved pergola, pulling her case behind him. Veronica had to hurry to keep up with him, his stride fast and long.

'It was my father's seventy-fifth birthday,' he tossed over his shoulder. 'It was also the weekend before Laurence died. Now, watch your step on this path. It's very steep but it's the quickest way up to your villa from here. There's another road for deliveries and such, but you have to drive a fair way round to get to it, and I don't keep a car on the island.'

It *was* steep, but she was fit and didn't have much trouble with the incline, or the rather uneven stone steps. Clearly, they'd been there a long time, as had the inhabitants of this island. Franco had given her a history lesson this morning during her sightseeing tour, telling her how the Roman emperor Tiberius had moved to Capri ages ago and had used the Blue Grotto as his private swimming pool. She'd possibly heard the same story when she'd been here before as a tourist but she'd long forgotten it. But she hadn't forgotten how impressed she was by all the beautiful white villas which dotted the island. Now one of them belonged to *her*. For a while, at least.

Her eyes lifted but the villa was hidden from view by a grove of olive trees. She could just glimpse the roof, which had terracotta tiles just like the Hotel Fabrizzi.

'Did you see Laurence that weekend?' she asked, glad to return her attention to the reason why she was here. Which wasn't to go gaga over Leonardo but to find out all she could about her father.

'I did,' was all he said.

'And?' she prompted.

'I've been trying to recall what we talked about. I knew you'd ask me,' he added with a wry glance over his shoulder.

'And?'

He stopped walking and turned to face her. 'It's difficult to remember. We spent many hours together over the last few years, Laurence and I. He taught me to play chess. But I never could beat him. He was way too good.'

'I've never played chess.'

'It's not an easy game to master,' he said, and started walking up the steps again, this time by her side rather than in front.

'Do you like red wine?'

'Not really.'

'Laurence was a red wine buff. He has the most incredible cellar.'

'I noticed he left you his wine collection in his will. Have you collected it yet?'

'No need. You're selling me the villa, remember?'

'Oh, yes. Yes, of course. I forgot. Oh!' Veronica exclaimed in surprise as the villa came into view.

It wasn't what she'd been imagining. Somehow she'd been picturing a smaller version of the Hotel Fabrizzi. But it wasn't like that at all. Yes, it was mainly white. And, yes, the roof tiles were terracotta. But that was where any resemblance ended. The building was rectangular, and all on the one level, with a cloistered veranda which ran the entire length at the front. Beyond this shaded area, the main wall of the house had a lot of sliding glass doors with no obvious front door.

'Come,' Leonardo said, and led her up a small cement ramp onto the wonderfully cool veranda. Once there, Veronica stopped and turned to gaze out at the Mediterranean.

'Oh, Leonardo,' she said with a sigh of both amazement and contentment. The olive grove stopped one looking down and perhaps having the magnificent vista spoiled by the sight of buses, towns and tourists. All you could see from where she was standing was crystal blue water all the way to the horizon, with just the occasional sailboat or yacht, which hardly seemed to be moving. Everything was peaceful, soothing and, oh, so beautiful.

'Perhaps now you understand why I want to buy this place.'

'Yes indeed,' she said, aware that he'd moved to stand close to her, so close that she could smell his aftershave, or his cologne, or whatever that wonderful scent was which emanated from his skin. She'd smelt it before in the car but had done her best to ignore the effect it had on her.

Ignoring it again, she turned and looked up at him.

'And if I decide not to sell it to you?'

For a split second, anger zoomed into his eyes. But then he laughed. 'You can't afford not to. The taxes on this place will be considerable.'

'Not so considerable if I can prove I'm Laurence's biological daughter.'

'And how do you plan to do that? He's been cremated, according to his wishes. You would need his DNA.'

'There must be something of his DNA in this place. A hairbrush, perhaps? Or a toothbrush?'

'Perhaps...'

'Don't look so worried, Leonardo. I *will* sell you the villa, but only after I've got what I came here to find out.'

'Which is what, exactly?'

'What my father looked like, for starters. There was a small article about him on the Internet, but no photos. Mum didn't have any photos, either. But, more importantly, I want to find out what kind of man he was.'

CHAPTER EIGHT

LEONARDO LOOKED DEEP into Veronica's lovely violet eyes and wondered if she'd be happy with what she found out. Laurence's looks wouldn't present a problem, since he had been a male version of her. But Laurence hadn't always been an easy man to warm to.

He'd been somewhat introverted, for starters, a typical scientist. Brilliant, but not the most sensitive of men. Leonardo imagined that as a young man emotions were not something Laurence had been familiar with.

His obsessive love for his wife must have thrown him for a loop. Because it clearly hadn't been in Laurence's nature to love like that. Her death had derailed him for a long time. Ruth had been the more social of the pair. She'd loved going to parties and entertaining at home.

It was obvious Laurence had just gone along with her wishes to keep her happy. After she'd gone, he'd sunk into a deep depression and had refused to accept any invitations, other than at Christmas, when Leonardo's *mamma* would force him to come down to the Hotel Fabrizzi for Christmas dinner. Even then, he'd been a right misery, leaving the table as soon as it was polite and sitting by himself, not talking to anyone.

Leonardo couldn't help having felt sorry for him, priding himself on having been the person to drag Laurence out of his mourning. Every time he'd come home to visit his parents, he'd made the effort to visit him up at his villa, their friendship deepening when Leonardo had broken his ankle rock climbing a couple of years back and had come home to recuperate. Laurence had become frustrated with watching Leonardo struggle up the path on crutches to visit him and had insisted he move in with him until his ankle healed.

It was during that time together that their real friendship had begun, Leonardo having confided to Laurence over a bottle of wine one night how devastated he had been when he'd been forced to retire early from competitive skiing. No one in his family had ever understood how upset he'd been at the time. His parents had simply been pleased that he was no longer risking his neck on the slopes. Uncle Stephano had been of a similar mind-set, saying there was just as much satisfaction in succeeding in business as in sport.

None of them had had a clue.

But Laurence had. He'd understood totally, his empathy coming as a surprise.

'There is nothing worse for a man, Leonardo,' he'd said gently, 'than to have a goal snatched away from him, right when it is within reach. I know how that feels. I was on the verge of making a huge scientific discovery when all my funding for that particular research was suddenly cancelled. There was nothing I could do at the time. It was at the start of my career and I had no reputation to fall back on. I felt quite suicidal. Fortunately, I met Ruth around that time, and she made me see that there was more to life than science. One day, my boy, you will find a new dream, one which you can fulfil. Meanwhile, try to enjoy what you have, which is a lot.'

It had been sound advice. Looking back, Leonardo could see that their mutual confidences had resulted in an affection for each other that was unconditional. Leonardo had accepted Laurence's flaws, and vice versa. It had made for an ease of companionship which hadn't required the usual male tendency to try to impress. With Laurence, Leonardo had been able to be himself. He missed that.

'Laurence was a good man, but he was basically a loner,' he told Veronica, couching his words carefully. 'Most scientists are, I would imagine. Their work is a huge part of their life. Ruth used to get him to socialise. She liked entertaining and having guests to stay. But after she died he reverted to type. *Mamma* often invited him to dinner and to parties but he usually declined, except at Christmas. I guess I knew him better than anyone on Capri. He was very open with me. But, even then, it's obvious he had his secrets.'

'You're talking about me,' she said.

'Yes. You came as a shock, I can tell you.' In more ways than one. Over the phone she'd come across as brusque and spinsterish, so he'd been expecting a plain woman. But Veronica was anything but plain. She was utterly gorgeous. Leonardo suspected that he would have difficulty keeping his hands off. Already he wanted to run his fingers through her hair, to pull her to him and kiss her until she forgot all about what her father had been like. Leonardo knew he could make women forget all sorts of things, especially once he got them into bed. Make himself forget too. Sex soothed the dissatisfied beast in him. That, and gazing out at this hypnotic and wonderfully relaxing view.

Leonardo turned to gaze out across the sea for a long moment. Soon Laurence's villa—and this view—would be his. But until then he'd have to make do with other methods of relaxation.

He turned back to face Veronica with his most charming smile in place, the one which always melted the ladies and made it oh, so easy when he came across a female he fancied. And he fancied this one. More than he had in a long time, Leonardo conceded. She actually reminded him of a girl he'd come across one night many years ago. A girl very similar to Veronica in looks. A girl who'd caught his eye but who'd rejected his drunken invitation with the disdain it had probably deserved.

She'd been Australian too, he suddenly recalled.

His brows drew together as he stared at her again. Surely not?

His eyes searched hers, then travelled down her delec-

table body and up again. It was a long time ago, and he'd
never known her name. All he'd known was that she was
Australian and that she'd worked as a masseuse at a neigh-
bouring ski resort. Sven had raved about her and asked her
to one of their after-competition parties. Leonardo's retirement party, as it had turned out.

'This might seem an odd question,' he said, 'but did you
ever work as a masseur in a ski resort in Switzerland? About
seven or eight years ago, it would have been...'

Veronica's stomach flipped right over. She hadn't expected
him to recognise her. Not on such a brief acquaintance so
many years ago. They hadn't even been properly introduced.

But it seemed he had recognised her. Or almost had.
What to do? Lie, or tell the truth?

She did so hate lies. Jerome had lied to her. A lot.

'I didn't think you'd recognise me,' she said simply. 'It
was so long ago.'

He blinked his surprise, then smiled a rather rueful smile.
'That's how you knew I was a skier,' he said.

'Yes,' she agreed. Not to mention a playboy.

'Why didn't you tell me we'd met before?' he demanded
to know, not angrily, but in a rather puzzled tone.

'I thought you might find the circumstances...embar-
rassing.'

He laughed. Not a loud, in-your-face belly laugh. Or an
amused chuckle. More of a harsh bark.

'I admit, it wasn't one of my finer moments.'

'Really? I got the impression it was your usual *après ski*
behaviour. None of the other people there seemed surprised.'

'I can't say I noticed. I was very drunk, Veronica. My
career as a downhill racer had ended that day and I didn't
take it well. One injury too many, I was told,' he added with
a flash of remembered pain in his eyes.

She just stood there in a stiff silence, not prepared to excuse his behaviour that night so easily.

He laughed again, this time with a flash of dry humour. 'I can still remember what you said to me. *In your dreams, mate.*'

'Yes, well, when I go to bed with a guy,' she said rather tartly, 'I like to have his total attention. I'm not big on sharing.' And wasn't that the truth!

'Believe it or not, I am usually a one-woman-at-a-time man.'

'If you say so.'

He smiled a crooked smile. 'You must have a very bad opinion of me. First, from that night. And then from what I told you about the business today in Rome.'

Veronica didn't want to offend the man, but she was way past letting him whitewash his behaviour. It galled her to think he imagined she would fall for his 'poor little me' act.

'Leonardo,' she said firmly. 'Let's not pretend. Your reputation precedes you. It always has, even back in your downhill racing days. You're a player. You change your girlfriends as often as you do your clothes. I've seen dozens of photos of you on social media. But never with the same girl on your arm.'

His eyebrows lifted, his dark eyes glittering with the most irritating satisfaction.

'You checked me out on the Internet?'

Veronica heaved an exasperated sigh. Trust him to take her admission as a measure of sexual interest.

'Of course I did,' she told him in a matter-of-fact manner. 'I'm not a fool, Leonardo. I wanted to know what kind of man you were these days. I wanted to see if you could be trusted.'

'And?' He still didn't seem offended or worried, that twinkle staying in his eyes.

'As a businessman, your reputation is spotless.'

'But not as a boyfriend,' he said with laughter in his eyes. 'Well…'

'Come, come—don't quibble. Australians are well

known for being straight shooters. Tell me what you think of me as a boyfriend.'

Veronica straightened her spine. 'I would say you weren't a very good bet in that regard. Not if a woman wanted commitment.'

'That would depend on the woman,' he countered. 'I have no objection to commitment when the time—and the woman—is right. But then, not every woman is looking for commitment. Take you, for instance…'

'What? *Me?*'

'Yes, you.'

'What about me?' she demanded to know, angling her head to one side as she glared up at him.

He smiled. 'You are in your late twenties and have no one serious in your life. Yet you are a very beautiful woman. I can only conclude that you have chosen to stay—what is the term?—footloose and fancy free.'

Veronica hadn't blushed in years and she didn't blush now. But she felt quite hot inside her body, the kind of heat which came from being turned on. He was turning her on, this devilishly handsome Italian, with his verbal foreplay and his suggestive smiles.

All of a sudden she thought about what it would be like to have sex with him. Would he be as good a lover as he obviously thought he was?

Yes, she decided, a decidedly erotic shiver rippling down her spine.

Sex wasn't something that had ever been that important to Veronica. It was the romance she enjoyed. The love. Orgasms for her had always been in short supply, even with Jerome, who'd been more than competent in bed. But he hadn't been all that passionate.

Naturally not, she thought bitterly. His passion—and his love—had lain elsewhere.

Veronica stared up into Leonardo's dark, sexy eyes and just knew *he'd* be passionate in bed. Passionate, uninhibited and extremely imaginative. There wouldn't be a form of foreplay or a sexual position he hadn't tried *and* revelled in. Any man who could have offered a threesome so casually was into anything. Orgies as well, no doubt.

Such thoughts made it difficult to speak at all, let alone find the right reply. Veronica licked her dry lips, then swallowed.

'I haven't been lucky when it comes to men,' she said quite truthfully.

'That is sad. But you are still young. There is no need to panic yet.'

Now it was her turn to laugh. 'That's a matter of opinion. It seems only yesterday that I was twenty. Now, in two years, I'll be thirty.'

'You wish to get married and have children?'

Veronica shrugged. Once upon a time, she would have said yes in a heartbeat. Now, she wasn't so sure. Marriage didn't seem as straightforward as it once had. She suspected that falling in love again would be difficult for her, for starters. And, without love, marriage was out of the question.

'Only if I meet the right man,' she said. *Which certainly won't be someone like you*, she thought, despite the desire Leonardo could evoke in her with shocking ease.

'When you sell me this villa,' he replied, 'You will be rich. And men will be chasing you like mad. Possibly not the right kind of man, though, so you will have to be careful. Come,' he said, and retrieved a key from one of the large pots full of geraniums that sat along the sunny edge of the veranda. 'Time for you to see your inheritance from the inside.'

CHAPTER NINE

'DON'T LOOK SO WORRIED,' Leonardo said as he inserted the key into the lock of one of the sliding glass doors. 'We don't have a crime problem on Capri. Perhaps a little pickpocketing, occasionally, but not serious crime. Laurence always kept a key in that pot so that Carmelina could get in when he wasn't around.'

'Carmelina?'

'One of my sisters. She used to clean for Laurence. And shop. I asked her to go through the place this week and stock up with food. And, no, you do not have to pay her. She was happy to do it.'

'That was very kind of her. Do you have her number? If she speaks English I would like to thank her.'

'Everyone in my family speaks English. And you don't have to ring her. You can thank her when you see her tonight. At dinner.'

'Oh, yes. Dinner…'

Dinner tonight with his family was going to be a trial, she thought. But not as much of a trial as handling Leonardo's disturbing presence right here and now. She needed a break from his overwhelmingly attractive persona so that she could get a grip on her treacherously excited body. Veronica had the awful suspicion that if she let him stay with her any longer she might do something foolish. Once they went inside together, they would be alone. In this gorgeous house. With bedrooms and beds. She didn't trust herself. *Or* him. Not that he would force himself upon her. She didn't think that. But it was obvious Leonardo would not waste time when he fancied a girl.

And he fancied her, if the looks he kept giving her were anything to go by.

'Leonardo,' she began as he slid open the first of the huge glass doors.

He swung round to set those incredibly sexy eyes upon her. 'Yes?'

'Would you mind terribly if I walked through the house without you? I just want to soak it all in by myself. And I really do need to ring my mother. Let her know I've arrived and everything's okay. She worries, you see.'

Veronica knew she was babbling, but Leonardo was the sort of man who could make a woman babble. She would have to get control of that before tonight. He was sure to seat her right next to him at dinner. Already she was wondering what to wear.

His smile hinted that he understood she was slightly afraid to be alone with him. Or maybe she was just imagining it. Guilty conscience and all that.

'Let me just put your luggage inside,' he replied, and turned to where he'd left it.

Panic almost had her screaming at him to leave it, but she held her tongue just in time, instead dredging up the cool smile she'd used on men for the past three years but which was in danger of deserting her. With Leonardo she wanted just to smile fatuously at him and agree with everything he suggested. She'd already agreed to let him take her sightseeing tomorrow. In a helicopter, no less.

Helicopters frightened the life out of her. She didn't like the idea that if the engine conked out and the rotor blades stopped you'd drop like a stone. No hope of gliding down to a soft landing. Not that you could do that in a big plane. Maybe she could suggest tonight over dinner that they cruise around in a boat instead. Not a small sailing boat. One with a big crew, to stop him from pouncing once they were at sea.

As soon as her black wheelie case was safely inside the enormous living area, he took her gently by the shoulders and gazed down into her ever-widening eyes. Lord, was he going to kiss her?

He didn't. She just wished he had. Instead, he shook his head at her, as if he knew what was going on in *her* head.

'You should have a rest this afternoon,' he advised. 'Dinner with my family is not a quick event. *Mamma* will want to impress you with all her best dishes, so don't eat too much before you come. I shall be here to pick you up at seven.'

'What…what should I wear?'

He shrugged. 'Nothing formal. If you wear a dress, then bring a wrap. Or a jacket. The evenings start warm but cool down quickly. *Arrivederci*, Veronica.'

And then he did kiss her. Not a big, swooping, passionate kiss. Just a peck, really. But on her lips. A light, lovely kiss which made her long for more. And then he was gone, not looking back once as he'd stridden away from her, his long legs carrying him down off the veranda and swiftly out of sight.

Veronica just stood there for long moment, staring blindly after him, not breathing, not thinking. Only yearning. No…craving. She *craved* Leonardo Fabrizzi. It was a stunning realisation. Because she'd never craved a man like that before. She knew it wasn't love she was feeling. It was lust making her heart thud and her lungs ache from not breathing. She gasped in then, sucking in the gloriously fresh air, clearing her light-headedness to a degree.

Crossing her arms, she hugged herself, then turned and stared through the glass doors at the view of the sea once more, using its soothing quality to find some common sense, asking herself what did it matter if she lusted after this man? What would it matter if she even had sex with him? It didn't have to lead anywhere. It *wouldn't* lead anywhere. Anyone who knew anything about Leonardo Fabrizzi would know that.

A slow smile spread across Veronica's face as she thought about Leonardo. What a devil he was. But a very charming devil. And sexy as hell. A girl would have to be dead to resist him.

'And I'm far from dead,' she said aloud as she unwrapped her arms and spread them wide. 'I'm over Jerome. I'm here on the gorgeous Isle of Capri. And I'm about to inspect my father's equally gorgeous house!'

CHAPTER TEN

It *WAS* GORGEOUS. The living area, especially. It was open plan, but not overly modern, though it did have all the mod cons. The floors were Italian marble in swirls of white and grey, the rugs very colourful. The furniture was an eclectic mixture of stuff one might see in an English home, the two sofas rather formal and chintzy, the armchairs large, squashy and very country. The dining table was oval-shaped, and made of an almost black wood, with six matching high-back chairs around it, the seats covered in green velvet. In the middle of the table sat the most glorious green glass... thing. Not a bowl. Or a vase. More of a sculptured shape with no visible purpose other than to be beautiful.

Possibly Murano glass, Veronica decided, having briefly visited Venice and the island of Murano during the Italy-in-a-week tour she'd undertaken when she'd been twenty-one. Whatever it was, she loved it. Had her father chosen it?

Thinking of her father sent Veronica hurrying over to the far wall where there was a selection of photos arranged on the mantelpiece above the fireplace. At last, she would see what her father looked like.

Her eyes immediately went to the wedding photo, which was black-and-white and showed the bride dressed in a long, straight gown and a heavy lace veil which had gone out of fashion aeons ago. She was short, slim and pretty in a soft blonde way. The groom was very tall, dark and handsome. Strong looking, with an air about him that was impressive at first glance until you looked a second time. His face was turned towards his bride, his expression both loving and vulnerable. Here was a man very deeply in love, with a love that surprised him.

Turning the frame over, she saw there was writing on the back:

Laurence and Ruth
On our wedding day, March 1968

Twenty-two years before I was conceived, Veronica thought.

The other photos showed them growing older, some of them alone and others in groups. Laurence had aged very well, keeping his thick, lustrous hair even when it had turned grey. His wife had faded with time, growing frailer with the years. But her smile remained bright and warm, her eyes loving whenever they were lifted to her husband. Which was often. He in turn always had his hands on her somewhere, either on her shoulders or around her waist. His body language was both protective and possessive. Yet not in any way threatening. Despite Ruth being the more fragile looking, Veronica suspected it was she who had worn the trousers in their relationship. Only one photo showed the colour of her father's eyes. They were, as everyone had pointed out, violet, just like hers. They were shaped like hers too.

It pleased her, then made her sad.

She would have loved to know her father when he had still been alive. Instead, all she could do was pick over other people's memories of him. And stare at old photos. Suddenly, the tears came, rolling down her cheeks and dripping off her nose. Thankfully, they didn't last long, Veronica pulling herself together by turning and looking through the mainly glass wall at the view beyond.

What *was* it about that view? It was only water, after all. Did the Mediterranean possess some kind of magic? Or was it Capri that was magical?

Whatever, it did the trick, bringing a sense of peace to her soul and an acceptance of the situation. At least she *had* some sense of her father's memories now. And photos. And this lovely villa. For a while, anyway. What a shame she could not live here permanently.

'Don't start wishing for the moon, Veronica,' she told herself sternly, then turned and went to discover the rest of her father's home.

Two hours later, after taking more photos than she could count, Veronica sent them to her mother's phone then rang her.

'Hel...lo?' came a very fuzzy voice after several rings.

'Oh, dear,' Veronica said, wincing. 'I've woken you up. Sorry, Mum. I forgot about the time difference.'

'No trouble,' she said, sounding a little more awake.

'What time is it?'

'Er...just after four. In the morning. What's up?'

'I'm here on Capri, in the villa.'

'What's it like? Not a crumbling ruin, I hope.'

Veronica laughed. 'Hardly. I've taken heaps of photos and sent them to you. Have a look and see for yourself.'

'Just a sec. Oh, yes. I've got them. Oh...wow! That is some view. Is that the view from the villa or somewhere else?'

'No, that's the view from the villa.'

'No wonder the place is worth heaps. That view alone is worth millions.'

'I agree. And the villa is fantastic.'

'Yes, it's lovely. Not very Italian-looking inside.'

'No. The decor is more English but the bones are Italian. Lots of marble on the floors and in the bathrooms. And the fireplace is very Italian. The kitchen is modern, despite the wooden benches. *And* the huge cooker.'

'Four bedrooms, I notice. Yet they didn't have children.'

'Leonardo said they used to entertain when his wife was still alive.'

'What's he like, this Leonardo chap?'

Veronica swallowed. To lie or not to lie? She didn't want

her mother worrying about her. And she might, if she said he was utterly gorgeous and she fancied him like mad.

'Oh, he's a typical Italian. You know the type. Very charming.'

'And very good-looking,' her mother said, startling her.

'How would you know that?'

'After you left I looked him up on the Internet. He's quite the playboy, isn't he?'

'Yes,' Veronica admitted. 'But harmless, once you know the species.'

Her mother laughed. 'Remember that Brazilian exchange student who chased after you during your first year at university.'

Veronica groaned. 'How could I forget?'

'He got you in the end, though, didn't he?'

'Mum! How on earth did you know that? I never said.'

'You always did like guys who refused to take no for an answer.'

She did, she supposed. Jerome had been like that. He'd pursued her like mad. She hadn't really wanted to go out with a doctor. Certainly not a surgeon. She knew the hours they worked. But she'd given in after the tenth lot of roses had arrived, and then she'd fallen in love with him, agreeing to marry him in a few short weeks. She'd never suspected Jerome had had a secret agenda. Never suspected anything.

'Has he made a pass at you yet?' her mother asked slyly.

Now she really did have to lie. 'No. He said something about a girlfriend in Rome. Though I *am* going to his family's place for dinner tonight. They own a hotel just below the villa. It's only a short walk down some stone steps. But first I must have a sleep. I'm exhausted.' And hungry, she suddenly realised.

'You might be exhausted but you sound happy. Happier than you've been in years. I was angry with Laurence for putting you in his will at first but now I'm grateful. This inheritance has been good for you, love. You're sounding like the girl you were before you met Jerome.'

Veronica blinked. 'Don't you mean before Jerome was killed?'

'No. I mean before you *met* that bastard.'

Veronica was truly taken aback. 'But I thought you liked Jerome. I mean…before we found out about him.'

'I just pretended to like him. For your sake. I always thought he was up himself. And so was his family. Talk about snobs!'

'They were on the snobbish side,' Veronica admitted.

'They thought you weren't good enough for their precious son. Little did they know he wasn't good enough for you.'

Veronica sighed.

'Now, none of that,' her mother said. 'Go back to the girl who rang me a few minutes ago. She's the girl you used to be before Jerome. She was a terrific girl who knew how to have fun. That man turned you into a try-hard. And then he turned you into a bitter cow like me.'

'Oh, Mum, you're nothing of the kind.'

'Yes, I am, and I hate myself for it. I don't know how you've put up with me all these years. The one thing I truly regret is that I didn't try to help you out of your unhappiness. To my shame, I just let you wallow in it.'

Veronica was so astonished by her mother's words she couldn't think of a thing to say.

'Of course, I liked it that you didn't have anyone else but me,' her mother confessed. 'And that you were living and working from home. I used to smugly think, *now she knows what it's like to have your trust in men destroyed*. Laurence's will was a wake-up call to me, I can tell you. When I saw how upset you were, it nearly killed me. I vowed then and there to stop being so selfish and to encourage you to get out there and make a life for yourself. I'm sure not all men are as rotten as Jerome, or that excuse for a husband I once had. There are good men out there. Men like your father.

He was a good man. Very loving and loyal to his wife. I'm sure there is someone out there just right for you. Meanwhile, if this Leonardo makes a pass at you, then go for it, darling. He's one hot hunk.'

'Wow, Mum, I don't know what to say!'

'You don't have to say anything at all. Just accept my apology and go have some fun. Oh, and one last thing.'

'What?'

'Please don't feel you have to ring me all the time. Nothing worse than going on holiday and feeling you have to check in with your mother. But feel free to send any photos and the odd text. Okay?'

'Okay,' she agreed with a smile on her face.

CHAPTER ELEVEN

Leonardo leapt up the stone steps two a time, excited by the prospect of seeing Veronica again. And having her meet his whole family. They were excited to meet her as well, his two sisters very curious over this girl who was Laurence's biological daughter.

Carmelina had liked Laurence a lot, but then she was the one who had seen him the most, being his cleaner as well as Ruth's sometime carer. She'd been astonished by the news that he had a secret daughter, and relieved when she heard that Veronica had been conceived through IVF and not some sordid affair.

The sun had set but it was still light, a golden hue hovering on the horizon. A silvery half-moon was up as well, bathing Laurence's villa in soft moonlight.

Leonardo bounced up onto the terrace and was about to press the front doorbell when the sliding glass door opened and there stood Veronica, looking even more beautiful than she had earlier that day. Gone were the jeans and simple striped top and in their place a sexy lilac sundress which left her shoulders bare, the halter neckline hinting at just enough cleavage.

Across her right forearm lay a black lacy cardigan.

'I won't need to bring a bag, will I?' she asked, looking up at him with sparkling eyes, their violet colour darker than they had been in the sunshine. Dark and sexier.

'Not on my account,' he replied with a smile. *Dio*, but she was delicious. Her hair was still up. Not severely but softly, with dark curls kissing her pale cheeks and throat. Her mouth was glossed in a plum colour, her eyes shadowed in a silvery grey which matched the moonlight. He couldn't wait to bring her home after dinner and take her to bed. She wouldn't say no. He could already feel the heat sizzling from her skin. Could feel his own as well, his hot Italian blood charging through his veins.

Thank God he was wearing loosely tailored slacks. They stopped his erection from being obvious. Leonardo didn't like being obvious.

She smiled back at him. 'I'll just lock up and put the key in that ridiculously obvious pot. I hope this building and its contents are insured,' she added as she did just that.

'They are,' he assured her, amused by her concern over security.

'Did you have a good look at everything?' he asked her as he took her elbow and guided her from the terrace.

'Yes. It's a lovely house. I had a look at some photos of Laurence as well. I do take after him, don't I?'

'You do. In looks. But you're much nicer.'

She halted at the top of the stone steps. 'What do you mean? Wasn't my father a nice person?'

Leonardo instantly regretted his tactless words. 'He was a very nice person,' he said, regrouping quickly. 'But you're even nicer.'

'Oh…' Her cheeks coloured a little, her eyes blinking with the most charming embarrassment. 'How can you say that? You don't really know me.'

'I am a quick judge of people. And a good judge, I believe.'

'You weren't with that girl in Rome,' she shot back, startling him into laughter.

'True. There are times when my hormones lead me astray.'

'I think your hormones lead you astray a lot,' she said drily, making him wonder if perhaps she would say no to him tonight. He hoped not, because he wanted this girl more and more with each passing moment.

'Come,' he said, and closed his fingers more tightly around her elbow. '*Mamma* is champing at the bit to feed you.'

'I don't think I could eat another bite,' Veronica whispered to Leonardo a couple of hours later.

'Try,' he whispered back.

'I hope you don't think it rude of me, Veronica,' Sophia said rather loudly from where she was sitting at the end of the table furthest from them. 'But I must ask you—your mother…why she not just get married if she wanted a *bambino*?'

'*Mamma,*' Leonardo chided with a wry shake of his handsome head. 'That *is* a rather rude question.'

'No, no,' Veronica said straight away, not wanting to offend Sophia, who was really a lovely person. Veronica already liked her enormously. She liked *all* of Leonardo's family. And there were twelve of them sitting at the table under the pergola that evening. Alberto and Sophia had three children, Veronica had learned when introduced properly. Elena was the oldest, followed by Carmelina and then Leonardo. Elena was married to Franco, the taxi driver, and they had three children. Marco was eleven, Bianca was nine with the youngest, Bruno, a precocious seven. Carmelina was the only shy one of the family. She was married to Alfonso, who worked at the Hotel Fabrizzi as a handyman-cum-gardener. They had a son, Luca, who was ten and a daughter, Daniele, who was eight.

'It is a fair question,' Veronica went on. She presumed Leonardo had explained how Laurence had come to be a sperm donor, but even he didn't know the reasons behind her mother's decision to have a baby that way. 'My mother actually was married when she was younger. But her husband was not a good man. He gambled away all their money, treated her badly then left her to run away with another woman. A rich widow. She had a nervous breakdown and lost her job. In the end she had nothing and could only get work as a housekeeper. She was very bitter about men and vowed never to trust one ever again. But as she got older she desperately wanted a baby.

'Around this time she was employed by Laurence. He was in Australia doing research at the Sydney University. His job came with a large house in nearby Glebe, along with a live-in housekeeper. That was Mum. She liked Laurence, said he was a decent man. They became friendly and one day she confided in him her plan to have a baby by artificial insemination.'

'And that was when Laurence offered his sperm instead of some stranger's,' Leonardo intervened. 'He didn't want to risk the baby having a bad gene, like Ruth apparently had. That was the reason Ruth didn't have children, by the way. She was worried they would inherit her bad gene. But Laurence knew his genes were fine.'

'Better than fine,' Leonardo's father said with a big smile on his face, his accent much stronger than Leonardo's. He waved his arms around a lot. 'Just look at the beautiful girl he produced. He would have been so proud of you, Veronica. You are *molto bella*. Your *mamma* must be very happy that she listened to Laurence.'

Other members of the family chimed in with their compliments as well.

Veronica tried not to blush. But, really, the whole family had been gushing and fussing over her all evening. She loved the attention but it was a bit overwhelming. She hoped and prayed that both Elena and Carmelina would get up and go soon. Unfortunately, the children didn't seem at all tired, and tomorrow was Saturday, after all. Not a school day. She couldn't claim she was wilting, either, having had a long nap this afternoon.

The beginning of a yawn took her by surprise.

'Tired?' Leonardo murmured in her ear.

'No,' she confessed with a soft sigh. 'Not really.'

'Good,' he said quietly so that only she could hear. 'I will tell everyone you have jet lag and need to go home to bed.'

Veronica was tempted, but when she turned her head and saw the devilish glint in his eye she found herself not wanting to do as he obviously wanted her to do. Not yet. As madly attractive as she found him, as fast as her heart was beating, her days of being a pushover with the opposite sex were well and truly over.

'No,' she said with a coolness which surprised even her. 'No, I don't want to do that. I'm not fond of lying.'

'A little white lie won't hurt anyone,' he grumbled. Clearly, he wasn't used to being thwarted.

'That's a matter of opinion,' Veronica retorted. 'Your mother would be offended. She's gone to a lot of trouble with this meal.'

'Very well, but be warned—I can't protect you from *Mamma's* never-ending questions if you stay.'

'What was that?' Sophia immediately jumped in. 'Are you talking about me, Leonardo?'

'Veronica was just complimenting you on the food, *Mamma*,' he said, showing Veronica how smoothly *he* could lie. 'She said you have gone to a lot of trouble.'

Sophia looked very pleased. 'She is welcome.'

Veronica smiled at her, glad now that she had stayed. But she almost wished she'd said yes to Leonardo's suggestion when Sophia went on to ask her a multitude of questions about her life back in Sydney, finally asking if there was a boyfriend waiting for her at home. It was a reasonable question, she supposed, but she was always reluctant to discuss her personal life. Or lack of one. It was a relief when Leonardo answered for her.

'Not at the moment, *Mamma*,' he said. 'I asked Veronica just that earlier today and she claimed not to be lucky when it came to men. Perhaps she will be luckier now that she is an heiress,' he added with a slight edge in his voice.

Sophia rattled off something exasperated in Italian before

apologising, then returning to English. 'I said you would not need the money to be attractive to men,' she told Veronica.

Veronica had a feeling she'd just been lied to, as everyone else at the table exchanged knowing looks. She'd heard Leonardo's name in there somewhere, not her own name.

'She might be divorced,' the precocious Bruno suddenly piped up.

An embarrassed silence settled on the table for a long moment.

'There's a thought,' Leonardo muttered. '*Are* you divorced, Veronica?'

CHAPTER TWELVE

SHE BLINKED UP at him, startled, he thought, by his question.

'Absolutely not,' came her firm reply. 'I've never been married.'

Leonardo wasn't sure why he was relieved at this news.

Why was he so pleased to hear Veronica wasn't in that category?

He had no idea. Neither did he wish to worry about it.

'But you do wish to get married?' Elena asked her.

Leonardo noticed Veronica's hesitation to answer. But then she smiled and said, 'Yes, of course. If I ever meet a man I can both love and trust.'

Ah, Leonardo thought. She *had* been burnt in the past. And burnt quite badly, by the sound of things.

'You should marry an Italian,' Elena continued. 'They make very good husbands.' And she gave Franco a loving glance.

My sister is as bad as my mother, Leonardo decided. *Always matchmaking.*

'I think it is time I took Veronica home,' he said, and stood up abruptly. 'She has had a long day, and I'm taking her sightseeing by helicopter tomorrow morning.' He knew that mentioning this would stop any objections to his escorting Veronica home. His mother and sisters would be satisfied with this news and could plan further matchmaking in their absence.

Not that any of it would work. Firstly, he didn't really want to get married just yet. And, even if he did, he wasn't about to marry an Australian girl who would be going home soon, never to return. Yes, he found Veronica extremely attractive. And, yes, he aimed to get her into bed before the weekend was out. Before this night was out, actually. But once she sold him the villa that would be the end of things. She would return to her life in Sydney and he would go on as before.

Leonardo looked down at Veronica who hadn't made a move to stand up. Surely *she* wasn't going to object?

She glanced up at him with those big violet eyes of hers, and once again it zapped between them—the sexual chemistry that had been there from their first meeting, and which he'd been trying to ignore all evening. It was impossible to ignore it any longer. It was like an electric shock, making every muscle in Leonardo's body contract as he battled to harness his desire into some semblance of control. But he knew, as surely as he knew he was on Capri, that the moment he took this glorious creature into his arms nothing would stop this night from reaching its inevitable conclusion.

And his satisfaction would be sublime!

CHAPTER THIRTEEN

VERONICA SUCKED IN her breath sharply. My God, the way he was looking at her. It was downright scary. But, oh, so exciting. And like nothing she'd ever experienced before. Jerome had never looked at her like that, as though he wanted to possess every part of her, body and soul. The thought thrilled her, then turned her on to the max.

Her lips dried as her heartbeat took off. So this was what real lust felt like—and she accepted only in that moment that this was something new to her. Yes, she'd been attracted to men before. Yes, she'd been to bed with a few. And, yes, it had been pleasant enough. But nothing to write home about. Jerome had been an improvement in the bedroom department. But then, she'd imagined herself in love with Jerome. And he'd obviously known what he was doing. He'd been in his late thirties, after all. But she'd never wanted him with this kind of passion, never felt her whole body react this way just to a look.

My God, she was on fire! She regretted putting on her wrap earlier, although she knew, deep down, that one small short-sleeved cardigan wasn't responsible for the heat gathering in every pore of her body.

'Come,' Leonardo commanded, and held out his hand to her.

Yes please, she thought with a jolt of uncharacteristic boldness. *Very* uncharacteristic. Veronica wasn't the type of girl whose focus in sex was constantly on having an orgasm. She'd always been more into how she felt about the man making love to her than if she came or not.

Not so with this man. He brought out the female animal in her, not the soul mate. She just wanted him to…

Veronica hated the F-word. But it was appropriate on this occasion. Because that was what Leonardo did to women. He didn't care about them. Or love them. He just screwed them silly till he got bored, and then he walked away.

His fingers closed around hers and he drew her slowly to her feet, then helped her slide out from behind the seat. Her knees held her upright, thank heavens, but it was a bit of touch and go. Thank heavens he kept a firm hold of her hand or she might have stumbled, a dizzying weakness having overtaken her. Veronica could feel everyone's eyes upon her. Could they see what was going on in her head? she wondered dazedly. Which was what, exactly? Nothing that children should know. Her mind was filling with R-rated images of herself and Leonardo tumbling together naked in a bed.

There were four bedrooms in the villa. She wasn't sure which one figured in her fantasy, her mind more on what they were doing, not where they were.

Somehow Veronica managed to say goodnight to everyone, as well as thank Sophia for the wonderful meal. She endured several hugs and kisses, and then Leonardo was leading her away—not hurrying, she noticed, for which she was both grateful and irritated. He obviously wasn't feeling the same urgency she was.

'I've remembered one of the things I talked to Laurence about that last weekend,' he said as he led her along the gravel path that led to the stone steps. '*Mamma's* infernal matchmaking brought it all back to me.'

'Oh?' was all she could manage in reply, until guilt arrived. What on earth was wrong with her? She'd come to Capri to find out about her father, not crave hot sex with the executor of his will!

She stopped and turned to face Leonardo. 'What was it?' she asked, doing her best not to think how handsome he was in the moonlight. And how sexy.

'I complained to him about *Mamma* going on and on

about my getting married and having a family. *Papa* was just as bad that weekend. He said he wanted me to have a son to carry on our family name. The only other Fabrizzi alive is my uncle Stephano and he doesn't have any children. *Papa* said it was my duty to get married and have a family.'

'But you don't *want* to get married,' she pointed out. Leonardo was a playboy. Always had been. Always would be. Hadn't his parents got that yet?

He pulled a face. 'I admit the idea of marriage doesn't appeal at the moment. I like my life the way it is for now.'

'Have you told them that?'

'Not exactly. I want to please them, but...' He shrugged, as though the decision was out of his hands. He turned and they headed up the ancient steps, Leonardo recapturing her hand.

As much as his touch sent an exciting charge shooting up her arm, this time Veronica refused to be totally distracted by it.

'What did Laurence say?' she asked. 'Did he give you any advice?'

'He said that I would change my mind about marriage when the right girl came along. He said falling in love did that to even the most confirmed bachelor.'

'That was naive of him, wasn't it?' came her slightly caustic comment. Because Veronica wasn't fooled by this man's charm, or his avid attentions. She doubted that Leonardo would ever meet the right girl. He was programmed to fall in lust but never in love.

He said nothing for a few seconds, not turning to face her till they reached the top of the steep incline.

'You are very cynical. Some man hurt you, didn't he? And, no, I don't want to hear the sordid details. I hate it when girls feel they have to tell you every moment of every bad relationship they've had. It is usually man-bashing. And boring. And turns me right off. Not that anything you said would turn me off tonight,' he added with a smile so criminally sexy that her toes curled up in her shoes. 'You could tell me you were the secret mistress to an Arab sheikh and I would still want to take you to bed.'

How did she keep a straight face? Somehow, she managed. Because she needed to show this arrogant Italian playboy that she had his measure. And was a match for him in every way.

'That's an interesting thought,' she said with brilliant nonchalance. 'No. I'm not the secret mistress of *a* sheikh. There are actually two of them. Mine are into horse racing. Plus riding of another kind,' she added with a saucy glance. 'And, my, they do keep me busy.'

It was only a momentary coup, but it was worth it to see his eyes widen in shock for a few seconds. But all too soon he realised that she was pulling his leg. His laugh was rueful.

'You are a devil in disguise, aren't you?'

'Not quite as much as you, Leonardo. But, yes, I do like being footloose and fancy free at the moment.' Lord, this lying business could get to be a habit! 'Though I do intend to get married. Eventually.'

'When you meet the right man,' he pointed out in an echo of what she'd said earlier.

'Exactly. Which I'm sorry to say is not you, Leonardo. I prefer my future husband to be a little less…travelled.'

He grinned. 'But not your lovers.'

'No. Not my lovers. There is something to be said for experience in the bedroom. Practice does make perfect, I've found.'

His eyebrows lifted. 'So you *have* had a sheikh or two in your bed?'

She gave him a coy glance. 'I'm not a kiss-and-tell kind of girl.'

'Thank heaven for small mercies,' he said, surprising her constantly with how well he spoke English, knowing all the right phrases and idioms. 'But let me remind you that I haven't even kissed you yet. Not a proper kiss, anyway.'

'No. You haven't.'

'Should I remedy that?'

'Not out here,' she said with a flash of panic, aware suddenly that she wasn't ready yet for their verbal foreplay to become reality. Maybe she would never be ready. The way she was feeling was quite frightening. So were the images which kept popping into her head.

Veronica's hand trembled a little as she retrieved the key from the geranium pot and unlocked the sliding door. It was cooler inside. Pity *she* wasn't. She didn't turn to see if he'd followed her—because she knew instinctively he would have. Instead, she switched on the lights then walked quickly over to the kitchen area, finding safety behind the long breakfast bar before turning to face him.

'Would you like something to drink?' she asked him. 'Coffee? Tea? *Water?*' she finished drily.

His smile showed he recognised her action for the delaying tactic that it was.

'I would prefer a glass of cognac. Or a port. Laurence has a magnificent one which he used to buy by the caseload. Have you been down to Laurence's wine cellar yet?'

'No,' she admitted. 'I couldn't find it.' In truth, she hadn't really looked.

'I'll show you where it is,' he offered, and held out his hand to her again.

'I need to go to the bathroom first,' she prevaricated. Although, now she thought about it, it was the truth. Her bladder had suddenly started protesting.

Veronica dashed off to the master bedroom which had an *en suite* bathroom. When she returned to the living area a few minutes later, Leonardo was there, his left arm resting on the marble mantelpiece as he stared broodingly into the empty fireplace.

'I still can't believe Laurence is dead,' he said, glancing back up at her with touchingly sad eyes.

Veronica was quite moved by his grief.

'He should have contacted you earlier,' he went on with an angry flash in his dark eyes. 'He was your *papa*. He was your flesh and blood. It was wrong of him to keep you a secret.'

'I think so too,' she agreed with a catch in her throat. 'But it's too late now.'

'*Si*. Much too late. I do not understand what he was thinking.'

'Neither do I.'

Leonardo frowned. 'Possibly he wasn't thinking at all. He was very depressed after Ruth died. Very grumpy too, at times. But I still liked him. He was good to me when I needed him. I miss him. Terribly. As strange as it might seem, he was my best friend, despite our age difference. He was always totally honest with me. And I liked that.'

'Honesty is a good virtue in a friend,' Veronica choked out, struggling a little with this conversation. *She* would liked to have been her father's best friend too.

'I have made you sad,' Leonardo said with a combination of regret and frustration in his voice. 'I did not walk you home to make you sad. Now, no more delaying tactics,' he went on with suddenly hungry eyes. 'I don't want coffee, or cognac. Not even that port I told you about. I just want you, Veronica. Only you…'

CHAPTER FOURTEEN

ONLY ME, VERONICA thought breathlessly as she watched him remove his arm from the mantelpiece and slowly walk towards her.

He could not have said anything more perfect. Or more seductive. If ever she'd needed to be wanted the way Leonardo professed to want her, it was now.

This time, she went into his arms without hesitation. And without any more qualms. Or worries. It was as though with those impassioned words he'd blinded her to the slightly sordid reality of the situation and turned their assignation into something sweet. Romantic, even.

Her arms wound up around his neck and slowly pulled his mouth down onto hers. But within seconds of his lips meeting hers the timbre of the moment changed. Suddenly, there was nothing sweet or romantic about his kiss. Or her response to it. The inner fire which she'd been desperately trying to douse all day sprang back into life with a vengeance. It was like the most savage bush fire, the ones which scorched everything in their path. Up on tiptoe, she pressed her open mouth to his like a woman dying of thirst, with the moisture of *his* mouth her salvation. When his tongue dived deep, her lips closed around it and sucked hard. He gasped, then moaned, then lifted her up off her feet. She wrapped her legs around his waist and he carried her like that into the master bedroom. There, he threw her across the bed, his breathing ragged as he glared down at her.

'*Dio*,' he muttered, shaking his head as he kicked off his shoes and started stripping off his clothes.

Veronica tried to think. Tried to will herself to move. But her mind was all on him, on this magnificent male animal whom she wanted as she had never wanted anyone before. Her hungry gaze ogled him shamelessly as he undressed, her eyes stunned by his rapidly unfolding beauty. Naked, he was everything she'd imagined and more. Not too big or too small. No flaws. Just perfect in every way. She loved the olive colour of his skin, and the sculptured look of his stomach muscles. She loved his broad shoulders and his long, strong legs. Skier's legs. But most of all she loved the length and strength of his erection.

When she started thinking of how he would feel sliding into her she *did* move, her hands reaching up under her skirt and ripping off her panties, uncaring that she'd ruined them. A need was possessing her, a need so powerful and impassioned that there was no room for shame. Or decorum.

'Hurry,' she choked out.

For a long moment he just stood there beside the bed and stared down at her, his expression stunned. Veronica groaned with frustration, lifting her skirt up and spreading her knees.

'Just do it,' she begged, her desire now desperate. She was so turned on she feared she might come with him still standing there staring at her. 'Please, Leonardo...'

Finally, he fell upon her, entering her with little finesse, taking her hands and scooping them up above her head, holding her captive against the bed as he pounded into her. Surprisingly, she didn't come straight away, moaning and groaning as her head whipped from side to side. He kept saying things to her in Italian. Not romantic-sounding words. Hard, hot, perhaps angry, words. After what felt like for ever she came, and he came with her, their bodies shuddering together, their mouths gasping wide. Veronica squeezed her eyes shut, afraid to look into his, afraid of what she might see.

Please God, not disgust!

He let her arms go with a sound she could not identify. Whatever, it didn't sound happy.

'I did not use protection,' he growled.

She opened her eyes, not to an expression of disgust, but anger.

'You did not give me time!' he accused her in harsh tones.

He was possibly right. But she hadn't exactly put a gun to his head and forced him to have sex with her. If he'd wanted to use a condom, he could have. She opened her mouth to apologise then closed it again. Why should she say sorry? Practising safe sex was as much his responsibility as hers.

'You don't have to worry,' she shot back at him. 'I won't get pregnant.'

Veronica knew her body well and her period was due next Monday. She should have ovulated more than a week ago.

He clasped the sides of her face and glowered down at her. 'You are on the pill?' he demanded to know.

His attitude both frightened and annoyed her. If she told him she wasn't, he would probably have a conniption. Or a tantrum. She could imagine that Leonardo would have had tantrums as a boy. He was spoiled rotten. That much was clear. She hated lies, but there were times when a little white lie was the only option.

'Yes, of course,' she said. 'What do you think I am, a fool? And, whilst we're asking each other personal questions, I hope you don't make a habit of practising unsafe sex.'

'Never!' he said, looking quite offended.

'Before tonight, that is,' she pointed out archly.

It shocked Veronica how quickly her feelings for Leonardo could go from uncontrollable desire to outright dislike.

He reared up onto his elbows with a strange look on his face. Was that shock in his eyes? Or just confusion? Clearly, he wasn't used to losing control as he just had.

'I think I should go,' he said and suddenly withdrew, scrambling up off the bed and reaching for his clothes.

Tears of hurt and humiliation stung Veronica's eyes. Suddenly, she felt both used and very cheap. She must have a made a sound because he turned and saw her distress.

'No, no,' he said hurriedly, sitting back down and pulling her up into his arms again. 'You were lovely. I am just not used to acting so foolishly. It has thrown me. There was this girl once. But no,' he said with a bitter laugh. 'I will not bore you with the details. Needless to say, it is a case of once bitten, twice shy when it comes to risking an unwanted child.'

Understanding dawned. He'd been targeted once before by a gold digger, some girl who'd tried to trap him with a pregnancy.

'I would not try to trap you with a baby, Leonardo,' she said gently, and stroked the back of his head, feeling suddenly tender towards him. Thank God she was certain there would be no unwanted pregnancy from tonight's mistake. 'It's a rotten thing for a girl to do.'

'It is.'

'Did she have a baby, this girl?'

He drew back and smiled a relieved smile. 'Happily, no. She wasn't pregnant at all. She just said she was.'

'What a wicked deception.' Veronica knew all about wicked deceptions. They scarred people. This girl had scarred Leonardo, trying to trap him into marriage before he was ready. And no doubt without love involved.

Leonardo sighed heavily, then stood up and started dressing. 'I would have married her,' he confessed as he zipped up his trousers.

'But why, if you didn't love her?'

'It is a question of honour,' he said, pulling on his shirt. 'The baby would have been mine.'

'That is a little old-fashioned, Leonardo. Honestly, an Australian man wouldn't have felt obliged to marry such a girl.'

'But to walk away from your own child,' Leonardo said, frowning. 'That is not right. I could not do that.'

'You didn't have to walk away. You could have paid child care and demanded visiting rights. Why marry when there's no love involved? To do that is not right, either.'

His smile was wry. 'Italians feel differently on the subject.'

Veronica shook her head. 'Then you are different, all right.'

'Apparently so. Now, I really must go, or *Mamma* will start getting ideas. She already likes you enormously,' he added, laughing. 'If I stay any longer she will be planning our wedding before the weekend is out.'

Veronica laughed too. 'Then you'd definitely better go.'

'I'll pick you up at ten tomorrow morning. Don't wear a dress or a skirt. We're going in a helicopter, remember?'

'Okay.'

'Ciao.'

She watched him leave, thinking that perhaps she should have told him she was afraid of helicopters. But she didn't want to sound like a scaredy-cat. She liked it that he saw her as a bit of an adventuress. Which she had been, once. She'd thought nothing of travelling to the snowfields in Europe on her own every year when she'd been doing her uni course. She would save up all year from her two part-time jobs and splurge the lot every January, backpacking from one ski resort to the next. It wasn't till the last year of her course that she'd been able to make it a working holiday, using her qualifications to get a job as a remedial masseuse at one of the top ski resorts.

That was where she'd run into Leonardo.

Who would have believed what fate had had in store for her when she'd rejected him that night? Veronica would never have imagined that she would actually have sex with Leonardo several years later. Or that she would jump into bed with him so quickly and so shamelessly. For years after the night of that party, she'd told herself firmly that she'd imagined how turned on she was at the time, and how difficult it had been to resist him. But she'd known, the moment he'd introduced himself over the phone two weeks ago, that he was the most dangerously attractive man she'd ever met.

Yes, she'd come to Capri to find out about her father. But she finally admitted that she'd also come because of Leonardo. To meet him again and see if all her sexual feelings about the man were just fantasies or the real McCoy. Well, now she had her answer, didn't she? The desires he could evoke in her—oh, so effortlessly—were real. Very real.

Not dangerous, though. Unless she did something stupid, such as fall in love with him.

Which Veronica resolved not to do. She wasn't a silly young girl any longer. She was an adult, with a wealth of experience behind her. She knew precisely what she was dealing with.

Leonardo was a playboy and a commitment-phobe. He pretended that one day he would settle down but she very much doubted it. Clearly, he didn't want to sleep with the same woman for the rest of his life. All he wanted to do with the opposite sex was have fun.

Well, that was what she wanted from him, Veronica decided. Just fun.

To want anything more would be crazy.

And she wasn't crazy. She was, however, crazy about Leonardo's body. Oh, Lord he was just so gorgeous. Her stomach lurched as she recalled how it had felt when he'd entered her. She could hardly wait till tomorrow.

Showing her Capri by helicopter wouldn't take long, Veronica imagined as she hurried inside. She had no doubt that when he brought her home afterwards he would stay for a while. Maybe even for the rest of the day. Things tonight had been so rushed. Thrilling, yes, and very satisfying. Had she ever had an orgasm like it?

All her internal muscles squeezed tight as she tried to relive the moment when she'd splintered apart in his arms. But the memory was already fading.

I needed to experience it again. And again. I don't want to ever forget.

Veronica reached the master bedroom where she stared at the indentations their bodies had made on the bed. Tomorrow, she vowed, they would not be having a quickie on top of the quilt. They would lie naked together *in* the bed. She would insist Leonardo make love to her more slowly, with plenty of adventurous foreplay. Veronica had never been into oral sex all that much, but she suspected she would be with Leonardo. Just thinking about going down on him made her quiver with anticipation. She could hardly wait. She would also insist that before he entered her he remembered to use a condom. Then, whilst she was totally protected, she would whisper for him to do *everything* to her.

A shudder ran through Veronica at this last thought. Her feelings for this man, she finally accepted, *were* dangerous. And threatening to run out of control.

Get a grip, girl, came her stern warning. *You will be going home to Australia in three weeks' time and Leonardo will become nothing but a memory. Have fun with him, like your mother said, but never forget that this will just be a fling, not a for ever moment.*

Veronica went to bed with this warning at the forefront of her mind. She fell asleep surprisingly quickly. And didn't dream. Which, when she woke, seemed a good portent for the day ahead. The weather looked excellent, the sun already up, the skies clear and cloudless. A good day for sightseeing, especially by air.

Now, what was she going to wear?

CHAPTER FIFTEEN

VERONICA DIDN'T DISOBEY Leonardo's instruction and wear a dress, despite being tempted, as she'd bought a couple of lovely sundresses for this trip. Instead, she sensibly chose three-quarter-length cuffed blue jeans, teaming them with a peasant-style pink-and-blue blouse and flat brown sandals. She gave in to vanity, however, and left her freshly shampooed hair down, hoping that her straw sunhat would control her sometimes wayward waves.

Not the only wayward thing about her, she accepted as ten o'clock approached. Despite all her warnings of the night before, her heartbeat took off and a perversely delicious tension invaded her lower body. Several deep breaths later, things hadn't improved.

Leonardo was right on time, his own outfit just as casual as her own. He too was wearing blue jeans, matched with a simple white T-shirt and lightweight navy jacket. The day might be sunny but it wasn't hot. She suspected his clothes were designer labels, because the fit and materials were superb. But she also suspected he would look just as good in anything. It was a case of the man making the clothes rather than the other way round. Leonardo was a total hunk who just exuded sex appeal. All of a sudden, Veronica wished they weren't going anywhere. She wanted to grab him and drag him inside. Wanted to spend the whole day in bed with him.

Hopefully, her eyes didn't say as much. She did have some pride left. Not a lot, she decided ruefully. But enough. Though, it wavered when he said how lovely *she* looked. Lord, but this was one wickedly seductive man.

'I'll just get the rest of my things,' she said, quickly putting her sunglasses on, then grabbing her straw bag and hat.

Locking up was achieved without any embarrassing fumbling, Veronica depositing the key in the geranium pot before glancing up at Leonardo.

'Let's hope all your wine is still there when we get back,' she quipped drily.

He grinned. 'It will be. Have you found the cellar yet?'

'No. I keep forgetting to look.'

'I'll show you where it is when we get back. This way,' he said, and cupped her left elbow, leading her not towards the stone steps but round the back of the house, where a taxi awaited them on the gravel courtyard.

It wasn't Franco's yellow convertible. This one was olive-green and much smaller. With a proper roof.

'Saturday is Franco's busiest day,' Leonardo explained as he steered her towards the already opened back door. 'This is Ricardo. Ricardo, this is Veronica, Laurence's long-lost daughter.'

Ricardo smiled at her. 'She looks like him,' he said, then just got on with the driving.

'Does everyone on Capri know who I am?' she asked quietly.

Leonardo shrugged. 'Pretty much. You can't keep any secrets on Capri. Why? Does it bother you?'

'I guess not.'

'By the way, the Hotel Fabrizzi is fully booked for tonight. With a group from America. I hate the noise, so I might have to throw myself on the mercy of one of my neighbours.'

Veronica's heart flipped over, but she managed to keep a poker face, determined not to let this devil know how excited she was by the thought of having him stay with her the whole night.

'Oh?' she said in a superbly nonchalant tone. 'Which neighbour were you thinking of asking?'

'There is only one who has a suitably large guest bedroom.'

'Will everyone on Capri know that you stayed at my place?' she asked him quietly, so that the driver couldn't hear.

'Not everyone. But *Mamma* certainly will.'

'Will that cause you problems?'

Leonardo shrugged. 'Nothing I can't handle.'

Veronica didn't doubt it.

'Let it be on your head, then, Leonardo,' she told him. 'Don't come crying to me when your parents mistakenly think your intentions towards me are serious.'

'Who says they aren't?' he asked with a look that she couldn't decipher.

It rattled her, that look. His dark eyes fairly smouldered at her from under half-lowered lids. She was still wondering what it meant when his tautly held lips split into a wide smile.

'Got you,' he said with a nudge against her ribs.

'You are a wicked man, Leonardo Fabrizzi,' she said, both annoyed and flustered that she would think, even for a moment, that Leonardo was anything other than a highly accomplished playboy.

Leonardo grinned. 'She says I am a wicked man, Ricardo. Is she right?'

'You, Leonardo?' Ricardo threw a shocked glance over his shoulder. 'No, no. Leonardo—he is a good man. When my Louisa got sick, he pay for her to go to the best doctors in Rome. The best hospital. He always do things like that. We all love Leonardo on Capri.' And he glared at Veronica in the rear-view mirror.

'I was only joking,' she said hurriedly. 'Tell him, Leonardo.' She poked him in the ribs.

'She was only joking, Ricardo,' he reassured the taxi driver. 'She loves me too, don't you, Veronica?'

Lord, but he was incorrigible. She rolled her eyes at him. 'But of course, Leonardo. How could I not?'

'I have no idea,' he retorted, his expression one of barely controlled amusement.

Her palm itched to smack him. The man was a devil, wicked to the core. Or so she wanted to believe. But some inner instinct told Veronica that his wickedness was only skin-deep, that he had a genuinely warm heart. His love for his family and his friends spoke of a different man from the callous playboy who flitted from woman to woman, using them for his pleasure without care or commitment. Without love.

It seemed odd to her, now that she thought about it more deeply, for an Italian man of Leonardo's family background not to want to get married and have a family of his own. She wondered what it was in his past that stopped him from settling down. She doubted it was that close call with the unwanted pregnancy. Perhaps it had something to do with his early retirement from the sport he'd been so passionate about. She might have asked him, if she'd imagined for a moment he would tell her the truth. But Veronica knew instinctively that he would not discuss his innermost feelings, certainly not with a woman who was just a ship passing in the night.

This last thought bothered her for a few seconds, until common sense came to the rescue. She *was* just a ship passing in the night. That didn't mean their brief encounter couldn't be both memorable and enjoyable. Veronica was determined not to complicate the weekend with qualms about what she was doing with Leonardo. She was an adult. She was entitled to a sex life, entitled to have some fun for a change. Even her mother thought so.

So why was she feeling as though she was running a risk in spending more time with this man? Why did the thought of his making love to her again bring a measure of anxiety along with the inevitable excitement? It annoyed her, this waffling in her head. *He* wasn't worried. Just look at him sitting there, totally relaxed in her company.

Their arrival at the helipad might have been a welcome distraction from her mental to-ing and fro-ing. Unfortunately, the sight of the helicopter brought new worries. She'd forgotten, for a moment, how frightened she was of flying in one.

'Oh, dear,' she said, her stomach somersaulting as she stared at the fragile-looking craft. It wasn't the large one Leonardo had arrived in yesterday. This was just a glass bubble with blades attached.

'What is it?' Leonardo asked straight away. 'What's wrong?'

'That helicopter,' she blurted out, pointing at it as they both climbed out of the taxi. 'Is that the one we're going up in?'

'Yes. Why?'

'It looks…small.'

'It is small. It's built for just two passengers.'

She turned to stare at him with wide eyes. 'But…but…'

'Don't worry. I'm a licensed helicopter pilot. And that particular helicopter is brand new.'

CHAPTER SIXTEEN

'ARE YOU OKAY?' Leonardo asked Veronica gently as he strapped her in. She did look a little pale.

'I… I suppose so.'

'Here. Put this on,' He gave her a headset that had a microphone attached. 'Once we're up and running, it'll be noisy and you'll need this to communicate.' He showed her how to put it on before turning and putting his own on.

'Have you always been afraid of flying?' he asked, never having experienced such fear himself. He loved flying, especially when he was the pilot.

'Only in helicopters,' she told him.

'I see. Don't worry. I won't let anything happen to you.' When he leant over and touched her cheek Leonardo was surprised at how tender he felt towards her. How protective. She seemed so vulnerable all of a sudden, nothing like the rather bold creature of the night before. He would have kissed her if the microphone hadn't been in his way. Instead, he smiled over at her, catching her eye and sending her a silent message of reassurance.

Veronica's heart flipped over at the almost loving look Leonardo sent her. For a split second, she almost believed he cared about her. This was his skill as a seducer, she supposed. To make women think he cared.

But he didn't. Not really. She knew that. Perversely, knowing the sort of man she was dealing with made no difference to her female reaction, either to his warm smile or the promise of safety in his eyes.

'We'll start with Capri, then I'll take you over for a bird's eye view of the Amalfi coast,' he told her as she started up the engine. 'We might even fly over Mount Vesuvius.'

'But…but…' she protested, having presumed that within fifteen minutes she'd safely be back on the ground. Capri was, after all, a rather small island.

'No buts today, Veronica. I've hired this little beauty for four hours and I don't intend to waste them. After you've seen the Amalfi Coast, we'll set down at Sorrento for lunch. I've booked us a garden table at the best *trattoria* in town. Then, if we have time, we'll fly south for a quick peek at Naples from above before heading back here. How does that sound?' he asked with a quick glance her way as they lifted off.

Veronica's stomach lifted off with them, so all Leonardo got in answer to his possibly rhetorical question was a sucked in gasp.

'Breathe,' he told her firmly. 'And stop worrying. I'm a very good pilot.'

She didn't doubt it. But his reassurance didn't stop her anxiety. Or the gymnastics in her stomach. His breathing advice did eventually work. Either that, or she was soon so distracted by the magnificence of the view below that she forgot to be afraid.

Leonardo circled the island three times, pointing out the same places of interest that Franco had shown her. But everything looked better from up in the sky. Better and even more beautiful. The ancient Roman ruins. The huge rocks jutting out of the sea. The small towns and the cute little beaches. Some of the villas they flew over were splendid, with ordered gardens and big blue swimming pools, whilst others were much smaller, surrounded by different types of garden. Clearly, these houses were owned by the ordinary people who'd always lived here, not the billionaires who'd bought properties on Capri for other reasons. Privacy, perhaps. But more likely to impress. Veronica suspected there were quite a few of those.

Not Leonardo, however. Veronica was sure he didn't want to buy Laurence's villa to impress. It wasn't that kind of place. Was it just the view he coveted, or something else? She would like to ask him but not right now. Right now she didn't want to say or do anything to spoil the memory of what she was seeing.

Suddenly, the helicopter swung to the right and set off away from Capri, heading for the mainland.

'Time for the Amalfi coast now,' Leonardo said into her earphones.

She'd thought Capri was amazingly beautiful from the air, but the Amalfi coast soon showed her why it was one of the most visited tourist spots in Italy. Veronica hardly knew where to look. It was just one spectacular town after another. All of them hugged the shore with lots of the buildings perched on the very edges of breathtaking cliffs which plunged into the sea. Once again, most of the villas were white, which at the moment shone brilliantly under the midday sun.

'You like?' Leonardo said when she sighed her admiration.

'Oh, Leonardo, your country is incredible. But also a little bit scary. I wouldn't like to drive on that road down there.' And she pointed to the one that hugged the cliffs.

'You would love it, in the right car. A Ferrari would be perfect.'

'And I suppose you own a Ferrari?'

'But of course. Unfortunately, it is in Milan. I could drive it down one weekend, if you would like me to.'

'Don't be silly. I wouldn't ask you to do that. It's too far.'

He shrugged. 'The roads are good. And the car is fast.'

'I don't doubt it, with you behind the wheel. You have a thing for speed, don't you?'

'Si. It is a passion of mine. To do things fast. I love anything which gets my heart beating. My uncle says I am an adrenalin addict. The only time I slow down is when I'm on Capri.'

'And not always then,' she said drily.

He laughed. 'If you're referring to what happened last night, then that was more your fault then mine. When we get back to the villa I will show you how relaxed I can be in bed. Sex is one thing I don't usually rush. I like to take my time with a woman. When she lets me,' he added, casting her a rueful glance.

Veronica was thankful she wasn't a blusher, but his pointed remark evoked a blossoming of heat deep inside her. She couldn't wait for them to get back to Capri. And back to bed.

Lord, but he made her totally shameless. But then he was shameless too. She'd never met a man who spoke so openly about sex, and who just presumed she wouldn't say no.

Which of course she wouldn't. She *couldn't*. Lust had taken possession of her body, a lust so strong and so fierce that it might have frightened her, if she hadn't been so turned on. The level of her sexual excitement propelled her past all common sense and conscience. She wanted Leonardo. And she would have him. After all, there was nothing to stop her, least of all Leonardo himself. *He* wasn't about to say no, was he?

'It's time for lunch,' he said abruptly. 'I don't know about you, but I'm suddenly very hungry.'

CHAPTER SEVENTEEN

LEONARDO DIDN'T WANT to bother with lunch. He wanted to take her straight back to Capri. It wasn't food he was hungry for. It was Veronica.

He didn't dare look at her again as he flew as fast as he could to Sorrento. That last glance had almost undone him in a way he couldn't begin to process. Because it was outside even *his* experience. Over the years he'd had countless sexual adventures with countless beautiful women. But Veronica was unlike any he'd ever encountered, a strange mixture of siren fused with the most bewitching vulnerability.

Uncharacteristically, he wanted to ask her about this man—or men—who'd hurt her in the past, but experience warned him against going down that road. Asking a girl about her emotional baggage was fraught with danger—the danger of getting emotionally involved himself. He didn't want that, especially with Veronica. Why, he wasn't sure. A reason hovered at the edge of his mind, a reason which threatened to derail him totally. So he ruthlessly pushed it aside and concentrated on what he was good at where women were concerned.

Sex.

Veronica had always been able to pick up on people's emotions by their body language. After she watched them for a while, she could see past their facade and tune into their pain, both physical and mental. It was what made her a good physio: the way she talked to her clients whilst treating them, the way she could find out what was bothering them and subtly offer some advice.

So, when Leonardo suddenly turned all stiff and silent

next to her, she knew something was bothering him. But what? This time she had absolutely no idea.

They landed safely, if a little roughly, in Sorrento, a strong breeze off the sea moving the small helicopter around a bit. Strangely, Veronica had ceased to worry about surviving the flight, her focus entirely on the man beside her. She ached to say something which would break the awkward silence that had unexpectedly developed between them. Finally, just as he shut down the engine and the blades started to slow, she thought of something suitably innocuous.

'Oh, Lord, I forgot to take any photographs,' she said with true regret as she took off her headset. 'When I woke this morning to such good weather, I planned to take pictures of everything and send them to Mum.'

When he took off his own headset and smiled over at her, Veronica's heart squeezed tight with relief.

'Don't panic,' he said, his eyes holding hers. 'You can take photos on the way back, both of Sorrento and Capri.'

'You're right,' she replied, once again struck by the beauty of Leonardo's eyes. 'I can do that. No need to panic.'

But if her thudding heart was anything to go by there was every reason to panic. She didn't want to fall in love with this man. That would be a disaster!

Keep it light and keep it sexy, she lectured herself. *Don't start worrying about what he was worrying about a minute ago. It probably wasn't anything serious, anyway. It certainly wasn't anything to do with* you.

'Gosh, we're up high here,' she said as he helped her down from the helicopter.

'Sorrento is built up on a volcanic shelf. Which reminds me. I didn't take you over Vesuvius. Sorry. I forgot.'

'That's all right. Flying over a volcano in a helicopter isn't on my bucket list.'

His eyes sparkled with genuine amusement, his earlier worries clearly gone. 'You're too young to have a bucket list.'

'Never too young for a bucket list,' she quipped back.

'Perhaps you're right.'

He took her elbow and directed her over to a waiting taxi.

'What would be on *your* bucket list?' she asked him on the way. 'If you ever made one, that is.'

'There isn't anything I want to do that I haven't tried.'

Except marriage and children, came the unexpected and unwanted thought. But then Leonardo didn't want marriage and children, did he?

Never forget that, Veronica. The man is a playboy. Which translates as a man who's stayed as a boy and who plays at life. Not a man to start having serious thoughts about. Or to care about.

'You should get your phone out and take some photos on the way to the restaurant,' he advised her. 'And again, once we're inside. This particular *trattoria* is a rather special place.'

It was. Very special. And very beautiful.

The formal dining room inside was extremely glamorous, worthy of a palace. Veronica snapped several shots of the plush surrounds and elegantly set tables. But they didn't eat there, Leonardo ushering her through to what could only be described as a garden room. It reminded Veronica of eating under the pergola last night. But this was on a much grander scale, with glass and iron-work tables instead of wood, and the plushest of cushions on the chairs. Above, across an intricate framework hung a canopy, not of grape vines, but an assortment of climbing vines which boasted scented flowers of all colours. The sky could be glimpsed through the odd break in the foliage, suggesting that this room would be unavailable if it was raining.

But it wasn't raining. The day was glorious, as was the setting, the service *and* the company.

'What would you like to drink?' Leonardo asked as he perused the drinks menu. 'I won't be having any alcohol myself. I never drink when I'm flying. I'll just be having mineral water.'

'Then I will too,' she said, not wanting to be tempted to get herself tipsy to soothe her nerves. If she was going to have a fling with Leonardo—which undoubtedly she was—then she preferred to do it with a clear head.

'Are you sure?' he asked. 'You don't even want one glass of wine?'

'No, your company is intoxicating enough,' she quipped flirtatiously.

Surprise flashed into his eyes for a split second, followed by a wry smile.

'You don't have to flatter me, Veronica,' he said. 'I'm a sure thing.'

She couldn't help it. She laughed.

'I'm so glad to hear that, Leonardo,' Veronica said, deciding this was the way to play it—light-heartedly and a bit naughtily. 'Last night was over far too quickly.'

'I fully agree. It was little more than an entree. But, speaking of food, here comes the waiter. Would you like me to order for you?'

'*Si,*' she said, and he grinned at her.

Veronica had no idea what he ordered but felt confident it would all be delicious.

The mineral water arrived quickly, as did a small plate of herbed bread.

'Would you mind if I asked you something personal?' she said once the waiter departed.

'That depends,' came his careful answer. 'I told you before, I don't discuss past relationships.'

Her smile was amused. 'You don't *have* any past relationships to discuss, from what I've read. No, I'm curious about why you want to buy the villa so much. Is it just the view, or somewhere private to escape to when you visit your parents?'

'I suppose it's a bit of both. But it also holds good memories for me. The weeks I stayed with Laurence after I broke my ankle were some of the happiest in my life. I learned to control my usual restless self and found pleasure in activities other than the physical. Of course, I have your father to thank for that. He was a man of the mind more than the body. And a very good teacher.'

Veronica found it hard not to feel jealous. How she would love to have spent weeks at the villa with her father; to be taught chess by him, and listen to his favourite music sitting by his side on the terrace. She might have even learned to appreciate wine.

Still, it was good to hear nice things about him, even if it was second-hand information.

'How did you break your ankle?' she asked. 'Skiing, I suppose.'

'No. Rock climbing.'

'Oh, Lord, you are a one, aren't you?'

He shrugged. 'I can't help it. I like physical challenges.'

'Perhaps you should stick to less risky ones.'

'Like making love all night, perhaps?'

Their eyes locked, Veronica seeing the sizzling hunger in his, *knowing* that her own eyes were just as hungry.

It was fortuitous that the entree arrived at that moment, a steaming pasta dish with bacon, aubergine and mushroom. Veronica welcomed the opportunity to look away from Leonardo's hot gaze.

'This is delicious,' she said after a couple of mouthfuls. 'Glad it's just a small serving, though. It's rather filling.'

'That's why I ordered grilled swordfish for the main, with just a light salad. I wanted to leave some room for dessert.'

Veronica winced. 'I hope it's not as fattening as that dessert your mother served me last night.'

'Not quite.'

When it finally arrived, Veronica gave him a droll look.

'You are such a liar,' she said as she eyed the large custard-filled pastry served with a huge dollop of whipped cream. But it was too mouth-watering to resist. Just like Leonardo.

'I thought you might need some extra calories to survive the night ahead,' he drawled.

Veronica tried to think of a witty comeback but she couldn't, her mind having gone blank at his provocative remark.

The dessert was followed by coffee which would have brought Lazarus back from the dead, and which left Veronica feeling quite hyped up. But underneath the caffeine-induced buzz lay some very female nerves. Silly, really, given she'd loved their passionate encounter last night.

But this was different, wasn't it? Last night had been brilliant but spontaneous. To *plan* sex, to anticipate it as she had done all day, was not conducive to calm. It was like sitting an important exam. No matter how many times you'd done exams before, no matter how much you'd studied the subject, there was always that fear of something cropping up that would throw you.

Best leave everything up to him, Veronica determined as he paid the bill then steered her out to another waiting taxi. *He obviously knows what to do. He's had enough practice.*

The flight back to Capri was still a welcome distraction, Veronica taking photographs of absolutely everything.

'Mum's going to want to come here for a holiday after I send her these,' she said at one point.

'Then she should,' Leonardo replied. 'She can stay at the villa.'

'It'll be *your* villa soon.'

'True.'

'She could stay at the Hotel Fabrizzi,' Veronica said with a mischievous glance. 'I can recommend it.'

'Would you come with her?'

'Probably. But if I did we wouldn't stay at your parents' hotel. Sophia might think I'd come back to see you and start matchmaking again.'

When he just shrugged at that, she shook her head at him. 'You really shouldn't encourage her, you know. She honestly thinks you're in the market for a wife.'

'I've found that to argue with *Mamma* only encourages her more. Besides, I *will* be in the market for a wife. One day. When the right girl comes along,' he added in a drily amused voice.

She snorted at that. 'Your *mamma* will be long gone by then. You are a cruel man, Leonardo.'

'Not at all,' he denied. 'I am a very kind man. But at the moment I'm also a very single man. And enjoying it,' he added with the wickedest glance thrown her way.

A sexually charged shiver rippled down her spine, heat spreading through her lower body. Her nipples hardened and her belly tightened. All from just a look.

Oh, my.

'Go back to taking your photographs, Veronica,' he ordered thickly. 'And I'll go back to making sure we get down safely. There's a strong wind blowing over Capri and this is a very light machine.'

He got them down safely, but he was right about the wind. It whipped her hair into a right mess on the way to the waiting taxi, which thankfully wasn't Franco's. No way did she want to make idle conversation with Franco who, she suspected, was somewhat of a gossip.

Finger-combing her hair into some semblance of order, she climbed into the taxi ahead of Leonardo, who told the driver to take them to the Hotel Fabrizzi. She winced at this, not wanting to endure talking to *any* of Leonardo's family, especially not his mother.

'It's all right,' he whispered to her. '*Mamma* will be busy inside. You can dash off up the path to the villa and I'll follow shortly. I just have to collect a few things for my overnight stay.'

'But what will they all think?' she whispered back.

He shrugged again, that dismissive shrug he used a lot.

'I refuse to live my life by other people's expectations. Now, hush up.'

She fell silent then. And so did he.

It was only a short drive from the helipad to the hotel. But the silence made it seem longer. It was so sexy, that silence, sending Veronica's head spinning with desire. By the time they turned into the courtyard she was agitated beyond belief. She hurried out of the taxi then rushed away from him, under the pergola and up the steep steps. She didn't look back. She knew he would soon come after her; knew they would soon be together.

Another erotic shiver raced through her as she dived into the pot to retrieve the front-door key. No, not a shiver this time. A shudder. The kind of bone-shaking shudder that a floundering ship might make. It reminded Veronica of her earlier idea that she and Leonardo were ships passing in the night.

If only that were true…

They weren't ships passing in the night, without consequences or complications. They were on a collision course.

Veronica shuddered again as she ran inside. She was still nervous but not afraid. She should have been afraid. Why wasn't she afraid? Why was it that she didn't care about consequences or complications? Was this what lust did to you—made you reckless and foolish? Made you uncaring of anything but the promise of pleasure?

Not that Leonardo was a promise of pleasure. He *was* pleasure.

Such thinking made Veronica feel hot and sticky all over. She winced at the thought that she might smell of perspiration. And other things…

She'd always been very particular about personal hygiene, hating it when clients came to her without having a shower first. Would she have time for a quick shower? she wondered.

It had only been a minute since she'd left Leonardo.

Surely it would be at least another five minutes before he made an appearance? His mother was likely to collar him and ask him innumerable questions about their day together.

Veronica was already stripping as she hurried towards the master bedroom with its lovely *en suite* bathroom.

CHAPTER EIGHTEEN

LEONARDO WAS GRATEFUL that the hotel was rather chaotic inside, with guests coming and going. He was able to slip into his room and get what he needed for the night without being accosted by his mother or father. Elena did grab him on the way out from where she was stationed behind Reception.

'Going somewhere?' she asked in Italian after eyeing his overnight bag.

'I'm staying in Laurence's guest room tonight,' he replied, also in Italian. 'I can't stand the noise when this place is full.'

'Veronica doesn't mind?' his sister asked with a knowing glint in her eye.

'Why should she mind? She came here to find out about her father. I had more to do with Laurence than any of you so I can tell her everything she wants to know.'

Elena smiled. 'She's very beautiful. She's also very nice. She would make some lucky man a good wife.'

He just smiled, told her not to meddle and left.

But his smile didn't last for long.

It annoyed him lately, how much his family were trying to press him into settling down. He had no intention of marrying some poor girl just to secure an heir. Who cared about carrying on bloodlines and family names these days? It was archaic.

Leonardo hurried as he headed for the path which led up to the villa.

Still…it probably *was* a mistake to stay the whole night with Veronica. He'd always kept his sex life away from Capri. He'd never brought a girlfriend to his parents' hotel, knowing that it was a bad idea. He came here to relax, not get himself into a total twist. Laurence's villa used to be his sanctuary, his refuge. When he'd sat on the terrace, soaking in the view and sipping some of Laurence's fine wine, all his inner demons used to slip away. He hadn't thought about that awful time when the true love of his life—competitive skiing—had been snatched away. He hadn't paced around like he did in his office. He hadn't needed sex to distract him. He'd actually relaxed.

He wasn't relaxed now, was he?

Hell, no. That witch of a girl had undone him, big time.

Leonardo charged up the stone steps two at a time, lust making him impatient.

The sliding glass door being open made him laugh. *Not too worried about security now, eh, Veronica?* Her mind was obviously on other things. He'd felt the sexual tension in her in the taxi. Seen the desire in her dilated eyes.

She wouldn't need much foreplay the first time, he decided as he walked in, dumped his bag in the guest room then went to look for her. The whole day had been foreplay.

When he heard the shower running, Leonardo strode purposefully in its direction.

He'd never actually been in Laurence's bedroom before. But it was a mirror image of the guest bedroom at the other end of the house, just with different furnishings. The bathroom was exactly the same too, the floor and walls covered in grey-and-white marble tiles.

Veronica was in the shower. Naked, of course, her nudity obscured slightly by the glass screen. Even so, he stared.

He hadn't seen her naked before. God, but she was lovely. He adored every inch of her slender but very feminine figure. She had just enough breast. Just enough everything. Leonardo had never been attracted to voluptuous women. He preferred athletic-looking girls.

She must have sensed him standing there in the doorway, staring at her, because suddenly her head whipped round and their eyes met through the wet glass. Did she blush, or was it the heat of the water making her cheeks pink?

When he stepped forward and slid back the screen, she snapped off the taps, then spun round to face him, nervously touching her hair that she'd bundled up on top of her head.

'I… I didn't think you'd be this quick,' she said shakily. 'And I was hot.'

That she was, he thought. But he wasn't crass enough to say so. Instead, he handed her one of the two white towels hanging nearby. She grabbed it and wrapped it around her dripping body, her eyes still touchingly vulnerable. Surely she couldn't be shy? She certainly hadn't been last night.

'I might have a quick shower myself,' he said. 'I could do with cooling down a bit.'

And wasn't that the truth. Leonardo already planned to make it an icy cold shower. The last thing he wanted was a repeat of last night's performance. He'd acted like some randy school boy, unable to control himself.

'Why don't you get us both a couple of glasses of wine?' he suggested. 'And I'll be with you ASAP.'

'Oh. Oh, all right. Does it matter what wine?'

'No. Whatever Carmelina put in the fridge is okay with me.'

Veronica tried not to think as she went in search of the wine; tried not to feel embarrassed at his catching her in the shower. After all, *he* wasn't embarrassed. She suspected that *nothing* embarrassed him. Certainly not nudity.

There were several bottles of white wine in the door of the fridge. Veronica selected a Chablis, then searched the kitchen cupboards for glasses. There were lots, especially wine glasses. One set attracted her. They were quite large, but with long, fine stems in a beautiful shade of green glass. Was it her father who'd liked green glass? she wondered. Or his wife?

This last thought reminded Veronica how quickly she'd

been distracted from her quest to find out everything she
could about her father. It was all Leonardo's fault, she decided when he walked in, obviously naked beneath the white
towel draped low around his hips.

Lord, but he was just so beautiful; the most beautiful
man she'd ever seen. She couldn't think of any model or
movie star who could compare. He was just so perfect. His
face. His skin. His body.

It was his body she kept staring at now. She'd become
rather used to his handsome face and his lovely olive skin.
But she wasn't used to seeing this much of his gorgeous
body. Last night was just a blur in her mind. Over far too
quickly. Her heart pounded as her eyes travelled over him
from head to toe.

Talk about every woman's fantasy come true!

Veronica had always been attracted to fit men. Not the
muscle-bound, weight-lifting type. She preferred the run-
ners and the rowers, men with flab-free stomachs and long,
strong legs. Leonardo had all that and more. His shape was
perfection in her eyes, from his naturally broad shoulders
to his flat stomach, his small waist and slim hips anchored
by long, sexy legs.

Her hand surprised her when it didn't shake as she
handed him a glass of wine.

He took it and lifted it to his lips, his eyes never leaving
hers over the rim. The air in the room suddenly felt thick
with a tension which she knew could only be eased one way.
But she stayed exactly where she was, lifting her own glass
and taking a deep swallow. Not that she needed any alcohol to make her body zing. Every nerve-ending she owned
was already electrified.

He drank the whole glass with agonising slowness, all
the while just looking at her. Not at her body, but deep, deep
into her eyes, searching for a sign perhaps that he could proceed. Either that, or he was just cruelly making her wait.

Finally, just when the anticipation became almost unbearable, Leonardo put his glass down on the nearby counter and closed the gap between them. A slow smile curved his mouth as he took her glass out of her hands and placed it next to his. When he turned back she thought he was going to kiss her. But he didn't. Instead, he reached up and pulled her hair down from the loose knot into which she'd wound it before her shower. It tumbled down around her naked shoulders, thick, soft and wavy. Her crowning glory, her mother always said.

'I've been wanting to do this all day,' he murmured as he ran his fingers through her hair.

Veronica blinked. 'But my hair was down all day.'

'I meant I wanted to touch it.'

'Oh…'

'And to touch *you*.' His hands left her hair and trailed down the sides of her throat then moved under her hair to her shoulders. He cupped them gently, then pulled her close, his mouth descending to hers as though in slow motion. Her own arms hung limply at her sides whilst her head grew light with the most dizzying waves of desire. Despite her seeming attitude of submission, her lips were already parted by the time his made contact, his low groan showing her that he was as turned on as she was. But still he didn't hurry, his tongue sliding sinuously into her mouth until she was beside herself with longing and need.

Her moan betrayed the extent of that need. Leonardo's head immediately lifted.

'*Si*,' he rasped. 'It is torture, is it not?'

She didn't answer him. She *couldn't*.

'You deserve to be tortured,' he ground out as he suddenly bent to scoop her up into his arms. 'You are the sort of woman who drives men mad, with your big violet eyes and your flirtatious ways.'

Veronica found her tongue as he carried her back to the master bedroom. 'I think you've got that the wrong way round, Leonardo. *You* are the sort of man who drives *women* mad. And you know it.'

He looked shocked for a second, and then he shrugged. 'I do have a good record with the ladies.'

Veronica couldn't help it. She started to giggle, and then she really started to laugh.

He threw her onto the bed as he had the night before, his hands finding his hips as he glared down at her.

'I don't see what you find so funny,' he growled.

'Don't you?' She stopped laughing but the corners of her mouth kept itching to smile. He, however, remained standing there with his legs apart, his hands clamped to his hips and his eyes all narrowed and angry. Talk about a typical Italian male! They really didn't have a great sense of humour. But she liked them all the same with their proud, passionate ways.

'I thought we were going to have sex, Leonardo,' she said. 'Not argue.'

His sensually carved lips pouted in the most deliciously sexy way.

'I do not want to have sex with you, Veronica,' he said in clipped tones.

Her eyes widened, her dismay acute. 'You don't?'

'No. I don't. We did that last night. Today, I want to make love to you.'

Her heart flipped right over. Okay, so they were only words, but they were lovely words. *Loving* words. It had been so long since she'd heard loving words said to her. Too long, perhaps. Leonardo's words touched the very depths of her soul.

Be careful here, Veronica, came the protective warning. *Be very careful.*

'I'd like that,' she said, trying not to sound too needy.

'Good.' His face softened as he reached down and plucked the towel away from her. But his eyes stayed hot. Hot and hungry.

'Bellissima,' he murmured, then tossed his own towel away.

He was the one who was *bellissimo*, Veronica thought, looking away from his stunning erection as she wriggled herself around on the bed so that the back of her head rested on the pillows. Leonardo climbed onto the bed, stretching out next to her. He propped himself up on his left elbow whilst he caressed her with his right hand, first one breast and then the other, his gaze intent on the reactions of her nipples, which tightened under his touch.

When she made a small gasp of pleasure, his eyes lifted to hers. 'You like that, don't you?' he said, smiling softly.

'Yes,' she choked out.

'What about this?' he asked, taking the nipple furthest from him between his thumb and forefinger, and slowly but firmly starting to squeeze.

'Oh, God!' she cried out as an electrifying shard of sensation rocketed through her body, making her belly tighten and her thighs quiver.

'And this?' he went on, holding the nipple with a hard grip and twisting it from right to left.

She moaned. It was not a moan of protest or pain. But it wasn't pleasure, either. This wasn't making love, she thought wildly. This was something else, something dark, delicious and troubling. Troubling because she liked it *too* much.

'No, don't,' she half-sobbed after he kept doing it. 'Don't.'

To give him credit he stopped straight away. 'I didn't mean to hurt you,' he said, his expression remorseful.

'Just kiss me,' she said shakily.

He did. And it was lovely. She wrapped her arms around him and drew him down on top of her. Soon, the kissing wasn't enough, of course. Dear heaven, but she wanted him so much. Her legs moved out from under him, spreading wide, her knees lifting in blatant invitation. He groaned, then obliged, sliding into her after only a momentary hesitation. It was fantastic, the feel of his flesh filling hers, the way he rocked back and forth inside her. Her hips moved with him, urging him deeper and deeper. He groaned again, the sound one of torment and frustration. When his rhythm picked up, the sensations were mind-blowing. She'd never felt such pleasure. Or such tension. She was panting and praying, wanting to come but not wanting it to end.

'*Dio,*' he growled, then came, his violent ejaculation propelling her into an orgasm that was as powerful as it was primal. Her fingernails dug into his back as her body bucked under his. Her mind was just as splintered, uncaring of anything but the ecstasy of the here and now.

CHAPTER NINETEEN

LEONARD COULDN'T BELIEVE he'd done it again. He'd lost control and not used a condom. Yet he'd put a couple on the bedside chest earlier, along with his phone and his watch.

Not that it mattered, he supposed.

Or did it? Could he really trust that Veronica was on the pill, like she'd said?

He withdrew abruptly, rolling away from her with a worried sigh.

'What is it?' she asked straight away. 'What's wrong?'

'Nothing,' he muttered, angry with himself now. 'Just…' He glanced over at her, not wanting to spoil things between them, but he simply had to say something. 'I didn't use a condom again.'

'Oh,' she said, blinking as though she herself had only just realised. 'I meant to ask you to use one. But I forgot.'

'I guess it doesn't matter, since you're on the pill,' he went on. 'But let's face it, even the pill isn't one hundred percent safe.'

Now it was her turn to sigh. 'True.'

He wished he hadn't brought the matter up. What they'd just shared had been incredible and he hated that he might have ruined the chance of more of the same.

'Look, Leonardo,' she said with an edge to her voice. 'Trust me when I say there's nothing for you to worry about. Aside from anything else, my period is due on Monday. If by some perverse twist of fate the worst happened, then I would handle it. I certainly wouldn't use a baby to trap you into marriage.'

He couldn't help being shocked. 'You'd have a termination?' He didn't believe in abortion; he had been brought up to think of all life as sacred.

'I didn't say that,' she snapped, sitting up and swinging her legs over the side of the bed. 'I need to go to the bathroom.'

Veronica just made it onto the toilet before the tears came. She didn't know why she was so upset. Perhaps because one minute she'd been lying underneath Leonardo's utterly gorgeous body, thinking she'd died and gone to heaven, and the next he'd rolled away from her, leaving her feeling both abandoned and unloved. He'd spoiled her little romantic fantasy with his worries about having unsafe sex.

It did bother her a bit that once again she herself hadn't thought of protection, especially after she'd planned to insist on it this time. But of course at the back of her mind she'd known she was ninety-nine percent safe. Did he honestly think she'd deliberately risk falling pregnant to a man like him?

The very thought appalled her. At the same time, it upset her that he would think she was anything like that other girl who'd lied to him so shamefully.

But you lied to him too, Veronica. By omission. You let him think you're on the pill but you aren't. Just because you know it's the wrong time of the month to conceive is not an excuse. You still lied to him.

Guilt had her biting her bottom lip. As did regret. The trouble was it was too late to tell him the truth now. He was a cynical man, and possibly ignorant of how well a woman could know her own body. He wouldn't understand that there really was very little risk. She was as regular as clockwork. The only time in years when it had been disrupted was when Jerome had died. Shock and stress, the doctor had said. But eventually everything had settled back into its normal rhythm, not missing a beat since.

Veronica sighed then stood up. Whilst washing her

hands, a quick glance in the vanity mirror showed a tear-stained face and very messy hair. Without stopping to think, she dived into the shower again, turning on the taps, squealing when it came out freezing cold at first. She squealed again when Leonardo suddenly pulled back the screen door.

'Are you all right?' he asked anxiously.

'The…the water was c-cold,' she stammered. 'It…it's getting warmer now.'

His frown smoothed out, replaced by an apologetic smile. 'I am a fool,' he said. 'I trust you, Veronica. Truly I do. Forgive me?'

He didn't wait for a reply, stepping into the shower with her and pulling her into his arms. They kissed under the warm jets of water. Then kissed some more. Leonardo ran his hands up and down her back, then stayed down, cupping her buttocks and yanking her hard against him. His head lifted then and he laughed. 'See what you do to me? Anyone would think I hadn't had sex in months.'

'Poor Leonardo. How long has it been, then?' she asked him with a coquettish glance. 'A whole week at least?'

'Longer than that,' he protested.

'*Two* weeks?'

'You really do have a bad opinion of me. Let me assure you that, since Laurence passed away, sex has been the last thing on my mind.'

His mentioning her father made Veronica sigh. 'I came here to find out about my father, and all I've wanted to do since I arrived so far is be with you. You're like a drug, Leonardo. A very addictive drug.'

'Is that a criticism or a compliment?'

'I'm sure you'll take it as a compliment.'

'If you insist,' he said. And he grinned down at her. 'Come. I'm not one for making love in showers. I much prefer the comfort of a bed.' So saying, he leant past her and turned off the taps before pushing open the glass door.

The nearest towel rail was empty, however, both towels still on the bedroom floor where Leonardo had dropped them.

'There are more towels in the utility room,' Veronica informed him—not very helpfully, since the utility room was some distance away.

'I think we'll just make a dash for the bedroom. Use the towels we left there.'

'All right,' she said, wringing out her hair so that it wouldn't drip too much.

They were like two naughty teenagers who'd gone skinny dipping in the sea and had to run for their clothes. They both made a dive for the nearest towel, actually having a mock tug-of-war before Leonardo gave in and let her have it. She didn't wrap it around herself this time, just rubbed herself dry then bent forward and wound it around her wet hair, before straightening and scrambling into the bed, where she sat up against the pillows with her arms crossed over her bare breasts and her turbaned head feeling ridiculously heavy.

'All done,' she said.

Leonardo shook his own head at her. 'No way,' he said. 'I'm not making love to you with a towel on your head. Take it off.'

There was something in his eyes which put paid to the momentary temptation to refuse. Leonardo, when crossed, was nothing like his usual smiling, charming self. His whole face darkened, his shoulders stiffened. No wonder he'd been such a fierce competitor on the ski slopes. He didn't like to lose. And he didn't like a woman to say no to him.

'My hair's still wet,' she complained, even as she removed the towel and tossed it away.

'I like you wet,' he replied, his good humour restored. As was his sexually charged persona.

Veronica tried to find something saucy to say back but he'd already climbed into the bed beside her, and then he pulled her down under him.

'None of this, either,' he said as he took hold of her arms

and placed them up above her head on the pillows. He didn't hold them there, thank God. She would not have liked that. Or maybe she would have. She seemed to like everything he did to her. She certainly liked it when he slid down her body and started making love to her with his mouth. She loved it, just as she'd imagined she would. He knew exactly where to kiss and where to lick. His lips and tongue were knowing enough, aided adeptly by hands which knew how to move and lift her to give that questing mouth better access to all of her.

He shocked her at times, but she never wanted him to stop. The only sounds coming from her open, panting mouth were the gasps and groans whenever she came: three times in as many minutes. She could hardly believe it. Multiple orgasms were unknown to her personally. She'd heard of them but thought they existed only in books and the imagination of fiction writers.

Not so. This was real. This was her, about to come again.

This time, Leonardo stopped just in time, sliding up her body and into her, taking her breath away with the size of his erection. Clearly, doing what he'd been doing had been a huge turn-on for him as well.

She expected to come straight away but, strangely, she didn't. Maybe she'd run out of orgasms for the day. But slowly, and quite deliciously, his steady rhythm stoked the fire back into her. Her hips began to move with him. He groaned, then whispered her name with the kind of warmth and passion that she'd never heard on any man's lips. Certainly not Jerome's. His love-making, whilst skilful, had been on the clinical side.

Suddenly, something broke within her. Something she could not identify. Not a physical thing but something deeply emotional, evoking a sense of bonding which compelled her to take her arms down from the pillow and wind them tightly around him.

'Leonardo,' she whispered back.

Only then did she come. And so did he, their bodies surrendering, not in a clash of wild shuddering but in gently rolling spasms which made Veronica want to cry. She did cry. But silently. The spasms seemed to go on for ever, which was just as well, giving her tears time to dry and for some common sense to return.

I have not fallen in love with Leonardo, she told herself sternly. *He's just very good at this. Very, very good. Get a grip, Veronica.*

She might have got a grip if she'd had time. And if she wasn't so exhausted. But sleep beckoned, a dark curtain having already fallen over her mind. Her body soon followed. She didn't see Leonardo frown down at her as he withdrew. She couldn't worry about his body language, which spoke of concern and confusion.

Leonardo lay beside her, unable to sleep, which was unusual for him after so much sex. He was troubled. The thought that he liked Veronica too much troubled him. Way too much.

Because let's face it, Leonardo, he thought to himself, *what you felt when you made love to Veronica just now far surpassed anything you've ever felt before.* It had been more than sex. It had felt suspiciously like what he'd imagined falling in love would be like.

The problem was he didn't want to fall in love with Veronica. He didn't want to fall in love with *any* woman just yet but, if it had to happen, he certainly didn't want it to happen with a twenty-eight-year-old Australian girl who carried way too much emotional baggage and who obviously believed he was some kind of man whore.

He wasn't. Not in *his* book. Okay, so his girlfriends didn't last very long. They bored him after a while, as did many aspects of life nowadays. But he only ever had one girlfriend at a time, and not nearly as many as social media suggested. He didn't cheat on them. Never. He always broke up with them before entering another relationship. Yes, he did have the occasional one-night stand. But only when he was between girlfriends, and only when he was in one of his dark, restless moods.

Leonardo could feel one of those dark moods descending right now. God, but he hated it when he felt like this. So out of control. He'd been out of bloody control ever since he'd met the girl beside him, who was sleeping like a baby with not a worry in the world. Damn her with her violet eyes and her oh, so kissable mouth. And damn Laurence for leaving his villa to her.

Laurence...

If only Laurence were still alive. He'd used to be able to get Leonardo out of his black moods. He'd put on some classical music, pour him some wine and they'd sit on the terrace, if it was summer, or by the fireplace in winter, not always talking, sometimes just listening and drinking. Relaxing.

He supposed he could get up and do that now. But it wouldn't be the same, doing any of that by himself. It wouldn't work, either. He needed Laurence's logical reasoning and pragmatic presence to do the trick. He'd had a way about him, that man. If Leonardo were honest, Veronica had a similar way. She was great company and very easy to talk to. He'd thoroughly enjoyed their sightseeing trip this morning. And their lunch in Sorrento. Unfortunately, the sexual chemistry flaring between them was difficult to ignore, bringing an irritation which he'd struggled to control.

That was what bothered him almost as much as possibly falling in love—his lack of control. Though maybe they were both wrapped up in the same package. He still could not get over not having used protection. What on earth had he been thinking?

But it was done now. And truthfully, it had felt fantastic. Was that what was tricking him, his level of physical pleasure? The sheer intimacy of it all?

Possibly. He liked that thought. It made sense. He probably wasn't falling in love with her at all. He was just blown away by how great it felt without using a condom. It was many years, after all, since he'd had the pleasure of spontaneous sex. He'd liked that there'd been no need to turn away and risk spoiling the moment. No matter how quick you were, that was sometimes very annoying.

A yawn captured him. Maybe he could sleep now that he'd worked out his emotions.

Leonardo rolled over and put an arm around Veronica. She snuggled back into him till they were like two spoons fitted together. Leonardo smiled with contentment, then fell fast sleep, happy with the thought that she would be there for him when he awoke.

CHAPTER TWENTY

SHE WASN'T.

Leonardo's eyes opened to an empty space next to him. He stretched, wondering what time it was and how long Veronica had been up. The blinds in the bedroom weren't down, and he could see that it wasn't yet night. Reaching for his phone, he checked the time. Not that late. Only six-thirty, and daylight saving meant it would be light for some time yet.

Rising, Leonardo headed for the bathroom where he'd dropped his clothes. Five minutes later, he left the bedroom in search of Veronica. He found her sitting at Laurence's desk, which was tucked away in an alcove in a corner of the living room. She was dressed too, a mug of steaming coffee at her elbow, her eyes fixed on the computer in front of her.

Laurence's computer.

'There you are,' he said, and she swung round in the chair to face him.

God, but she was beautiful, he thought. Even without make-up and with her hair up.

'I didn't want to wake you,' she said coolly, and picked up her coffee, 'So I had a shower in the guest room and got dressed there. I've been trying to get into my father's computer, but it's password protected.'

'I know the password,' he offered.

'You do?' She blinked up at him in surprise.

'He gave it to me when I was staying here with my broken ankle. I couldn't sleep some nights so I would get up and play poker on the computer. What are you hoping to find?' he asked as he came over and tapped in the password, which wasn't exactly obscure. Just Ruth with her birthdate after it. Of course, he had to lean over her shoulder to do that, his nostrils immediately assailed with a faint but tantalising scent. Not perfume. Possibly just shower gel.

'Anything, really,' she said, and quickly stood up. 'Would you like some coffee?'

'*Si. Grazie.*'

'Why are you speaking Italian all of sudden?' she demanded to know.

He shrugged. 'Does it matter?'

'No. Yes. I mean, I understand a few words, but I'd prefer you to use English.'

'Fine.' He smiled at her then sat down in front of the computer. 'Let's see if I can find anything enlightening for you.' He brought up Laurence's email account and tapped in the same password, guessing that it would be the same.

It was. Of course, there was a whole heap of spam, sent after Laurence's demise. He deleted it all then backtracked to the days before Laurence had left for London. One email jumped out at him. It was from a private investigation firm in Sydney and was accompanied by a PDF. Leonardo downloaded it, frowning as he began to read, his frown deepening by the time he'd read the report, which wasn't overly long, but which included an attached photograph.

'I remembered from lunch that you liked your coffee black and strong,' Veronica said as she set a steaming mug down on the desk next to him. 'Have you found something?'

Had he found something? *Dio*, had he ever!

Veronica peered over Leonardo's shoulder at the computer screen.

'My God,' she gasped, pointing at the screen. 'That's me.'

'That it is,' Leonardo said slowly.

'But…but…'

'It's attached to a recent report from a private detective agency based in Sydney,' he explained. 'Clearly Laurence wanted to find out how you were faring before he died. Also clearly,' he added, glancing up into her widening eyes,

'What he discovered made him decide to change his will and leave you his villa here on Capri.'

'What…what does it say about me?' she asked, obviously shaken by this news.

And well she should be, Leonardo thought, not sure if he felt sad for her. Or furious that she had deceived him.

'I think it best that I print out the report and let you read it for yourself,' he said with creditable composure.

'All right,' she agreed.

'Perhaps you should also sit down.'

Veronica sank onto the nearest dining room chair, her heart sinking as well. She knew exactly what the report would say, her mind scrambling to find some excuse she could give to Leonardo as to why she'd let him think she'd been out there, socialising and having an active sex life, one that required her to take the pill. Oh, Lord! She had to keep that lie going. Leonardo would be understandably furious if she told him she wasn't on the pill.

Her stomach tightened as the printer spat out the report.

She wondered if the investigator had found out the whole truth about Jerome as well.

Possibly not. He'd hidden his affair well.

'Here,' Leonardo said, and slapped the pages down on the dining table. He was angry with her, she could see. Which was understandable.

The report wasn't long. Only three pages. But it spelled the situation out exactly as she'd feared. It made her sound like some grieving widow, not the bitter wronged woman she actually was. Or had been.

But she wasn't that woman any longer, was she? Leonardo had shown her she'd been a fool to hide away, nursing her grievances and shunning the opposite sex. Okay, so he wasn't the kind of man to pin any future hopes on. Which was bad luck. She did so like him. But he'd still been good for her, giving her back her libido, along with a more optimistic way of looking at the opposite sex. She would remember him for the rest of her life.

Veronica decided then and there to embrace the truth. Though, not as far as Jerome's affair. Leonardo had already said he didn't want to hear any man-bashing. And, really, it was none of his business. Neither would she be telling him she wasn't on the pill.

'Well?' Leonardo prompted, having drawn out a chair opposite her and sat down. 'What have you got to say for yourself?'

Veronica's lifted her eyebrows in a nonchalant gesture. 'There's not much I can say. The report has spelt it out and it's all true. My fiancé was killed in a motorcycle accident just before our wedding. I was devastated, then deeply depressed for a long time. And, yes, ever since then I've lived the life of a nun. There haven't been any sheikhs or any other men in my life, or in my bed, for three years.'

'Not exactly the impression you gave me, is it?' he threw at her.

Her shrug was a brilliant echo of the shrugs he often used. 'What can I say? When I found out Laurence was my father and that he'd left me a villa on Capri, I finally saw the error of my ways. I decided then and there to throw off my nun's habit and start living life again.'

His lips pursed, his dark eyes narrowing with obvious distrust.

'So when did you start taking the pill?' he demanded to know.

'Girls take the pill these days for many reasons,' Veronica said haughtily, but with her fingers crossed under the table. 'It protects you from osteoporosis, as well as reducing premenstrual tension. It is not always about avoiding an unwanted pregnancy, although nothing beats a condom for safe sex,' she added tartly for good measure.

The best defence was always attack. Or so she'd read.

He looked both distracted and offended. 'You keep on

saying things like that,' he snapped. 'I assure you, I am perfectly safe. And I am not as bad as you think.'

'Yes you are, Leonardo. But no sweat. I like you the way you are. You're great fun, and fantastic in bed. On top of that, I certainly won't have to worry about leaving you behind with a broken heart when I go back to Australia.'

His mouth opened then closed like a floundering fish's.

She might have laughed if her last words hadn't made her own heart lurch all of a sudden. Maybe *she* was the one who should worry about going back with a broken heart.

Leonardo finally found his tongue. 'I don't know what to say,' he said, sounding totally flummoxed.

'You don't have to say anything, do you?'

CHAPTER TWENTY-ONE

LEONARDO TRIED TO keep his outrage going, but it was hard in the face of her nonchalance over the situation. When she smiled at him, he simply had to smile back.

'Truly,' he said with a shake of his head. 'You are impossible!'

'So my mother tells me. Oh, Lord, that reminds me,' she said, jumping up and leaving the report on the dining table.

'Where are you going?'

'To get my phone and send Mum the photos I took today. I might ring her as well. You go drink your coffee and see if you can find anything more on that computer. Then afterwards you can show me where the wine cellar is. I also might have to rustle up something for us to eat. I don't know how late it is, but I'm starting to feel darned hungry.'

She dashed off, leaving Leonardo staring after her with hunger of a different kind.

Shaking his head at himself, he reached over and picked up the report, reading it through again. Nothing new struck him, though this time he felt more compassion for Veronica's plight. It must have been very hard for her, losing the man she loved shortly before their wedding. The first time he'd read the report his reaction had been shock, plus anger at the way she'd deceived him. Leonardo was never good with female deception. Now, admiration crept in with his compassion. It had been brave of her to throw off her depression and come to Capri. Brave to adopt a brighter, happier personality, instead of the dreary one which came across in that report.

Laurence had done a good thing, leaving her this place. Though, damn it all, he should have contacted his daughter earlier. She was his flesh and blood. Okay, so she might not have been conceived in the normal way, but what did that matter? She was still family.

When Leonardo folded the pages over then stood up, a memory teased his mind, a memory of Laurence doing exactly the same thing that last weekend. Clearly, he'd been reading this very report when Leonardo had come to visit him. But, also clearly, Laurence hadn't wanted to tell him about it. Instead, he'd folded the pages and hurried away, hiding the contents from him. Why? Leonardo was puzzled. They'd been very close friends. With Ruth dead and Laurence himself dying, there'd been no reason why he shouldn't have told him that he had a daughter in Australia. They could have discussed the situation together.

But Laurence had remained silent on the matter, choosing instead to drink wine and make idle conversation with Leonardo about *his* family's constant pressuring him to get married. Leonardo felt quite hurt that his friend hadn't confided in him about his secret daughter. Instead, he'd hurried off to London, changed his will then died without explaining why he'd structured his last wishes that way.

Leonardo could only speculate. He didn't *know*. He supposed it had to have been to get Veronica to come here personally. Though, there had been no guarantee of that. She could have sold the place from Australia and never darkened this doorstep. Still, Laurence wouldn't have thought of that. He really hadn't had a great imagination. If he'd decided something would happen a certain way, then it had to happen that way. It was as well that he'd made *him* executor of the will. Leonardo suspected that, if he hadn't met Veronica all those years ago, she might not have come to Capri.

What a terrible thought!

So was the thought that Veronica would soon be leaving. He wondered how he could persuade her to stay longer. It wasn't just the sex. It was her company—rather like having Laurence still here, only better.

He had just sat down at the computer again when Veronica returned.

'I didn't ring Mum,' she explained. 'I just sent her the photos and a text. She told me the other day that I didn't have to ring all the time and that I should just have a good holiday away from everything. I took her at her word this time. Did you find anything more on the computer?'

'No,' he replied, not wanting to admit that he hadn't even looked, that he'd been reading the report again.

'Oh, well. At least we have an idea now about why he left me his house. He must have known Mum would tell me he was my father and that I'd want to come here and find out all about him.'

Leonardo had his doubts about that, but declined to say so. Laurence had had a very unemotional way of looking at most things. His daughter had some of his pragmatism but, being a physiotherapist and not a geneticist, this possibly inherited characteristic had been softened by her more caring profession and her sex. She could be tough, he could see that. But she was still all woman, with a woman's tendency to surrender herself totally in bed. Just thinking about how she felt under him fired his testosterone once more. It pained him to think that one day she would just be a dim memory.

But she's not gone yet...

Leonardo walked over to her and took her in his arms. 'If he hadn't left you this villa,' he said, 'today would never have happened.'

'What a horrible thought,' she said, her voice teasing but her eyes sparking with instant desire.

'I'll get some pizzas delivered afterwards,' he pronounced as his mouth slowly descended.

'What about the wine cellar?'

His lips hovered above hers, his heart thundering in his chest as he fought for control. 'I'll take you down there afterwards as well. Though, you might find it a little chilly without your clothes on.'

He thrilled to her widening eyes, plus his recent knowledge that she wasn't nearly as sexually experienced as she'd pretended to be. Hell, he was the first man she'd slept with in three years. He vowed to make this weekend something she would never forget. But to do that he would have to concentrate on her pleasure, not his. Even now he could feel his body racing away with him.

He breathed in deeply, telling himself that making love was not the same as a downhill skiing competition. It was not a case of first to finish in the shortest possible time. It was more like ice-skating, where technique and artistry instead of speed won the day.

He kissed her slowly, doing his best to concentrate on *her* reactions and not his own. If only she hadn't wrapped her arms up around his neck. If only she hadn't pressed her breasts against him. If only she hadn't moaned…

It undid him, that moan.

To hell with taking things slowly! All thought of control was abandoned as he started stripping her where they stood.

CHAPTER TWENTY-TWO

'THIS IS ONE of the best pizzas I've ever tasted,' Veronica said truthfully as she took another large bite.

They were sitting out on the terrace, night having descended. They were fully dressed again, a necessity with the evening air having turned fresh.

'But of course,' Leonardo said smugly. 'It's Italian. But this wine is French.' And he picked up one of the glasses of red which sat on the small table between them.

He'd finally shown her where the cellar was, the entry behind a doorway that she'd mistaken for a closet. It was an enormous basement and, yes, chilly, with wall-to-wall shelves only half-filled with wine. Veronica had stared at the empty spots and felt sad at the thought of how much her father must have drunk to get liver cancer.

'I did know it was French,' she said with a roll of her eyes. 'Even an Aussie philistine like myself can recognise a French label when they see it. I'll have you know that I know a few Italian words as well.'

'Oh, really? Tell me some.'

'Let's see… There's *pizza*, and *arrivederci*, and *grazie*, and *bellissima*. And the best one of all. *Si*. I like that one. *Si*.'

'You'll be speaking like a native in no time,' he said drily.

'*Si,*' she repeated, her eyes smiling at him over the rim of her wine glass.

His eyes twinkled back at her.

'So how come you speak such good English?' she asked after she'd put her glass back down and picked up her slice of pizza.

'I did learn English at school. But I'd have to say my command of the language was mostly due to the fitness trainer my uncle hired for me when I became serious about my skiing. He was English and he refused to speak anything but English. His name was Hugh Drinkwater and he was quite a character. He was also a very bad skier. But that didn't matter. He wasn't teaching me to ski. I had a coach for that. He taught me the discipline of fitness. Believe me when I say there is no one better than an Englishman when it comes to discipline. He was ex-army and took no prisoners.'

'But you liked him,' she said, having heard the affection in his voice.

Her statement seemed to surprise him. 'Yes. Yes, I suppose I did. But he was a hard taskmaster.'

'A necessity with you, I would imagine, Leonardo.'

'What do you mean?'

'Come, now. You've been shockingly spoiled all your life. You would have needed someone tough to whip you into shape.'

He laughed. 'You could be right there.'

'I am right. So, what happened in the end? What were the injuries which forced you to retire before you wanted to?'

'Too many to enumerate. I broke practically every bone you could break at one time or another. And pulled just about every muscle.'

'I read that you were a very reckless skier. But very brave,' she added, not wanting to offend him.

'I was a risk-taker, that's true. You have to take risks to win. Apparently, I took after my grandfather in that regard. Though his risks were in business, not on the ski slopes. My uncle inherited his talent for making money, but not my father. He hated the cut and thrust of the business world. When my grandfather died, *Papa* took his share of the money, put most of it into the bank and bought that hotel down there with the rest.' He nodded down the hillside to where the Hotel Fabrizzi stood. '*Papa's* a hard worker but he likes a simple life. Running a small hotel suits him.'

'And your mother?' Veronica asked. 'Does she like life on Capri?'

'She loves it. So do my sisters. I love it too, but only in small doses. It's too quiet for me. When they came to live here, I stayed in Milan with Uncle Stephano. I wanted to ski professionally and I couldn't do that from here. He sponsored me and taught me the textile business during the off season. There's nothing I don't know about manufacturing and selling fabrics.'

'Do you still miss it?' she asked. 'The skiing life?'

When he shrugged, she saw that that was what he did when he didn't want to answer a question, or face something.

'You couldn't do it for ever, Leonardo,' she pointed out. 'Age would have caught up with you, even if injuries didn't.'

'I would have liked to do it a little longer,' he bit out. 'I was favourite to become world champion that year.'

'We don't always get what we want in life, Leonardo,' she said with a touch of her old bitterness.

'True,' he said, not picking up on her change in mood. But it had changed, the happiness which Leonardo's company brought to her spoiled by thinking about Jerome's treachery.

She stood up abruptly, having found that doing things was the best antidote for unhappy thoughts. At home, she would distract herself with work. Housework, if she wasn't seeing a client at the time.

'What are you doing?' he asked her.

'Cleaning up,' she replied as she swept up the dirty plates.

'I can see that. But why? It can wait, can't it? You haven't finished your wine and I was enjoying our conversation.'

'Really?'

'Yes. Really. Talking to you is like talking to Laurence. He used to make me open up and tell him my worries. It's a relief sometimes to confide in someone else, especially someone nice and non-judgemental. And it's far cheaper than seeing a therapist.'

Veronica stood there, holding the plates, genuinely surprised by his admission.

'I can't imagine you ever seeing a therapist.'

'I did for a while. Being forced to retire affected me terribly. But, in the end, I realised that going over and over my feelings wasn't doing me any good, so I stopped.'

Veronica put the plates back down and settled back into her chair.

'Yes, I'm not sure that's the right way to get over things. The world seems obsessed with celebrating anniversaries at the moment, especially ones remembering quite wretched events. I honestly think it's a bad thing to dwell on the past. I did it for far too long. You have to accept reality and then move on.'

Even as she said the brave words, Veronica recognised it was a case of easier said than done. After all, until recently she'd hugged her misery around her like a cloak, afraid to move on, afraid of some other man hurting her as Jerome had done. But at least she had finally moved on. And she doubted Leonardo would hurt her. She wouldn't let him, for starters, this last thought crystallising her decision to end their fling tomorrow. It was too much of a risk to keep on seeing him. He was way too attractive. And way too good in bed.

But she wouldn't say anything until she had to. Hopefully, he wouldn't take it badly, or as a blow to his ego, which was considerable.

Veronica picked up her wine glass and took a deep swallow.

'You are meant to savour this type of red wine,' Leonardo chided. 'Not drink it like water.'

'Ooh. Pardon me for breathing. I did tell you that I prefer white wine but you insisted on my trying one of the reds.

Is this better?' she asked, lifting the glass to her lips and taking a delicate sip.

'Much better. I apologise if I sound snobbish. It's just that this particular wine is one of the best ever bottled and needs to be sipped to be appreciated.'

'It *is* nicer when sipped. Okay, I forgive you.'

'*Grazie,*' he said, and smiled over at her.

Her heart lurched anew, warning bells going off in her head.

Veronica searched her mind for the best subject to quell any growing emotional involvement with this man.

'Tell me, Leonardo,' she said. 'On the night we first met, all those years ago, if I'd said yes would you have really enjoyed a threesome with me and that blonde bimbo?'

His dark eyes glittered. 'But of course. Though my mind would have been on you all the time. I wanted you like crazy.'

Veronica's fingers tightened around her wine glass. Why, oh, why had he had to add that last bit? 'Were you in the habit of having threesomes?' she asked stiffly.

'No. Like I told you, I was very drunk that night.'

'Your friends didn't seem shocked by your suggestion.'

'My friends were also pretty drunk. And stoned, some of them.'

'Yes, I noticed that.'

Leonardo sighed. 'It was a common thing in the circles I moved in.'

'And what about now? Do you take drugs now?'

'I never took drugs back then. I didn't like them.'

'I see…' Did she believe him? She supposed she had to, since he would have admitted it if he had taken them. He wouldn't see any reason to hide his actions.

'And what about you, Veronica? You went to university which, I am told, is rife with drugs. Did you ever indulge?'

'Never. I hate drugs.'

'That is a good thing. They ruin people's lives.'

'They certainly do,' she said.

They both fell silent for a few moments, Leonardo being the first to speak again.

'We are getting too serious. After we've finished our wine, we shall go back to bed.'

For a split second his presumption—and his arrogance—annoyed her. But the thought of the pleasure that awaited her in bed with Leonardo trumped any sense of feminine outrage.

Whilst she sipped the rest of her wine, her mind was already there, naked in bed with him. The only concession she made to her pride was that, this time, *she* would be the one making love to him. First with her mouth, then with her whole body. *She* would be the one on top, with him at her mercy. She would thrill to his moans and wallow in his arousal. She would do to him what he'd done to her. She would not stop until he begged her to.

CHAPTER TWENTY-THREE

'I HAVE TO GO.'

Veronica looked up from where she was loading the dishwasher to see Leonardo standing there, showered and dressed with his overnight bag in his hand. She herself was still naked underneath her bathrobe.

'But you haven't even had breakfast yet,' she said on straightening.

Leonardo dropped the bag and come forward to take her into his arms. 'I know,' he murmured into her hair. 'But it's almost eleven. The hotel guests will have left and *Mamma* will be expecting me for Sunday lunch. After that, I have to return to Milan. I have an important meeting in the morning which I must attend. Still, it's best I go whilst you still have some reputation left. I will claim I slept in the guest room but I doubt anyone will believe me.'

She pulled back and lifted cool eyes to his. 'You told me I shouldn't care what other people think.'

'*Mamma* and *Papa* are not other people. They are my parents. Now, don't make a fuss. I will return. Though, not next weekend I'm afraid. I have things on.'

'What things?'

'A charity ball on the Saturday night which my company sponsors every year.'

'Oh. And I suppose you'll be going with some glamorous model on your arm?'

'No. I told you, I have no girlfriend in my life at the moment, other than you. If I asked you, would you come with me?'

Her heart fluttered at his invitation. She was seriously tempted, until she remembered her decision last night to end their affair today. It was a painful decision but a necessary one. 'I came here to find out about my father, Leonardo, not go flitting all over Italy to attend fancy dos. And I am not your girlfriend,' Veronica pointed out a little tartly.

'You could be. All you have to do is stay here in this villa and I will make Capri my second home.'

Exasperation joined temptation with this particular offer. Because it was a typically selfish suggestion on his part. He didn't want her on a for ever basis. He just hadn't had enough of what she'd given him last night. And, brother, she'd given him a lot!

'I don't think that would work, Leonardo,' she said archly. 'I'm not cut out to be mistress material.'

His dark eyes glittered. 'Oh, I wouldn't say that.'

'I would. Besides, what would your parents think? Not about me but about you. They would finally have to face up to the fact that you're an incorrigible playboy with no intention of getting married.'

'Maybe you could change my mind on that score.'

She laughed. 'Please don't insult my intelligence.'

His frown contained frustration. 'Why do you persist in thinking so badly of me?'

'Let's not argue, Leonardo. I've had a lovely time this weekend and I want to remember it fondly.'

'How long are you actually staying?'

'My return flight is in three weeks' time. I leave on a Sunday.'

'Then you'll still be here the weekend after next.'

'Yes…'

'What say you meet me in Rome that weekend? By then you will have found out everything you can about Laurence. I will show you the city and we'll have another great time together. My uncle has a lovely townhouse he'll let us use. Or I can book us into a hotel.'

Don't say yes! came the savage warning from deep inside her. *You'll regret it.*

At least she didn't say yes straight away. There again, she didn't say no, either.

'I'll think about it,' was what she said.

He smiled, looking supremely confident in her saying yes in the end.

'I will ring you tonight.'

'Please don't.'

'I will ring you tonight,' he repeated, giving her a brief peck before picking up his bag and striding away, not glancing back over his shoulder even once.

She stared after him, her heart thudding fast in her chest, her head in a whirl. Because she was already looking forward to his call tonight.

Oh, Veronica. You should have told him no straight away. You should have put an end to this once and for all. Tell him tonight. Be strong. Be firm. Now, ring the airline and make an earlier booking. You need to go home ASAP. Before it's too late.

She didn't ring the airline, of course. She procrastinated, spending the next couple of hours going through the drawers in her father's desk, looking for Lord knew what. She didn't find anything enlightening, only the typical stuff you found in household drawers. Papers of every kind, copies of old bills, receipts for things bought over the years, pamphlets and brochures. There wasn't anything about her, or his will. After that, she tried to open his computer but it had shut down again, and she needed his password, which she didn't have. She hadn't thought to ask Leonardo to write it down but she would tonight, if and when he rang.

She wasn't so sure that he would ring. Out of sight was possibly out of mind where Leonardo was concerned. Not so in her own case. He was constantly in her mind, her thoughts troubling her. For they were no longer thoughts of lust but…dared she think it?…thoughts of love…?

Her memory recalled several times during the night when

their love-making had taken on a highly emotional edge. At least for her it had, especially when she'd followed through with her idea to be the one in control. That was a laugh. She had never been in control. Not once, either of her body or her soul. It seemed it was impossible for her to be that intimate with this man and not have her heart join the proceedings.

Leonardo himself made it extremely difficult for her to remain the sexual sophisticate she'd vowed to be. His passion was her undoing, plus his tenderness, especially after she was recovering after yet another explosive climax. He would always hold her close and murmur sweet nothings in her ear. He didn't tell her he loved her, instead using other euphemisms which any foolish female would swoon to. Sometimes he talked to her in Italian, possibly saying dirty things. She had no way of knowing. But the words didn't sound dirty. They sounded…romantic. No matter how much Veronica tried to tell herself this was just lust between them, she no longer believed it. Not on her side, anyway.

Leonardo, of course, was a different story. He was an accomplished seducer. And lover. A playboy, let her never forget. He operated in the bedroom on autopilot, knowing exactly what to say and do. Yes, he wanted to see her again. Why not when the chemistry between them was so good? Clearly, he hadn't had his fill yet.

Veronica knew that to spend another weekend with him, this time in Rome being wined, dined and romanced, would be very silly indeed. At the same time, how could she resist it?

Oh, Lord…

Sighing, Veronica rose from her father's desk and went in search of further distraction. She found some in a pile of photo albums she discovered on the top shelf of the linen press. They were numbered from one to five, tracing Laurence's life from when he'd been a baby. Veronica soon became engrossed in them, marvelling at how much they'd looked alike as infants before their different sexes had too much of an influence. It was also a shock to see a mirror image of herself in his mother. Clearly, the maternal genes had been the dominant ones, Laurence's father being a very ordinary-looking man with pale eyes and hair.

Each album showed her father at a different stage in his life. She went through them slowly, enjoying the glimpses into Laurence's life at various stages. His school years, then his days at university, where it seemed he must have been quite good at athletics. There were several photos of him running in races, a few of him crossing the line in first place. Veronica had been quite a good runner herself at school, though she preferred skiing.

Album number three was totally devoted to his wedding to Ruth and their honeymoon, which had obviously been spent in Italy. They'd toured most of the major cities, as well as visits to Sicily and Capri. Possibly this was where their love affair with the island had started. Album four covered the middle years of their marriage, with lots of pictures of Laurence at work and Ruth in her garden. Veronica gasped when she saw a group shot taken at a party, with her mother in the background serving drinks. What surprised her most was that she was smiling. It made Veronica wonder if this was after she'd fallen pregnant. Nora had always claimed that the day she'd found out she was expecting was the happiest day of her life. Laurence wasn't in the same photograph, but Ruth was, smiling her usual warm smile at the camera.

Album five followed the later years of their marriage, including snaps of various holidays, plus lots of the renovations they'd made to this villa. It had been a bit of a wreck when they'd bought it, though the view had always been great. This last album wasn't full, ending abruptly with a photo of Ruth looking very fragile, and Laurence hovering protectively behind her chair, his violet eyes worried.

Veronica suspected that Laurence's will to live had died with his wife's death. She wouldn't mind betting that that was when he'd started drinking heavily. Sad, really. If only he'd reached out to *her* instead of killing himself slowly. They could have become friends. She could have given him a reason to live. Instead, he'd just withered on the vine, so to speak, not caring about his health or his long-lost daughter. Leonardo seemed to be the only person in the world he cared about. And that was possibly only surface caring.

Or was it?

Veronica's anger at her father's actions regarding herself was making her judge him harshly with others. Clearly, he'd been very fond of Leonardo. And very trusting of him as a man. You didn't make a person executor of your will if you didn't have good faith in their integrity and honesty.

Honesty and integrity were not words she normally associated with playboys. Yet, strangely, they did seem to apply to Leonardo. Just because he wasn't in a hurry to marry and have children didn't mean he wasn't a good person. He had remarked more than once that she had no reason to think so badly of him. Veronica vowed to be fairer in her assessment of his character in future. Though fairer did not mean stupider. It was still risky to keep on seeing him. She really didn't want to fall for him any more deeply than she already had. At the moment, her heart was still relatively safe. Leaving Leonardo would hurt, but she would survive.

As Veronica closed the last album and put it on top of the pile, something slipped out of the back pages and fluttered to the ground. It was a small photograph, she saw on picking it up. Of herself as a newborn baby. On the back was written her name, her date of birth and her birth weight. Nothing else.

Had her mother sent it? Or had her father hired another detective agency all those years ago?

Only one way to find out for sure, she supposed.

Veronica carried the photograph into the bedroom where she'd left her phone. She tried to work out what time it was in Australia but she had no idea; her brain seemed to have gone on holiday. She'd just have to take a chance that her mother wasn't asleep, because she simply couldn't wait.

Her mother answered fairly quickly, and without sounding fuzzy.

'You're still awake,' Veronica said, guessing that it had to be close to midnight.

'I never go to bed too early. You know that. What's wrong?'

'Nothing's wrong. I just need to ask you something.'

'What?'

'Did you send my father a photograph of me after I was born?'

'What? Oh, yes, actually, I did. It was one of his conditions. But I wasn't to send it to his house. It went to his place of work back in London. He was worried that his wife might find it by mistake.'

'So he did care about me, then?'

A heavy sigh wafted down the line. 'I suppose so, love.'

'Why do you doubt it?'

'It was just something he said at the time, back when he found out I was pregnant. He seemed keen to see how much you were like him. He had this thing for passing on good genes, as you know. He lived and breathed his work.'

Veronica pulled a face. 'Sounds like I was just an experiment for him.'

'No, no, I wouldn't go that far. It was only natural that Laurence would be interested in seeing what you looked like. You have to understand…he probably would have liked to have a relationship with you. To love you like a real father. But he couldn't. He was hamstrung by his love for his wife. He adored her. She came first with him.'

'Then why didn't he contact me after she died?' Veronica snapped.

'I don't know, love. Oh, please don't get all worked up about this. Life and relationships are complex things. And people don't always do the right thing. I dare say Laurence regretted a lot of things in the end. Maybe he tried to make up for his absence in your life by leaving you that villa,' her mother suggested. 'You have to admit, it's a very beautiful place.'

Veronica opened her mouth to tell her mother he'd had her investigated recently, but then decided against it. She needed to think about her father's reasons for doing what he had without her mother confusing her with endless speculations.

'Maybe he didn't expect you to sell it,' Nora went on regardless. 'Maybe he wanted you to live there.'

'Maybe. I guess we'll never know now, Mum,' Veronica said, hoping to stop her mother from any further speculating. 'Anyway, I can't live here. Not permanently.' She could not bear the thought of running into Leonardo whenever he came home, or being within a short plane trip of wherever he was.

'Why not rent it out as a holiday place? You'd get a good rental. And then you could holiday there yourself occasionally.'

'No, Mum. I need to come home,' she said firmly.

Her mother was always good at picking up her feelings. 'It's because of that man, isn't it?' she said sharply. 'Leonardo Fabrizzi.'

'Yes, Mum.'

'You haven't fallen for him, have you?'

'I think I might have. A little.' She gave a dry laugh. 'Actually, more than a little. So I need to get out of here before it gets more serious. On my side, that is. Leonardo isn't the kind of man to get serious over any woman.'

'Oh, dear. It's all my fault, telling you to get out there and have fun. I should have known you'd be extra vulnerable after all these years of having no man in your life.'

'It's not your fault, Mum. I'm just a fool. Anyway, I'm going to ring the airlines and move my flight forward a week. So expect me home on Friday week. There's no risk before then. Leonardo can't make it back here until that weekend, by which time I'll be safely gone.'

'Lord. You make it sound like you're afraid of him.'

'Not of him, Mum. Of my own silly self.'

'Is he that irresistible?'

Veronica closed her eyes, her mind immediately conjuring up an image of him looming over her in bed last night, his dark eyes glittering wildly, his voice rough with desire as he told her what he was going to do to her. All night long.

'He is to me,' Veronica choked out. And possibly to all the swathes of women who'd come before her.

'Then you had better come home.'

CHAPTER TWENTY-FOUR

BY THE TIME Leonardo picked up his car at Milan airport he'd come to the conclusion that he was actually falling in love for the first time in his life. He'd missed Veronica like mad within minutes of leaving her. At first, he'd put his feelings down to missing the fantastic sex they'd had together, not realising that his feelings came from something way deeper than that.

Lunch with his parents had been tedious as he tried to sidestep their escalating hopes over his relationship with Veronica. He'd lied, saying that they weren't romantically involved, but he could see they weren't buying it. They kept looking at each other with that knowing glint in their eyes until in the end he stopped bothering with the lies, saying instead that, yes, he liked Veronica a lot, but she was going home to Australia in three weeks' time and there was no point in pursuing the girl. He scoffed at the suggestion that he invite her to stay with him in Milan for a while.

He was no longer scoffing at that idea. In fact, he thought it was a very good idea. He could not wait to ring her and suggest it. It was a pity that the ski season hadn't started yet. Then he could have taken her skiing. But no matter. There were many other places he could take her. Venice, perhaps. Girls loved the romance of Venice.

By the time Leonardo arrived home—he owned a house not that far from the airport—he could hardly contain his excitement. Of course, he couldn't tell her he loved her. Yet. That would be premature. And not conducive to achieving his goal, which was her loving him back. He could see Veronica was wary of relationships, though why that was, he wasn't sure. Her fiancé had been killed. He hadn't run off

with some other woman. The hurt he sometimes glimpsed
in her eyes when talking about men must have come from
some other earlier man's treatment of her.

Yes. That had to be it.

Leonardo hurried inside, the house very quiet. He always gave his housekeeper the weekend off when he went
to Capri. Francesca was a widow in her fifties and lived in
most of the time, but on her weekends off she liked to visit
her daughter who lived in Florence, so she wouldn't be back
until the morning. A glance at his Rolex showed it wasn't
too late to call Veronica. It was only twenty-past nine. Pulling out his phone, he hurried upstairs and lay down on his
bed, stretching out before bringing up her number and hitting the dial icon.

She took her time answering. The thought that she'd seen
who was ringing and simply didn't want to answer was a
worrying one.

'Hi,' she said at last. 'I'm glad you rang.'

His spirits rose immediately.

'I have something I wanted to ask you,' she went on, her
voice brisk and businesslike, reminding him of the voice
she'd used when she'd discussed arrangements with him
over the phone from Australia. It made him rethink his
tactics, knowing instinctively that she wasn't just going to
say yes to what he wanted. Maybe he should concentrate
on getting her to come to Rome in a fortnight's time. Asking her to come visit him in Milan seemed a step too far at
this early stage.

'What is it?' he replied, trying not to sound crestfallen,
which was something Leonardo rarely felt when it came
to women.

'I need the password to Laurence's computer,' she said.

Leonardo frowned. 'What for?'

'I've been going through his things. I thought I should
go through his computer as well, have a look at his search
history. It might give me a few clues.'

'Clues to what?'

'To why he left me this place, for starters,' she said sharply. 'Which reminds me, what happened to his phone?'

'His phone?'

'Yes. I would imagine my father was well up on technology. He was an intelligent man. He would have carried a smart phone with him everywhere.'

'Yes, he did. I have it in a drawer at work, along with his wallet and his watch.'

'Oh.'

'If you want them, I could give them to you when we meet up in Rome,' he offered.

Her hesitation to answer straight away was telling. Leonardo's heart sank.

'I… I haven't made up my mind about that yet,' she said carefully.

At least she hadn't said no outright. Still, Leonardo wasn't used to women waffling where his invitations were concerned. He wasn't sure what to say next.

'If you don't fancy Rome, then how about Venice?'

'Venice?' she echoed.

'Yes. The city of love.'

'I thought that was Paris,' she returned, her voice quite cool, making him instantly regret his use of the word.

'You sound like you're not too keen,' he said, knowing that *he* sounded put out, but unable to harness his disappointment.

'I told you, Leonardo. I think it's best we don't keep seeing each other.'

'You don't really mean that.'

'You're just not used to girls turning you down.'

'Possibly. But I honestly believe we have something special. I'd like to explore things further between us.'

She laughed. She actually laughed. 'I know the kind of exploring you mean and I'm sorry, Leonardo—I do find you terribly attractive, but I can't see any future for us.'

'How do you know?'

'I just know.'

'Is it my playboy reputation which worries you?'

'Partly.'

'I'm not as bad as the media make out.'

'If you say so.'

She didn't sound convinced and Leonardo was beginning to despair. So he played his trump card.

'What if you're the right girl Laurence said would come along one day?'

He heard her suck in her breath sharply.

'You're just saying that,' she bit out.

'No,' he said firmly. 'I'm not. Look, I'm as surprised as you are. But surely you can see the chemistry between us is stronger than usual?'

She said nothing, though he could hear her breathing down the line. It was very fast.

'For pity's sake, you can't go back to Australia without giving us the chance to find out our true feelings for each other.'

'You promise me you're not just saying this to get me into bed again?'

'Cross my heart and hope to die.'

Her sigh was long. 'If you're playing with me, Leonardo, then you just might die. By my hands.'

Her passionate words excited him. And gave him confidence. She must care about him to feel that strongly.

'I'm not playing with you,' he reassured her.

'I hope not.'

'I can see you have had your trust in men severely damaged. I can only think some man in your past treated you very badly. A player, is my guess. Am I right?'

'Yes and no. He wasn't what you would call a player, just an extremely selfish man who thought of no one's wishes but his own.'

'And you think I'm like that, thinking of no one's wishes but my own?'

'*Don't* you?'

'No,' he denied hotly. Though he suspected he was guilty of some selfishness.

'In that case, please do not ring me again until next Sunday evening, at which point I will give you my answer about the following weekend.'

'What harm could there possibly be in my ringing you? I like talking to you, Veronica. You don't sugar-coat your answers. You certainly don't flatter me the way most women usually do.'

'*You're* using flattery now to get your own way.'

He ground his teeth with frustration. 'You constantly misread me.'

'I don't think so, Leonardo, but you could prove your good intentions by doing what I ask.'

'Very well,' he bit out. 'I won't ring you until next Sunday evening.' With that he hung up, too annoyed with her even to say goodbye. Lord, but she was one difficult woman!

CHAPTER TWENTY-FIVE

VERONICA DIDN'T SLEEP well that night, tossing and turning until well after midnight, then waking with the dawn. For a long time she lay there, thinking about Leonardo. Already she was regretting her tough stance of the night before, knowing full well that when next Sunday came she would say yes to spending the following weekend with him. Which meant she wouldn't be ringing the airlines today and changing her flight to an earlier one.

The romantic side of her wanted to believe he was falling in love with her, but the sensible, pragmatic side kept warning her that it was too good to be true. It was just as well, she decided in the end, that she'd forbidden him to ring her this week. At least that way she wouldn't be swayed by his sexy voice and, yes, his flattery. Veronica vowed to keep her head and to use this week to do what she'd come here to do: find out everything she could about her father.

It was a stroke of luck that at eleven that morning, after Veronica had spent hours going through her father's computer without finding a single enlightening thing—he obviously only used it for the most basic correspondence and banking—the front doorbell was rung by the one person who possibly knew more about Laurence than anyone else living on Capri.

Carmelina, Leonardo's sister and Laurence's part-time housekeeper.

'Good morning, Veronica,' she said when Veronica opened the sliding glass door, her English more formal than her brother's. 'I am sorry if I woke you.'

Veronica sashed her bathrobe and smiled at Carmelina.

'You haven't. I've been up for hours. I was just too lazy to get dressed.'

Carmelina smiled back. She was in her mid-to late thirties and still very attractive—as all the Fabrizzis were—with dark eyes and hair and the loveliest olive skin.

Good genes, her father would have said. Veronica smiled at the thought, pleased that she could think of her father without feeling frustrated with him.

'I have come to do the cleaning,' Carmelina said. 'Leonardo. He is a messy boy. He drops towels and does not pick up.'

'Oh, no, no, no,' Veronica said. 'I couldn't possibly let you do that. I am quite capable of doing my own cleaning. Trust me. I am not *that* lazy. I have all day and nothing much else to do. But, now that you're here, I would like to talk to you. About my father,' she added quickly when Carmelina looked a little alarmed.

They had coffee together out on the terrace, Carmelina also admiring the view, despite no doubt having seen it countless times. The day was warmer than the previous day, and the sea breeze delightfully cooling.

'I wish I didn't have to sell this place,' Veronica said.

'Do you have to? I would like you to live here. You would be a very nice neighbour.'

'I can't afford the taxes,' she said, having realised that proving Laurence was her father would be virtually impossible. There wasn't a single personal item of his in his bedroom or bathroom, everything having been cleared out and the whole house thoroughly cleaned.

'If you married Leonardo,' Carmelina said, 'he would pay the taxes. He is very rich.'

Veronica smiled at the wonderful simplicity of Carmelina's solution. If only life was that straightforward. 'You all want Leonardo to get married, don't you?'

'*Si,*' Carmelina said. 'But only to someone nice. Like you.'

'We've only just met, Carmelina.'

'No matter. I love my Alfonso the first day I meet him. Leonardo likes you very much. I can tell.'

'Yes, but…'

'You like him too.'

'I do, but…'

Carmelina frowned over at her, waiting for her to continue.

'I don't think Leonardo is ready for marriage yet.'

'Oh, pah! He is ready. He just needs a push.'

'Pushing doesn't always work, Carmelina. Not with someone like Leonardo. He has to make up his own mind. You should tell your mother and father to back off.'

'Laurence thought he needed a push.'

'What? What did you say?'

'I said Laurence thought my brother was ready for a wife. He said he just needed the right girl. Maybe he was thinking of you, Veronica.'

It was a stunning thought, and one which Veronica would never have imagined. But it was possible, she supposed. Maybe that was why he'd left her this villa. And why he'd made Leonardo the executor of his will. So that they could meet and fall in love. It was a hopelessly romantic idea which seemed uncharacteristic of what she'd learned about Laurence.

But maybe it was true. It certainly appealed to her own romantic side.

'Tell me, Carmelina, what kind of man was my father?'

Carmelina tipped her head on one side as she considered her answer.

'He was very English,' she said at last. 'He did not like to show his feelings. Not like Italians. When his wife died, he did not cry. He just sat out here and did not speak. For days and days.'

Veronica's heart turned over. 'Oh, how sad.'

'Yes, that was what he was. Sad. Very sad.'

'Was that when he started to drink too much?'

'*Si*. He try to hide it but I see the empty bottles.'

Tears pricked at Veronica eyes. *If only he'd contacted me*, she thought. *If only he...*

She stood up abruptly. 'I don't think I want to talk about that any more.'

Carmelina shook her head as she stood up also. 'You are just like him. You are afraid to show your feelings. Come. You need a hug.'

The rest of the day went very well. Carmelina helped Veronica give the house a quick tidy-up while the sheets and towels were in the washing machine. After remaking the bed with fresh linen and replacing the damp towels with fresh ones, Veronica jumped in the shower. Half an hour later both girls left the house arm in arm to go shopping. Not for clothes or even food. It was more of a look-but-not-buy expedition where Carmelina showed Veronica the best places to buy both, as well as the easiest ways for her to get around. They walked some, caught a bus and finally, when they were tired, they called Franco to come, pick them up and drive them home.

'You ladies look like you have fun,' he said in his usual jolly manner.

'We did, Franco,' Veronica assured him. 'Carmelina was a marvellous guide. Almost as good as you,' she added with a sparkling smile.

Franco beamed, catching her eye in the rear-view mirror. '*Si*. I am the most best guide on Capri. With the best car too. You call me any time you need ride, Veronica. I will not charge you.'

'Ooh. I will tell Elena,' Carmelina said cheekily.

'She will not care. Elena knows I love her. She not jealous.'

Carmelina laughed. 'She's very jealous of any pretty girl who smiles at you.'

Veronica grinned. 'Then I will try not to smile at him when he gives me a lift.'

'*Si*. Good idea.'

Franco drove round to the delivery entrance to the villa, probably to avoid his wife seeing Veronica in his car. But Veronica was just grateful that she didn't have to climb those steep steps. Her new sandals were starting to rub and she suspected she might have the beginnings of blisters. Saying goodbye to both Franco and Carmelina, she took herself wearily inside, ready to have a siesta. It wasn't late—only three—but Carmelina had wanted to get back before the children arrived home from school.

Veronica immediately went down to the bedroom where she dropped her bag by the bed, slipped off her sandals and crashed onto the cover, sleep finding her in less than a minute. When she woke the light outside showed that the sun was very low in the sky. Sighing, she rolled over and reached for her bag, rifling through it for her phone. Once retrieved she checked the time. Six twenty-three. She'd been asleep for over three hours.

She rose and made her way to the bathroom. It wasn't until then that the thought occurred to Veronica that her period hadn't arrived yet. She wasn't overly worried. Although her period was usually as regular as clockwork, her poor body had been through the mill lately, what with the shock of finding out about Laurence, followed by the nervous exhaustion of travelling here, not knowing what she would discover.

Veronica suddenly recalled how her reproductive system had shut down for a while after Jerome had died. This might be something similar. It didn't cross her mind that she might have fallen pregnant. The thought did occur to her, however, that if her cycle had been disturbed she would have to ask Leonardo to use condoms, if and when she went away with him again. Which could present a problem. What reason could she give when she'd already had unprotected sex with him many times?

Oh, dear. Perhaps she just shouldn't go away with him. After all, her female intuition kept warning her that he was all hot air about their sexual chemistry being extra special, implying that he might be falling in love with her.

Unfortunately, at the same time, her own feelings kept overriding common sense, tapping into his appeal to give him a chance to show her he wasn't the player she thought he was. It would be difficult to deny him that chance when she was absolutely crazy about him.

But if he put a foot wrong that weekend then that would be that. And putting a foot wrong could include making a fuss when she asked him to use protection. If he cared for her as he said he did, then he should just do as she wanted, no questions asked.

Suddenly she regretted demanding he not ring her until Sunday. She would so like to hear his voice. Dared she ring him herself?

No. Perhaps not. Nothing good ever came of a girl seeming too eager. She would content herself with reading one of the very interesting looking novels her father had in his bookshelf next to his desk. It seemed he'd liked spy stories, a genre which had never overly appealed to her. But she supposed if her father had liked them then maybe so would she. So she selected a medium-sized tome with the provocative title of *One Spy Too Many* and took it out onto the terrace. There she settled, soon engrossed in what turned out to be a real page-turner.

It was hunger pains which finally forced Veronica to lift her eyes from the book. That, and the light fading so much that she was forced to go inside if she wanted to continue to read whilst she ate. Either that or turn on the outside lights. But that always attracted insects.

Dinner was poached eggs on toast. More of a breakfast than a dinner meal but it was enough for now. She'd had a huge plate of pasta at lunchtime. She hadn't come to Italy to get fat, though it would be easy…the food was so delicious.

When her period still hadn't arrived by the time she'd finished the book late that night, Veronica resigned herself to her cycle temporarily having gone walkabout. When it had happened before she'd gone to the doctor in a panic, thinking she'd contracted some dreaded disease, but after an examination and some tests the doctor had told her that she was perfectly fine. The worst thing she could do, the doctor had said, was worry. His advice had been to eat healthily, take plenty of exercise and do things she enjoyed. Which had been a little hard back then when nothing had made her happy.

Not so on the Isle of Capri.

Veronica decided to follow that doctor's instructions to a T. The next morning she rose early and went for a walk before breakfast. Nothing too adventurous, just down the road and back again. Then after breakfast she made her way carefully down the steep path to the Hotel Fabrizzi and asked Elena—who was sitting at a computer behind the reception desk in the coolly spacious foyer—if there was a map of Capri she could borrow. Elena showed her a stand on the wall which contained maps, as well as lots of brochures of tourist activities on Capri. Veronica sorted through them and took one of everything which interested her.

'Thank you, Elena,' she said.

'You are welcome,' came her warm reply. '*Mamma* said if I saw you to ask you to come to dinner tonight. Nothing like the other night. It will just be her and *Papa*.'

'How nice of her. That would lovely. Is she here?'

'She is busy doing the rooms with Carmelina at the moment. Can I say you will come?'

'Of course. What time do you think?'

'Seven. And don't eat too much before you come. *Mamma* likes to feed her guests until they burst.'

Veronica laughed. 'Yes. I did notice that last Friday night.'

'Have you heard from Leonardo?' Elena suddenly asked.

'He rang me on Sunday night to thank me for letting him stay. But not since then.'

Elena frowned. 'He was strange at lunch on Sunday.'

'Strange? What do you mean?'

'I do not know. He was not the brother I am used to. He was too quiet. I wondered if you had argued with him.'

'No. Not at all.'

'*Mamma* does not understand Leonardo. She and *Papa* keep pressing him to marry but he is not ready to settle down yet.'

'Leonardo will never be ready to settle down,' Veronica said, any foolish dreams she'd been harbouring totally shattered by voicing the truth out loud.

Elena's eyes showed her surprise. 'You know him well enough already to know that?'

'We met briefly many years ago,' Veronica explained. 'I knew then what kind of man he was.'

'He is a not a bad man,' Elena defended hotly, dark eyes flashing.

'No, but he is restless. And dissatisfied with his life. He never got over his retirement from competitive skiing. I hope your *mamma* and *papa* don't think he's going to marry me. Because he won't.'

Elena sighed. 'They must have hope, Veronica. Please don't say any of this to them tonight.'

'Okay. I'll just play happy tourist.'

'You are more than a tourist. You are Laurence's daughter.'

Veronica left the hotel with her map and several brochures, troubled by her conversation with Elena. Perhaps because she'd finally accepted that loving a man like Leonardo was a sure path to misery.

Seeking distraction, she set herself the task of familiarising herself with all the established walks, as well as exploring the towns of Capri and Anacapri. Both were beautiful towns—quaint and historical—but she preferred Anacapri because it was smaller and out of reach of the day-trippers. She sat down at an *al fresco* table in the piazza there and had a lovely lunch—though not too big, given she was going to the Fabrizzis' for dinner that night. After lunch she bought a bottle of water and set off for another walk which took her down a steep, winding path to the most delightful little beach. There she sat on a smooth rock for a couple of hours, sandals off, her hot feet cooling in the tepid water.

The walk back up was not so delightful, but she took her time, though vowing not to do quite so much the following day. Her period still hadn't come but she'd decided not to worry about it. She couldn't *will* it to come, could she?

Once back at the villa, she had a long shower, followed by a short nap before dressing for dinner. Nothing too fancy, just a pair of black cotton culottes and a black-and-white wrap-around top that had elbow-length bat-wing sleeves. She left her hair down, having freshly washed and styled it.

'How lovely you look,' Sophia gushed before giving her the obligatory hug. 'But you have caught the sun, have you not?'

'I have,' Veronica confessed. 'I was silly and took off my hat while I was at a beach. The breeze and the water tricked me into thinking I was cool.'

'A little sun doesn't do any harm,' Alberto said, and came forward to give her a hug also.

Veronica wondered if she'd ever get used to all the hugging, then realised she wouldn't have to. Soon, she'd be back home in Australia and back to her less demonstrative lifestyle.

It was a rather depressing thought.

'We do not have any guests in the hotel tonight,' Sophia told her. 'We can eat in the dining room, if you wish. Or on the big table in the kitchen.'

'Oh, please, in the kitchen.'

Sophia beamed at her, her wide smile very satisfied. 'Good. Come. Alberto wishes to give you some of Alfonso's prized limoncello before we eat.'

'It is very good,' Alberto said. 'You will like.'

She did like. And she said so.

'Alfonso also makes his own wine,' Alberto added.

'He's very clever, then,' Veronica said.

The table in the kitchen was quite large. Sophia had set just one end with Alberto at the head and herself and Sophia flanking him. The food,, as Veronica had expected, was simply delicious, but not too over the top, just a meatball and spaghetti dish, all washed down with what she suspected was some of Alfonso's home-made wine. Dessert was a coconut cake which was very tasty. The coffee afterwards was strong, but Veronica didn't say anything, just added cream and sugar and gave up the idea of sleeping until the wee hours of the morning.

Not that it mattered. She didn't have to go anywhere tomorrow.

The meal ended around nine, Veronica surprised that not once had Sophia and Alberto brought up the subject of their son. In turn, she resisted the temptation to question them about her father, deciding she wanted just to enjoy their company and forget about everything else for tonight. They asked her about her job, which she explained, confessing that she worked six, sometimes seven days a week. They looked horrified, claimed she must be in need of a holiday, then made a lot of suggestions about how she should spend the rest of her time on Capri. They insisted she see the Blue Grotto again, but warned her to go very early in the day or very late, so that she didn't get caught up with all the day-trippers. Also on the list was the chairlift up the mountain, both of which she agreed to do.

After another round of hugs, and a promise to join the whole family for lunch next Sunday, Veronica left to walk home slowly, thinking what lovely parents Leonardo had. Much nicer than Jerome's parents.

Jerome...

For the first time in three years, Veronica was able to think about Jerome without feeling one bit upset, or even bitter. Finally, she was able to look at what he had done more objectively. Yes, it had been wicked of him to lie to her about loving her when he had loved another woman— a married doctor with whom he had worked. Even more wicked to plan to marry her and have children with her because he wanted a family, because the so-called love of his life refused to leave her husband and children and marry him. At the same time, she hadn't wanted to give Jerome up. She'd wanted to have her cake and eat it too. Veronica would never have found out the horrible truth if the woman hadn't broken down at Jerome's wake and confessed everything.

Veronica still hated Jerome and his lover, but they no longer had the power to destroy *her* life. She was free of them at last.

She had her father to thank for that. Her father and, yes, Leonardo.

A sigh came to her lips, a sigh for a dream which she accepted was just a dream. Leonardo wasn't going to change. Leopards didn't change their spots. He was taken with her because she was different, that was all. And maybe she was taken with him because he was different from the Australian boyfriends she'd had. Not just better looking but more passionate. More...exotic. And definitely more erotic.

A shiver ran down her spine when she thought of how much she loved the ways he made love to her. Nothing seemed wrong to her when she was in his arms.

Another sigh wafted from her lips, this one the sound of resignation.

There was no use pretending she could resist the temptation to spend another weekend with him, especially if she could spend it with him in Venice. She would insist on that. If she was going to risk another broken heart, then she could at least have it broken in Venice.

Her mind made up, she decided to tell him the good news when he rang her on Sunday evening.

CHAPTER TWENTY-SIX

By THE TIME Friday morning came, Veronica really started to worry about her missing period. It was no use. She couldn't help it. She knew the odds of her being pregnant were very small, but not impossible. Her stomach somersaulted at the thought.

Because what if she *was* pregnant? Lord, what a disaster!

Logic told her she was panicking for nothing, but logic didn't always figure in life. She kept telling herself that she didn't *feel* pregnant. There was no light-headedness, or being sick in the mornings, or swollen nipples. Of course, all those symptoms usually came later, not after just one week.

Sighing, she arose and dressed, still not having fulfilled her bucket list of activities for Capri. This morning she planned to go on the chairlift up the mountain, then later in the afternoon she would take a trip out to the Blue Grotto. Sandwiched in between she would walk, walk and walk some more. If nothing else, all the walking should make her sleep tonight. She didn't want to lie there worrying about having Leonardo's baby growing inside her body.

It would have been a marvellous day, Veronica thought as she finally trudged up the steps to the villa just after six, if that last horrific thought hadn't plagued her mind every five minutes. Not that having a baby was horrific. It was having *Leonardo's* baby that horrified her. Because the stupid man would offer to marry her. And the last man on earth she wanted to be married to was a playboy—hardly a recipe for happiness for ever. Okay, so she was in love with the man. Stupidly. Hopelessly. And, yes, if there was to be a child, she would be severely tempted to say yes if he proposed. After all, she had personal experience of growing up without a father and she wouldn't wish that on any child.

And in truth Leonardo would probably be a good father. But he would be a hopeless husband. And undoubtedly unfaithful. That was something she could not bear, not after her experience with Jerome. If and when she married, she wanted her husband to be so besotted with her that he would not even *look* at another woman.

Veronica retrieved the key from the geranium pot, let herself in, dumped her hat and bag on the lounge then walked over to the kitchen area. There, she put on some water for coffee before heading for the bathroom, where a visit to the toilet showed nothing of note.

Naturally.

Cursing under her breath, she flushed the toilet, washed her hands and went back to make herself the coffee. Cradling the mug in her hands, she wandered out to the terrace in the hope of finding some peace with the soothing water view. She didn't. For the first time since coming here, she found no pleasure whatsoever in gazing out at the Mediterranean. Her mind was too full of worry to find pleasure in anything. She was severely tempted to ring her mother and talk things out with her. They were very close, and rarely kept their problems from each other. Not only that, her mother was much less emotional than she was, and not given to dramatising situations or making mountains out of molehills.

The intelligent part of Veronica's brain told her that the odds of her being pregnant were very low. But she needed someone else to reassure her that she was panicking unnecessarily. So, as she sat there sipping her coffee, she worked out what time it was in Australia. All you had to do, she'd discovered after putting the question into her father's computer, was take off two hours from the current time, then change the a.m. to p.m. and vice versa. By eight tonight, it would be six in the morning in Australia, the time her mother usually rose come rain, hail or shine.

It was just after seven here now, and Veronica decided to get herself something to eat. By the time she picked up the phone an hour later, a nervous tension was gripping her stomach. She didn't want to worry her mother with what was possibly a non-existent problem but she desperately needed her advice.

'Veronica?' her mother answered. 'I didn't expect to hear from you. What's up?'

Trust her mother to twig straight away that there was something wrong.

'Nothing, I hope.'

'That sounds ominous.'

'Sorry, I'm not trying to alarm you. I just want to run something by you. Mum, you know how I'm always very regular. With my period, I mean.'

'Yes…' her mother said warily.

Veronica sighed. 'Well, I'm late.'

'Ah.'

'Yes, ah. I don't think I'm pregnant, but it is possible if ovulation was delayed.'

'Are you telling me you had unprotected sex with a play-boy?'

She sounded aghast. And highly disapproving.

Veronica steeled herself. 'Yes. I'm afraid so.'

'Oh, for pity's sake! How come? I would have thought this Leonardo Fabrizzi would be more careful than that.'

'The first time, it just sort of happened. I mean…we both got carried away.'

'That doesn't sound like you.'

'It's not. But I did. Then when Leonardo came to his senses he asked me if an unwanted pregnancy was on the cards. I told him it wasn't. At the time I assumed I'd already ovulated. The trouble was *he* assumed I was on the pill.'

'And you let him think it.'

'Yes.'

'After which he was happy not to use a condom, like any man.'

'Yes,' she said again, but this time with a deep sigh. 'Oh, dear…'

'You think I'm pregnant, don't you?'

'Not necessarily. But it's well known that a girl is always extra vulnerable to a man at the time she ovulates. It's Mother Nature.'

Veronica began to feel sick.

'Look, that might not be the reason you lost your head over this man. You did say he was pretty irresistible.'

'He is.'

'You'd have to be very unlucky to be pregnant. Look, why don't you buy a pregnancy testing kit and find out one way or another?'

'I can't do that. Not here on Capri. Everyone knows everyone on this island. It would soon get around and Leonardo's parents might hear.' She shuddered at the thought. 'Anyway, it's way too early to get a reliable result.'

'Not necessarily. I saw a show on TV that said those tests can tell pretty early these days.'

'I suppose I could catch a ferry over to the mainland and buy one there.'

'Buy two. That way, you can take a test a few days apart and be sure.'

'That's a good idea. Thanks a lot, Mum. You always know what to do.'

'Not always. But at least it would put your mind at rest. Now, are you still coming home early, or has that idea gone by the board?'

'I'm not sure now. I haven't changed the flight yet.'

'Let me know what you decide. And what the results of the test are. What do you think you'll do if you are pregnant?'

'Come straight home.'

'And do what?'

'I don't know yet. I'll cross that bridge when I come to it.'

CHAPTER TWENTY-SEVEN

NEGATIVE. *IT WAS* NEGATIVE!

Veronica stared at the testing stick for a long time before dropping it on the bathroom floor then burying her face in her hands. *Oh, thank God, thank God.*

After a few sobs of relief, Veronica dropped her hands from her face, picked up the stick and threw it into the small bin under the vanity.

It wasn't that she didn't want a baby. Just not Leonardo's. At least, not right now. If by some miracle he was genuinely in love with her and wanted a future with her then, yes, having his baby would be the best thing in the world. She'd always wanted children, but only after she was married. No way did she want to go down the single mother road, like her own mother.

Not that she could be absolutely sure yet that she wasn't pregnant, she thought as she stripped off and stepped into the shower. It was still early days. But the girl in the chemist yesterday—it was called a *farmacia* in Italy—had assured Veronica that this particular test was the latest and best and could detect a pregnancy as early as a week. Given it was now Sunday morning, nine days after she and Leonardo had first had sex, then the test should be accurate. But she would take the test again in a few days, having followed her mother's advice to buy two kits.

But she wouldn't worry about that today. Today, she could at least go to lunch with the Fabrizzi family without having to pretend that everything was fine. But first she would text her mother with the good news.

* * *

'Veronica,' Elena whispered to her during dessert. They were sitting next to each other in the middle of the long table under the pergola, with children on either side.

'What?' Veronica whispered back, immediately tensing up at the urgency in Elena's voice.

'I need to speak to you after lunch. Alone.'

'All right.'

About what? Veronica wondered, her stomach rolling over with sudden alarm. *Nothing good, that's for sure.*

Finally, after lunch was over and all the thank-yous and goodbye hugs had taken place, Veronica looked at Elena and said, 'Would you have the time to walk back with me, Elena? I know you must be good with technology since you do all the bookings for the hotel and I need some help with Laurence's computer.'

Elena smiled at her inventiveness. 'Yes, of course. Franco, would you look after the children for me?'

'So what did you want to talk to me about?' Veronica asked as soon as she had Elena safely alone.

Elena stopped walking. They were halfway up the stone steps.

'Are you going to see Leonardo again?'

Veronica decided not to lie to Elena. 'Yes. Next weekend.'

Elena frowned. 'Here?'

'No. We'll meet up somewhere. Rome, possibly. Or Venice.'

'Are you in contact by phone?'

'He's going to ring me tonight.'

Elena frowned. 'Do you know where he went last night?'

'Yes. To a charity ball in Milan.'

'Do you know who he went with?'

Veronica stiffened. 'No. Who?'

'Lila Bianchi. She's an Italian model. Very beautiful. Very sexy.'

'He...he said he was going alone,' Veronica choked out.

Elena stared at her, then shook her head. 'I knew it. You *are* in love with him.'

'I...' Veronica closed her eyes against the dismay which flooded through her. She'd known all along what kind of man Leonardo was. But even she hadn't thought he would lie to her like that.

'Come,' Elena said, and took her arm. 'I will show you the photos. They are all over social media this morning.'

When they got up to the villa, Elena pulled her phone out of her pocket and brought up the photos of the ball. There were several of Leonardo with this Lila woman draped all over him. In one photo they were dancing cheek to cheek. In another, she was kissing his neck. The final straw, however, was the one of him going arm in arm with that creature into some apartment building.

Nausea swirled in Veronica's stomach, bile rising into her throat. She swallowed, then looked away. 'I don't want to see any more,' she said. 'I've seen enough.'

'I am ashamed of my brother,' Elena said forcefully. 'He is not worthy of you.'

'No,' Veronica agreed. 'He isn't.'

'Are you going to see him again?'

'No.'

'Please don't tell him I showed you the photos. He will be very angry with me.'

'I won't even mention that I have seen them. I'll make up some excuse and tell him that I'm going home ASAP.'

'Oh. Now I feel awful. I should not have told you. I have spoiled your holiday.'

Veronica's smile was sad. 'You did the right thing, Elena. And I thank you. Please don't worry. You've saved me from making an even bigger fool of myself.'

'Leonardo is the fool,' Elena snapped.

'He will be a lonely old man one day,' Veronica muttered, then came forward to give Elena a hug. 'He won't ever have what you and Carmelina have. Yes, you're right. He is a fool. Now, go back to your husband and children and be happy. I have to ring the airline and change my flight.'

After Elena left, Veronica slumped down on the terrace and tried to get her head around those awful photos, especially the last one she'd looked at. Impossible to pretend there was any logical explanation for them. They spoke for themselves. Leonardo had gone to the ball with that creature and no doubt taken her to bed afterwards.

This last realisation brought a wealth of pain. And a rush of tears.

How could Leonardo have lied to her like that? she agonised. What kind of man was he?

The kind of man you've always known he was, came the bitter answer.

A playboy and a player.

No way, Veronica determined as she dashed away the tears, was she going to give him the opportunity to lie to her again. And he would lie, if she confronted him with those photos when he rang her tonight. No…she intended to do what she'd said to Elena. Make up some excuse why she had to go home ASAP and then cut him dead.

CHAPTER TWENTY-EIGHT

LEONARDO HAD TO have a lie-down late that Sunday afternoon, something which he couldn't remember doing in years. Last night had been a nightmare, with Lila having latched onto him as soon as he'd arrived at the ball and made it impossible for him to extricate himself from her clutches without being rude. If she hadn't already been contracted as the main model for next season's ski-wear, he would have told her to get lost in no uncertain words.

Of course, she'd been totally stoned. On top of that, she'd had an argument with her boyfriend and come alone, determined to find some man to make the boyfriend jealous. Leonardo had been an excellent mark, since he was handsome, rich and, in a way, her boss. He'd been in a no-win situation from the start, unable to get rid of her, yet knowing full well that everything he did would be photographed and misinterpreted, fodder for all the gossip websites and magazines.

Never had a night seemed so long, or so emotionally exhausting. He'd had to smile and make speeches, all the while worrying what Veronica would think if she saw reports of him dancing with Lila at the ball. Not that she was likely to. Capri was rather isolated when it came to mainland gossip. Though there was always social media. Nowhere was safe any more. Best he tell her about it upfront tonight, even the part about having had to see the stupid girl safely home at some ungodly hour. She would understand. Surely? Veronica was quite the pragmatist. And not given to dramatising things.

A glance at his watch showed it was just after four in the afternoon. He'd promised to ring her this evening. When did evenings start, exactly? he wondered. Seven? Eight? He wanted to hear her voice. Wanted to hear her say, *yes, Leonardo, of course I'll spend next weekend with you. Wherever you like, darling.*

He doubted she would go that far. Just 'yes' would do for now.

Dio, he was tired. Yawning, Leonardo closed his eyes and drifted off.

Veronica couldn't get a flight until Wednesday, not on the same airline and without spending a small fortune by upgrading to business class. She supposed she could last until then. Her flight took off early in the morning, so she would make her way to Rome on the Tuesday then stay at one of the airport hotels that night.

She spent the rest of the afternoon keeping busy so that she didn't fall into a depression. She packed, cleaned the bathroom then returned to the living room to read another of her father's books. This time, it didn't hold her attention. In the end, she put it down and went out onto the terrace.

By the time her phone rang just after seven, she felt very down. But furious as well. When she saw Leonardo's name on her screen, she wanted to throw the damned phone against the wall. But she didn't. Her fingers tightened, as did her lips.

'Leonardo,' she said in a rather droll tone. 'You remembered to ring.'

His hesitation to answer showed he'd heard the sarcastic edge in her voice.

'But of course,' he replied at last. 'Did you doubt me?'

Doubt him?

No, she didn't doubt him. She'd known he would ring.

'I don't have a lot of faith in the opposite sex,' she said truthfully. 'But I'm very glad you rang,' she swept on. 'Unfortunately, my mother is not well and I have to go home earlier than expected, so I'm afraid I can't join you next weekend.'

Again, a few seconds went by before he spoke. 'What is wrong with her?' he demanded to know, as though sensing she was lying to him.

'She's always had a weak chest. When she gets a cold, it quickly becomes bronchitis, which sometimes turns into pneumonia.' Actually, this was quite true. But of course Nora didn't have a cold at the moment.

'She has pneumonia?'

'Not yet. But it's heading that way if she doesn't rest.'

'I see.'

'I'm sorry to disappoint you, Leonardo, but it's a case of family first. My flight leaves on Wednesday morning. Anyway, it's not as though we were going anywhere. It was just a fling, as you very well know.'

'No, I do not know,' he bit out. 'Maybe it was to begin with but I thought... I hoped...'

He actually sounded upset.

Too bad, Veronica thought angrily. The man was a bastard. And a liar. The only thing he hoped for was more sex.

'I'm sorry,' she said with little apology in her voice, 'But I did warn you. Now, about the villa...'

'You want to talk *business* with me?' His astonishment was obvious.

'Why not? You still want the villa, don't you?'

'I don't feel like talking business with you right now,' he said coldly. 'I will contact you via email after you arrive home. Goodbye.' And he hung up.

Veronica blinked at the abruptness with which he'd ended the call, all her anger dissipating in the face of the reality that it was over. Never again would he kiss her. Never again would he hold her in his arms. Never again...

Before she could work out her emotions, she threw herself down on the lounge and wept long and hard.

CHAPTER TWENTY-NINE

IT SEEMED TO take for ever for Tuesday to come. On the Monday Veronica bit the bullet and walked down to the Hotel Fabrizzi, repeating her lie about her mother's illness and saying her goodbyes, as well as quietly reassuring a worried Elena that she hadn't mentioned anything to Leonardo about the photos she'd shown her. All the Fabrizzis seemed genuinely sorry to see her go, which made Veronica feel even worse than she was already feeling.

Later that day she rang her mother and did her best to sound composed.

'I'm coming home even earlier than I said. My flight leaves Rome on Wednesday morning.'

'Oh, that's a shame. You really needed a long holiday.'

'Perhaps. But not here.'

'I see,' she said with a wealth of knowingness. 'Have you taken the second test yet?'

'No. I'll do it when I get home.' If by some awful twist of fate it was positive, she didn't want to be here when she found out.

'Right. Do you want me to meet you at the airport?'

'Heavens, no. That madhouse? I'll catch a taxi home.'

'Are you sure you're all right?' she asked, sounding worried.

'I'll survive, Mum. See you on Wednesday. Take care.' And she hung up before she could burst into tears again.

When Veronica finally came to pack the second pregnancy test, she stared at it for a long time. Then curiosity— or maybe it was masochism—got the better of her. So she carried it into the bathroom and did what she had to do.

Afterwards, she put the stick down on the vanity and

walked out, unable to stand there waiting. Was it her imagination or were her breasts suddenly tingling? Surely fate
couldn't be that cruel? She paced around the bedroom for
the required time then charged back into the bathroom,
snatching up the stick.

'Oh, no!' she cried when she saw the result. 'It can't be!'

But it was. It very definitely was. She was pregnant with
Leonardo Fabrizzi's child.

Her stomach suddenly heaved and she only just bent
over the toilet in time. After flushing away her dinner, she
washed out her mouth and returned to the bedroom, where
she collapsed on the bed. Her head continued to whirl and
she could hardly think straight.

How could this have happened? she wailed to herself.

The usual way, you idiot, returned her pragmatic side.
*You took a risk and now you're going to have to pay the
price. Serves you right for relying on the rhythm method.
What sensible girl does that these days? And what sensible
girl sleeps with a playboy like Leonardo Fabrizzi without
using condoms?*

'Oh, God… Leonardo,' she groaned aloud.

He was going to be even more upset than her when she
told him. More than upset. He'd be furious with her for having lied to him about the pill. But she would have to tell
him about the baby at some stage, because no way was a
child of hers going to be brought up without knowing who
its father was. Lord, no!

Perhaps she wouldn't tell him until she was safely past
the three-month stage when the threat of miscarriage had
passed.

Thinking about miscarrying her baby made Veronica
realise that deep down she didn't want that to happen any
more than she wanted to have a termination. This was her
child growing inside her, a child born out of love. She could
at least admit to herself that she loved Leonardo. Which was

perverse, given the kind of man he was. But then life was perverse, wasn't it?

Her hands came to rest across her stomach as she contemplated what it would be like to be a mother. She hoped she would be a good one. Kind and caring, but not a helicopter mother. Her own mother hadn't been that, for which she was grateful. She'd allowed Veronica considerable freedom as she'd grown, encouraging her to work as well as to study, to become her own person. She knew she had considerable strength of character when needed. And she would need it now.

The next morning she had a good breakfast, after which she washed everything up—there wasn't enough to load a dishwasher—then finished off packing her one case. At eight-thirty she locked up and placed the key back in the geranium pot. Thankfully the weather was still good, if a little cloudy. She hadn't called a taxi, Franco having insisted that he would pick her up from the Hotel Fabrizzi to drive her down to the jetty. She stood for a long moment on the terrace, gazing out at the gorgeous view and putting it into her memory bank, though she suspected it might not be the last time she saw it. Leonardo would not let his child go easily. Neither would Sophia and Alberto. But she would not think about that yet. Time enough when she had a healthy ultrasound in her hands.

As she headed off towards the path, tears pricked at her eyes. She turned to have one last, longing look at her father's villa, wondering at the same time if he'd ever envisaged this happening when he'd made his will. Had he hoped that she and Leonardo would end up together? It seemed rather fanciful.

Dragging her case behind her, she started walking down the steep path, dashing away tears at the same time. It happened so quickly. She caught her heel in something and pitched forward. A scream of terror burst from her lips as she crashed down onto the uneven stone steps. Her head hit something and everything went black.

Veronica woke slowly to a dull headache and a strange bedroom, not to mention a strange man sitting on a chair beside the bed she was lying in. He was quite elderly with a neat white beard and white hair—though perhaps he was not as old as he looked, since his blue eyes were clear and his face not too wrinkled.

'Where am I?' she asked groggily. 'And who are you?'

'You're in a guest room at the Hotel Fabrizzi, and I'm Dr Waverly.'

She blinked at him. 'You're English.'

'Yes. I semi-retired to Capri many years ago but continued to practise for people who wanted an English-speaking doctor. I was Ruth's doctor until she died. And Laurence's, when he deigned to go to a doctor. Which wasn't often. Sophia called me in because she thought you would be best with an English doctor. So, how are you feeling, my dear?'

'Rotten.'

'I can imagine. You had a bad fall and you've been unconscious for over a day. Concussion. Would you mind if I examined you?'

Veronica blinked, struggling to remember the circumstances of this fall.

'What kind of examination?'

'Nothing too intrusive. I just want to check you over. Make sure you're on the road to recovery.'

'How long did you say I've been out of it?' she asked as he took her blood pressure.

'Just over twenty-four hours.'

'Oh, Lord!' she said, sitting up abruptly. 'I've missed my flight. I have to ring Mum and tell her.'

'Leonardo's already rung her and explained.'

Veronica gaped at him. 'Leonardo's talked to my mother?'

'It seems so. And he wants to talk to you. Shall I call him in? He's just outside.'

'No!' she cried out.

'He knows about the pregnancy, Veronica.'

She slumped back on the pillows, her head thumping. 'But how?' she choked out.

'You never stopped talking about it when you were semi-conscious. You were worried that you might lose the baby.'

'Oh…'

'You haven't, by the way. Your baby's fine.'

Veronica closed her eyes, tears of relief leaking out. Being pregnant by Leonardo wasn't ideal, but she didn't want to miscarry.

'It is Leonardo's, isn't it?' the doctor asked gently.

She nodded wearily.

'Are you absolutely sure you're pregnant?'

'I did one of those tests. It was very positive.'

'No need for a blood test, then.'

'You can do one if you like.'

'Knowing Leonardo, perhaps it would be best.'

'Yes, I would imagine so,' she said, somewhat bitterly. 'Though he needn't worry about my trying to trap him into marriage. Because I wouldn't marry him, no matter what!'

The doctor made no comment, just got a syringe out of his bag and took a sample of her blood. 'You don't love him?' he asked after a while.

She refused to answer, her emotions a mess, anger and distress mingling with fear. Leonardo was here. And he'd talked to her mother! What had they talked about? What had Nora told him?

The doctor looked perplexed. 'I think I should tell Leonardo to come in.'

Before Veronica could protest, he stood up and carried his bag outside. Through the open door she could hear the murmuring of voices. And then there he was, standing in the doorway, looking as handsome as ever but rather strained.

There were dark shadows around his eyes which held an expression of real concern.

Or possibly she was mistaken about that. Maybe it was just controlled anger fuelling the tension in his face.

After a momentary hesitation, Leonardo came in, closed the door and sat down in the chair the doctor had vacated.

'Dr Waverly said you must rest easy for a few more days,' he said coolly. 'Your blood pressure is up.'

'I feel fine,' she returned stubbornly, and looked away from him.

A silence fell in the room, Veronica aware of the pulse beating in her temples.

'Were you ever going to tell me about the baby, Veronica?' he demanded to know. 'Or was I just to be a sperm donor, like Laurence?'

Outrage had her head whipping back to face him.

'Do you honestly think I would deliberately get pregnant by you? Or that I would choose to be a single mother? I know how hard that life is.'

He nodded. 'Yes, I can appreciate that. And, no, I don't think you *deliberately* set out to get pregnant. But you were never on the pill, were you?'

'Oh, God. Mum told you I wasn't, didn't she?'

'No. I was just guessing. Your mother did tell me about Jerome, however. I think she wanted to explain why you mistrusted my intentions so much, and why you would try to bolt home once you realised you were pregnant. Which, by the way, was news to your mother. She said you did a test and it was negative.'

'The first time it was,' she muttered. 'I did a second test later on and it was positive. If you don't believe me, ask Dr Waverly. He's taken a blood sample to double-check. I thought you might want proof,' she threw at him, her top lip curling with contempt.

'No,' he denied with amazing calm. 'Not really. I can

see that you're not lying. But you did lie to me about being on the pill, didn't you?'

'Not at first,' she said with a frustrated sigh. 'You asked me if there was any danger of a pregnancy and I told you there wasn't. That was because I'm always very regular and I honestly thought there was no risk of conceiving that weekend. You just assumed I was on the pill and it seemed easier to let you think that.'

'So what went wrong?'

'I don't know!' she wailed, stuffing a fist against her trembling mouth and shaking her head. 'I guess finding out about my real father upset my cycle somehow. I could hardly believe it when I was late.'

'I see,' he said slowly. 'Don't you want my baby, Veronica?'

She opened her mouth to snap that of course she didn't. But then she shut it again. She could not keep lying to him. She just couldn't. So she didn't say anything.

'*I* want it,' he said softly into the silence. 'And I want you. I love you, Veronica.'

Her eyes grew wide with shock, and the most awful hope.

Oh, Veronica, don't fall for the 'I love you' ploy, she told herself sternly.

'You're just saying that because you want your child.'

'I am not in the habit of lying,' he returned. 'Which reminds me,' he continued before she could laugh in his face. 'Elena told me about the photos she showed you. Of me and Lila at the ball. I didn't lie to you, Veronica. I went to that ball alone. Lila threw herself at me as soon as I got there and it was impossible to extricate myself from her cling-on tactics without making a scene. I wouldn't have been so tolerant if she hadn't been hopelessly drunk and very upset over a fight with her boyfriend. She wasn't making a serious play for me, Veronica. We've known each other for years and there's nothing between us. She was just trying to make her boyfriend jealous. And it worked too. They're back together again. I was going to tell you all about it when I rang last Sunday night but you didn't give me the chance. If you don't believe me, I'll have her come down here personally so that she can explain her behaviour.'

Veronica stared at him for a long time without blinking. Could he be telling the truth? Maybe he did care for her. Maybe he even loved her. Just the hope of it sent her head into a whirlwind.

Leonardo leant over and took both her hands in his. 'I care deeply for you, Veronica. It took me a while to accept my feelings but they are real, I assure you. When I rang you last Sunday and you said what you said, in such a cold voice, I was devastated. Because I'd arrogantly thought you cared for me back.'

'I… I do care for you,' she said hesitantly. 'But…'

'But you think I'm a playboy who is incapable of commitment and true caring.'

'Yes…'

'I have been a bit of a bad boy in the past, I admit. But I haven't been all that bad for some years now. Yes, my girlfriends don't last long. Perhaps because I didn't fall in love with any of them. But I never cheated or treated them shoddily. If nothing else, I've always been a gentleman.' And, lifting her hands to his lips, he kissed every finger gently. Reverently. Lovingly.

Veronica's heart turned over.

His head lifted at last and he looked deep into her eyes. 'I love you, Veronica. More than I ever thought possible. Dare I hope you love me back?'

She could not speak, her heart too full. Tears flooded her eyes. It was all too good to be true. She found it almost impossible to believe.

His sigh was heavy. 'I see you still don't trust me. Understandable, considering what you went through with that other unconscionable bastard. But, if you just tell me that you love me, I will move heaven and earth to prove to you that I am a man of my word.'

'I... I do love you. But how...how do you propose to prove yourself?' she asked, moved by his passionate declaration.

'By not proposing marriage, for starters, even though that is my dearest wish—to have you as my wife. I have a lovely home in Milan where I think we could be very happy together. But I can see you are not ready to take that step yet. So this is what I propose instead. Your mother said I was welcome to stay at her home whenever I liked, so I will take her up on her offer. I can run my business over the Internet. I have excellent staff who are very capable. So I will come to Sydney and live there with you—without sex—until you can see first-hand and up close what kind of man I am. An honourable man who will make you a good husband and a very good father.'

'You would do that for me?' she choked out, overcome with emotion.

'I would do anything for you.'

'Oh!' she exclaimed, sitting up and throwing her arms around his neck.

He held her close, kissing her hair and telling her over and over how much he loved her.

Veronica could scarcely believe the wave of happiness that claimed her. She'd been so unhappy for so long. So cynical as well. But Leonardo had blasted that cynicism to pieces just now with his incredible offer. She wasn't too sure about the 'no sex' part, but if he could do it then so could she.

And so it was that just over three months later, on the evening after they went together to have their first ultrasound—the baby was healthy and a boy—Leonardo took Veronica out for dinner where he produced the most glorious ring and asked her to marry him.

* * *

Leonardo would remember the look on her face for ever. It was filled with a joy which came not just from love but absolute faith. It had taken time for her to totally trust him. Time and sacrifice on his part. He was not a man used to denying his male urges. But it had been worth it in the end.

'You were the right girl that Laurence talked about,' he said as he slipped the diamond ring on her finger. 'This was what he wanted when he made sure that we would meet.'

'That thought did occur to me once too,' she replied, surprising him.

He was very thankful now that he'd never told her what he'd found on Laurence's phone. He hadn't been sure that she would be pleased with her father researching the female biological clock the day before he'd gone to London and changed his will. He would not have liked Veronica to assume that her father was more concerned about her being childless than anything else. It was possible, he supposed, but Leonardo preferred to believe that his friend wanted his daughter and his friend to meet, fall in love and hopefully marry.

Whatever his motives, it had all worked out in the end.

I have found a new dream, Laurence. A better one. I am going to be the best husband and father in the whole of Italy. Maybe even in the whole world!

Hopefully, if Laurence were able to observe things from heaven—or wherever he was—he would approve.

As for Leonardo's own family, they would be over the moon now that marriage was on the horizon. His *mamma* was already making preparations for a big wedding on Capri. Nora had been in constant contact with her and the two women were happy little conspirators.

He smiled over at Veronica, who was touching her ring and looking very thoughtful.

'What is it?' he asked, very in tune with her feelings by now.

'I was just wondering…'

'Wondering what?'

'If I could spend tonight in the guest room. With the man I adore.'

Leonardo took a deep breath, letting it out slowly as emotion claimed him. He'd always thought that nothing would ever surpass winning a race on the ski slopes.

He was so wrong.

EPILOGUE

March the following year...

'YOU LOOK ABSOLUTELY BEAUTIFUL,' her mother said, her voice catching.

They were alone in the master bedroom of Laurence's villa, getting ready for what was going to be the wedding of the year on Capri. The official invitations numbered over three hundred, with guests coming from all over the world, their expenses paid for by Leonardo. The wedding was to take place in Santo Stephano, the main church on Capri, the reception at the Grand Hotel Quisisana, a five-star hotel which exuded both history and luxury.

Veronica didn't like to think of what the bill might be, Leonardo having brushed aside her worries with his usual *savoir faire*.

'I am not going to stint on our wedding, Veronica,' he'd said when she'd broached the subject. 'You deserve everything I can afford to give you.'

It seemed that what he could afford was one hell of a lot. Her wedding dress had been designed by one of the best designers in Milan, with Veronica not even having been told what it had cost. And the gown was, in truth, a breathtakingly lovely creation, designed to hide perfectly her six-and-a-half-month baby bump without compromising on elegance.

There was a floor-length under-dress made in white chiffon, which was princess-line in style and sleeveless, with a scooped neckline and softly gathered skirt. Over this lay a long, white lace coat that had long sleeves and flowed out the back in a train. There was only one button, just under her bust, though one could hardly call it a button. It was a jewelled clasp, made of pearls and diamonds, as were the drop earrings that Leonardo had given his bride as an additional wedding present. Her hair was up, a circlet of flowers crowning her dark tresses. Attached at the back was a simple tulle veil that had a small face veil which could be brought over her face then lifted during the ceremony.

Veronica looked at her mother and smiled. 'I do look good, don't I?'

'I think that's an understatement, my darling daughter. Laurence would be so proud.'

'I like to think so,' she said, still feeling a little sad when she thought of the missed opportunities with her father.

'Come, now. No sad thoughts today. You are on your way to be married to one of the nicest, most sincere men I have ever met. Not to mention the most generous. But first, we have to join the others and have photos taken on the terrace.'

The 'others' were considerable. Veronica had been unable to resist asking both Elena and Carmelina to be her matrons of honour, Leonardo going along with her by making Franco and Alfonso his best men. All their children were in the wedding party as well as flower girls and page boys. They were thrilled to pieces to be asked and promised to be very good, even the precocious Bruno having given his solemn word. The matrons of honour were in sky-blue silk and carried white bouquets, the flower girls in white with white-and-blue posies. All the men—and boys—had chosen to wear black tuxedos, all made in Milan, their lapels carrying white roses.

Nora—as mother of the bride—had chosen pale lemon, her elegantly styled suit also having been made by a top designer in Milan. She looked lovelier—and happier—than Veronica had ever seen her. Her mother was in the process of selling her home-help business and moving to Capri, where she would live in Laurence's villa, looking after it for Veronica and Leonardo for when they could come and stay.

Which Veronica vowed would be often. The happy couple had already made their permanent home in Milan, the nursery all ready for their son's arrival. Francesca, Leonardo's housekeeper, was very excited at the thought of having a baby in the house. Luckily, she and Veronica liked each other, which had pleased Leonardo greatly.

Last in the wedding party was Dr Waverly, who'd agreed to give Veronica away. He'd seemed a good choice, being a friend of her real father, and of his vintage.

The photos took a good while, the sky being a little cloudy, though every now and then the sun would peep out. At least it wasn't raining. The weather on Capri in March could be very capricious. At last the photos were all finished to the photographer's satisfaction and it was time to head to the waiting cars, the bride having chosen to travel in Franco's yellow convertible, the rest in other equally colourful taxis. Just as Veronica made her way off the terrace, the sun came out again, bathing the villa in glorious light. Veronica glanced over her shoulder and thought how her father's home had never looked more beautiful.

Her father…

Yes, she hadn't known him in life, but she'd got to know him in death, lots of people having filled her in on his character. No, he hadn't been a perfect man, but he had been a good man, and a brilliant scientist who'd made a difference in the world through his work. He'd also been a man capable of great love. Veronica felt she had inherited that quality from him, because she loved Leonardo and their unborn baby more than she could ever have thought possible. She could not wait for her son to be born and to see what their genes would produce. A very special child, she was sure. Very special indeed.

But none of this would have happened, she thought as she gazed back at the villa, if her father hadn't left her his home in his will.

'Thank you, Dad,' she murmured, her heart filling with gratitude and love. 'Thank you.'

Their son was born in May, three weeks early, obviously impatient to come into this world. He was perfect in every way, captivating everyone who saw him. They called him Antonio Laurence Alberto Fabrizzi. His grandfather was thrilled. At last, a boy who would carry on his name. Antonio's two grandmothers were besotted, but not as much as his parents, who vowed to have more children as soon as possible.

* * * * *

MILLS & BOON

Coming next month

THE ITALIAN'S CHRISTMAS HOUSEKEEPER
Sharon Kendrick

'The only thing which will stop me, is you,' he continued, his voice a deep silken purr. 'So stop me, Molly. Turn away and walk out right now and do us both a favour, because something tells me this is a bad idea.'

He was giving her the opportunity to leave but Molly knew she wasn't going to take it – because when did things like this ever happen to people like her? She wasn't like most women her age. She'd never had sex. Never come even close, despite her few forays onto a dating website which had all ended in disaster. Yet now a man she barely knew was proposing seduction and suddenly she was up for it, and she didn't care if it was *bad*. Hadn't she spent her whole life trying to be good? And where had it got her?

Her heart was crashing against her rib-cage as she stared up into his rugged features and greedily drank them in. 'I don't care if it's a bad idea,' she whispered. 'Maybe I want it as much as you do.'

Continue reading
THE ITALIAN'S CHRISTMAS HOUSEKEEPER
Sharon Kendrick

Available next month
www.millsandboon.co.uk

COMING SOON!

We really hope you enjoyed reading this book. If you're looking for more romance, be sure to head to the shops when new books are available on

Thursday
1st November

To see which titles are coming soon, please visit
millsandboon.co.uk

LET'S TALK
Romance

For exclusive extracts, competitions
and special offers, find us online:

f facebook.com/millsandboon

⊙ @millsandboonuk

🐦 @millsandboon

Or get in touch on 0844 844 1351*

For all the latest titles coming soon, visit
millsandboon.co.uk/nextmonth